KID DETECTIVE ZET - THE EGYPTIAN MYSTERIES

SERIES COLLECTION BOOKS 1-4

SCOTT PETERS

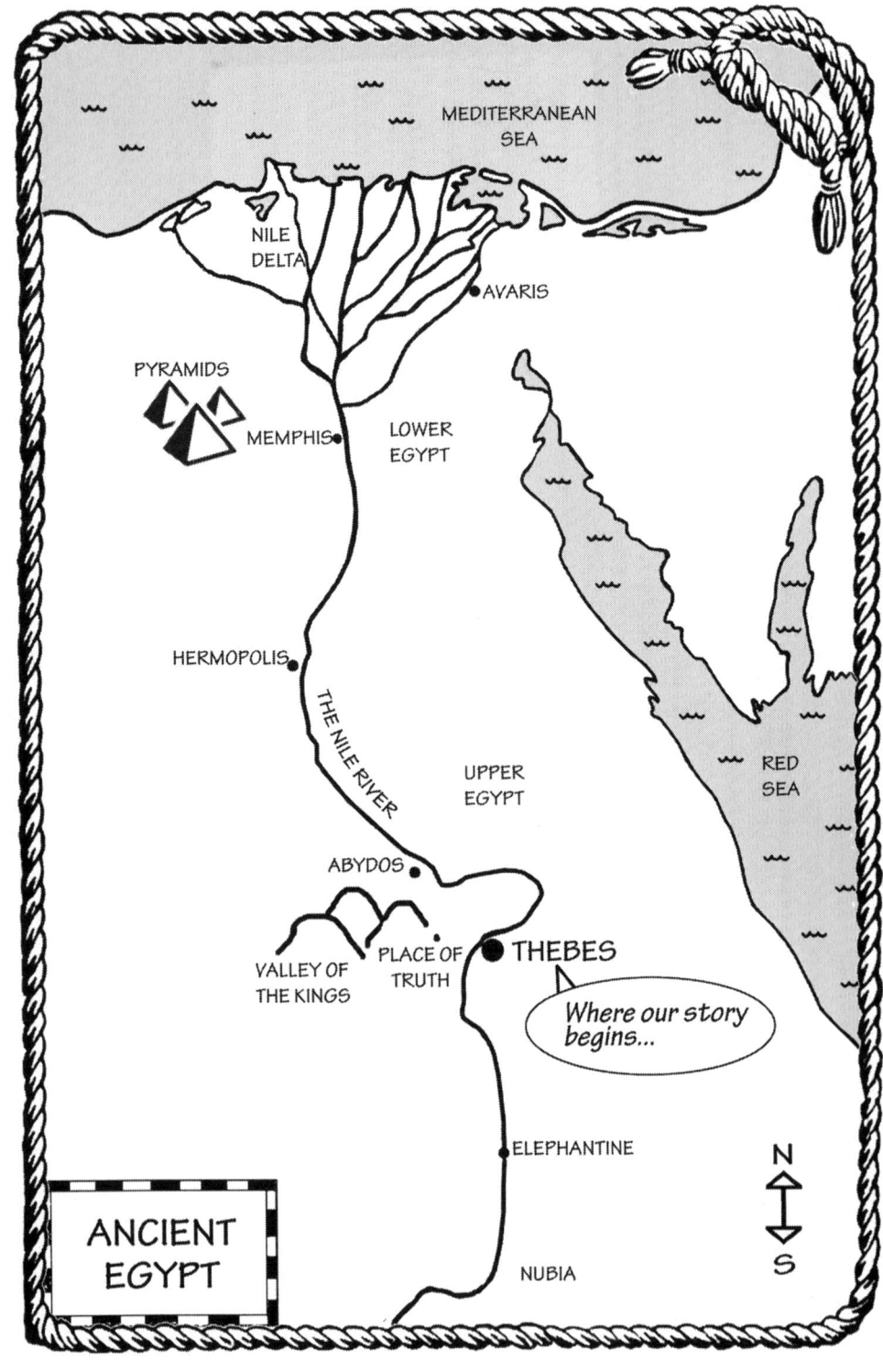

CONTENTS

MYSTERY OF THE EGYPTIAN SCROLL   1
Zet's First Case
By Scott Peters

MYSTERY OF THE EGYPTIAN AMULET   101
Zet's Second Case
By Scott Peters

MYSTERY OF THE EGYPTIAN TEMPLE   245
Zet's Third Case
By Scott Peters

MYSTERY OF THE EGYPTIAN MUMMY   387
Zet's Last Case
By Scott Peters

Author Resources   506
Acknowledgements and Sources   507
More Great Stories by Scott Peter   508

MYSTERY OF THE EGYPTIAN SCROLL

ZET'S FIRST CASE

BY SCOTT PETERS

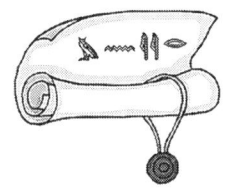

THE THIEF

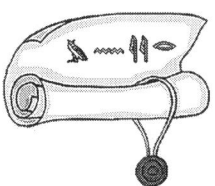

Dust hung thick over the Thebes marketplace. Standing before a mountain of clay pots, twelve-year-old Zet swatted a fly from his shoulders. The fly dive-bombed his head, and he swatted it again.

"Pots and dishes!" he shouted, waving a plate in the air.

"You're supposed to be drawing customers over here," his sister Kat said. "Not scaring them away!"

"Sorry!" Still, Zet gave one last warning swipe at the fly.

With a grin, he turned and leaped over the pots. He landed where his sister sat studying the record of trades. She didn't bother to look up. She was too busy staring at her calculations. Kat was eleven, and good with numbers and writing. Not that he'd ever tell her that.

"We need to do something," she said. "We haven't sold a single thing all day."

"Make that all week," he said.

She pushed her dark bangs from her eyes and glanced up at him. She looked worried.

"Maybe it's the heat," Zet said. "No one likes cooking when it's this hot."

"Maybe it's because we're kids?" She held up the pottery shard covered with her neatly printed hieratic. "According to these, for every week that father's been gone, sales have dropped."

She wasn't the first one to think it. Zet had been wondering the same thing. He glanced across at a vegetable seller. Under his shaded awning, two women browsed the baskets loaded with beans and cabbages. A third bartered a length of fabric for her purchases.

"If it's true, that's not fair. Our father is off fighting Hyksos to keep Egypt safe," Zet said.

Maybe Zet was a kid, but he was as capable at running a stall as any of the adults. He'd promised he could take care of his family until his father returned, and his father trusted him. Maybe they were hungrier, but they wouldn't starve. Zet wouldn't let them. So why did he have this terrible knot in his stomach?

He jumped up. "We just need to make things more interesting. I could learn to juggle. I could juggle dishes, that would bring people over."

"Yes, but there would be nothing left to buy, because everything would be broken."

"Have some faith!" Zet said.

"We should rearrange the stall."

Zet groaned. "Again?" Move the mountain of clayware a fourth time? No way. He'd already fallen for his sister's logic once too often.

"Don't make that face," Kat said. "I've been taking notes, and when certain things are placed in view, those things draw customers over and—"

A scuffle of feet and shouts broke out by the goat stall.

Zet glanced across the market square. A man, deeply tanned, head shaved and wearing a threadbare tunic, broke free of the crowd and burst into view. The man sprinted around the goat pen, glanced back, and slammed into a basket of dates. The dates flew like cockroaches in every direction.

"Stop!" the date-owner screeched.

The man kept running.

"Not this way!" Zet said, darting forward as the man bumped into a stack of pots. Zet grabbed the stack, righted it, and then flew through the air to catch a falling dish. He landed belly first, with the plate in perfect, pristine condition. He rolled over and looked for Kat.

"See that? How's that for juggling?"

Kat's eyes were on the far alley. So much for proving a point. He turned to see three medjay officers sprint into view. Two carried wooden staffs, one had a curved bronze sickle, and another had a dagger on his belt and a fiber shield in his left hand.

"Where did he go?" one officer shouted.

The date-stall owner, an old man named Salatis, pointed to where the man had disappeared. Two of the medjay tore after him. The clank of their weapons echoed down the alley and disappeared.

The third medjay stood catching his breath. He was unarmed, but his gleaming insignia marked him as important, and his fists looked big enough to crush several thieves at once. The running had winded him. Zet wondered how long they'd kept up the chase.

The medjay mopped sweat from his dark face. He bent and picked up one of the fallen baskets and handed it to Salatis.

"I'd like to ask you a few questions," the medjay said, his voice deep and rumbling.

"Why?" Salatis said.

"I wondered if you recognized the man," the medjay said.

"Me?" Salatis said, in almost a shriek.

Zet rolled his eyes. It's not like Salatis was in trouble. Still, no one wanted to be associated with thieves. That much Zet agreed with. You might get your hands cut off, or worse, your head.

"Maybe you'd sold dates to him before," the medjay said.

"How would I know?" Salatis said. "He was here and gone. And I don't remember my customers."

The medjay hooked his thumb into his kilt. "I'm not accusing you of anything, vendor. I just want some help here. Did you see his face?"

"All I saw were my dates, flying. Look at them!"

The medjay looked at the dates scattered in the dust.

"I can't barter them now, can I? Who's going to pay for this waste?"

Kat nudged her brother and whispered, "Look at Salatis, piling them into that reed basket. He's going to barter them anyway, isn't he? Even though they're all dirty!"

Zet nodded, wrinkling his nose.

The medjay's face turned red. He stepped up to Salatis and grabbed him by the collar of his dirty tunic. "Stop that. Show some respect when an officer's questioning you."

"I'm a victim here!"

"And I'm trying to do my job. I'd appreciate your cooperation. This is no ordinary thief we're hunting."

"They never are," Salatis snapped.

The medjay sighed and looked skyward. He reached into a pouch and pulled out a coin. "There's a deben of copper in it," he said, holding the shiny piece of metal to the light.

At this, Zet started. A deben of copper? The medjay was willing to pay? He shoved the plate he'd saved into Kat's arms, much to her surprise. Then he sprinted across the hot paving stones toward the officer.

2

A REWARD

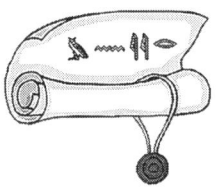

Standing in front of his date stall, Salatis seemed to have forgotten all about his ruined wares. He rubbed his hands together, eyes on the medjay's sparkling coin.
"Well, now, come to think of it . . ." Salatis began.
"I saw the thief!" Zet called. "I can describe him!"
The medjay wheeled, his insignia gleaming.
"Ignore that meddlesome boy!" Salatis said.
"And who might you be?" the medjay asked.
"I run the clay pot stall over there," Zet said, drawing himself up.
"And you say you saw the thief?"
Zet nodded.
The deep grooves in the man's face relaxed a little. "Go ahead. Tell me then, what did he look like?"
"The deben, first please," Zet said, holding out his hand. He knew from his father to ask a customer for money before goods were transferred.
The medjay laughed. "Pay you?"
Zet's hand dropped a little. "You told Salatis you were going to pay for it."

"Boy, if you saw something, tell me now or I'll drag you down to the office of the head medjay."

Zet's hand fell to his side.

He *had* seen the thief, and there was one distinct detail he remembered clearly. But he didn't see why he should give it up for free, just because he was a boy instead of a man. And with his father gone, he *was* the man. He needed the money as much as Salatis. More. Salatis lived alone, and Zet had not only his sister, but also his mother and his new baby brother back home.

He glanced at the stall. Kat was staring at him, open-mouthed.

He thought fast.

"All right. I'll tell you what I know, as a free gift," Zet said.

"It's not a gift, it's your duty."

Zet ignored this. "But what's the reward if I hand over the robber, too?"

The medjay laughed.

"I mean it! I want to know. If it's a good business venture, I'll undertake it."

Throwing his head back, the medjay laughed even harder. "A good business venture? Boy, I think your father taught you well in the ways of bartering. I'd offer a reward. But there's no point. You don't stand a chance of finding him."

Zet liked the way the huge medjay's eyes crinkled around the corners. Here was a fighter with a sense of humor. Even if he was laughing at Zet, he was still listening to him. Zet wondered if he'd ever be that big one day.

"Then take a gamble and give me a figure," Zet said.

"Twenty deben of copper." The medjay tossed out the huge number with a reckless grin.

Zet gasped, and so did Salatis. He could barter that for ten sacks of grain; enough to feed them for months!

The thief must have stolen something incredibly valuable! "Twenty deben!" Zet said.

"Yes. But camels have a better chance of flying than you do of seeing those twenty deben."

"Shake on it," Zet said, making sure to seal the deal.

The man's strong, leathery hand grasped Zet's and shook it.

"And where will I find you?" Zet said.

The medjay rolled his eyes. "You're a persistent one, aren't you? You'll find me at the central office. Ask for Merimose, that's my name."

"Merimose," Zet said, committing it to memory.

"Now that business is complete," Merimose said, "How about my free information?"

Zet cleared his throat. "The man you were chasing wore two different sandals."

"Two different sandals?"

Zet nodded. "They didn't match."

"That's your information? And you wanted me to pay for it?" Merimose put his thick fists on his hips. "I should cuff you for wasting my time."

But it was good information! And even if it wasn't the only information he had, it was free. Zet darted back to his stall in case Merimose tried to get in a smack or two.

"What was all that about?" Kat said, still clutching the plate.

She followed him to the back of the stall.

"Listen to this!" Zet said.

When he explained the way he'd argued with the man, Kat said he was showing off. Still, he was pretty sure she looked impressed. And that was before he told her about the reward.

"Twenty deben!" she practically shouted. "That's more than we make in three months!"

Zet grinned.

Kat looked skeptical. "But I don't see how you can find the thief."

"Think about the sandals," Zet said. "I told him they didn't match, but I didn't tell him I knew where the sandal-owner lived."

"But you don't know—" She paused. He watched the realization dawn in her eyes. "That doorstep we pass, on our way home!"

Zet nodded. "How many times have you grabbed my arm and

made me look at those stupid sandals, lined up side-by-side, even though they're two different designs?"

Her mouth hung open. "Zet, that's true!" Kat's face was bright. He could see her imagining writing the entry—twenty copper deben reward for finding a thief—on her pottery shards.

"I'm going to go there," he said. "Watch the stall."

Kat grabbed her brother's wrist. "Wait."

"What is it?"

"Be careful."

"Of course I'll be careful," he scoffed. Then, seeing she was truly concerned, he grinned at her and gave her braids a tug. "Don't worry about me, little sister."

3

THE STRANGER'S DOOR

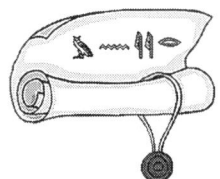

*Z*et bounded over the pots and headed out of the marketplace.

A cool alley quickly swallowed him in shadow.

The air felt good on his hot skin. Doves cooed, nestled in eaves over doorways. Underfoot, a few sleepy pigeons rose, flapping, disturbed by the slap of his bare feet. He passed the woodcarver's open door; the sweet smell of cedar shavings floated in the stillness.

Zet flew around a corner, and then slowed. He was almost there.

What if the thief kept running right out of town, instead of going home? But then he saw the sandals, lined up on the stoop. His heart leapt. He was in luck. He could almost feel the deben in his hands. A big, heavy bag of copper. He could barter that copper for ten sacks of grain, or any manner of things. What would his mother say? She'd be so proud! And he'd tell her he was simply doing his job and taking care of them. Just like father asked.

Zet crept up the steps.

Rather than a proper door, a heavy curtain shielded the house from the alley.

He approached and gently pulled it. Just enough to peek inside.

He wanted to make completely sure it was the same person, before raising the alarm.

As he lifted the curtain, however, he suddenly realized the danger he was putting himself in. A thief lived here. No ordinary thief, according to the medjay. Zet couldn't hope for help from a passerby. The alley behind him was empty. And Zet had no weapon.

Before he could change his mind, two strong hands grabbed him by the shoulders and hauled him inside.

"What's this?" the man growled. "A spy?"

"Let go!" Zet said, struggling.

"Why should I?" he said. "What are you doing, sticking your head in my door?" His sun-darkened face was the color of old leather. A scar ran down one cheek, and mud stained his calves.

"You're a thief!" Zet said. "Let go, or you'll be in more trouble! They'll come for you!"

"Who have you led to my door?" he said.

Zet was about to say medjay, hoping the man would believe him and let him go, when a woman hurried into the room. Flour covered her hands.

"What's this? Let go of the poor boy! What's come over you?" she cried.

"He followed me," the man said, but the anger had gone out of his voice.

The woman wiped hairs from her cheek, leaving a streak of flour. She was dressed simply, and her black hair hung in a neat braid. "Why would he do that? And what's got you so upset?"

The man slumped onto a three-legged stool. "Medjay were chasing me."

"He's a thief!" Zet said.

"Will someone please tell me what's going on?" the woman said, looking from Zet to her husband and back again.

"Now, Ama," he said, "Do you really take your good husband for a thief?"

She planted a hand on his shoulder. "Of course not." She brushed away her floury prints. "What happened?"

"First, bring me and the boy some water. I think we're both thirsty from running." He looked at Zet for confirmation.

Zet nodded. Seeing the man now, he realized he was telling the truth. While he'd looked frightening in the doorway, he could see he was simply a hard worker. And the laugh lines etched deeply around his eyes and mouth spoke of kindness.

The man stood and offered Zet his stool, and went in search of another. The house smelled good, like flowers. He searched for the source of the smell and was rewarded by the sight of one of their big clay bowls on a low table, filled to the brim with fragrant, flowering herbs. The bowl was etched all around with blue water birds; funny how he remembered liking it when he was little—and now here it was like a long-lost friend. They must have bought it years ago.

The man returned, and Ama came back a moment later with three clay cups balanced on a tray of woven straw. The water tasted pure and cool, and Zet drank thirstily.

The man set down his cup.

"I'll tell you both what happened. My name is Padus. I'm a papyrus farmer. I have a plot of land on the bank of the Nile, where I tend my papyrus plants. It's a small plot, but it yields enough reeds to barter with the paper makers and feed me and my Ama here."

"Why were those medjay chasing you?" Zet said.

He smiled and held up a calloused hand. "I'm coming to that. It started when I was leaving my field. I was walking through my reeds, slowly, checking for insects and rot, that sort of thing. They're very tall this time of year—much taller than me. I overheard a man talking. I was surprised, because few people just wander into my plot." He shrugged. "There's no reason to. There's nothing worth stealing, and it's not particularly interesting, unless you're a farmer."

He took a deep sip of water, then set his cup down.

"As I said, I heard voices. Given the thick vegetation, I couldn't see who was speaking. But I did hear one man say, *Now that we have the building plans, we're set. All you need to do is to make sure our buyer is at* —" Padus paused, and color suffused his cheeks.

"At what?" Zet said.

"That's the problem. I don't know." He ran a hand over his head. Frustration was clear on his face. "That's the last I heard. I was so stupid to let them see me! I didn't think. I just stepped out into the open. And they stopped talking."

Zet groaned. If Padus had held back just a little longer, they'd be able to solve the case.

"I know," Padus said, as if reading Zet's thoughts.

"What did they look like?" Zet asked.

"One was quite fat, a large man with a short, beaded wig. Wealthy. Rings on every finger. And in one hand, he had what looked like a large scroll wrapped in leather."

"A scroll—the building plans they were talking about," Ama said.

"Exactly," Padus said. "But building plans for what, I don't know."

"What about the other man?" Zet said. "You said there were two."

"Yes. The other one was tall and thin and bony, with a long neck. He looked like a boiled chicken, if you know what I mean."

Zet grinned. "So what happened after they saw you?"

"I looked at them, and they looked at me, and the fat one shouted, 'Get him!' Well, I could have told them they were trespassing, but that didn't seem like a good idea because the thin one pulled out a knife. I didn't wait to find out if he planned to use it. I just started running! I ran for town, hoping I'd lose them in the alleys."

"So then why were the medjay chasing you?"

"I think the big man must be some kind of official, because a medjay recognized him, and he yelled that I was a thief and that I'd stolen something. I was lucky to make it home."

Zet nodded. It had been close. "It's good you're a fast runner."

"That won't do me much good now, though. I'm afraid to leave my house. They've seen my face. You know what happens to thieves. And if he's official, and it's state business, it's death for certain. But if I don't leave home, how can I tend my fields?"

Ama looked stricken. "But you're innocent!"

Zet jumped to his feet. "That reminds me, you'd better bring your sandals inside!"

"Why?" Padus jumped up, hearing the warning in Zet's voice.

4

THE LIST

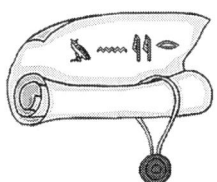

Zet was closer to the door. He ran for it.

"I told a medjay the man they were chasing had mismatched sandals," he told Padus.

Throwing the curtain aside, Zet snatched them up. Barely had he done so when a medjay turned into the alley. Zet clutched them to his chest. The medjay glanced curiously at Zet.

"Good morning," the medjay said. His muscled shoulders shone with sweat.

"Good morning," Zet replied. "Just—er—getting my sandals here!"

"Those look a little big for your feet, boy."

"Oh! Yes. Growing into them."

The medjay stopped and scanned Zet's face more closely. "Do I know you? You look familiar."

"Me?" Just his luck. That was the thing about working in the market. People sometimes recognized him. "I don't think so."

The man grunted. After a moment he said, "Have a nice day." And he kept going.

Zet let out a huge sigh of relief and slid back into the house.

"Just on time," he said, handing them to Padus. "But keep them inside until the real thieves are caught."

"I don't see how that will happen." Padus said, rubbing his neck.

"I'm going to solve this mystery, that's how," Zet said.

Padus shot him a typical adult look. One with doubt written all over it.

"I found you, didn't I?" Zet said. "I'm already ahead of the medjay."

"That's true."

Zet said his goodbyes and told them he'd return with any good news. He left, pondering all the things he'd learned. When he reached his market stall, Kat was nearly frantic.

"You've been gone forever!"

He pulled her back into the shadows. "You won't believe what I've learned."

Crouching behind the tall piles of stacked clay pots, he told Kat everything that had happened. Her look of terror when he told her about Padus yanking him through the door was definitely satisfying. She whacked him when she realized he was scaring her on purpose. When she knew everything, she sat back, looking thoughtful.

"Let's take stock of everything we know so far," she said, reaching for her brush and ink.

"Why? It's not like I'm going to forget."

She found a scrap of broken pottery and pulled out the cake of ink. "Because it might be helpful. Maybe we'll get more ideas." Kat mixed the ink with a little water, and dipped the brush. "Go ahead, tell me what to put first."

Zet told her, and she began to write.

When she finished, the list looked like this:

Who:
Man #1 has a big belly and wears gold rings.
Man #2 is tall and thin. Looks like a boiled chicken.
Where:
Padus's Papyrus plot
What:
Large leather-wrapped scroll with building plans on it

Zet's heart leapt looking at the list. "We know a lot!"

"A lot more than the medjay," Kat said. "Do you think he'll pay for this list?"

Zet considered it. "Possibly. But I told him I'd bring the thief."

"Well, did you get any other ideas while I was writing?"

"Maybe we should write what to do next? How about, 'Look for the two men', and then, 'Figure out why building plans are important'."

Kat added them both. "That's a good question. How could building plans be so important? Is it for a new building, I wonder?"

They pondered this, both lost in their own thoughts.

Overhead, the sun god Ra was nearing the end of his daily voyage across the sky. Soon, he would reach the horizon. Sunlight slanted across the rooftops. It bounced off the copper plates in the market stall across the way. The stall-owner sang as he gathered them up and stacked them in two locked trunks for the night.

"We'd better pack up, too," Zet said.

They draped their pots up with linen cloths, and tied the linen down. It wasn't the most secure way of closing shop, but they couldn't exactly carry everything home. And it's what their family had always done. So far, they'd been lucky. People respected the market at night, and medjay had a habit of crossing the square frequently, knowing it was full of goods.

The date-seller left just as they did.

"Goodnight, Salatis," Zet called.

"Meddlesome boy," Salatis complained.

"Uh oh," Zet said to Kat. "I guess he's not too happy with me."

"He'll get over it, the old grump," Kat said.

He hoped Kat was right. He didn't like the idea of having an enemy, especially one in his market.

On their way home, Zet and Kat kept an eye out for the two men Padus had described. They passed dozens of people. A scribe with a sack of writing tools. A barber with a box of razors and shaving oils. A woman carrying a baby in one arm and leading a goat with the other.

But none of them matched the description Padus had given.

5
HOME

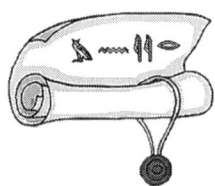

Soon Zet could see their doorway up ahead. Cozy lamplight spilled through the front window into the narrow street. The air smelled of rich stew and baking bread. Zet's stomach roared with hunger. He turned to his sister and said,

"Let's not tell Mother about this, all right?"

She frowned. "Why not? You mean lie?"

"I don't mean lie. I mean, just don't mention it."

"I'm not going to keep things from her. Why should I? First, she'd probably think it was interesting. And second—"

"And second, she'd think it was dangerous, that's what she'd think! And she'd tell me not to do it!"

"Well then maybe you shouldn't. Maybe you should be focusing on the stall instead of wasting time chasing after a thief. That's the medjay's job!"

Zet stared at her open mouthed. "You were excited about it before!"

"Yes, well that was before I had to keep it all secret."

"Kat, Mother has barely been out of bed since she gave birth. She's finally up and well enough to get around a little. I don't want to worry her! But this deben could mean a lot. Think of it! We need it."

She stared at him with that stubborn set of jaw he hated. "I am thinking of it. You'll be off running around on some wild chase, and I'll be at the stall alone. And it's hard enough getting customers with two of us!"

"I'll do both. I promise, I'll figure out a way."

Kat's lip jutted out a little, and she wound her braid around her fist. He could tell she was beginning to waver.

"Just one day," he said quickly. "Tomorrow. And if I can't figure out any more clues, we'll forget it. Deal?"

Kat blew out a breath. She glanced at their home, and back at Zet again. "Fine."

He grinned, elated.

"But just until tomorrow!" she said, rolling her eyes at his victory dance.

Over dinner, the mystery was temporarily forgotten. The family sat comfortably on overstuffed cushions before a low table. Lamplight danced on the whitewashed walls. Zet, Kat and his mother talked and laughed. It felt so good to see their mother back to her old self again.

Their baby brother, Apu, earned the most attention; he was trying to walk. The three cheered him on. The baby rewarded them by taking his first three unsteady steps. Then he squealed with delight and fell over.

Everyone wanted their turn to give him a hug of congratulations.

Later, while everyone got ready for bed, Zet knelt before the household shrine. Their statue of Bastet, the cat goddess, was small but made of the finest ebony. She had been the household god of his father, and his father's father before that. The statue had been handed down from father to son for many generations. One day it would be his. Age had softened her features. He lit a stick of incense and prayed to her for help in finding the thieves.

"Because it's not right to steal, and Padus shouldn't have to live in fear for something he did not do."

He rubbed Bastet's carved, ebony head. Even though she was a statue, he felt sure she enjoyed it.

He climbed up to the rooftop. During the very hot months, he and his sister liked to bring their sleeping pallets up there where it was cooler. Zet lay down under the vault of stars. For a long time, he tossed and turned. Finally, he pushed the linen sheet from his shoulder and sat up.

"Are you still awake?" he whispered to Kat.

"Yes," she mumbled.

"I want to go to the papyrus field. There might be a clue we're missing that the men left behind."

"Good idea. As long as you get up early and go before work."

"No. I'm going right now. What if those men go back to check and make sure they didn't leave anything?"

Kat struggled upright. He could see her staring, wide-eyed, in the moonlight. "That's exactly why you shouldn't go tonight. It's too dangerous!"

"I'll be careful," he said. He pulled on his kilt.

"I'm coming with you," Kat said.

"Forget it. Like you said, it's too dangerous."

She fastened her hair behind her neck in a low ponytail. "That's exactly why I'm coming. Someone has to keep an eye out while you search."

He had to admit it was a good idea. He could use a look-out.

He nodded. "All right. But we have to be quiet leaving."

"I know that!" she said. "I might be your younger sister, but I'm not a baby."

They crept downstairs. Zet found the oil lamp in the kitchen, along with a flint and an extra wick. Barefoot, they padded outside.

In the narrow streets, they kept to the shadows. Even though they weren't doing anything wrong, people would question why two kids were out at this hour. They didn't need strangers slowing them down with questions. They needed to move fast, before their mother awoke and found them gone.

"How far is this place?" Kat whispered.

"Past the old palace, and then down the long road that leads south out of town."

"All the way out there?"

"You're the one who said you wanted to come. Now come on, let's hurry up."

It was hard to find their way in the dark. Things looked different at night.

"I recognize that chapel," Kat said. "It's the chapel of Mut. Look, there's the goddess's Hearing Ear shrine. I'm pretty sure we turn left."

She was right. There was the niche on the chapel's side wall. Inside was the shrine with the stele—the stone carving—covered with dozens of engraved ears. During the day, the Hearing Ear shrine would often be crowded with worshipers coming to speak to the goddess. They'd ask her for favors or help with whatever ailed them. Now, it was empty.

Moments later, they were passing the old palace.

Soon, they reached the road out of town. The air smelled different. Night-blooming flowers perfumed the soft breeze. Mixed with the flowers came the brackish smell of the Nile River.

It felt strange and exciting and dangerous to be out walking at this late hour.

"I think we're almost there," Zet whispered. "He said there was a white road marker, followed by a stand of acacia." He pointed. "There's the road marker."

"And there's the stand of acacia!" Kat said.

And beyond that, they could easily see the thick shoots of papyrus rising to meet the dark sky. Zet, excited, sprinted ahead. Kat caught up quickly.

He paused before a path that led into the dark, towering plants.

6

THE SEARCH

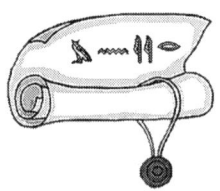

Zet looked at Kat, whose eyes were wide.

"I'm not standing guard out here, if that's what you're thinking," she said.

"Then let's go. This has to be where the men entered."

Kat stood rooted to the spot, peering into the black, murky pathway. "Maybe we should leave."

"We're not leaving! We came all this way."

"And we can just as easily go all the way back," she said. Still, she followed him into the inky tunnel of plants.

"Ow!" Zet stopped and she banged into him.

"Why did you stop?" she whispered.

"Because that's the fourth time you stepped on my ankle!" he whispered back.

"Oh. Sorry."

They carried on. Soon, the ground turned soft and muddy under their bare feet.

"Wait!" Zet whispered suddenly.

"What is it?" came Kat's frightened reply.

"We might be stepping on evidence."

Kat whacked his shoulder in the dark. "You almost scared me to death! I thought you heard someone."

"At this hour? Don't worry, we're alone," he said. *He sure hoped it.* "Let's light the lamp. Here, hold it while I do the flint."

A moment later, light sprang up. Kat's face looked eerie, all shadows and bouncing light. She set the lamp near the ground. They both got down on all fours to search. They scoured the ground for some time in silence.

"Anything?" Kat whispered.

"It's muddier up there. Keep going. I think I see something."

Sure enough, a chaotic jostle of footprints had been etched deeply into the mud.

"This must be where they saw each other!" Zet said.

There were three distinct sets of footprints. One set, whose soles didn't match, which clearly belonged to Padus.

"And look, these deeper ones must belong to the fat man," Kat reasoned. "Since he weighs more."

There was a third set; the feet were huge, but failed to make deep impressions. They had to belong to the tall thin man.

Together, Zet and Kat combed the area for other clues. He'd hoped maybe they'd left something behind, like a ring or a piece of torn fabric. Some kind of information they could use.

"Nothing," he finally said, when he'd gone over everything three times to be sure. "You?"

"Nope." Kat sounded as disappointed as he felt.

"We better go," Zet said.

He doused the lamp and they headed for the road.

"What a waste of time!" Kat said. "And I was really starting to get hopeful."

"It wasn't a complete waste of time," Zet said. "At least we know Padus was telling the truth."

"True," Kat said. "But still. What more can we possibly learn about the thieves? All we know is their description. Thebes is a big city, and even if we did see a fat man and a skinny one, there's no crime in that. It could describe dozens of people."

Zet's heart sank, because he knew what she said was true. And he'd felt so certain he could solve the case! The medjay was right. Zet had been foolish and arrogant to think he could do a better job than the official medjay.

"I guess this whole thing was a dumb idea," he said. "Sorry I dragged you out here."

He was glad Kat didn't say 'I told you so', even if she *was* obviously thinking it.

Papyrus stalks brushed his bare shoulders. The fluffy plant tops wavered overhead. Beyond them, a sea of stars sparkled in the black sky. Tomorrow he'd be back at his market stall, praying for customers. Just like any other day. Except things would be worse now. True, they were rich in pots. But one couldn't eat clay. And he'd imagined the money so clearly!

"Who passes there?" came a voice.

Kat squeaked in fright.

Zet spun, crouching, ready to attack.

At first, he saw only a pile of rags in the ditch alongside the road. But when the rags moved, he stepped closer. It was a beggar woman. Her bony arms jutted from an old linen tunic that was at least six sizes too big. Deep wrinkles lined her face, but her skin looked soft for someone who clearly spent her life outdoors, and was the color of washed linen.

"We're just on our way home," Zet said.

"I'm sorry we don't have anything to give you," Kat said. "I wish we had!"

"Thank you. You're kind," the old woman said.

Zet suddenly had an idea. "Were you here yesterday?"

The old woman nodded. "My ears were listening."

Kat and Zet looked at each other. It was a strange answer, but clearly it meant she'd been here. He could feel his heart increase in speed. Maybe she'd seen something. Maybe they'd get some more information.

"I wondered if I could ask you something?"

She nodded, and turned to him.

Silver moonlight lit her face, and he saw her fully for the first time. Although she was old and wrinkled, he could see that she must have been pretty once. But it was her strange eyes that drew his attention.

Without thinking, he sucked in his breath.

"Yes," she said. "I am blind."

"I'm sorry," he said, understanding the curious answer she'd given earlier. "We shouldn't bother you."

"Ask me your question, young man. You may be surprised by the answer."

"All right." He glanced at Kat, and then went on. "Some men came here yesterday and chased a friend of ours. Did you . . . *hear* anything?"

She smiled. "I did. My ears remember it well. The men were quite rude, as a matter of fact. One of them, a heavy fellow, cursed me." She rubbed her throat as if in remembrance. "He's not a good man."

Zet wasn't surprised to see Kat scowl at the news. She always wanted to take care of the helpless. She made a habit of putting out food for stray cats, and carrying handouts for the downtrodden.

"That's terrible!" Kat said.

Zet agreed. Then, realizing it was getting late, he told her they had to go. He couldn't help feeling disappointed. For coming such a long way, and risking their mother's anger, they hadn't learned much at all.

"Wait!" the blind woman said. "I haven't told you what I know."

"There's more?" he said, hopeful but wondering what more she could tell them, being blind.

"You sound surprised. I may no longer have my sight. But I've found ways to make the other senses keener. So let me tell you this. First, one of the men you seek, the big one who stepped on me, smells of temple incense."

Zet nodded, taking this detail in. True, it was something they didn't know. But not particularly useful. He couldn't walk around smelling people and hope to find the thief.

"And second, his accomplice speaks with a stutter."

"A stutter!" Zet cried. "That's a good clue! We could use that!"

She smiled, satisfied, and nestled back into her rags.

"We'll bring you lunch tomorrow," Kat said suddenly.

"Good idea," Zet said. Even though it would be a busy day, he more than wanted to help this kind woman. He wanted to thank her for the information.

"Thanks are not necessary," she said. "It is I who thank you for finding the thieves."

"But we want to!" Kat said.

"You are a good girl." She paused, and after a long moment inclined her head. "I look forward to it."

Finding the thieves would not be easy; he knew it was a long shot. But the old woman had given him hope.

7

THE THIN-MAN

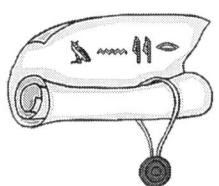

As they made their way home, Zet and Kat talked about the poor old woman camped along the roadside. How awful it would be to have no home.

They reached the dark city and wound through the silent streets. The paving stones felt almost cold at this time of night. They made a wrong turn into a short alleyway that stank of rotting fish and vegetables.

"Ugh," Kat said, covering her face. "Someone's using the dead-end as a garbage heap."

Plugging his nose, Zet backed out at a run.

Soon, they were back on familiar territory.

"Now that we know the thin one stutters," Zet said, "This should be easy!"

She didn't look quite as certain. Still, she said, "People probably would remember a stutter."

"Exactly! Tomorrow, we can ask everyone who comes to the stall. Someone will recognize their description."

"Everyone? I agree we should ask around, but I, for one, am not going to pester everyone. And neither should you!"

Zet laughed. "Okay, not everyone. But admit it. You're excited too!"

She grinned. "Maybe I am."

Think how proud his mother would be if he brought home the ransom! Her eyes would shine, and she'd tell him that his father would be happy to know what a good son he had.

Kat broke into his thoughts. "I can't help wondering about those building plans."

"What about them?"

"Just that they must be very important. I wonder what building the plans belong to?"

"I don't know, but you're right. What if they're for something official?"

She nodded. "I think they must be."

In the light of this, Zet felt even more urgent about finding the stolen scroll.

Back home their mother and the baby slept on. Zet and Kat tiptoed into the kitchen and cleaned their muddy feet as best they could. It was difficult in the dark. By some miracle, no one woke up. Together they crept up to the roof, thankful their departure had gone unnoticed. As soon as Zet's head hit the sheets, he nodded off to sleep. It had been a long day.

The next morning, Kat shook Zet awake.

"Come on! Mother's changing the baby."

He wiped the sleep from his eyes and groaned. "What's the big rush?"

"The third lunch. Remember? Unless you want to explain where we were last night?"

"Oh. Good point."

In the kitchen, they quickly set out three clay bowls. Into each they put chickpea salad, left over from the night before. On top of the salad went a thick hunk of bread. On top of the bread they put a handful of sweet, dried apricots.

"Can I help you in there?" their mother called.

"No!" Kat answered, quickly tying the bundles in linen.

"Hurry," Zet whispered, and shoved them into his sack.

Packed and ready to go, they said goodbye to their mother and headed outside.

Despite the early hour, hot sunshine cooked the paving stones. In some streets, laundry hung overhead on lines that attached clear across the sky—from building to building. The laundry cast rectangular shadows on the ground. In their bare feet, they hopped from one dark rectangle to the next, enjoying the coolness of the shaded spots.

Every time they met a person, Zet stopped to describe the men they were looking for. But no one had heard of them. They must have asked two dozen people. And the answer was always the same.

Kat wound her braid in her fist, then flung it over her shoulder. "I can't believe no one's seen them! No one!"

In silence, they untied the linen coverings from the neat stack of pottery dishes, bowls and pots. Zet took a stand up front. Despite Kat's warning, he still asked everyone who came to browse their wares.

A young woman who'd bought dishes there before stopped to chat with Kat. Zet's mouth dropped open when he overheard Kat ask about the two men. When the conversation broke up and Kat came out into the sunshine, Zet was grinning to himself.

"What's that look about?" she demanded.

"Nothing."

"I'm curious, too, all right? So there." She stuck out her tongue.

He broke out laughing.

Kat fetched the sack of food. "Come on, jackal-head. Let's go to Padus's field. It's lunch time."

They closed up the stall, tying sheets of linen over their wares. Zet picked up the sack of food. Time was short, so they ran most of the way. The clay pots thunked together in the bag, bouncing against his back. It was a good thing Kat had tied the bundles so tightly, or they'd have spilled everywhere.

Both gasping and out of breath, they reached the entrance to Padus's field.

The old woman smiled up at them.

"You've come back," she said.

"How did you know it was us?" Zet said.

At this, her cheeks dimpled. "Still so little trust in my powers of observation, I see!" She patted the ground kindly, like a grandmother welcoming them to her house. Her hands were gnarled, but a fine gold chain circled her wrist.

"Come, sit," she said. "It's not often I have such loyal visitors. Let me enjoy my treat."

Together the three sat and ate, talking and laughing. The old woman asked them all about their stall in the market. She asked about their mother and father, and baby brother. She asked what it was like to be young and have the freedom to run around Thebes with quick legs and healthy, seeing eyes. They talked, eager to entertain her. She listened, rapt, hanging on their every word.

Finally the time came to go. Kat looked a little sad, and the old woman patted her hand.

"You've made me very happy today. Now go. And Zet?"

"Yes?" he said, bowing to her.

"Catch your thieves."

"I'll try," he said.

She nodded, satisfied. "I know you will give it your best."

After wrapping up their things, Zet and Kat hurried down the road. They needed to get back to their market stall. They couldn't afford to miss any buyers that might come looking to barter for some clay pots.

They had walked for several minutes, when a tall man burst out of a neighboring field. Dirt caked his calves. Scars marked his whip-like arms. His legs were long and thin.

Zet watched absently, wondering why the strange man was in such a hurry.

8

THE CHASE

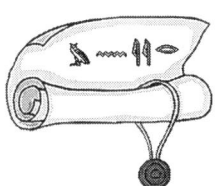

There came the sound of hooves approaching from behind. Zet tore his eyes from the odd looking man up ahead, and glanced back. Two donkeys approached, kicking up clouds of dry, red dust. Flies buzzed around the donkeys' furry gray ears, which flapped in earnest.

Seated on the bigger donkey was a squat man in a thick tunic.

"Hi!" Zet called as the man passed.

"Afternoon!" The man's red cheeks puffed into a grin. Up on the donkey, he jostled left and right. He looked surprisingly comfortable doing it—especially since his feet almost scraped the ground. His right hand held a rope, which pulled the second donkey along.

The animals trotted onward, tails flicking like fly-whisks.

Suddenly, up ahead, the thin-legged man stepped out into the donkeys' path.

"S-stop!" he cried.

Zet froze, his ears on alert.

"What do you want?" the donkey owner said.

"I n-n-need a ride. To t-town," the man said.

Zet gasped. He glanced at Kat, who stared back, wide-eyed.

"It's him!" she whispered. "He *does* look like a boiled chicken."

He put a hand on her arm. Was it possible the thief had walked right into their path? He thought of his prayers to Bastet the night before and said a silent *thank you*.

The thin-man grasped at the donkey's bridle. "I'm in a h-hurry!"

Zet's muscles tensed, ready for the chase. But the donkey owner kicked him away.

"Get back, dog!" he roared. "I don't like your filthy legs. And my donkey's not for rent." He kicked his animals into action and carried on down the road.

Zet let out a breath of relief. "Don't let him see we're following him."

"I won't," Kat scoffed.

They hung back, allowing the thin-man to get ahead some distance. On the open road, it was easy to keep him in view. His tall, thin shadow lurched along at a fast clip. Twice, he glanced back, seeming to take no notice of Zet or his sister.

The walls of the city rose in the distance, brown mud brick growing ever clearer. Voices of people and sounds and smells of industry filled the air: clanks of hammers, the pungent odor of the leather tannery, shouts of people offering their wares. Fishing boats clustered along the wharf. Ruddy fishermen hauled out their catch, while customers stood watching. The full nets hit the paving stones, the silver fish inside still struggling and leaping against their bonds.

Ahead, the thin-man turned into an alley.

Zet and Kat darted to catch up.

Three chatting women with marketing baskets on their arms blocked their view.

Zet and Kat squeezed past, desperate not to lose their quarry.

But the thin-man was gone.

"Quick!" Zet cried. He took off, running. An alley ran crosswise. He glanced down it just in time to catch sight of the thin-man.

"Down there!" he said, "He just turned left! Come on!"

Their bare feet slapped against the ground. A man in a gold-edged tunic growled at them to slow down. They kept running. Zet flew around a corner. He recognized the small town square with the fruit and vegetable market ahead.

"He must be up there somewhere," he said, breathing hard.

Kat kept pace with him, her keen eyes searching.

They flew into the open market. He glanced right, past the herb stall. Baskets with pyramids of colorful spices blocked any view of the far alleys.

"Split up. Meet on the other side!"

Zet wove left. Around the bags of grain. He banged into a man who was lifting a sack over his shoulder. Wheat flew everywhere. Zet's bag with the three empty bowls clattered across the ground. He snatched it up and kept running.

"Stop!" the man shouted, cursing.

Zet kept running. He glanced back over his shoulder to see if the man was following him. He didn't see the basket of lemons until he tripped over them. They rolled under his feet, sending him flying one way, his bag crashing the other.

"Boy! My lemons!" the stall owner cried.

"Sorry," Zet gasped, scrambling to his feet and taking off.

At the far end of the stalls, Kat was running to meet him. With a glance back, he spotted the man from the wheat stall, and the lemon seller. Both were red-faced. Both were running.

Both shouted, "STOP!"

Zet grabbed Kat and kept going.

"Did you see him?"

"No, you?"

"Nope."

They flew headlong until finally, the men gave up. Seeing the alley behind them was clear, they slowed to a walk and caught their breath.

"We had him!" Zet cried. "I can't believe we had him! That was our one chance. We'll never find him now."

"Zet?" Kat asked.

He glanced at his sister. Color flushed her cheeks, and her damp bangs stuck to her forehead.

"I don't know if you noticed," she said. "But that thief was really big. And really scary. What, exactly, were you going to do if we caught him?"

Zet shrugged. "I don't know. Something."

She put both hands to her glistening forehead and slowly wiped away the sweat. Then she flopped back against a wall and crossed her arms over her chest. "This is way too dangerous."

"If we'd followed him, we'd at least know where he was going. Maybe he was going to his house. We could've waited until he left and searched it for the stolen papyrus."

She bit her lip. "Maybe."

"Anyway, it doesn't matter now," Zet said, unable to hide his disappointment. "We better head back to our stall."

Glancing around, he took in the unfamiliar surroundings. They'd run far, up and down the city's maze of twisting alleys.

"Which way?" Kat said.

"We might as well go straight. Maybe we'll come to something recognizable."

TEMPLE OF AMENEMOPET

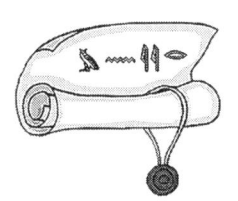

Zet and Kat walked in silence, scanning for familiar landmarks.

He wondered if any customers had come to the stall. It would be just his luck that the one time they weren't there, half a dozen buyers had shown up and left empty-handed. His mother had commented last night at dinner that they were running very low on grain and beans.

Straightening his shoulders, he strode forward. Enough with this thief business. It wasn't turning out, and it might even be costing them money. He'd lost his bag with three of his mother's good bowls. She'd be crushed when she found out they were gone. Even worse, Kat was right—it was dangerous. What if Kat had been hurt? She might be a brat sometimes, but still.

He'd never forgive himself.

"Look!" Kat gasped, her fingers wrapping around his wrist and yanking him to a halt.

They'd reached a wider avenue. Crowds were coming and going. Beyond the people, great stone steps rose to the entrance of a temple. And on the steps, speaking with a young, acolyte priest, stood their thief.

"The temple of Amenemopet!" Zet said.

Despite having seen the temple once before, it was no less impressive today. Six huge statues of Pharaoh Ramses towered out front—two seated, four standing. A matching pair of stone pylons loomed on each side of a giant wooden door.

Zet's heart plummeted as the acolyte led the thief toward the entrance. They'd never be allowed in there.

Kat nodded, her face glum.

"Stay here," Zet said suddenly. He had to get in there. He had to try.

As he took off, running, Kat kept up with him. "I'm coming with you."

"No way! You're the one who said it was too dangerous!"

"I changed my mind."

Zet groaned. But there was no time to argue. They wove between pedestrians. They pounded up the steps. Six granite faces of Ramses stared down at them. The statues looked even sterner from this angle. People weren't supposed to just barge in. The temples were sacred. There were strict rules about who could enter.

So then why had the thief gone into such a holy place?

He made up his mind. He had to get inside. They reached the door. He couldn't believe their luck! The acolyte had left it ajar.

One hand on the thick wood, Zet paused and turned to his sister. "Promise me. If anything happens, run. Even if I'm caught. Agreed?"

She nodded.

He took a deep breath. He expected someone to shout at them from the street. No one did.

Pushing it open just enough to squeeze past, he and Kat slipped inside.

The hush was instant. After the noisy crowd outside, it felt as if a blanket of silence had dropped over them. Thick, sweet incense hovered in the stillness. Although the occasional chink of light shone down from holes in the roof, overall it was heavy with shadows.

Zet let his eyes adjust.

A forest of colossal pillars stood before them. Even from where he stood he counted dozens. They were spaced closely, at even intervals across the hall. Hieroglyphs had been chiseled up and down their length. Zet was unable to read the complex hieroglyphic symbols. Still, he guessed what was on those pillars.

Powerful magic. Curses to ward off intruders.

He shivered.

In the distance, he heard low voices.

Zet motioned Kat forward. Their bare feet whispered against the cool floor. They went on tiptoe from pillar to pillar. The voices grew clearer.

"I warned you not to come here!" a deep-voiced man growled.

"I had to t-t-tell you, didn't I?" came the answer.

"So he wasn't at his field. And no one knows where he lives?"

"No. I s-s-searched. And n-no one would t-t-talk to me."

So they were still looking for Padus. That's why the thin-man had been over there. But why, what were they going to do to him? A thread of fear tugged at his belly. How would Padus ever go back to his fields with these two after him?

Zet risked a peek. The two men stood in a dusty shaft of light. The big one wore a magnificent leopard skin draped over his thick shoulders. His kilt was long and expensively pleated. The belt around his waist glimmered with gold, and items of holy power hung from various loops. And just like Padus said, rings glittered on every finger. Zet had never seen so much wealth worn on a single person. The effect was almost god-like.

"Never mind," the big man said, brushing at the fur on his leopard skin. "After tomorrow night, it'll all be over. We can clean up our mess later."

Clean up their mess later?

Zet swallowed and ducked back out of sight. He didn't like that sound of that! Apparently, neither did Kat, because she'd begun to tremble all over.

"That's what I wanted to t-t-talk to you about," the thin-man said.

"Eh? What do you mean?" growled the big man.

"It's j-just, I don't know if I l-l-like—" He stopped and gulped, audibly. "If I l-l-like s-selling the plans to Pharaoh's p—p-palace."

The last was said so low, that Zet had to crane to hear it. But when he did, his jaw dropped.

"Shut your mouth," growled the large man. "And keep it shut, or I'll have to do it permanently. Don't think I won't, either. We might go back a long way, you and I, but this is the biggest deal we've had. And I don't need you mucking it up."

"B-b-but—"

There was a long silence. Then the big man broke out in a laugh.

"Don't grow a conscience on me now, old pal," the fat man's voice had grown friendly. "We'll do our deal. Stop worrying, that's your problem!" He grunted. "We just hand it over at the Rose Bark tomorrow night, and then we can forget all about it. We'll go out and celebrate. All the food and drink you could want. All right?"

Zet risked a peek.

The thin-man stared at the floor, but nodded. The other slapped him heartily on the back.

"What are you doing here?" came a man's voice, right behind Zet.

Zet turned quickly. Kat cried out as the young man seized both of them by their elbows.

It was the young acolyte priest they'd seen outside on the steps. Apart from a single sidelock of hair, braided and tied in a tight coil, the rest of his head was shaved. His tunic was of the purest white linen. He looked down with distaste at Zet and Kat's filthy legs and feet. They were both sweaty and dirty from running in the dusty streets.

"This is a holy place! You defile it with your filth!" he cried. "What are you doing in here?"

"We just—"

"Who's there?" growled the big man.

Zet gulped and looked at Kat. Her eyes were wide with terror.

HIGH PRIEST

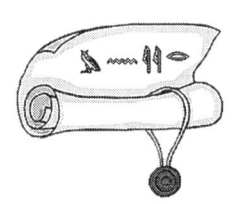

The acolyte yanked Zet and Kat from their hiding place behind the pillar.

"My apologies, High Priest."

High Priest? The big man with the rings was High Priest of the Temple of Amenemopet?

How was that possible? What did this mean?

The acolyte bowed low, and forced Zet and Kat to do the same. "Two children," he said, still bent forward as if speaking to the floor. "They must have snuck past me when I was returning to the steps."

"Come here, my children," the High Priest said.

"Go," the acolyte said, and shoved them forward.

Zet didn't know whether to keep bowing, so he just kept his eyes on the ground. He remembered what their friend, the beggar woman near Padus's field said: the big one smells of temple incense. Now he understood why. The sweet smell was all around them, wafting through the shadows. It mixed with his terror, making him dizzy.

This was who they were up against? The medjay, Merimose, would never believe Zet when he told him the High Priest was a thief! Zet knew they were in much bigger trouble than he could ever imagine.

Not only could he never win, he and Kat might lose their lives. And the High Priest could order it done.

He wanted to run, but that would only show their guilt. So he kept walking carefully forward, keeping his eyes cast down.

Kat took Zet's hand. Her damp fingers shook.

He had to think fast. He had to say something that would get them out of there. But what? What could he say?

The High Priest made a dismissive wave with one jeweled hand at the acolyte.

"Leave us," he said.

The acolyte kept his head down. "Yes, Your Grace."

"And count yourself lucky I'm in a lenient mood," the High Priest told him. "But do not forget your duty in this holy temple. Next time, you won't get off so easy."

"I understand, Your Grace," the acolyte said. He sounded truly upset.

The High Priest waited until the young man's footsteps died away.

"So." He turned to Zet and Kat. "Come closer and let's have a look at you, shall we?"

Trying to keep his knees from knocking, Zet came forward. He stopped a few feet away from the High Priest and the now silent thin-man. Kat still held Zet's hand. Her grip was so tight, his fingers were turning numb.

"Look at me," the High Priest said. His voice was kind enough, but his eyes were like small, black stones.

Zet guessed the High Priest was trying to figure out what they'd overheard.

"Do you know where you are?" the High Priest asked.

Zet swallowed, and then nodded. "A temple," he said, deciding to play dumb.

"Not just any temple," he said. "This is the great temple of Amenemopet." He waited to see what sort of impression this made.

"Oh," Zet said.

"And do you know who I am?"

"That man, the one with the hair-lock, called you the High Priest."

"Indeed, I am."

Zet got to his knees, and dragged his sister down with him. He pressed his face to the floor. "We are so very honored. I never imagined I might be in the presence of such a great man." He didn't need to pretend to be impressed. His voice trembled of its own accord. "We . . . well we came from the fields, you see. For help."

"Ah. Indeed?" The man's voice still sounded suspicious, but a note of curiosity crept into it. "You risked the anger of the gods, and my anger, for help?"

"Yes, Your Grace."

"You are a brave boy, then. And you are farmers?"

"Look at my legs, Your Grace, and my sister's," Zet said, still speaking to the floor. "You must know that we come straight from the fields. We did not realize our filth would be a stain on this clean holiness in here."

Zet could feel the High Priest's eyes, drilling into his skull. Several moments passed. Sweat dribbled down his neck. He didn't dare move.

The man broke the silence, and there was the hint of a smile in his voice. "It's true, you are dirty. But farmers keep our good people fed. We cannot forget that. Egypt is forever grateful to our field workers. And I like bravery. It amuses me."

Zet didn't dare raise his head; he feared his relief would give them away.

The High Priest laughed. "Come now, you may rise. I'm not Pharaoh." It was clear to Zet, however, that he was enjoying his power over them. And that realization just might let them escape.

"We are too lowly to stand in your presence, Your Grace."

"Now, now," he laughed. "It was wrong of you to come here, but I will hear your petition."

Zet swallowed. "The reason we have come is because we have fallen on hard times. Our father has gone to fight in the war. My sister here and I must tend to our . . . work, by ourselves. And this has not been a good year. I don't want to burden you with our problems.

They are too complicated to explain. I just want to tell you that soon, we will be in dire straits."

"The temple is not a bank," the High Priest said, annoyance creeping into his voice.

"We did not come asking for that kind of help."

"Then what is it you want?"

"We simply want your blessing. A blessing from a man as powerful as yourself. You have the ear of the gods. You have the ear of Amenemopet himself. We simply ask that you include us once in your prayers, that we may find relief from our troubles."

The High Priest stepped forward. "You are a good boy." He touched Zet's shoulder, and Kat's in turn. "I grant you my blessing. And I will do as you ask. I will put in a good word to Amenemopet for you."

"Thank you! Oh, thank you," he cried.

Kat, still clinging to Zet's hand, nodded frantically.

"Now run along. And heed what I told my acolyte. You were lucky to find me in good spirits."

"Yes, thank you again, Your Grace, thank you!" He and Kat ran for the exit.

"Boy!" the High Priest called.

Zet turned.

The fat man's face was a mask once again. His eyes looked dark and frightening, shadowed as they were in the dark hall. "Do not dare set foot in my temple again."

AN UNWANTED VISITOR

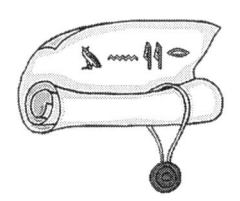

Zet and Kat squeezed out through the temple's tall wooden door. On the steps, the acolyte priest scowled at them. But Zet was too relieved to feel very sorry for him. Still, he and Kat apologized. Then they hurried off down into the crowded boulevard.

"I was sure we were dead!" Kat gasped.

"Me too," Zet said.

"I don't know how you thought up that whole business about the field," she said.

"It was true, we were at a field, and we do need help," he said.

She started to giggle. "Oh my gosh, and he gave us his blessing and everything!"

They were running, and Zet started laughing too. One of those crazy, relieved laughs. After they'd gone a little way, their laughter sputtered out. Kat put her hand to her chest. She pulled him off to the side of the road and sank down against a wall.

"Let's just catch our breath a moment. I feel sick," she said.

"I don't feel so great myself."

With the adrenaline draining from him, he felt suddenly exhausted.

It was some time later that they roused themselves and joined the crowds.

"I can't believe he's the High Priest!" Zet whispered.

"I know," Kat said, shock clear in her voice. "He has everything. Why risk this?"

It felt like his whole world had been turned upside down. The temples had always seemed so sacred. So overwhelming. So steadfast and true. To think that the High Priest of the Temple of Amenemopet was corrupt made him feel unsteady. He didn't want to believe it. But he had no choice.

"Not all the priests are like that. Do you think?" Kat said.

Zet took a few moments to consider this. "No," he said. "No, I don't. That acolyte wasn't."

She nodded. "No, I think you're right."

"But this is bad, Kat. The High Priest, selling plans to Pharaoh's palace? I don't know what the buyer wants with them, but it can't be good."

"We have to go to the medjay," she said. "This is too big for us."

"And say what? No one would believe us."

They turned down a familiar street. They were nearing their little market, and the safe familiarity of their stall. He ran his hands along the wall of the building next to him as he walked. Then he smacked his fist into the bricks in frustration.

"You're right. For once, I agree with you. But don't get all gloating on me," he said. "I'm not going up against the High Priest of Amenemopet. But I'm not going to tell the medjay either. They'll figure it out, it's their job!"

Kat bit her lip. "Will they, though?"

"Look, we can't win! We need to get back to the stall and start trying to make some sales. I'll die if I find out customers came and we weren't there."

Business was in full swing when they reached the square.

A man was arguing with a stall-owner over the price of beer. Salatis was filling a customer's shopping basket with dates. Their own stall looked strange, still closed and wrapped in its linen sheets. One of the sellers frowned his disapproval as Zet and Kat hurried over and began to pull the covers off.

A few moments later, the sheets were folded and put away. They stood, eager to draw customers.

"Clay pots!" Zet called. "Clay pots for sale! Sturdy pots and bowls!"

Kat added her voice to his. It was nice to hear their shouts ringing off the stones. The frightening experiences they'd had over the last two days were quickly fading. He'd been crazy to strike up that bargain! Only the thought of poor Padus and his wife kept him from being happy.

"The best clay pots in Thebes!" he called, trying to sound brighter than he felt.

"Hey, boy!" called Salatis.

Zet glanced over.

"Come here," Salatis called.

Zet looked at Kat, shrugged and then crossed the distance to the date-seller's stall.

"You missed out. Someone came to your stall earlier."

It was exactly what he'd feared. After days of no sales, someone showed up the one time he was gone. "Did you tell them we'd be back?"

Salatis nodded. "They waited for you, you know," he said in a sour, disapproving voice. "For a long time."

Zet's shoulders sank. "Thanks for telling me. Something happened to keep us away. I just hope they'll come back. We really need to sell our pots."

"They weren't here for the pots."

Zet's head shot up and he stared into Salatis's cold, droopy eyes. "What did they want? Who was it?"

Salatis rubbed his stubbly chin, as if enjoying Zet's concern. "Someone asking about that thief."

"A medjay?" Zet said, heart hammering.

"Nope. Nosy as the other one, but nope. He said he was doing some special investigating. For the High Priest of Amenemopet. And that he heard about some pot-seller boasting about seeing the thief. I told him that was you. I pointed out your stall, and like I said, he waited around a long time. Seems your information is in demand, boy." He laughed, and his rough laugh turned to a fit of coughing.

"I see," Zet said. "Well, thanks for telling me." His heart slammed in his ears as he headed back to where Kat stood.

She hopped from foot to foot, anxious to hear what Salatis had said.

He told her, quickly.

Kat blanched.

"If they come back—"

"Not if. They're coming back!" Zet said. "They could be here any minute."

"What if the thin-man comes with them? What if they take us to the High Priest for questioning? He'll recognize us, he'll connect everything! He'll know why we were in the temple." Kat was shaking all over.

"We need to cover the stall. We need to leave. Now."

In a frenzy, they threw the sheets over the mountains of clayware. Salatis and the others looked on in surprise. The market didn't close for some time yet. Just as they tied the last piece of linen down, Zet spotted a familiar face headed their way.

"The thin-man!" he gasped. "Duck!"

"Oh, no!" Kat cried, shaking in terror as she crouched toward the back of the stall.

"He's coming." He pushed her through a narrow gap between the stacks. "Run!" he cried, struggling out after her.

IN HIDING

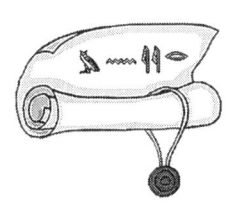

Zet and Kat darted between stalls. Their neighbor vendors stepped out of the way, their mouths open in shock.

"Hey! You!" came a shout.

Zet glanced back. The thin-man had someone with him. A huge man with a knife strapped to a belt at his waist. He wore his chest bare, and his muscles bulged. Recognition dawned on the thin-man's face.

"S-s-stop!" he cried.

Zet ran for his life.

He was already spent from the last few hours. He dug deep within himself to try and find a store of energy somewhere. Kat was flagging. She'd begun to trip. He held her by the arm, dragging her along.

"Don't stop," he gasped. "Keep going."

She nodded, breathing hard.

They'd never make it home. They needed somewhere to hide. But where?

He hauled her around a corner. Then he knew.

"Quick, this way," he said.

Footsteps pounded close behind as they turned a corner, and then another. Zet and Kat were making headway, but not by much.

"Just a little further," he said. "We have to sprint."

Together, they pulled out a blast of energy from nothing. He glanced back. They'd lost the men. Together he and Kat plunged through the curtained doorway into Padus's house.

Ama was in the middle of cleaning the floor. She glanced up in surprise.

"Zet!" she said, recognizing him at once.

He was bent forward with his hands on his knees, breathing hard. "We need to hide," he said.

"Upstairs." She hurried them to the second floor. At the top was a small, bright room, filled with tools and buckets. In the center, on a great open space on the floor, lay a giant piece of thick, wet papyrus paper. Next the paper lay several mallets. A trap door led to the roof.

"There are piles of old burlap sacks up there that Padus uses for his plants. Maybe you could wrap yourselves up in them. I'm sorry I don't have a better suggestion!"

"Where's Padus?" Zet said.

"He decided to risk going to his field. A customer was meeting him, and we can't afford to lose the business."

Zet nodded, knowing exactly how Padus felt. "I hope he doesn't get caught."

They hurried onto the roof.

Rather than hiding themselves, they inched up to the edge of the building and looked down. Below, the thin-man and his burly helper wandered into the alley. They were no longer running. Instead, they looked frustrated and tired.

"How could you lose them?" the muscled man said.

"It w-w-wasn't my f-fault!"

"Let's just head back. The kids are long gone by now."

Zet breathed a sigh of relief, and Kat did the same. They rolled onto their backs and stared at the bright afternoon sky.

"We're in big trouble, huh," Kat said.

"That's for sure," Zet agreed.

They'd been pulled in deeper than he ever thought possible. This whole situation was turning into the worst, scariest mess he could ever imagine. It would ruin them. They couldn't go back to their stall. They couldn't resume their old sales.

What would they tell their mother?

They lay silent for a very long time, each of them adrift in their own frightened thoughts.

The trap door creaked open.

"I heard you were here," Padus said.

Zet nodded, not knowing what to say. He realized he was in shock.

"Why don't you two come downstairs. It's safe. No one knows where we live. No one knows you're here."

Zet helped Kat to her feet. They climbed down into the workroom with its tools. It smelled clean and earthy, like dried plants. Ama was there. Zet made the introductions, explaining that Kat was his sister.

"As brave as your brother, I see," Padus said.

"Brave or not," Ama said, looking worried, "You'd better wait here until after dark."

Padus agreed. "After sun-down, I'll do my best to see you home safely."

"What happened out there?" Ama asked, her brows knit in a frown.

Zet ran a hand through his hair and blew out a sigh.

Ama found some cushions and smiled kindly at them. "I'm sorry, that was nosy of me. Sit down and relax. You must be exhausted. I'll bring up some water, and I've just baked fresh seed cakes."

"Thank you," Zet said. He needed some time to gather his thoughts. The fact that he could no longer go back to his stall had hit him hard. Kat looked even worse. She was white as a bird's feather. He wondered if she might faint.

Ama headed down to the kitchen.

"Look at this, Kat," Zet said, pulling his sister over to Padus's work area. Zet glanced at Padus's face. "What are you working on in here? Is that paper you're making?"

Padus caught on and quickly nodded. "I like to do a little paper making of my own up here, to earn extra. In addition to growing the plants of course. I'd make more of it, but we don't have the space."

"I've always wondered how it was made," Zet said, "Haven't you, Kat?"

She swallowed, then nodded, stepping closer to the giant sheet on the floor.

"Do you want me to show you how it's done?" Padus asked.

"That would be great!" Zet said.

Padus led them to the corner where several tall stalks of papyrus rested against the wall. He explained that he first peeled away the outer fibers, to get to the soft pith inside. Using a blade, he peeled one a little to show them.

The pith inside was pale yellowish-white, and much softer.

"Then I cut the pith-core in long strips. I make them as thin as possible. Of course, the center strips are the best because they're the widest. But I try to use as much as possible."

The next step, after the strips had been cut, was to soak them in water.

"That's what's in the buckets?" Kat asked. Her color had begun to return.

He nodded. Just then Ama appeared with the snacks.

"Don't bore them with that, husband," she said.

He grinned. "They asked."

"He's not boring us," Kat said, accepting a cup of water.

Zet took a seed cake, suddenly starving. "These are delicious!" They really were. And not just because he was starving. Ama was an excellent baker.

Ama smiled.

"It's the honey," she confided. "A trader from upriver brings it to barter for the reeds."

After they'd all eaten a little, Padus carried on with his demonstration.

"Now, I lift the slices out like so, and lay them across the floor. As you can see, they're very soft and spongy."

"And almost transparent," Kat said.

"Exactly. That's what we want. Sometimes I cut them to the length I want at this point, but usually I just pound them flat like so." He hammered them with the mallet. The slices grew flatter and wider.

"The last step is simply to lay a number of them side by side in a giant sheet, overlapping just a bit. Then I add a second layer at right angles to the first. When that's done, I pound the whole sheet, and leave it to dry for around six days or so. The sugar inside the plant makes it stick together. This big piece is around half dry. When it's ready, I'll cut it up into a dozen or more sheets."

"That's a lot of work!" Kat said. "No wonder papyrus is so expensive."

Padus nodded.

"Speaking of papyrus," Zet said. "We found out what's on the stolen scroll."

ROYAL BUILDING PLANS

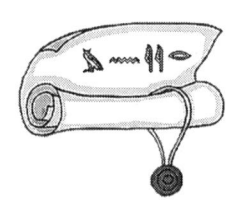

Zet's words rang in the stillness of the workroom. As if unable to believe that Zet had somehow seen the stolen papyrus, Padus and Ama stared at him with their mouths wide.

Padus finally swallowed. "But how did you manage that?"

"Is that why you were being chased?"

"Yes," Zet said.

He rubbed his neck for a minute, wondering where to begin. Finally, he started at where they'd seen the thin-man on the road. He described the chase through the streets. Kat, back to her old self again, chimed in, filling in bits. When Zet described sneaking through the door into the sacred Temple of Amenemopet, Ama and Padus gasped.

"What choice did we have? We had to follow him."

"You wouldn't have gotten me to sneak in there. No way," Ama said. Her cheeks were flushed, her eyes wide with excitement. "I would've been terrified beyond belief. So what did it look like in there? The Temple of Amenemopet! Think of it," she said, turning to her husband.

He made an impressed sort of grunt and nodded for Zet to go on.

"It was all shadows, with enormous pillars. A forest of them in stone."

"And all carved with spells," Kat added. "And since we're still here, I suppose the gods must not have been too angry with us."

"No, I suppose not," Ama agreed.

"We snuck up and heard them talking. The thin-man and the big one. And the big man is the High Priest."

A shocked silence filled the workroom.

"The *High Priest?*" Padus said.

"It gets worse." Zet took a deep breath, thinking of what they'd learned about the stolen papyrus, and about how they'd been chased all the way to their stall. He picked at the thin strip of papyrus Padus had pounded as an example of how paper was made. "That scroll he stole is much more important than you'll ever guess."

"What is it?"

"The original building plans for Pharaoh's palace. They're going to sell them tomorrow."

Padus stood and began pacing the room. "Do you know what this means?"

Kat said, "That whoever buys them will know the layout of Pharaoh's home. They'll be able to get in there and steal things. The sacred relics."

"I'm afraid it might be worse than that," Padus said. "It may be about theft, you are right. But if that were the case, they'd more likely spend their efforts trying to rob the tombs. That's where the true wealth lies. Buried with the Pharaohs who've come before." He picked up one of the heavy mallets, turning it over in his hands.

"Then what?" Kat said.

"I think the most likely reason someone wants it is to make an attempt on Pharaoh's life."

Kat sucked in her breath.

"You think someone wants to kill Pharaoh?" Zet said.

"Given that the High Priest is involved, I fear this is much larger than a simple robbery. There have been rumors of unrest in the Royal

House. I think it's possible we've put ourselves right in the middle of a plot to overthrow the throne."

The delicious seed cakes Zet had so greedily eaten now formed a lump in his stomach.

Ama nodded. "I agree. That palace must have all sorts of secret tunnels in it. Ways for Pharaoh to get around undisturbed, shortcuts and things. No doubt tunnels that go straight into his sleeping chamber. If someone else had access to them, it would be easy to kill him and get away."

"Not only is Pharaoh in deep trouble. We are too," Zet said. "They came to our stall, looking for us."

Kat tugged on her braids. He could see beads of sweat forming on her forehead.

"Oh, no," Ama said.

"That's why we ran. And I'm sure the thin-man saw us, and he knows now that we were the ones in the temple, that we overheard them talking." Zet pushed his fingers through his short hair. It was just hitting home now, the depth of the trouble they were in.

"We should go to the medjays," Kat said in a trembling voice. "They'll know what to do, won't they? Can't we just tell them everything, and we'll be safe?"

Padus shook his head. He went to the roof hatch and opened it to let out some of the stifling air. But there was no breeze, and it made little difference.

"I don't think they'd believe us," Padus said. "That's the problem. We could tell them, but it would be our word over that of the High Priest. Who do you think would win?"

The question wasn't even worth answering.

"But what can we do?" Kat cried. "There must be something!"

Zet was afraid his sister was about to start sobbing. He went and put an arm around her. She wrapped her arms around her knees and leaned into him. He thought of their abandoned stall. He loved that stall. Until this afternoon, it felt like home. Until this afternoon, it was their family's means to get by in the world. To keep hunger at bay. To keep a roof over their heads.

What would they do without it? What would he tell their father? That he'd gambled his family's safety away over the hope of some copper deben?

"We'll make it," Zet said, as much to convince her as himself. "We'll figure this out."

"You said they were going to sell the scroll," Padus said. "Let's keep our heads here. Did you get any more information on that?"

Bleary-eyed, Zet looked up. "Yes. Yes, we did. They said they were meeting someone tomorrow night at a place called the Rose Bark." Zet got to his feet. "That's it," he cried, suddenly energized. "Don't you see? All we need to do is find the Rose Bark, and bring some medjay there. They'll be caught red-handed, and we're safe!"

"The Rose Bark? I've never heard of such a place," Ama said.

They looked to Padus, who shrugged. "Neither have I. But it doesn't mean we can't find it. We have until tomorrow night, right?"

Kat nodded. The color had begun to return to her cheeks.

The sunlight that once shone through the overhead slats was quickly fading. Soon they'd be safe to leave.

They discussed a plan for tomorrow. Everyone would spend the day discreetly searching for and inquiring about the Rose Bark. Ama offered more water, and asked if they'd like to stay for dinner.

Zet and Kat shook their heads. "We'd better go—"

Before they could finish speaking, Padus leaped up and grabbed Zet by the shoulders. His face had gone white. His fingers were like vice grips.

"Does anyone else at the market know where you live?"

"I—I'm not sure!"

"Think!" Padus said, and shook him. "Do they or don't they?"

"Maybe, I never thought about—" Zet stopped. A sick feeling twisted his stomach. "Mother!" he gasped and tore for the stairs.

14

A MEAGER MEAL

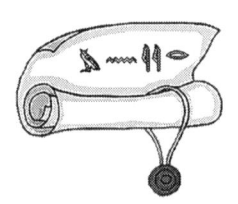

*Z*et, Kat and Padus ran from the house. They tore through the streets, all caution gone. It may have only been a few minutes. To Zet, it seemed to take forever.

Lamplight flickered through the familiar, cozy open window ahead. The three of them slowed, found an alcove and pressed themselves to the wall. The front door was shut, which Zet took as a good sign. When his mother crossed in front of the window, her movements calm and composed, he sucked in a great breath of air.

"They're not here," he said.

Padus said, "Which means you're safe for tonight. With the market empty and the vendors home for the evening, the High Priest and his men will have to wait for morning to inquire about your address. What a relief."

"Thanks for coming with us," Kat said. "And for keeping us safe today."

He patted her on the back. "Don't worry, everything will be fine. Tomorrow, we'll find this Rose Bark. We'll tell the medjay, and it will all be over. I promise."

"Thank you," she said.

Padus stood watch until they reached the front door. As Zet

stepped inside, he glanced out before closing it. Their friend waved good night and disappeared into the darkness.

Kat ran to her mother and threw her arms around her waist.

"Hello," their mother said with a smile. "It's late, I was getting worried. But what's all this?" she cried as Kat stifled a sob.

"I just, I missed you, that's all," Kat said, wiping her nose and smiling up at their mother.

"Well! I missed you too, sweet one." She stroked Kat's braids. "I think you've been working too much, haven't you? I know it's a burden on you children, I wish it weren't so. But I'm proud of you. And your father would be too."

Zet stared at the floor, unable to agree, but not wanting her to see his face.

"Let's have dinner, and you can tell me all about your day," she said. "I'll just check on the baby. Wash up, and then sit down at the table, I'll be there."

They washed in silence in the kitchen. Kat looked exhausted. Zet felt exhausted.

"Let's try not to worry mother," he said.

She nodded. He wondered if they'd fool their mother. At least he'd regained his appetite. That would make her happy! She liked to see them eat well. At the table, he put on a happy face, and Kat did the same.

"Aren't you going to eat?" Zet asked his mother, after he and Kat had been served.

She waved a gentle hand. Her comforting, motherly perfume smelled faintly of baking and flowers.

"I'm not hungry," she said. "You go ahead."

"Did you eat earlier?" Kat asked, putting down her piece of bread.

"Oh, I had a little here and there. I was baking," she said vaguely.

"Mother, what's going on? Please, we want to know."

She dusted the table, smoothing her fingers over it, despite the fact it was clean. "Children, I don't suppose you made any trades today?" she finally said.

"I'm sorry," Zet said quietly. "We didn't."

She nodded. "That bread you are eating, I used the last of the wheat to bake it."

When both Zet and Kat dropped their bread on the table and looked at her in astonishment, she stretched out her arms. "Come here," she said.

The two of them sidled up to her and she gathered them close. Zet leaned into her side, wishing he were four again, and that his father was home, and that he was still running around clamoring to go outside and play.

"I only tell you this because you ask, and because you are old enough to know. You are out there running the stall, so I know you realized this might be coming." She stroked Zet's back. "But we'll get by. Something will change. The gods won't forsake us."

The sound of her voice, and the steady warmth of her hand began to comfort him. Just for now, he'd allow himself to believe they were safe. Just for now, he'd let himself relax.

"Then let's share what we have," he said. "We'll make a feast of it, together."

And somehow, once they'd divided the food between the three of them, there was more than enough. They ate and talked of old times; they shared stories about their father and all the wonderful, funny things he liked to do. Their mother told them each about what Zet and Kat had been like when they were small children, and the mischief they got into—which got gales of laughter out of them.

Despite the hard times, despite their father being gone, it was one of the best evenings Zet could ever remember. It had almost felt as though their father were with them.

On the roof, he lay and stared at the stars.

"I've been thinking about tomorrow," he told Kat.

She propped herself onto one elbow.

"It's not safe for Mother to stay here," he said.

"What should we tell her? How can we explain?"

"Here's my plan, and I think it's a good one. We need to convince mother that you and she should spend the day together. With the baby, out of the house. It's been too long since you've had time together. We'll tell her that I'll man the stall. She knows we're not busy. And then while you're out with her, you can ask around about the Rose Bark."

"Do you think she'll say yes?"

"She has to. She can't stay here, Kat!"

"I know."

"Plus, if you and I split up, we'll have more chances of finding someone who's heard of the Rose Bark, and we'll be less recognizable apart. They'll be looking for two of us."

"I'll do it. And I think it is a good idea," she said. She rolled onto her side. "Now I need to sleep. After everything, I'm just so tired."

He bid her goodnight and rolled over himself. Despite his exhaustion, he doubted he'd be able to sleep. But he drifted off shortly after, and awoke with a start as the first rays of Ra shot over the horizon.

Bleary eyed, he stumbled downstairs to find Kat in the kitchen talking with their mother.

"I think it's a wonderful idea," their mother said, beaming. "A whole day with my daughter? As long as Zet doesn't mind."

"I don't!" Zet said, grinning.

From a pile of cushions of the floor, Apu gurgled and laughed and clapped his hands.

Kat went over and swept him up. "And you agree!" she cried, swinging him in a circle.

Since this was currently Apu's favorite thing, to be swung around and around, he shrieked in delight. Zet took a turn too. When he finally handed his baby brother over to their mom so she could get the child ready for his outing, Kat pulled him aside.

"You're not going back to the stall today, are you?" she whispered.

WHAT REMAINED

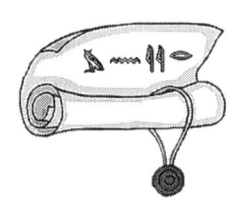

Zet and Kat faced off in the kitchen. She looked furious that he'd even think of going back to the stall.

"The thin-man knows it was us! He'll come back! You can't possibly be stupid enough to go back." She was so upset, her face was red.

He shrugged. "I might. Just for a little while."

"It's too dangerous! We were lucky to get away!"

"And we need to eat. What do you want me to do, Kat? Let us starve? I promised father I'd take care of us. So don't call me stupid. I'll do what I have to." He knew he sounded sullen, and he didn't care. It was the truth.

Kat was beyond angry. She looked terrified. "Where will we meet?" she said, changing the subject.

He thought about it for a moment. "The Chapel of Mut. Meet me near the shrine of the hearing ears. Do you remember where it is? You pointed it out that night, when we were going to the papyrus field."

"Of course. What time?" she said quickly. Their mother was coming.

"Sun down."

"And if you're not there?" she said, her brows tented in fear. "What then?"

"I'll be there."

"What's all this whispering?" their mother said with a good-natured laugh. "It sounds as if you were plotting some big secret!"

Zet managed a grin, although inside he felt like his world was falling apart. "I better get going! Have to get to the stall on time."

"Thank you, Zet," she said, handing him a package. "Lunch. Dried fruit mostly," she said.

Looking into her eyes, he knew then that despite her smile and light-hearted tone, she felt as worried as he did. And out of everything, that frightened him the most.

"Have a good day!" she called.

"You too!" he called back, and ran from the front door. He couldn't bear to see her that way.

Please, let me sell at least one pot. Please. Just one.

He prayed like that as he walked. At the woodcarver's house, he paused before the open door. The man crouched and chiseled at the lid of a half-completed, ornate trunk. Sweet-smelling cedar-wood dust hung in the hot air.

"Excuse me?" Zet said.

The shirtless man glanced up. He wiped a bead of sweat from his brow.

"I'm looking for a place called the Rose Bark. Do you know where it is?"

The woodcarver thought for a moment. He shook his head. "Nope, sorry."

Zet carried on. He asked dozens of people as he went. No one had heard of the place. It was strange. Thebes was big, but someone had to have heard of it.

He took the long way around, cutting north up two extra streets. He approached the market from a different angle to get a clear view of his stall. He wanted to check things out in advance, from a distance. Who knew if men would be posted up, waiting for him?

To his relief, all was calm.

It was just like any other day. Blue sky crowned the hot square. The dusty, shuffling sounds of morning preparations were like a balm to his soul. Soothed by the familiarity, he padded across the paving stones to his family's beloved business.

The other vendors greeted him, curious but friendly enough.

It was only as he drew closer that he noticed something was wrong. The linen sheets that covered their precious wares hung at odd angles. The tall, covered stacks were shaped differently. Shorter. Lumpier. Bulging in odd places.

A tremor of fear started in his belly. It spread outward, claiming his arms and legs, making his head spin. His hearing went all funny, as if he were going to pass out. He forced his legs forward. Faster. Sweating, he broke into a run.

With both hands, he yanked the closest sheet up.

Broken pottery shards spilled out. An avalanche of them. Tumbling and clattering and smashing to the ground. Zet stumbled backward, pulling the sheet with him. Nothing was recognizable as having once been a beautiful dish or pot. Instead, he faced a mountain of destruction. He fell to his knees, clutching the sheet to his face. He nearly threw up.

Zet forced himself to his feet. He ran to the other covered piles. Pulled the sheets free. By now, every vendor had abandoned their stall to come and stare in horror.

"Who could have done such a thing?" the goat-vendor cried.

So much beautiful work had gone into making the earthenware. Zet and his father had often made trips downriver to purchase the items in bulk from the artisans who made them. To see it destroyed was sickening.

Forcing back tears, he crunched over the remains. One item caught his eye: a shard with Kat's handwriting on it. He bent and picked it up.

Their list.

They thought they'd been so clever, making a list with all the facts of the case. He dropped it and crushed it underfoot.

"Fetch the medjay, boy!" said a spice-merchant. "This is an outrage to all of us!"

Zet glanced up at him, barely registering the gathering crowd. With a nod, he left the square. But he had no intention of fetching the medjay. For all he knew, they were on the High Priest's side now and they'd take him into custody. If that happened, he'd have no hope of stopping the meeting at the Rose Bark.

Shaken, he forced the horror of what he'd seen from his mind. Because if he thought about it, he'd break down and wouldn't be able to carry on.

He was angry. He was frightened. And he was determined to put an end to this.

The morning passed in a blur. Zet went everywhere. He felt as if he asked every person in Thebes about the Rose Bark. No one knew if it was a tavern or a shop or a little square with a tree in it. No one had ever heard of it.

The whole thing was beginning to baffle him. It was too strange. How could no one have heard of the place?

It felt like a dead end.

Not knowing what else to do, he decided to head for Padus and Ama's house. He slipped through the familiar heavy curtain. With relief, he found he was in luck. They were both home.

"We both just came in ourselves," Padus said.

Ama called them into the kitchen. "This is a stand-and-eat lunch," she said, laying out some dried meat and bread, and pouring water for the three of them.

Zet pulled out his packet of dried fruit, but Ama told him to save it for later when he might need it. They still had a well-stocked pantry, and she'd make sure he was full before he left. He nodded in gratitude.

The three of them settled in to compare stories.

TRANSFORMATION

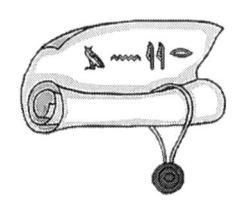

As it turned out, Zet, Padus and Ama had all had similar experiences trying to find the mysterious location.

"No one has heard of it!" Ama said.

"I'm beginning to think it's more complicated than it seemed," Padus said, rubbing his chin.

"What do you mean?" Zet asked.

"Maybe it's a code of some sort?" Padus said.

"If that's the case . . ." Zet trailed off. A code? They had no time to break a code. Not without some further clues as to its meaning. And how would they manage that? It was past midday. The meeting at sunset was now only hours away. They had no hope.

His mind went to his stall. Frustration took over. He put his water cup down harder than he meant to. It slammed against the wooden table.

Ama jumped.

"Zet," she said, looking at his face. "What is it? What's happened?"

He sighed and put his fingers to his eye-sockets, trying to rub away the nightmarish vision of what he'd seen. Finally, he let his hands drop, and he met their curious stares.

"It's our stall," he began.

He told them of the destruction. Their mouths dropped, and their faces turned white as sheets.

"Buying new pots would cost a fortune. We'd never be able to do it. My father trusted me. My family has been selling clayware there for generations. And in two days I lost it all. What am I going to do?"

"Something," Padus said. "We're all going to pick ourselves up and think of something!"

"Not to make things worse than they already are," Ama said, "But I overheard a medjay asking about you, Zet. Apparently they're searching for you. It's too dangerous for you to go back out!"

Zet toyed with his cup, turning it slowly. Padus started pacing. Ama cleared the lunch things away.

Needing some space to think, Zet wandered out into the front room. He pulled the curtain aside a few inches and stared into the street. The silence of post-midday-mealtime had settled on the city. Many people were napping, waiting for the world to cool down. With Ra, the sun-god, at his high point in the sky, the heat was almost unbearable. It radiated up from the sun-bleached paving stones.

Zet felt eyes watching him. Glancing up, he caught sight of a cat nestled under the shady overhang of a rooftop. They stared at one another for a time. Then the cat closed its feline eyes, but Zet knew it was still aware, still watching him with some sixth sense, in the way cats seem to do.

He turned his attention back to the deserted street. How could no one in the city know of the Rose Bark?

It was a riddle. A question with no answer. He had no time to go down that route any longer. He needed to switch paths. And he had an idea.

"Ama!" he called, hurrying into the kitchen.

She turned, wiping her hands on a cloth.

"Ama, I need you to shave my head."

Clearly this was the last request she was expecting.

"And Padus, can you write?"

"Of course! I may be a lowly farmer, but as a papyrus maker, I made it a point to learn the craft of writing."

"I have a great favor to ask of you."

"Name it. Whatever I have is at your disposal," Padus said.

"I need you to write a letter."

When he'd told them his plan, they agreed that although it was dangerous, it was the best hope they had. In addition to the shaved head, Ama had a few ideas of her own to add to Zet's transformation.

Letter in hand, Zet stepped out the door. To any observer, he no longer looked like the boy who manned the pottery stall in the market. He looked like an official city courier. The dark waves of hair that his mother loved were gone. Instead, his head was clean-shaven. Thick black lines of kohl surrounded his eyes. At his waist, he wore a belt of blue-dyed fabric, which Ama had made by folding one of her scarves. She attached a leather pouch at his hip, and made a number of loops for holding things at the back. One of the loops held the letter Zet had dictated to Padus.

He looked so official, Ama worried someone would stop him and ask for his services.

"Don't worry," Zet said. "I'll be running too fast for that to happen."

They wished him good luck.

"Thank you," he said, and sped out the door.

It wasn't long before he reached the office of the medjay. He slowed, his heart pounding at the sight of all those officers coming and going. Sweat trickled down his ribs.

It was now or never.

Summoning his courage, he strode the last few steps to the door. A medjay was exiting just as Zet came up the low steps. Zet started when he realized the man looked familiar. It was the muscular thug who'd come looking for him with the thin-man the day before. But today, the thug was in uniform.

Zet's mind screamed, *run!* But he stayed his ground, praying the costume worked.

It did. The thug shoved past with barely a glance and headed into the street.

Inside he found himself in a front office. He approached a desk, where an official sat making notes on shards of white ostraca. The official glanced up.

"Got a message?" he said.

"Yes. It's for Merimose, the head medjay." Sweat poured down his sides, but not from running. Zet hoped the man wouldn't notice he was sweating in fear.

"Give it to me, Merimose is out of the office."

Zet expected this to be the case, which is why he'd written it all down. Everything—about the High Priest, about the stolen plans to Pharaoh's palace. So that if he was caught today, Merimose might still have a chance of working things out. And if he did, he'd know Zet was telling the truth.

"When will he be back?" Zet said.

"The day after tomorrow."

THE MIGHTY BULL

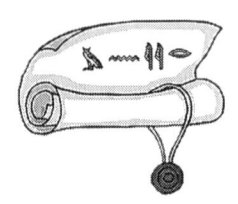

Zet stood before the officer, reeling at the news.

"You're certain?" Zet said. "Gone until the day after tomorrow?"

The officer looked suddenly curious. "Why, what's it to you, boy?"

"It's just, my orders are that the document is important. He needs to see it today!"

"They're all important. That's the way it is in this office."

"But this one . . ." Zet paused. "Are you sure there's no chance of him coming back today?"

"Not a hope. He's on the opposite bank, investigating a crime in the tomb builder's village." The man gestured in the general direction of the Nile.

Zet knew that if you stood on the bank and squinted into the distance, you could see brown, desert hills. Egypt's Pharaohs were buried in those hills, in secret tombs, but he knew little more about them than that. What he did know was that it took hours to get there from here. He had no chance of going to the tomb builder's village to find Merimose. Not now, it was too late.

If what the man said was true, he was completely out of luck.

"I see," Zet said.

"Give it to me, I'll put it in his box," the man said.

What else could Zet do? He handed over the sealed scroll and watched the man set it into a small cubby.

"Is there anything else?" the officer said.

Zet shifted from one foot to the other. Should he tell him? Should he trust this man? The sun was a good deal past noon. Time was running out. He swallowed.

"No," Zet said. "No, thank you. I'd better get on with my work."

The man nodded and turned back to writing on his ostraca shards.

Wandering out into the streets, Zet tried to think what to do. He'd barely gone two blocks when he cursed himself for handing over the papyrus. He should have taken it to the palace! He could have entered as a messenger, and handed it to one of Pharaoh's own men!

Maybe it wasn't too late. He could have Padus make another.

When he reached Padus's street, however, medjay swarmed the narrow lane.

"It's that house," a woman was saying. "He's the one with the two different sandals. He used to leave them on the step all the time."

Zet hung back and watched in horror as two big, armed medjay entered through Padus's curtain. He heard Ama's cries. Then, a moment later, the men came out with Padus between them. Zet's stomach almost heaved at the horror.

They would kill him. Impale him on a stake, or burn him to death. That was the punishment for crimes against the state. And it was Zet's fault. He was the one who'd given Merimose the clue that had eventually led the men to Padus's door.

Padus turned and Zet stepped fully into the alley. Their eyes met. Padus made a tiny movement with his head.

No, his friend's eyes said. *Don't give yourself away.*

A medjay remained on guard in front of Ama and Padus's house. The others marched Padus right past where Zet stood. He could have reached out and touched his friend, they were so close. But there was nothing Zet could do. A suppressed cry caught in his throat.

His whole world had fallen to pieces.

All because he'd sprinted across the square two days ago, on that cursed afternoon, in hopes of a handful of copper deben.

Zet's feet carried him to the palace. He didn't know what he was going to do; he simply hoped the answer would present itself. Men marched up and down in front of the grand entryway. He approached the first one he saw and tried to explain he had an important message for Pharaoh.

"Where's your scroll, boy? Or an ostraca?" the guard asked, his eyes searching for the expected item.

"That's just it, I'm to give the message by word of mouth."

"No one gives Pharaoh messages by word of mouth. Get away from my gate."

At that moment, trumpets sounded.

Weapons clanked as men rushed into position.

"Pharaoh's coming, make way!" said a man.

Zet darted back, pressing himself to the ground.

A procession appeared, marching down the wide boulevard. First came a handful of royal soldiers, with swords at their waists and pectorals over their chests made of hammered silver and inlaid with gold. Then came ladies, some carried on litters, others walking, all in gowns of white and trimmed with precious metals and jewels. They chatted and fanned their faces, laughing. In a large litter, carried by six powerful men, sat the Mighty Bull, the Great God on Earth.

Pharaoh himself.

The curtains had been pulled back, so all might look upon him.

It was a rare glimpse, and one Zet had never dreamed of experiencing. Not only did Pharaoh normally remain hidden from his people, with the war in Hyksos, he'd been traveling much of late. Rumor was that he'd spent a good deal of time leading the soldiers himself, but that he'd come back now to deal with matters of state.

Zet raised his head for a better look, and at that moment the Mighty Bull happened to glance down. Their eyes met.

Pharaoh's were dark and his lids were heavily painted with green malachite, gold dust, and black carbon. Despite the overwhelming glory of his appearance, it couldn't hide the bluish pouches under the Great One's eyes.

The Mighty Bull looked worn, and Zet wondered if he knew of the plot on his life. Surely he'd heard of the royal scheming, if Padus had known of it. Between that and the war, it must be taking its toll. Even on one so great.

Zet had no idea why he did it, but despite everything, he smiled at Pharaoh. To his utter surprise, Pharaoh smiled back. His eyes crinkled at the corners, causing the make-up to bunch into little wrinkles. The Great One raised a jeweled hand, as if waving and blessing Zet all at once.

The action emboldened Zet.

This was his chance. He had to warn Pharaoh!

He stood. As he did, a guard shot out as if from nowhere and grabbed him by the arm.

"Get back," he ordered.

In the next instant, the litter had passed through the gates. Pharaoh was gone. The doors clanged shut once again. His opportunity was lost.

"Get moving, or I'll cite you for causing a disturbance," said the guard, still crushing Zet's arm in his powerful grip.

Zet glanced at the fingers and the man let go.

"I know that was an amazing sight for a boy like you," he said. "Now run along. You'll have a good memory to tell your friends and family."

Out there in the street, Zet realized he had nowhere to run along to.

He'd lost his family business. They couldn't go home, they could never go home. Even once today was over, the High Priest would track him down and kill him and his family. A man like that wouldn't want witnesses. And he couldn't go to Padus and Ama's. They'd been caught, too.

He thought of his childhood friends. His best friend Hui had left home several months ago to become an apprentice at the Kemet Workshop. Hui might have had some idea what to do. As for the others, there was no way he'd even think to bring them into this nightmare.

His life as he knew it was over.

The thought nearly crushed the breath from his chest. He and his mother, sister and baby brother would have to leave town with nothing. But where would they sleep? How would they eat?

How would his father ever find them?

Zet wanted to lie down right then and there. He wanted to escape into a corner, curl up into a ball and close his eyes against the world.

Instead, he stumbled down to the Nile.

UNDERSTANDING

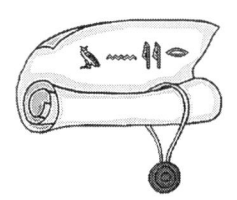

The broad river sparkled up ahead. Zet headed for it.

He had a vague idea of finding a boat headed for the far bank. Maybe he'd find a person who was headed for the tomb maker's village. Maybe they could carry a message to Merimose for him. Saying what, he had no idea. And the chance of finding someone to help was next to impossible.

Time was ticking away. He'd need to meet Kat and his mother and baby brother soon. She'd be worried if he didn't show up. And he needed to prevent them from going home at all costs. But he still had a little time.

Around the curve in the river, he spotted the crowded water-steps. Near the fishing boats, skiffs made of papyrus stood ready to taxi passengers up and down river, or across to the far bank. Zet approached, drawing ever closer as the events of the last two days roiled around in his mind.

Something was bothering him. Some little thing that he couldn't quite grasp.

He tried to figure out what it was. He went over the facts, but the point he was searching for kept eluding him. A ferryman helped two passengers onto a skiff. A second boat pulled up to the steps and threw out a line. A boy caught it and tied the rope to an iron cleat, which was fastened to the stone stairs. Further down, three fishermen scrubbed the deck of their vessel.

Then he had it.

The Rose Bark.

Bark was another word for boat.

His feet carried him flying to the shore. He skidded to a halt in front of the fishing boat with the three men on board. It was a large skiff made of papyrus reeds tightly lashed together.

"Hey!" he shouted.

The nearest man glanced up. His face was deeply tanned. He quirked his brow.

"I'm looking for the Rose Bark!"

The fisherman wiped sweat from his face with his forearm. "The Rose Bark?" he said, as if searching his memory. He turned to the others. "Do you know it?"

They shook their heads.

"Sorry, messenger," he called. "We don't usually dock in Thebes. Try that boat down there. Maybe the captain knows it."

"Thanks," Zet called back.

He headed for the boat. It was larger than the others, and unlike most it was made of wood. Cedar planks, glued with resin, and it had a large square sail made of linen cloth.

"Hello?" Zet called.

He waited.

"Hello!" he shouted a second time.

"Coming, coming," said a reedy voice. A little old man poked his head over the side. He wore a wig, but it was all off kilter. He looked like he'd been sleeping. His eyes lit up at the sight of Zet. "Oh good. You have a message for me?"

"I'm sorry to say I don't."

The old man's scrawny shoulders drooped a little. He reminded Zet of a friendly, bony cat, all lean with big dark eyes. "Oh. That's a disappointment. Can I help you with something, then?"

"I'm looking for the Rose Bark."

"Rose Bark . . . Rose Bark . . ." he put a finger to his lips. "Aha!" he raised his finger in the air. "I have it! You must mean the boat with the roses painted along the hull. Am I right?"

"I'm not sure! That's all I know, that I need to get to the Rose Bark."

The old man shot Zet a toothless grin. "Then I woke up for a good reason. Always nice to help a fellow in need. Yes, it's the boat with the roses you want. Only one that would match that description. Roses painted all down each side, twining into each other if you know what I mean. Pretty thing it is."

Zet's heart was in his throat. Finally. Finally someone knew of it!

"Where can I find it?"

"Some official owns it. Try down near Pharaoh's palace. At that set of water-steps where the nobles like to dock."

"Thank you so much!" Zet cried.

The old man laughed and waved. "Glad to be of service!"

Overhead, the sun-god was sailing swiftly for the horizon. Cool shadows slanted across the waterfront. He needed to get to Kat and his mother soon. They'd be waiting outside the Chapel of Mut, as planned.

As he made his way there, Zet went over everything in his mind. He thought about his family, their stall destroyed. He thought about poor Padus, locked up in jail and awaiting death; and Ama, home alone and terrified. He thought of Pharaoh with his kind, world-weary eyes, and the threat on his life. And then he thought of the medjay, Merimose, called away to a village in the desert.

It's true, he knew of the Rose Bark now. But what he would do with that information he had yet to figure out. Everything he knew and cared about had fallen into ruin. And it seemed there was nowhere to turn for help. No one would believe a boy like him. And the man in power, the High Priest, wanted him dead.

A DECISION

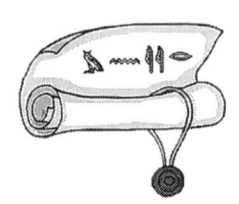

Kat, their mother and little Apu were already outside the chapel, waiting. He spotted them from a distance, seated to the right of the Hearing Shrine. Zet's heart swelled at the sight of his family. And at the same time, he wondered if this was a foretelling of things to come. Would they be left to the streets, the four of them, their happy home gone forever?

Apu saw Zet first. The baby gurgled and clapped his chubby hands. Zet swept him up and hugged Apu tight. Their mother was smiling, but her smile faded at Zet's appearance.

"Your hair," she cried, touching his shaved head. "And this uniform, what's going on?"

Zet desperately wanted to lie. He wanted to tell her everything was fine. But what excuse could he give for not letting her go home?

He let out a huge breath. "I have to tell you something. And it's not good."

Kat was shaking her head frantically, but Zet ignored her.

His mother's eyes were wide. "Did something happen with the stall?"

Apu was touching Zet's face paint with a curious finger. Zet sat down against the wall, still holding his baby brother.

"Do you remember how father asked me to take care of things while he was gone? And you were still in your birth bed, and Apu was only days old and I said I would?"

"Of course!"

"And you both trusted me? That I could do it?"

At this point, Kat had her face in her hands, as if she couldn't bear to hear what he was going to say next. A woman with a marketing basket approached the Hearing Ear shrine. She made an offering, and spoke in low tones. Zet waited for her to leave, and took another deep breath.

"Here's the thing," he said. "I need you to keep trusting me. Just for tonight. Something has happened, many things. Terrible things. All I ask is that you let me try to deal with them now, without asking questions."

His mother studied his face. "Perhaps I could help you."

"No." He shook his head. "It's something only I can fix."

"If there are terrible things, I'd like to know about them. I'm your mother."

He wished he hadn't used those words, because now it was clear she was curious and worried. He stood and handed her the baby. "I know you'll be angry with me when I tell you there isn't time, but that's the truth. I have to go. Right now. And you'll be even angrier when I tell you that you can't go home tonight, but you can't. Men are looking for me. Evil men. And they'll hurt anyone they find at our house. That's why I'm dressed in this disguise."

"This can't be true! What could you have possibly done? I don't believe it. You're exaggerating."

"Look at Kat's face. See how scared she is?"

It was true, Kat had begun to shake, knowing it had come to this. They couldn't go home. They were stuck in the street.

"Kat knows it's true. That's why she took you out today. I'm sorry we created this lie to get you out of the house, but I love you and am terrified for you, for all of us."

"Men are after you? At least give me some hint why!"

Zet glanced at the sun. It was nearly at the horizon. He drew himself up to his fullest height. The time for arguing was over. "If you love me, if you love this family, you'll do what I say. You'll let me go, and you'll stay away from our house. What is your decision, Mother?"

She looked taken aback.

"I'm running out of time!" he said.

"All right." She nodded, quickly. "Clearly, you give me no choice. I'm not happy, but we'll stay here, we'll wait for you."

"Thank you!" He threw his arms around her neck and kissed her cheek. She smelled of flowers. She smelled of home. She smelled of everything good he stood to lose.

"I'm coming with you," Kat said.

"No. It's too dangerous. I'll be back as soon as I can." Zet turned and sprinted away.

He heard footsteps and turned to see Kat running after him. He slowed to let her catch up. "Kat, I mean it! It's too dangerous."

"It's my responsibility, too," she said. "So don't argue. And you'll need help. And I'm not going to sit around when our family is in trouble."

He groaned, but kept going.

"Where are we going? Did you find out about the Rose Bark?"

He told her everything as they ran. About their pots being destroyed, and how he'd found them all smashed to pieces. He told her about meeting the Pharaoh in the street. About Padus and Ama. About the papyrus he'd tried to deliver to the medjay. And about the discovery that the Rose Bark wasn't a restaurant, or a tree, but that it was a boat.

Suddenly, he saw it.

"Out there, on the water!" Zet cried. "Look!"

Sure enough, there it was. A lavish, private river cruiser. The boat was long and crafted of cedar. Its sail was unfurled, and a gentle breeze tugged it shoreward. All along the side of the boat, below the polished rail, were beautifully painted roses. Leaves and stems twined around them, so that it looked like it was festooned with a long garland of flowers. The prow, which arched upward in a graceful curve, was crown by the head of a wooden ibis bird.

Kat caught her breath. "It's beautiful," she said.

Together they stood watching in awe. It made a beautiful picture. On the Nile's opposite bank, mountain peaks cradled the setting sun. Overhead, long streaks of red and purple stained the sky. There was very little wind. Water lapped gently at the stone wall that bordered the river, and the air smelled fresh. The sun winked, sparkling. Then it dropped out of sight.

From the pier-side, two men strode into view—the High Priest and the thin-man. The High Priest wore a gilt-edged, ankle-length kilt, which had been pressed into countless knife-sharp pleats. The thin-man followed close behind, his sandals flapping as he walked. Over one shoulder, he carried a large basket filled with what appeared to be the makings of a lavish picnic. Zet had no doubt that secreted beneath the fruits and flagon of wine was the precious scroll, well-wrapped in leather to keep it safe.

The High Priest turned, as if sensing someone watching.

"Get back," Zet said, grabbing Kat's hand and pulling her behind a pile of reed baskets.

20

THE ROSE BARK

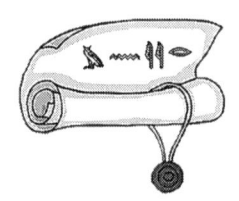

*Z*et and Kat ducked back just in time.

The High Priest scanned the waterfront. Behind the baskets, Zet held his breath. The air smelled of old fish. He wanted to gag. After a moment, the priest glanced away, turning his attention to the boat.

On the water, the boat came closer. A tent-like structure occupied much of the boat's deck. Colored ribbons flew from its four corners, and the sides were trimmed with thousands of golden beads. Four servants guided it shoreward, using long paddles. One leapt out when they reached the water-steps. A second threw out ropes, and the servant on shore fastened the boat in place.

When the boat came to a gentle halt, the curtains of the tent were thrust aside.

Out stepped a man with broad, muscular shoulders, on which rested a collar of shining gold. A striped cloth covered his head, held in place with a gleaming circlet. Everything about him seemed regal. There was a grace and power with which he surveyed his deck. His servants bowed low, but he brushed them aside, ordering them ashore.

The tent flap was pushed aside a second time, and a beautiful young woman stepped out. A white sheath hugged her slim upper body; it flowed away in billows down her legs. Around her shoulders lay a delicate, short cape that looked as if it had been sewn from threads of pure gold. A formal, black wig with beads of turquoise framed her high cheekbones. Her wide, almond shaped eyes looked neither cunning nor evil, and Zet wondered if she was aware of the purpose of the meeting.

Beside him, Kat sighed at the sight of her.

"Who is she?" Kat whispered.

"I don't know. Look, the man's inviting the High Priest and the thin-man on board. This is it, Kat."

"What are we supposed to do? We can't just run over there!" she said.

That was just it. He didn't know what to do. It could all be over in moments, and their chance would be lost forever. He stood, frozen in place, unable to do anything except watch. On the boat, the four people greeted one another. The High Priest seemed on good terms with the man, for the man clapped his back and their laughter echoed over the water.

The High Priest gestured at the overflowing basket of goodies, which the thin-man now clasped with both arms. It looked heavy. Smiling, the group ducked into the tent.

To anyone on shore, it appeared to be a small, private evening party.

The servants took up a post on shore, some distance from the boat.

Clearly the men on board wanted privacy to make the transaction. Why else order the servants away? It would also make it impossible for a stranger to get on board, with all four men standing near the gangway.

Two stood guard, facing the city. They were armed with short daggers and clubs, fastened at their waists. The other two sat on the steps. One unfolded a game of Senet, laying the playing board on the ground. When they began throwing knucklebones, the servants standing guard drifted closer to watch.

The red, dusky streaks were fading overhead. Twilight had begun to fall. A huge yellow moon glowed on the horizon. Over the water, an ibis bird flew low and called out in a lonely cry. There was no response.

Zet turned his attention to the boat. On board, inside the tent, lamplight flickered to life. It danced against the white linen walls.

"What are we going to do?" Kat whispered.

"I don't know!"

Zet let out a breath of frustration and sank down with his back to the baskets. He drew his knees up and put his head on his folded arms. What could he do? He was just a single boy. How on earth could he fight four armed servants, and then four more adults if he did somehow miraculously get on board? It was impossible.

"I don't know, Kat," he said again.

"There must be something we can do!"

"Like what?"

She didn't answer.

He'd never thought he could sink so low in life. He never thought a beautiful evening like this could be so disturbing and bleak.

"Zet," Kat said. "Padus will be killed. And Pharaoh too. We're the only people who can stop it. We're the only people who know."

He looked at his sister, whose wide eyes were staring into his own as if searching for an answer. She hadn't even mentioned what would happen to her. It was so like his little sister, to think of everyone else. If a stranger were drowning, she'd throw herself into the river and drown herself trying to save him.

Wait—that was it! He had an idea!

"Kat! Quick. Run for the medjay. Go to the head office if you have to."

"Why? They'll just arrest you!"

"Trust me, just do it."

"Why? What are you going to do?"

"I'm going to get on that boat."

"It's too dangerous."

"Do you have a better suggestion?"

She bit her lip.

"Then run!" he said. "It's our only chance."

She grabbed his wrist. "What if they won't come? What should I tell them?"

"Anything! Tell them I'm trying to murder the High Priest if you have to!"

She let go of him and her hand dropped to her side. Her chin was trembling and she blinked back tears. "All right, I'll do it," she said. She put her arms around his neck in a quick hug. Then she took off running.

Zet turned to face the boat. It was a crazy idea. But with everything lost, it was his only choice left. He'd stop the thieves, he'd free Padus and his family name, and he'd stop the enemies plotting to kill Pharaoh. Or he'd die trying.

ACTION

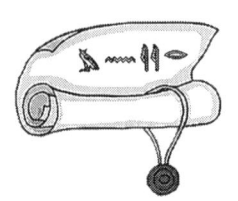

Keeping one eye on the guards, Zet crept out of his hiding place and made his way to the river. When he reached the water, he slipped in. The bottom felt soft and muddy against the soles of his feet. Silt squished between his toes as he waded toward the water-steps, staying low.

The closer he came, the deeper the water got. Soon he had to tread water to keep his head above the surface. He wasn't the best swimmer, but he managed to dog paddle along with one hand on the wall to guide him.

He kept moving, trying desperately to stay silent. Finally, he reached the first rope that tied the boat to the wharf. Pulling himself up, he risked a peek on shore. The servants were still playing their game of Senet. No one glanced his way, but from this distance their daggers looked longer and sharper, and their arms, muscled from rowing, looked deadly.

The rope had been wound several times around a cleat, and then knotted securely. He worked the knot free, his legs furiously treading water. Then he unwound the rope from the cleat. The rear of the boat floated out a little, but not so far for anyone to notice.

Not yet.

Praying it would stay that way, he swam for the second rope. This went more slowly than the first. The knot was more complicated, and his legs were growing tired. He kept sinking below the surface, and his wet hands were slippery.

On shore, one of the men shouted. Zet looked up, frantic, and saw he was shouting about the game. The shouts were followed by laughter.

The second rope was free.

Zet didn't allow himself time to rest. He tied the rope around his waist and then pushed off the wall with his legs. The current caught hold of the boat and he swam with it, towing the boat from shore. So far so good, but he needed to get to the oars before someone else did.

The polished rail was incredibly slippery. His wet hands found purchase on the bow where the rope had been tied. Feet kicking, he clambered up the hull, climbed over the ledge, and landed with a wet thunk.

He lay, breathing hard, waiting to see if anyone would come investigating.

Someone laughed inside the canopy, and glasses clinked together.

Quietly, he undid the rope from his waist. On hands and knees, Zet crawled forward and found the first oar. He slid it gently over the side. One down, three to go. He found the second and third easily, and worked his way around the tent to find the fourth.

The party inside was seated just on the other side of the thin fabric. His heart pounded. The oar was on its side, and part of the paddle was wedged under the tent. He'd have to pull it out. Zet heard Pharaoh's name mentioned.

"We will see a new Egypt," the High Priest said.

"Indeed," answered a male voice.

Zet got his fingers around the oar and began to slowly pull it toward him.

The man kept talking. "And I presume you'll want more than compensation?"

"Only what Your Eminence deems just, of course," said the High Priest.

The man laughed. "Such modesty does not become you."

He had it. He had the paddle! Zet swung it wide. He didn't mean to let it go so quickly, but it flew out over the water and landed with a splash.

That's when the alarm when up. The servants on the shore shouted. The four people under the enclosed canopy ran out on deck. The High Priest spotted Zet first. His eyes narrowed, but then flew open as recognition dawned.

"You!" he cried.

Zet backed away. He turned, climbed over the rail and jumped into the water.

"Get that boy!" the High Priest shouted.

"Where are my oars?" cried the man next to him. "Get an oar and row!"

Zet was swimming clear of the boat as fast as he could.

"They're in the water," cried the woman. "We're drifting!"

There came the splash of bodies as the four guards on shore plunged into the river. Zet scanned the waterfront, hoping desperately for a glimpse of Kat. The boat had floated out a good distance, but the servants were surprisingly strong swimmers. Zet dogpaddled toward an oar and grabbed hold of it for protection. The instant he had it, though, he knew it would be of little use. It was too unwieldy.

"He's over here! This way," shouted the boat's owner, guiding his men toward Zet's position.

Zet was quickly losing strength. He saw the nearest man approach. Water streamed off the man's thick shoulders. His muscles flexed with each powerful stroke. A scar ran across the man's shaved head, and his nose looked like it had been broken a dozen times.

Maybe if he swam around the boat, the other way! Maybe he could buy some time.

He dogpaddled in terror, glancing back at the man closing in.

The man grinned, showing a mouth full of broken teeth.

"No point, boy," he said.

Zet saw what he meant. Another guard cut across the water from the stern.

The powerful man reached him and they struggled. The servant easily pushed him under, holding him down until Zet thought his lungs would burst. Somehow, he bit the man's arm. Hard. The hand released him.

Zet popped to the surface, gasping, his lungs on fire.

The huge guard grabbed for him again, but Zet found the oar and punched it toward the man's ribs. It hit home so hard the man grunted, momentarily winded.

His score was short lived. From behind, strong arms grabbed him in a headlock and shoved him down. He had barely a second to gulp a mouthful of air before he was pushed under water. He fought, kicking out, knowing every move he made robbed him of precious oxygen. Through the silty water, he could see nothing. Then he felt something hard brush his shoulder. The side of the boat.

With his last burst of life, he kicked free of the man and swam down deep. Using his hands, he felt the underside of the boat, maneuvering himself under it. He needed to breath! By the gods, if he didn't breathe soon, his life would slip away.

He felt a blackness hovering behind his eyes. Water, all around. Warm, liquid death, clasping him in its powerful embrace.

There was no escape.

Without air, there was no life.

22

UNDER MOONLIGHT

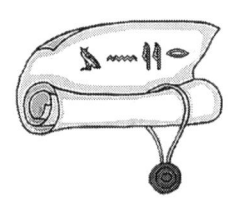

Hands barely aware, they moved upward. Searching. Through his delirium, some part of him knew he'd reached the far side of the boat. He was rising. He could see the surface. The beautiful, shiny surface, with the round yellow moon glowing warmly overhead.

And then he broke through.

Gasping and gasping.

"There he is! There's the rat! Get him!"

With arms like lead, Zet struggled shoreward.

Two men closed around him.

And a whistle sounded from shore.

"This is the medjay!" a man shouted. "I repeat, this is the medjay! Bring the boat in immediately!"

A thick arm wrapped around Zet's torso.

"Not a word," the man growled.

As long as he didn't push Zet under a third time, he was more than willing to comply. He was too exhausted to fight.

"We're drifting!" came the boat owner's reply. "We have no paddles!"

"Stay as you are. We'll come out to you."

There was a hasty argument on board. Meanwhile Zet could see men running down the shore to where several papyrus skiffs had been pulled out of the water. He saw a smaller form in a white short dress, and knew it was Kat. She'd done it. She'd brought medjay. Lots of medjay. With the reflected moonlight, everything looked bright and eerie, a sick, bluish green.

"Forget the boy," said the boat's owner. "Get those paddles and get us out of here!"

The burly servant abandoned Zet, giving him one last shove. Then he and the other men scrambled through the water and pulled themselves on board.

"Hurry! Paddle. They're coming!"

"Stay as you are!" shouted the medjay, powering his skiff through the water.

At this, the boat owner seemed to realize it was no use trying to get away.

"We're trying to row to shore," he called. "A boy sabotaged our party! He threw our oars overboard."

Zet's legs were giving way under him. He swallowed a mouthful of briny water. He couldn't tread much longer.

Two hands grabbed him under his shoulders. He was hauled onto a skiff, his drenched clothes scraping over the woven papyrus. He lay coughing and sputtering.

The medjay who pulled him on board shouted, "You are ordered to stay as you are!"

"We've done nothing wrong! Give us our oars, and let us continue our evening in peace."

"We cannot do that. Your Eminence, we have orders to search your ship. Tell your guards to stand down, or you will all be taken prisoners immediately. We have you surrounded."

And indeed, they did. Zet struggled upright.

The medjay had paddled six skiffs out. Every man was armed with clubs and swords.

When Zet saw the face of the man who'd saved him, he started in shock.

"Merimose!" Zet said in disbelief. "But you were supposed to be—"

"I know." Merimose tapped his skull. "A bit of ingenuity on my part. I wanted them to think I was out of town. I just had no idea where the deal would take place. Thanks to you, we made it."

"So you knew they'd stolen the plans to Pharaoh's palace?"

"Actually, no. But we did get a tip that something like this might be in the works. And we still don't have that precious scroll."

The skiffs had reached the side of the Rose Bark. They tied up along its sloping rail.

"This is an outrage," said the High Priest.

"I'll have you all excommunicated," said the boat's owner. "Do you know who I am?"

"I do, Your Eminence," said Merimose. "And I apologize deeply. But I am under orders to search your ship. And I must do my duty. I'm sure you understand?"

"No. I don't understand. This is my boat. You have no right to come and disturb me!"

"I have every right. I am here on Pharaoh's orders."

And with that, the men swarmed on board.

Zet watched the chaos that ensued. The tent was dismantled. Objects were systematically searched from one end to the other, while the High Priest, the thin-man, and the one they called Your Eminence, stood under guard. The woman cowered in fear near the stern. She'd begun sobbing softly, the beautiful beaded wig hiding her delicate face. Her dress billowed around her like the wings of a caged bird.

Zet saw her hand move, pulling something from the folds of her dress. It was white and rolled into a tight scroll, and blended with her clothing so well he couldn't quite understand what she was doing. She leaned closer to the rail, her other hand over her sobbing face.

"She has it!" Zet shouted. "The girl!"

Everyone turned.

The girl was no longer sobbing. Instead she stood and flung the papyrus as hard as she could out over the water.

With his last burst of strength, Zet dove in after it. Barely a corner had touched the surface when he grabbed hold and lifted the thick paper skyward. He struggled back to the skiff and climbed on board. He had to see. He had to make sure.

He found a cloth on the bottom of the boat and dried his hands. Then, holding one edge carefully so as not to drip on it, he unrolled the papyrus just one hand's width. He stared down at the black, neatly made diagram. Even from what he could see, it was obviously huge and detailed, with numbers and floor plans. He recognized the front entrance, where he'd stood and tried to speak to Pharaoh. It was, without doubt, the complete layout of the Great One's palace.

"This is it!" Zet shouted.

On board, Merimose ordered the three men and the woman bound.

"What is this? We've done nothing wrong!"

"You are under arrest for treason, and conspiring to kill the Pharaoh."

WHEN CAMELS FLY

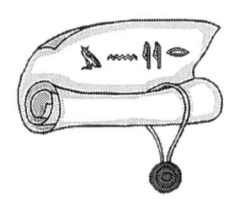

They'd done it. They'd truly done it. Zet whooped as waves of relief washed over him. On shore, his sister was leaping from foot to foot. She screamed with joy when Zet stumbled, dripping, onto the water-steps.

"Good job," he told her. "You did it. You brought them."

"I'm sorry it took so long! I couldn't find anyone! They'd all gone to the temple. They had it surrounded. They wouldn't come away!"

Merimose approached. "Not until Kat told me she was your sister," he said. "Then we came running. That's for sure."

"So does that mean I'll get my reward?" Zet asked. He sure needed it!

The medjay laughed. He clapped Zet on the back. "I misjudged you. Clearly, I shouldn't have set the price so high! I should've known a persistent one like you wouldn't stop until he got his pay." But the man was smiling from ear to ear. "Of course you will. I'll be happy to pay it. You and your sister here deserve every bit of it. Come tomorrow morning. I'll be waiting."

"Actually, there's one more favor I have to ask," Zet said.

Merimose glanced skyward. "Oh no. Here we go with the bargaining. I never was much good at bargaining." But he was grinning. "Go ahead."

"It's about a friend of ours. He was arrested earlier today." Zet told Merimose about Padus.

Merimose nodded. "I'm on my way. He'll be free within the hour."

"We better go too. We need to find our mother," Zet said. "She's waiting for us." And then, realizing how good it sounded, he added, "We need to go home."

It was a happy reunion when they returned to the Hearing Ear Chapel and told their mother they were safe. She was proud when she learned that Zet and Kat had stopped a plot to kill Pharaoh, and added that their father, a fighting soldier himself, couldn't ask for anything better for Egypt.

The only thing Zet and Kat hadn't told her about was the ruined stall. They'd be getting their reward, but it would be nowhere near enough to buy back the stock they'd lost. They'd have to start small. It was going to be a hard road, especially given the times.

The following morning, their mother insisted Zet and Kat dress in their finest to accept the reward. So, cleaned and wearing a fresh linen tunic, Zet headed out the door. Beside him, Kat's hair shone in two thick black plaits, and she wore a white dress with a colored sash around her waist and her mother's necklace made of painted wooden beads.

They giggled at the sight of each other.

"I feel stupid," Zet said.

"And I feel pretty. Come on, let's run!"

At the head office, they stepped up the stairs and through the door. A cheer went up. Everywhere Zet looked, men in uniform were on their feet, clapping. People stepped forward to congratulate the two of them. Zet's heart swelled with relief. He and his sister shared a glance of amazement.

Merimose bowed low and handed them the deben.

"I may not have seen a camel fly," Merimose said, "But I have witnessed bravery that was even more astonishing. This will not be forgotten. Thank you."

When they finally left, Zet felt as if he were humming with gratitude. They'd survived. They walked through the streets. There was someone they needed to visit.

Before long, the familiar curtain came into view.

Padus stood outside on the stoop. He wore his mismatched sandals. His face spread into a huge grin at the sight of them. The three piled inside, and Zet and Kat took turns telling what happened after Padus had been hauled away.

Ama brought tea and bread.

"And what happened in jail? Did they hurt you?" Kat wanted to know.

"I was fine. They held me in a room, but so much effort was being put into the search that the men mostly ignored me."

Zet took out the bag with the reward. "That reminds me. We wanted to share this with you. Because if it wasn't for your help, we'd be dead. And if it wasn't for me seeing you that day, we'd never have this at all."

Padus shook his head and held up a calloused hand. "I won't hear of it!"

"No, children," Ama said. "We are fine. And you have your stall to think of."

"Well, there is someone else then, that we want to give some of the reward to," Zet said.

Padus raised his brows, curious.

"The old woman by your field," Kat said.

"Old woman?" Padus looked puzzled. "What old woman?"

"The blind one. She stays out by the entrance."

"I've never seen a blind woman by my field."

Now it was Zet and Kat's turn to look puzzled.

"But she was there, twice. We visited her." Zet stood. "We'd better go now to find her. Maybe she's already wandering somewhere else. I'd hate to miss her."

Taking their leave, they headed out the door. Zet and Kat made their way mostly in silence. There was so much to think about. So much had happened, it felt like months had passed, rather than just a few short days.

They left the city behind and wandered along the dirt road. Soon the papyrus stand came into view, tall and weaving in the gentle breeze.

The depression in the grass where they'd sat with the old woman still remained, but there was no sign of her. Together they wandered up the road for some time, searching, hoping desperately to find her. No one had seen her. No one remembered the blind old woman who'd been so kind to Zet and Kat.

Kat brushed away a few tears. "I so wanted to find her."

"I know," Zet said. "I did too. We'll come looking again. Maybe she'll turn up."

Despite the joy they'd felt, they headed home with heavy hearts. Zet hated to think of the woman, alone somewhere.

They were met by a commotion in their alley. It seemed like hundreds of guards filled the street, although there may have only been twenty or thirty. A beautifully decorated litter lay outside their front door. Next to it, a dozen litter bearers stood at attention.

Zet and Kat eyed them in astonishment, and ran up the front steps.

24

AN UNEXPECTED GUEST

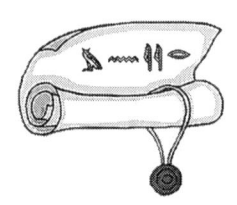

Inside, their mother looked flushed and breathless. She sat at their dinner table, and cups had been laid out. Across the table, seated on Zet's plump cushion, sat the little old woman.

Instead of rags, however, she was dressed in royal colors. A sumptuous gown flowed from her thin shoulders.

"Is that you, children?" she said, turning her blind eyes toward them.

"Yes," said Zet. "But you are—"

"The Royal Mother. Yes. Come, sit by me and I will explain."

She told them of how she'd feared for her son's life. She'd heard the rumors, and had sent her men everywhere, but no one knew for certain who led the plot. She'd had the High Priest followed. And so, when she learned the High Priest had gone to the field and met the thin-man, she asked to be brought there herself, that night. She too believed they might come back to cover their tracks, and she wanted to confront them herself.

"But I met you instead!" she said.

"Why did you come back and eat with us the next day?" Kat cried. "You are the Royal Mother, and we are just children."

"I couldn't turn down such a kind offer," she said softly.

And he knew she meant it.

"When I said you'd made me a happy woman, I meant it. That was one of the loveliest days in memory."

They reminisced about it, telling their mother how they'd eaten bowls of leftovers. Their mother laughed, amazed.

"You are a good cook!" the Royal Mother said. "I've still been dreaming of that chickpea salad. You'll have to give me the recipe!"

"Still, it wasn't safe," Zet said. "What if someone recognized you?"

"My guards were all around me. Hidden in the field."

Zet shook his head, amazed. "But why didn't you just arrest the thin-man. Or the High Priest? Or search the temple? Why wait?"

"How could we? The High Priest cannot be touched by regular laws. And how could we accuse him? On what evidence? He was a very cunning man. As for the thin-man, there seemed to be little point. It was better to let him go. We hoped he would lead us to some kind of answer. The only way we could succeed was to catch the High Priest in the act."

The morning passed swiftly, with much talk and laughter. Baby Apu crawled around, gurgling his delight at all the happy people.

Finally, the Royal Mother said it was time for her to get back to her son at the Palace.

Zet helped her up.

"My son and I will be forever grateful," she said, squeezing his hands.

The family went outside to see her off. People crowded the streets, unable to believe a Royal visitor had come to the house of a market family. They watched in awe as Zet and Kat and their mother said goodbye.

Seated in the litter, the Royal Mother took Zet and Kat's hands in her small, wrinkled ones.

"I know you suffered great struggles. But you did the right thing. I will never forget this. And neither will my son."

Zet watched her go, barely able to believe that the kind woman they'd shared lunch with was the same great lady who rode in a litter surrounded by dozens of guards.

He trailed after his family, up the steps and into the front room.

"What's that?" he asked his mother, seeing a box near the front door.

"The Great Mother brought it for you. I don't know, I'd forgotten all about it."

"I wonder what it is?" He and Kat went to it and knelt before it.

The box was beautifully carved, inlaid with gold and turquoise and bore the Pharaoh's mark.

"This box must be worth a fortune!" Zet said.

"Open it," Kat cried.

And he did. He lifted the lid and gasped. On top was a small piece of papyrus, with a neatly printed note. Beneath the note lay a shining mound of deben. Kat took out the note and read it.

"For goods lost in the line of duty. Please accept with our thanks," she read. "And it's signed by Pharaoh himself!"

Zet thought of the man he'd seen with the dark eyes, and closed his own eyes in thanks.

Their business was saved. Pharaoh knew, and understood. He'd taken the time to find out what Zet had gone through, and what he'd lost. And what lay inside this box was beyond generous. They could easily buy back their pots. And they wouldn't have to worry about starving for a long time.

"Goods lost in the line of duty?" his mother said.

"Uh . . ." Zet looked at his sister. "Do you want to explain?"

"No way!" she said.

They both turned to their mother, who was studying their faces.

"All right children. Just what goods, exactly, are we talking about?"

And so they told her about the stall, and even about the three favorite bowls he'd lost in the chase. It's true, she was upset, but in the end they organized a wonderful trip down river to visit the village where the potters made their beautiful wares.

It took several boats to bring their haul back to town.

The stall looked incredible when it was done. Everything was new and fresh.

They even had little toys made of clay.

"I'm so glad everything's back to normal, aren't you?" Zet asked his sister.

"That's for sure," she said. "I hope nothing like that happens ever again. Don't you?"

At that moment, a medjay ran into square. His insignia shone at his throat, and his sword and club banged at his hip. He looked this way and that, and then beelined for the stall.

"Are you the boy called Zet?"

"I am."

"Merimose sent me. He wondered if you'd like to make a little extra deben?"

Zet and Kat glanced at each other.

Zet shrugged at his sister, and was unable to keep the grin from his face. "It couldn't hurt, if it's for a good cause, right?"

She rolled her eyes. "May the gods protect us."

"Hurry!" the man said.

"I'm on my way," Zet replied. And together, they took off into the sunlit afternoon.

SCOTT'S HISTORICAL NOTE

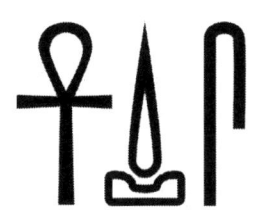

Although this is a story, Zet and Kat's world is much as it would have been. Little remains of the old city of Thebes beyond the great monuments. Certain places however, such as the Temple of Amenemopet with its forest of stone pillars, can actually be visited today.

The Egyptians kept good notes. Using their records, we can imagine what life was like—from their clothing to the marketplaces, from their foods to their customs. Most families kept a household shrine, and Bastet, the cat deity, was a popular god. Citizens did not visit temples in the way churches are visited today. Only priests were allowed inside. The Hearing Ear shrines were a great way for people to make requests of their gods.

The medjay began as troops during wartime, but evolved into a regular police force. Crimes were tried in court but unlike today, the punishments could be brutal. The best a thief could hope for was the loss of a hand. The worst was burning at the stake, a terrible fate for an Egyptian; they believed that destroying their body meant they wouldn't go on to the afterlife.

Download the study guide at ***bit.ly/egyptstudy***

MYSTERY OF THE EGYPTIAN AMULET

ZET'S SECOND CASE

BY SCOTT PETERS

SNAGGLETOOTH

Twelve-year-old Zet stood outside a tall, narrow gate in the artisan quarter of Thebes. Time had blackened the metal with soot and age. It had taken human hands, however, to sharpen the tops of the bars into knife-like blades. Zet studied them a moment.

They'd be hard to climb over without getting ripped up pretty bad.

All around him, late afternoon shadows crouched low and dark. The dank smell of a leather tannery drifted from somewhere nearby, tugging at his stomach. It smelled like old urine. He tried breathing through his mouth. It didn't help.

"Hello!" he shouted through the gate.

No one answered.

He rattled the handle. Locked.

"Hello?" he shouted again.

It was hard to imagine his best friend Hui locked up in this creepy place. Locked up probably wasn't the right word, since Hui was there as a jeweler's apprentice. Still, it seemed like a jail, with its big, ugly unmarked entry.

Zet had been angry the whole way through town. You'd think Hui could've answered at least one of his letters in six months. Sure, Hui was probably busy. But that busy? Who forgets their best friend just because they land an important position at the Kemet Workshop?

He gave the bars a hard shake. It was still working hours. Where were these people? "Anyone home?"

A big man lumbered into view on the far side of the gate. His shoulders almost filled the narrow entrance as he approached. He was stripped to the waist, and sweat stood out on his barrel-shaped chest.

"Get away from here," he said.

Shocked, Zet frowned. "Isn't this the Kemet Workshop?"

"What's it to you?"

"I'm looking for a friend. He's an apprentice here."

"Apprentices don't get visitors. So beat it."

"But I just—"

"Beat it!" the hulk of a man said.

When Zet didn't move, the man cracked his meaty fingers. He took a key that hung from a loop on his leather belt and unlocked the gate. Zet stepped back a foot or two, but the man grabbed his arm and twisted Zet into a headlock.

"Makes a funny noise," the man said. "When your neck breaks. Crunch-like."

"I get it," Zet managed, seeing stars. "Let go."

The man spun him lose with a laugh, and Zet slammed face first into the dirt. Zet got to his feet, furious but trying not to show it. What would be the point? It was obvious the man would win any fight.

The man grinned, showing a set of jagged teeth. "We don't like snoops."

"I wasn't snooping. Just tell my friend Hui I was looking for him."

"Hui, huh?"

Immediately, Zet wished he hadn't said it. What if he got Hui in trouble?

Snaggletooth went inside and slammed the gate shut and locked it. "Hui," he repeated with a nod. "I'll tell him."

The thug walked away, knuckles cracking as he ground them into his fist. Zet swallowed and watched him go.

Something strange was going on behind that gate. Maybe there was a reason Hui hadn't answered. Zet wanted to climb over the knife-like bars, sneak past the guard and find him. But the workshop was probably a maze of rooms and corridors.

And who knew how many other Snaggletooth-like men lurked back there?

Running a hand over his short-cropped hair, he let out a frustrated breath. It took all his determination to turn his back on that gate, on Hui, and head for home.

2

MISSING ORDERS

The next morning, Zet walked to work in a grim mood. The sun god spilled his rays over the rooftops as Zet wound through the narrow streets. He said nothing to his little sister, Kat, about last night's eerie visit to the Kemet workshop.

Still, she plodded along looking equally gloomy.

A woman stepped onto her front stoop, holding a broom. She shook it out. Dust rose in the still air.

"Good morning," she called.

"Morning," Kat said.

"Got to get things clean and ready for the Opet Festival," she said.

"Right!" Zet said, trying to sound cheerful. Her words, however, made sweat prickle on his neck. Sure he was worried about Hui, but he had another problem to deal with. And the problem kept growing worse.

He and Kat ran the family pottery stall—ever since their father had gone to fight the Hyksos invaders. Up until now, they'd managed pretty well. But things were going downhill fast. People had ordered a large number of special dishes and bowls for the festival parties, and the orders hadn't come.

Out of earshot, Kat spoke in a shaky voice. "Do you think the shipment arrived?"

"It better have."

"What if it hasn't? Our customers are really upset. They're saying things about us, like we can't keep up our end of the bargain."

"It'll come," he said.

"But it's been weeks. And like that woman said, the festival's almost here. People paid us in advance, Zet. They paid us a lot!"

He groaned. "Tell me something I don't know."

They reached the familiar marketplace. They were early, and none of the other vendors had arrived. The tented booths were still wrapped up, silent and deserted.

All, that is, except theirs.

Zet gulped. "Uh oh."

Half a dozen women waited. Frowning. Arms crossed.

Zet forced an uncomfortable smile.

His gaze flicked hopefully from the women to the surrounding area. He surveyed the whole marketplace, praying to see a crate had been delivered during the predawn hours.

But there was no crate.

"Maybe we should run away," Kat whispered.

He looked at her like she was crazy. "What, not open the stall? Come on, let's go."

Moments later, the complaints were flying.

"What was I thinking?" shouted a woman. "I never should have trusted a pair of silly little children."

"I planned three whole parties around the plates and platters I chose," said another in a trembling voice. "I've had table linens made to match, and centerpiece flowers and everything." She looked like she was going to start crying.

Anger Zet could handle, but tears were awful.

"They'll be here," he said. "I promise."

"For your sake, boy, I hope so," said the first. "Or I'll see you lose your stall for this."

With that, she and the others left.

To make matters worse, other vendors had arrived. They looked disgusted. They didn't want shady, unreliable businesses around.

Zet's stomach clenched. Lose the stall? But they'd starve. Sure, he'd earned a big reward several months ago, but he'd spent almost all of it repairing the damage to their business. And he'd promised his father that he'd take care of his sister, his mother and his baby brother.

His ears burned in shame. The thing is, everything the women said was true. They'd paid, and Zet hadn't delivered. The Opet Festival was just days away.

What could have happened to delay the orders?

On top of everything, he'd paid for them himself in advance to have them made.

Zet set out clay pots and colorful plates in the sunlight. The sun god's rays gleamed in the glazed dishes. He dragged a vase forward; taller than his waist, it scraped across the paving stones as he hauled it front and center.

His mind drifted from the stall's problems to Snaggletooth. Things might be bad here, but what was going on over at the Kemet workshop? Was his best friend, Hui, in trouble? Nothing about his visit the night before seemed normal. The more he thought about it, the stranger it seemed. Why would Snaggletooth put Zet in a headlock, just for asking to see his friend?

He glanced over at Kat. Her cheeks were still bright red. One woman had called her a crook, and a whole lot of other mean things. Kat stood alone, plate in hand, polishing it carefully. Even from here, he knew her well enough to see she was shaken. Sure, he and his sister fought like crazy, but she definitely wasn't a crook.

Kat really cared about making their customers happy. And so did he.

Noon came. The air felt stifling. Heat radiated up from the paving stones. The droves of shoppers slowed to a bare trickle.

"Kat," Zet called, wiping his brow.

His sister spun, black braids flying, a hopeful look in her dark eyes. Seeing his face, however, her look quickly faded.

"Oh!" she said. "I thought—well, I thought you saw the delivery people coming or something."

"No. I was just going to say we should go to the watersteps to eat."

She brightened. "And we can check for the pottery guild's shipping boat."

"Exactly."

"Wait . . . I don't know if we should." She crossed her arms and got that super practical look of hers. "It could get busy quick."

"We won't be gone that long," he said. "Come on, it will be nice and cool, and it would be good to relax."

She groaned. "I know. But you go. I'll stay. We can't afford to lose any sales."

"No. I'm in charge, and you're coming."

Which was true, seeing that he was a year older. Not that he ever made a big deal out of the fact.

"Thanks for the reminder, big brother," she said, rolling her eyes.

"Just come on," he said. "We need a break."

Kat glanced around the hot square. "Okay. But not for long."

Together they quickly tied a few linen sheets over their wares. From the stall next door, Geb, the herb-vendor, watched them over his baskets. His woven containers held herbs and spices for cooking, medicine and dyes—deep red powders, and mustard yellow, and Zet's favorite, bright blue woad—all piled high and shaped into cones.

When Zet and Kat picked up their lunch parcels and began to leave, the wizened old herb-seller shot them a surprised look.

Zet colored.

With their bad reputation growing, disappearing in the middle of the day was just making them look worse.

"We're not going far," Zet said.

"We're coming straight back!" Kat added.

Geb nodded. But the old man didn't smile.

3

NO RECOGNITION

Kat twisted her braid as they exited down a shady lane that led to the Nile. Neither of them said anything about Geb's disapproval, not to mention the rest of the market vendors. More than one glare had come Zet's way.

Clearly wanting to change the subject, Kat said, "Don't you think it's strange we still haven't heard from Hui?"

Zet shot her a look. All he said was, "Yeah."

"It's been six months. I'm sure they have scribes there. He could have at least dictated a message. You know, like, 'hello, I'm having fun making jewelry, and I have a million new friends, so I won't be writing to you anymore', or something."

Zet was silent.

Somehow, he doubted friends had anything to do with Hui not writing.

"I've sent him seven letters," she said.

Which didn't surprise Zet. She'd actually been glad when their father hired a boring old writing tutor. And she'd actually paid attention. Then again, boring or not, unlike most people, Kat could write, and fairly well.

"They were long letters, too," she said.

At this, he couldn't help a small grin. "They would be."

"What? What's that supposed to mean?"

Zet glanced at his little sister's red face. "*Someone has a crush*," he sang.

"I do not!" Kat said, punching his arm.

"Ow." He laughed and leaped sideways. "Kat likes Hui!"

The bright patches on her cheeks deepened. "Quit it."

"Okay, okay."

Kat glared at him.

"Truce. Forget I said anything about Hui." He pointed ahead. "Look, there's the river. Come on, let's see if the boat's there."

A broad avenue ran along the river's edge. Here and there, wide steps led down to the water. People milled about. A musician sat plucking out a tune on a lute. Two men played a game of Senet, while a third watched.

The Nile sparkled, all full of bobbing birds and floating watercraft. Some boats ferried goods, and others carried passengers.

But the one boat they wanted to see wasn't there.

They stood in the shadow of a large Sphinx statue. Zet frowned at the spot where the potters usually tied up to unload their goods. He wished, by force of will alone, he could imagine the potters' boat into existence.

Suddenly, Kat gasped. "Look!"

At her tone, Zet's head snapped to where she was pointing.

A small boat held four people. In the back, poling them downriver, stood a huge, scary looking thug: Snaggletooth. In the front stood a second guard. A padded seating area filled the boat's midsection. In it lounged a man in a gold edged tunic. And beside the richly dressed man, sitting bolt upright, was none other than Hui.

Zet stared, unable to believe his eyes.

Hui looked different. Stiff and formal—completely unlike the joker Zet once knew.

The man in the expensive tunic said something to Hui.

Hui nodded, his expression blank and controlled.

On shore, Kat darted down the water-steps.

"Hui," she shouted. She cupped her hands around her mouth. "HUI!"

Everyone in the boat turned.

On land, Zet dove behind the stone Sphinx. From his hiding spot, he watched Hui's eyes fasten onto Kat's face. If he recognized her, he showed no sign of it.

"Hui," Kat shouted again, and waved wildly. "Hey!"

In the boat, Hui made no response. Instead, he simply turned away and stared straight ahead.

Clearly stunned, Kat let her arm drop. She watched the boat drift out of view. Then she turned to Zet.

"Did you see that?" she cried.

Zet nodded, mute.

"He didn't even know who I was. Did you see his face? He didn't recognize me."

"Maybe he couldn't see you clearly," Zet said, wishful.

"Of course he could. He looked right at me. Maybe he was hypnotized." She gulped. "Or possessed."

At this, Zet looked skyward. "Possessed? Come on." That was so like her, to think up something crazy.

"Well if he wasn't possessed or hypnotized, then—" She broke off. "Hey, wait, what were you hiding for?"

"Hiding?"

"Yes, hiding. When I turned around just then, you were all ducked down behind the Sphinx."

Zet rubbed his neck. It was gritty with dust and sweat. He wiped his palm on his kilt. "Well, here's the thing." He knew she'd be mad he'd kept it secret, but plunged ahead. "I went to try and visit Hui last night and it was all weird over there."

"Why didn't you tell me before?"

"Because we have other stuff to worry about. Look, I don't want to argue. Do you want to hear what happened or not?"

She snapped her mouth shut.

"They have this big black gate at the workshop, which is locked. And when I yelled to see if anyone was around, that thug in the boat came out and put me in a headlock for asking if I could visit Hui."

"He put you in a headlock?"

Zet showed her the bruises. "You weren't wondering where I got these?"

Kat's face had gone pale. "Not really. I mean, you're always getting bruises and stuff. Oh my gosh, Zet, that's totally creepy." She wound her fingers together. "Maybe he was hypnotized."

"I don't know . . . Maybe he's just busy with his new life. Maybe they don't like visitors over there."

Kat knit her brows together.

Zet hated to say it, but felt he had to. "Maybe Hui just doesn't want us around."

"That's ridiculous. Listen to what you're saying. Hui?"

Zet shrugged. "Maybe he's changed."

"Into a totally different person?" Kat demanded.

His eyes went to the boat, tiny now in the distance. It was true, that sure wasn't the Hui he knew—zany best friend and famous neighborhood trickster. Hui could throw his voice so it sounded like it came from a rooftop, or a doorway, or a window, among other crazy skills. That stiff Hui looked like he'd never stolen his mom's face paints and given himself fake bloody gashes and black eyes. He looked like he'd never jumped out and terrified Kat. But he had, a lot, and it had been totally hilarious.

Zet rubbed his face. "I don't know," he said. "Look, let's just go back to the stall. It's getting late."

She nodded, biting her lip. "I'm not hungry anymore, anyway."

"Hey," Zet said, trying to sound brighter than he felt. "You know what, I'm sure there's some explanation. Don't worry about it. Hui is Hui. He's probably got some scheme going on, and we'll find out about it eventually. Right?"

She let out a little laugh. "If Hui was just teasing me right then, pretending not to know me, I'll kill him."

From out of nowhere came a horrible thought:

If someone else doesn't kill him first.

4
THE LETTER

Shadows closed over the city streets as evening fell. Alleys grew dark, doorways even darker. Overhead, red streaks stained the sky. Cool air brushed Zet's neck. He shivered, and walked a little quicker.

"Where are we going?" Kat asked, running to catch up.

"To talk to Hui's mom."

He rounded another corner and spotted Hui's house up ahead. It was two blocks from theirs. A lamp flared in the window. Even from outside, the chatter and shouts of Hui's little brothers—Akiki, Sefu and Moss—could be heard.

Zet and Kat mounted the steps and knocked on the wooden door.

"Coming!" called Hui's mom, Delilah.

She opened the door, looking cheerful as ever. Normally plump, now she was hugely pregnant. Her cheeks were flushed. Her hair, which she wore in ringlets, had a smudge of bread flour next to one ear. Her grin widened at the sight of them.

"Kat, Zet, hello."

"Hi," they said.

Instantly, Zet felt relieved. Obviously, everything was fine with Hui. His mom didn't look the least worried. Behind her, Akiki and

Sefu ran past shouting. Over her shoulder, Zet spotted Moss climbing a ladder. Moss got his feet into the rungs, hung himself upside-down, and waved at Zet.

"Get down from there, Moss!" Delilah said, without even turning around.

Moss slipped and landed with a crunch and a wail. She went over, dusted Moss off, and set him on his feet.

"You'd better come in, and close the door," she said.

They did.

"I wanted to see if you heard from Hui," Zet said.

They followed her through the house, which somehow always had scrubbed floors despite the piles of wooden toys everywhere. In the kitchen, she gave a delicious smelling pot-full-of-something a stir.

"Got a letter yesterday," she said.

"You did?" Zet asked, baffled. If Hui had written to her, why not to him and Kat? Was his friend mad at them for some reason? It didn't make sense. "And he's okay?"

"Why wouldn't he be?" She pushed curls from her face and wrinkled her forehead.

Zet's fingers went unconsciously to his bruised neck, where Snaggletooth had grabbed it with his meaty hands. "I'm sure he is. That's not what I meant, I just wondered if he's happy. What did he say?"

"Actually, the letter wasn't from him." She paused. "Is something going on I should know about?"

Zet and Kat shot each other a quick glance.

"No," Zet said quickly. "It's just, we haven't heard from him, that's all."

"Well, if it makes you feel any better, neither have I. Not directly. It was a formal letter inviting me to what they call the six-month visit. It's very structured over there. But he's just busy, you know how things are, fitting in at a new place."

"There's a six-month visit? When are you going?" Zet asked.

"I'm not, unfortunately."

"Why not?" Zet and Kat said at the same time.

"Look at me, I could never walk to the other end of Thebes like this. It's too far. And besides—"

Moss shot past, shouting and holding a wooden horse high overhead, with Akiki and Sefu in pursuit.

"As you can see, it would be difficult, to say the least," she said with a laugh.

"But you have to go," Zet said.

"He'll be expecting you," Kat cried. "He hasn't seen his family for six months. And it's not like he's in another city, he's right here. Think of how sad he'll be if you don't show up."

"Exactly." Zet crossed his arms over his chest. "I bet he'll be the only kid without a visitor."

At this, Delilah's cheeks flushed. Zet cringed, regretting his last comment.

"I'll stay here," Kat said, "And babysit."

"And you can lean on me," Zet said. "I'll help you walk there."

Some adults might have gotten mad at them by now. But Delilah wasn't like most adults. She threw her arms in the air.

"You kids will be the end of me," she cried. "But fine. All right. I'll go."

"Yippee!" Zet said.

"And I'm going to do it in style. I'm going to hire a litter to carry me." She held her belly with one hand. "The gods know I don't indulge in luxury much. So why not?" She smiled, but then looked suddenly concerned. "I don't know, though, Kat. Are you sure you're up for the chaos?"

"Of course," Kat said, and gulped.

Zet was relieved as they worked out the details. They left Hui's house and headed home. Soon, he'd get to see Hui. Then he'd know for certain what was going on.

5

HOME

Back home, the delicious scent of dinner met them as they opened the door. Zet's stomach made a ferocious growl.

Kat laughed.

Having skipped lunch, he was starved. "I could eat a hippo."

"Gross," Kat said. "I bet it would be really chewy."

At this, he grinned.

"Dinner's on the table," their mother called.

Moments later, the whole family was seated on cushions—Zet, Kat, their mother and baby brother, Apu. They didn't talk. They were too busy stuffing their mouths. Their mother had splurged and made a roast goose, along with a salad of sliced fennel and onions in a tangy lemon dressing. For dessert, there were soft, ripe dates stuffed with honey roasted almonds.

Finally, Zet groaned and leaned back, full.

"That was so good."

"Long day?" their mother said, smiling and clearly pleased at his enjoyment of her cooking.

Zet nodded, his mind roaming to his problems at the stall. He and Kat hadn't told their mother about the angry customers, and how the pottery hadn't arrived. They didn't want to worry her. But it had come to the point where he needed her advice. She knew the people at the pottery guild better than he did. She'd been there often, first with their father, and more recently with Zet and Kat.

"There's something I wanted to ask you about," Zet said.

He glanced at Kat, who bit her lip.

"What is it?" their mother said. "Is something wrong?"

Zet began to explain. It all came tumbling out in a rush; how the orders had been placed and paid for by the women, how Zet had paid the potters with their remaining savings, and how the orders hadn't come.

"We'll have to repay the women," Zet said.

"And they're spreading terrible rumors," Kat added. "People might stop buying from us. And everyone in the market is angry with us, too. We might even lose the stall."

"I wish you'd told me earlier," their mother said. "It's getting so close to the festival."

"I know . . . we just, I thought we could handle it," Zet said, coloring.

"Oh dear." She looked upset. Worried. She stood abruptly and carried the dishes to the kitchen.

Zet and Kat hurried to clear the rest.

"Well," their mother said. "At least you've told me. For now, you'll just have to tell the women they can choose a second set of dishes. Either they'll get their orders, or we'll deliver the second set. And when their orders do eventually come, which they will, they can keep both sets."

"Both sets," Zet gasped. "Do you realize how much—"

"That's my decision. It's better to take the loss and keep our reputation, don't you think?"

Zet nodded, mute. What good was a reputation, if they went out of business?

Kat's face had gone pale. She kept the records of trade. She knew they could never afford that.

"Don't worry." Their mother pulled them both close. "It will all work out." She kissed the top of their heads. "My guess is the shipment will arrive in the morning. You two go to work, and I'll take Apu on a little outing to where the pottery guild docks their boat. If they're not there, I'll find out what's happened. All right?"

Zet let out a huge sigh. "Okay."

A short time later, Zet climbed the ladder to the roof. He and Kat liked to sleep up there on hot nights. He lay down on his pallet and stared up at the river of twinkling stars.

Somewhere in the distance, a jackal howled. Hairs prickled along Zet's arms. Usually, the vicious animals didn't come into the city. It had to be lost. Or maddened. Or crazy.

Or possessed by Anubis, the jackal-headed god of the underworld.

Thoughts of Hui and Snaggletooth and the angry women swirled in his head.

He groaned and rolled over, and soon fell into a restless sleep.

In his dreams, a pair of wild jackals with glowing red eyes chased him into a dead end. The two animals were huge, with slathering teeth. Cornered, Zet tried to climb to freedom. The walls were slippery.

He was trapped.

He had to get out!

The two jackals inched closer and closer, eyes like flaming coals, enjoying his panic.

CHILLING NEWS

The following day dawned bright and hot.

On their way to work, Zet and Kat passed dozens of unusually silent people sweeping and polishing door-handles, and burning fragrant incense cones to perfume the air. Everyone liked to spruce up their homes and entrances for the Opet Festival. The city's stone streets gleamed as they always did at this time of year.

Despite that, it felt as if an unseen darkness hung over the city.

And the dark feeling had nothing to do with Zet and Kat's problems.

People were acting downright strange. He passed a man painting a protection symbol on his front door, and chanting what sounded like a spell. Had he heard the jackal in the city last night, too?

Farther along, a woman opened her door and peeked left and right before stepping outside with her marketing basket. Her fingers clutched the handle so tightly, her knuckles looked white.

Zet shot Kat a questioning look. She shrugged.

"Weird," she whispered.

But that wasn't as weird as the sight that met them when they first entered their marketplace. A new stall stood near the entrance.

The stall owner was a stooped man, with thick black hair and large, bloodshot eyes. Protection amulets of every kind swung from his awning. There were oil lamps with strange symbols Hyksos spirits probably; heady, acrid-smelling incense burned, and he was stirring liquid in a pot and chanting.

The chant sounded a lot like the one the man had been chanting outside his door.

"Who are you?" Zet asked, approaching. "What is all this stuff?"

The man's bulging eyes fastened on Zet. "I am Akar. And it is well that you ask, my boy," he said. "I take it you haven't heard the news."

"What news?" Zet said.

A slow, oily smile spread over Akar's features. "An evil army of spirits is coming."

"An evil army of spirits?" Kat gasped. "What kind of evil army of spirits?"

Zet frowned at the bug-eyed man.

"The dead souls of Hyksos invaders!" Akar said.

"That's ridiculous," Zet said.

"Is it? Already, they're creeping into town. Stirring up trouble. Casting dark dreams. Can't you feel it, children?"

"No. I can't," Zet said. But he suddenly remembered his jackal dream.

Kat grabbed Zet's wrist and whispered, "Maybe that's why our pottery hasn't come. And why Hui's acting so strange."

Zet turned to the bug-eyed man. "And what are these spirits supposedly doing?"

"My boy, don't you know? There have been thefts. A large number of them. They're stealing scarab amulets. All the golden, jeweled ones they can find. And you know how important scarabs are to Egypt. They ensure long life. They ensure birth. Creation. Balance. Be afraid. Very afraid."

Zet glared at him. "A spirit army, stealing golden scarabs? Sounds more like a jewel thief to me."

"Careful," Akar said. "And stay out of the streets at night."

Zet took Kat's elbow, before she could hear any more. It was exactly the kind of stuff she'd believe. He propelled her across the square.

"Come on, we have to open up," he said.

"But Zet—" she said.

"You're the most logical person I know. So why do you fall for all that stuff?"

"It could be true. The Hyksos spirits probably are mad. And you know they can't be burying the enemy Hyksos soldiers properly, with the war going on. They're not going to the afterlife. They're restless, and wandering, and want revenge. And what better time to take revenge than now? During the festival? When tons of people are in town, and Pharaoh and the royal family plan to make their procession and everything."

Zet grimaced. He hadn't thought of that.

"I'm not saying it's not possible," Zet said. "But there could be dozens of explanations for the scarab thefts. A spirit army is the last one I'd worry about."

As they made for their stall, Zet considered paying a visit to the medjay police.

Merimose, the head medjay, had become a friend. Zet had helped him solve the Mystery of the Missing Scroll, and had even earned a reward for doing so. It didn't mean Merimose would share restricted information, but there was a chance Zet could learn more about the thefts.

Because at the mention of stolen jewels, even though he hadn't said it out loud, his mind had gone right to Hui and the Kemet jewelry workshop.

Maybe he could escape and drop by the station for a few moments sometime during the day.

When they got to the stall, he realized there would be no time. As soon as they opened up, things got busy. Customers jammed the square. Zet and Kat had to focus on sales. And maintaining the shreds of their dying reputation.

If nothing else, tomorrow was the day he'd be visiting Hui. At least then he'd be able to see his best friend in person. He doubted

Kat's crazy fears that Hui had been hypnotized, or worse, possessed. But he did want to know why Hui had pretended not to recognize her, and why Snaggletooth had attacked Zet just for asking about him.

That evening, they headed home, hoping to hear good news from their mother.

Zet prayed in silence, all the way. *Please, let her have found out about the shipment.*

Instead of good news, however, they found her packing.

"Where are you going?" Zet and Kat cried.

"Down river, to find out what went wrong."

"But right now?" Kat said, looking frightened.

Zet knew Kat was worried about being left in the city with the demon army coming.

Their mother nodded. "I know you can manage on your own. I'm leaving with baby Apu at sunrise tomorrow."

7

UNDERWAY

The next morning fell on a market-closing day. It was still dark when Zet and Kat saw their mother off at the dock.

"You were lucky to find a boat, Ma'am," said the steersman who helped her on board. "Everyone is hired out because of the festival."

"But you weren't?" Zet asked him.

"I was, but fortunate for you, the fellow who hired me canceled. Now don't you kids worry, I'll take good care of your mother here," he said.

The man leapt into the boat, cast off the ropes and poled the boat away from shore. Moments later, their mother and baby Apu looked tiny as they waved goodbye and disappeared in the river traffic.

A flash of sunlight shot over the horizon, painting the world red.

"We better run if we want to get to Hui's house on time," Zet said.

As the sun rose higher, so did his mood. Finally, they were putting an end to the stall's problems. His mother would get to the bottom of this, he was sure of it. Meanwhile, in a short while, he'd get to see Hui, and all his questions would be answered.

He and Kat were grinning and laughing by the time they reached

Hui's house.

A fancy looking litter rested on the street just outside the door. It was made of two long poles, with a covered seating area in the middle, and linen drapes on either side. Two large men in leather sandals stood waiting next to it.

"Sorry we're late," Zet shouted, spotting Delilah.

Delilah's eyes were twinkling. "Not to worry. I knew you'd come. Shall we go?"

And so they were off, leaving Kat with a houseful of three rowdy boys.

Zet trotted after the two men and their swaying contraption, letting the litter bearers lead the way.

Despite the heat, the two men moved with a minimum of effort. Their breath flowed in regular rhythm. Their footsteps made a light patter. Only a telltale line of sweat down the closest man's back showed how much work was involved in holding Delilah steady. High on their shoulders, the litter seemed to almost float down the street. A very pregnant Delilah, meanwhile, lounged like royalty amongst the pillows.

The small group cut down twisting back streets. Zet was shown all sorts of shortcuts through the city.

After thirty minutes or so, they reached the edge of the artisan quarter. The tannery with its foul smells greeted them with such force that Delilah coughed in the acrid air and Zet shielded his nose and mouth with his arm.

Further on, he glanced sideways through an open door, into a room that glowed red and billowed heat. Inside, a man stood next to a forge, banging a long metal blade into shape over a stone. Zet slowed to watch. The roof was open to the sky. Sparks wound upward, twirling into the morning air.

He was falling behind, and ran to catch up to the litter.

The delicious aroma of baking bread stopped him short. He spotted the bakeshop and his stomach roared. Beyond a curtained entryway, plump loaves of date-studded bread stood on open shelves. He loved date bread.

"Here we are, madam," said one of the litter bearers.

Zet spun to see them put the litter down. They were there? Then he realized that they really had reached the Kemet Workshop.

But it looked different.

A bright carpet had been laid at the entrance. Two slim male servants stood to greet them. They were expensively dressed: blinding white tunics, a large turquoise pin at each man's shoulder, gold bands on their wrists, and braided reed sandals. Only the tattoos on the palms of their hands marked them as Kemet's servants.

There was no sign of Snaggletooth. As for the horrible black gate with its creepy, knife-like points on top—well, it was hidden in shadow. All pressed back against the inner wall, so no one could see.

Zet stared.

"You are here to visit an apprentice, my lady?" the nearest servant asked.

"My son, Hui," Delilah said.

"Then welcome to you. Please, let me help you," he said.

"Thank you." Delilah took his hand and stepped out onto the carpet. She'd brought a sack of things for Hui, and reached down to lift it out.

"I'll take that for you," the closest servant said.

"Don't worry yourself, I can manage."

"As you wish, my lady," the servant said, and bowed. There was a note of disapproval in his voice, as if he thought her coarse for wanting to carry her own bag. "Please, enter."

Clearly excited at the promise of seeing Hui, Delilah moved past him, into the narrow entrance.

Zet started to follow, but the servant sprang in front of him with surprising speed. The man stretched out both gold-braceleted arms and barred Zet's way.

"I'm with her," Zet said.

"You are Hui's brother?"

"His best friend."

"It is not allowed."

8

AN UNWELCOMING

Zet's hands unconsciously formed into fists as he stared in surprise at the servant blocking his way.

"What do you mean, it's not allowed?" Delilah said. "He's with me."

The servant frowned. "As I said—"

"I heard what you said, young man. Where's Kemet?"

"Madam, please. Those are the rules."

"I want to speak to Kemet. Immediately."

"Madam! But he's—"

"Now." Delilah was usually the kindest, gentlest person around. But threaten anyone close to her and she turned into a lioness. Her cheeks had turned that angry shade of red that meant someone was about to be in big trouble. Zet, Kat and Hui were all terrified of that look. Her being pregnant didn't help matters.

The servant shuffled his feet, and glanced at the man next to him.

"Young man, did you not hear me?" Delilah said.

"Hear what?" came a pleasant voice from the dark doorway beyond.

Everyone turned as a man emerged from the shadows. He was a

little shorter than average, and laugh lines radiated around his gray-blue eyes.

"What's seems to be the trouble, my lady?"

"I want to speak with Kemet."

"I am he."

Zet stared. It was the man in the boat! The rich man who'd been speaking to Hui.

Today Kemet wore an expensive looking gold-bordered tunic, but on close inspection, it was clear he'd seen a lot of hard work. Burn scars dotted his arms and wrists, no doubt from melting and shaping hot metal. Zet's eyes went to Kemet's fingers and he stifled a gasp.

Kemet may have worked hard once, but he couldn't make jewelry anymore; the craftsman's hands were swollen and curled into useless, gnarled claws.

Ignoring Zet, Kemet's smile widened as he approached.

"Welcome to you, my lady. And how may I be of assistance?"

Delilah wrapped her arms around herself. "I'm Delilah. I'm here to visit my son, and your servant won't let my companion in."

"I see. And this is your companion?" he asked, nodding at Zet.

"Yes. Zet's like a son to me. And I brought him to help me." She clutched one hand to her belly. "Not that I should even have to explain. What kind of place is this?"

Kemet laughed. "I see you've never visited a jeweler's workshop before. We simply need to be cautious given the wealth of materials we handle. But come in, both of you." He waved them forward. "This way."

The servant scowled at Zet and took up his post at the gate once again.

Turning his back on him, Zet followed the crippled owner. All was silent as they headed for the shadowed door at the far end of the narrow entranceway. When they reached it, Kemet stood back and let them enter.

Zet found himself in a cool, dark hallway. He squinted, waiting for his eyes to adjust.

"I'm going to assume you're trustworthy," Kemet said, close at his elbow.

"I don't even have pockets," Zet said. "Even if I wanted to steal something. Which I don't."

"You'd be surprised at the creative way people have of hiding things. But enough of that unpleasant topic. All our boys are in the forecourt. They're quite excited to have the day off," Kemet said, leading them ahead. "Hui is eager to see you, my lady."

"Is my son happy here?" Delilah asked.

"Very. He's my star-apprentice," Kemet said.

She flushed and smiled. "Really?"

"He's the best I've ever seen."

It was clear Kemet meant it. Zet couldn't help feeling impressed.

They passed an open door. Inside, Zet spotted forges blackened with use. In the next room, racks of shelves held a dizzying array of tools. Further, he glanced into a room and saw dozens of shelves stacked with stoppered containers of various sizes.

Kemet was suddenly at his side. "Like I said, expensive materials." He waved at the jars. "Those contain jewels and precious metals."

"Oh. Why is the door open?"

"To let our guests see the workshop. Normally we keep it locked."

"A guest could take something."

He shrugged. "It's a risk."

This seemed weird. Totally out of line with Kemet's earlier worry. They kept walking, and Zet suddenly noticed a small, narrow slot in the wall. It was so well placed, he only spotted it because something moved in the darkness beyond the hole and caught his eye.

Were they being watched?

He noticed more slots as they made their way down the corridor.

He walked past one, pretending to ignore it. At the last second, he turned, spun, and looked directly through the hole. He caught the whites of someone's eyes.

Then nothing.

It was downright creepy.

They were definitely being watched.

Was it like this all day long? The idea of having eyes on him all the time made him shudder. He couldn't wait to hear what Hui said about it.

THE KEMET WORKSHOP

"Now, it's Zet isn't it?" Kemet asked, turning to him. "What about you, boy? You're not apprenticed anywhere?"

"I work for my family."

"I see."

"Oh, Zet's being modest," Delilah said with a laugh. "He runs the most popular pottery stall in Thebes."

"Indeed? You're an artist then? You make earthenware?" Kemet asked.

"Actually, no. We buy our wares from a potters' guild downriver."

"Well, we can't all be artists," Kemet said with a laugh.

Zet frowned.

"Zet might not be an artist, but he has some special talents," Delilah said. "He solves crimes. Isn't that right, Zet?"

"I guess," Zet answered with a shrug. It was the last thing he wanted to talk about, even if Kemet seemed friendly. He didn't want to put the man on guard. "Where's the forecourt?" he asked, trying to change the subject. "Are we almost there?"

"Nearly," Kemet said. But he wouldn't be thrown off so easily. "What are these crimes you've solved?"

"Nothing really. It's not that interesting."

"Not interesting?" Delilah stopped. "Zet, you saved Pharaoh's life!"

"Pharaoh?" Kemet stopped to look at him. "Indeed. Now that is something I find very interesting."

Delilah said, "Zet stopped a group of criminals from sneaking into the palace. They were going to kill Pharaoh. The city police—the medjay—even gave Zet a reward. Isn't that right, Zet?"

Kemet was watching Zet's face.

Zet shrugged. "Luck."

Kemet studied him with eyes like a serpent—cold, calculating and deadly. After a moment, he said, "Luck only favors the skilled."

Then the jeweler turned and walked quickly toward a sunny, open door.

Zet swallowed and glanced at Delilah. She didn't seem to notice anything strange in the man's behavior.

Together, they stepped from the cool hallway into the blistering light of a walled courtyard.

"The forecourt," Kemet said, gesturing.

Zet blinked in the brightness, scanning the crowded outdoor area. Tables held groups of people chatting in excited voices. It was easy to spot the trainees—each one wore a tunic with Kemet Apprentice stitched in gold hieratic script.

It took a moment to spot Hui. Then he saw him. In the farthest corner, away from the crowd, Hui sat at a table beneath a shaded awning.

Hui looked shocked to see Zet.

Zet watched his best friend quickly cover his surprise.

"Hui," Delilah cried. One hand on her belly, she waddled at almost a run.

Zet followed more slowly. A guard stood in the corner, no more than ten paces from Hui. He had his arms crossed over his bare, barrel-shaped chest.

Snaggletooth.

The huge guard turned and spotted Zet. Zet hoped the thug wouldn't recognize him, but he was out of luck. Snaggletooth's lip curled up on one side in an ugly grin. He bent his thick, muscled arm like he was grabbing Zet in a chokehold, and flexed his bicep.

Was that supposed to be a joke? If so, it wasn't funny.

Zet kept his face like a stone mask and walked the last few paces to his friend. He wouldn't give Snaggletooth the satisfaction of seeing how freaked out he was inside.

Hui had his arms around his mom. Which wasn't easy, given the size of her belly. Still, he squeezed her for a long moment before pulling away.

"Wow, I almost started to go all sappy or something," Hui said. "Guess I've been cooped up in here too long."

Hui raised his fist, and Zet bumped his knuckles like they always did. Hui certainly didn't look hypnotized, or possessed, or anything weird like that. He looked like good old Hui. Still, it was clear Zet's best friend was guarded. His eyes seemed to shoot Zet a warning —*don't mention seeing me in the boat.*

Out loud, Hui said, "I can't believe you're here."

"Ha! Same," Zet said. "It's pretty boring without you around."

Hui grinned. "What, no new terror squad's replaced us?"

"What's all this about a terror squad?" Delilah said.

"Joking, Mom. We're not a terror squad." Hui winked at Zet. "Except in Kat's mind, of course."

"That reminds me, Kat sent you something," Zet said.

He reached into a fold in his tunic for the gift Kat had sent. At the mention of Kat, Hui colored a little. It was obvious he was thinking of how he'd ignored her shouts.

"Oh?" Hui said, sounding awkward.

"Yes. She sent you a clay donkey." Zet held it out.

Taking it, Hui's mouth quirked in a grin. "A donkey, huh. Now there's a message for you." His eyes twinkled. "Let me guess, she's trying to remind me I behaved horribly. Well, tell her I apologize. And it wasn't my fault, by the way."

"No, I didn't think so," Zet said, knowing they were talking about the boat. "But you seem strangely happy about her choice in presents."

In a grand, funny voice, he said, "Tell Kat I shall treasure it forever. Hui, the donkey boy. Watch this." He ducked and shielded his mouth.

A second later, the sound of a donkey braying burst from the far hallway. Everyone turned to look. One guard even darted forward, and ran halfway to the door before he realized he'd been tricked. He stopped and glanced around slowly, narrowing his eyes. Hui wore the most innocent expression imaginable.

"Hui," Delilah said in a stern voice that barely disguised a laugh. "I hope that's not how you've been behaving!"

"Never." Hui's face was solemn.

"Humph. And somehow you're still Kemet's star apprentice." But her eyes twinkled and it was obvious Delilah was glowing with pride.

10

STRANGE BUSINESS

"I should show you some of my work," Hui said. "Want to see?"

Zet and Delilah nodded. Hui unwrapped various items bundled in soft cloth.

Hui's work was incredible. Zet was seriously impressed.

There were amulets of gold, all studded with jewels. Zet thought of the new vendor in his market, and how Hui's work made those amulets look like the worst, cheapest trinkets.

"Look at this one," Delilah said with a tiny sigh. "It's beautiful."

It was a tiny gold statue of Maat, Goddess of Truth. The goddess looked ready to do her job—to greet people when they arrived in the afterlife. She'd weigh your heart against her feather, to judge if you deserved to live for all eternity.

At a prod of Delilah's finger, the scales actually moved.

"You can take the feather off of the scale," Hui said.

"Wow," Delilah said.

"It was my test project to be Kemet's new partner," Hui said, but colored suddenly.

"Kemet's partner? What do you mean?" Delilah said.

Hui laughed, nervous, as if he'd said something he shouldn't have. "Er . . . well, sorry, that just slipped out. Kemet's partner left recently, and so I'm doing some extra projects. That's all. Don't mention it to Kemet though, it's kind of a secret."

"All right," Delilah said, frowning.

As Zet took in this news and the strange expression on Hui's face, he flashed back to seeing Hui in the boat that afternoon. Were the special projects and the boat trip connected? Something strange was going on here. But what?

He glanced around, and couldn't help noticing just how many sentries there were. Several barrel-chested men per family. Huge and dark, as if they'd been baked in the same pottery mold. A shiver ran down his back.

"There sure are a lot of guards here," Zet said in a low voice.

Instantly, Hui's face changed. He still wore that good-humored look, but there was something serious underneath that only a good friend like Zet would detect.

"Oh, yeah," Hui said lightly. "That's the jewelers' business for you."

"I saw these creepy slots everywhere."

"Slots?" Delilah said.

But it was obvious Hui knew exactly what Zet meant. His eyes darted to Snaggletooth and back. "You know, all that guard stuff is boring." Hui's expression turned cold—a clear warning that Zet's probing questions were off limits.

Zet whispered, "Hui, I need to know if—"

Hui shook his head. Under his stiff smile was a look of sheer terror.

Zet picked up a wide, pectoral neck-collar made of such delicate links that it felt like fabric. "I mean, what I was wondering is, are you sure you're not pulling my leg? You really made all this stuff?"

Hui's expression changed to relief. He laughed. "Yes. And you don't have to look so shocked about it."

Zet grinned. "Okay. I guess the master trickster is allowed to be a pro at something else, too."

"What did I tell you?" Kemet said, appearing out of nowhere. "Good, isn't he?"

The crippled jeweler had come on them so swiftly and silently that Delilah nearly dropped the pendant she'd been studying.

Delilah put her hand to her chest. The jovial man smiled at her.

"My apologies," Kemet said. "I didn't mean to startle you." He gestured at Hui's work with one claw-like hand. "Impressive, isn't it?"

"Amazing," Delilah said.

"Really good," Zet agreed.

"So, what's all this about a master trickster?" Kemet asked.

Zet's best friend colored and his shoulders tightened.

Kemet had been listening in?

"Not for real," Zet said, on guard.

"I see. Then why did they call you a trickster, Hui?"

Delilah said, "Boys will be boys." She waved the topic away. "Kemet, I must say you're a wonderful teacher. I never realized he'd be doing work like this already. And I admit I've been worried about the workshop being so off-limits, but now I see it's having a good effect on my son. Hui seems very grown up."

"Mother, thanks. I'm sitting right here," Hui said.

Kemet barked out a laugh. "So you are, my young friend. I can teach until I'm blue in the face, but takes a good student to actually learn." The wrinkles around his eyes deepened. "Still, a trickster? Now that's news. I enjoyed playing a joke or two when I was young." He grinned. "These visitor days are good for us as well as the families. We find out all sorts of things about our boys."

The statement hung for a moment.

Kemet bowed. "I must move on to the next group. Lunch will be served shortly. Enjoy."

"It's nice he's so proud of you. I'm proud of you, too." Delilah hugged her son. "I'm so glad we came today."

"Me, too," Hui said. Still in her arms, he shot Zet a meaningful glance.

But as to what he meant by it, Zet had no idea.

What was going on here? They needed to talk, but how?

Still, it didn't make sense. Why would Hui be in danger? This was a proper business, a workshop. And he was Kemet's star pupil.

QUESTIONS WITH NO ANSWERS

On their way to lunch, they detoured by the sleeping quarters.

Zet hoped they could talk as they walked, but his hopes were cut short. Snaggletooth followed a few paces behind.

"My domain," Hui said, showing him the small cell he shared with another boy.

A sleeping pallet lay against either wall.

"That one's mine," Hui said.

Next to Hui's pallet, a table was heaped with possessions. In the middle, overseeing Hui's collection of things, stood a statue of Bes—Hui's family god. Grinning troublemaker himself. The funny little dwarf god fit Hui's zany family perfectly. Sure, he protected their household, like all family gods did, but Bes also loved to stir up trouble. Generally of the entertaining kind. It was no wonder Hui loved joking around.

At Bes's feet lay a half burned cone of incense. Beside that lay a big old hippo's tooth.

"You still have that?" Zet said.

"Of course."

"Remember when you found it?" Zet said.

"After nearly losing my foot to an angry old croc? Yes." Hui laughed.

"I think that's the last time Kat went swimming in the Nile," Zet said, grinning. "But I still don't believe there was a croc after you."

"It was under the water, all right. Why do you think I leapt out, screaming?"

"Uh—to scare the living ka out of Kat?"

"Would I do that?" Hui said, all innocent.

"Definitely."

Hui cut in on Zet's thoughts. "Before you leave, don't let me forget I have gifts for you." He hauled a sack out from a trunk. "And don't say you don't want them. But you can look at them later. When you get home." He held the sack close to his chest. "Now let's go eat."

"I want to open them here, with you," Delilah said.

A sheen of sweat appeared on Hui's forehead. "No, really. Let's go, mother."

"Whatever you like," she said.

Lunch was served in a smaller, adjoining courtyard. Finely made spoons, carved of out ivory, lay at each place. Holding his spoon up, Zet could see the light through it.

"I hope I don't break this thing by eating with it," Zet said.

"Which is why I'm going for the bread option," Hui said, tearing off a piece. Using it like a spoon, he scooped up a bite full of thick, rich stew, and shoved his mouth full.

Zet copied him. "Good bread."

Hui's face was bent over his food. "They make it next door," he said, speaking into his dish.

Zet spent the rest of the meal trying to think up ways to communicate with Hui.

Hui looked pained, as if he was trying to figure the same thing.

But it was impossible. There were people and guards all around.

The meal finished way too fast. And then the visitors were all being politely, but efficiently, ushered toward the door. People were saying good-bye, hugging, telling their boys to write.

There was a line to get outside. They filled the narrow entryway that led to the outer gate. Zet, Hui and Delilah craned to see what was going on. Ahead, a family stood talking to the servants who'd first greeted them when they arrived.

"We need to check your bags," one of the servants said.

The father of the family shrugged and put his belongings on a table for inspection.

Zet glanced at Hui. His best friend's cheeks had gone pale. His eyes had turned to pinpoints, watching the search. He still carried the bag of gifts, and Zet noticed his hands were trembling.

SEARCHED

Zet's heart had begun to race. What was in that bag that made Hui so nervous?

The servant at the door motioned to the three of them. "Come forward, we're ready for you," he said. "Please, put your belongings on the table."

Delilah shot him a look of distaste. Clearly she hadn't forgotten their earlier run in with the man, when he'd tried to stop Zet from entering.

"This all seems a bit over the top," she said.

"Sorry. Routine check."

Annoyed, Delilah asked, "Why, by the gods, would we take anything?"

"Those are the procedures, madam, unless you want to leave the bag behind."

"It's fine," Hui said. His face showed nothing as he handed it over. "Just the gifts I made. The materials I used are all recorded in the daily log."

The servant referred to a sheet of papyrus. He moved his finger down the line of text, read what had been written, and reached into the sack. He pulled out several parcels, all wrapped in linen. Then he started to unwrap them.

Hui swallowed, and let out a little laugh. "I guess your presents won't be a surprise."

"That's all right," Delilah said.

The first contained a tiny kitten pendant carved of jade on a thin gold chain.

"For Kat, obviously," Hui said.

Everyone knew she loved animals, especially homeless strays. She was always putting out water and food for them in their street.

There were little trinkets for his baby brothers and something for his mother. For Zet he'd made a perfectly round ball out of polished ivory. It was large, and a wadjet eye had been carved on the surface. It was the moon, ruler of the stars. Like the spoons at lunch, the ivory looked breakable. But Zet couldn't wait to put it on display back home.

"Wow," Zet said. "That's for me?"

"Thought you'd like it," Hui said.

The servant rolled it around in his hands, checking to see if it opened.

"Careful. It's fragile," Hui said sharply.

"Don't worry, I'm taking care," the servant said. Still, his tattooed hands treated it more carefully. Deciding it didn't open, he replaced it in its covering and set it aside. Then he turned the empty satchel upside-down and shook it.

Hui pulled Zet back a few steps. "Don't worry if you break the ball. It's yours. Really, I won't be offended."

"I won't break it."

"Really. I don't mind."

"Okay," Zet said with a laugh.

Still, it was funny because Hui knew he was good at handling fragile things. He did it all day long in his stall, with the earthenware. And maybe he wasn't good at math and writing like his sister Kat, or at creative things like Hui with his metalwork and pranks, but he was good at others. Like being quick and incredibly agile. If something fell, he'd catch it, sometimes even if he were across the room. He could dive like a hawk, and land like a panther.

Well, so his mother said anyway. And he liked to think it was true.

"Wish we could've talked," Zet said so quietly that it was little more than his lips moving. "It's like we were under guard all day."

"I know."

"When are they going to let up on you?"

"Tell Kat I liked the donkey."

"The donkey?" Zet sensed someone behind him. "Oh, right. Yeah, I will. And she said to say hi to you." He turned to see Kemet. That man could sneak around like a desert breeze. How had he come up on them like that?

"I came to say good bye," Kemet said. "Thanks for visiting. I'll take good care of my star apprentice here."

At the table, the servant finished putting everything back in the bag.

"You're all clear," he said.

It was only then that Hui seemed to relax. Was something in the bag? There couldn't be. The man had checked it thoroughly. So why had Hui seemed so tense?

"Have a nice trip home," Kemet said.

Hui hugged his mother and Zet. The gate was closed between them. Delilah climbed back into the waiting litter.

The visit was over.

A PLAN

All the way back to Delilah's, Zet puzzled over Hui's reaction to having the bag searched. He stopped in with her to find Kat and the boys playing a game of hide and seek. At the mention of gifts, Hui's brothers cheered. They ran around with their little prizes, holding them in triumph. Kat screamed with delight over her kitten pendant.

Zet, meanwhile, took the empty bag and searched it again himself.

Nothing.

"We'd better get going," Zet said to Delilah.

Delilah's cheeks were rosy "Thanks for everything," she said. "Especially for twisting my arm. And Kat, for taking care of the boys."

"It was fun," Kat said.

"Are you sure you won't stay for dinner?"

"Mother left food for us," Kat said. "We'd better eat it or she won't be too happy with us."

Moments later, they were out the door. Zet almost ran the short distance home.

"What's the hurry?" Kat called.

"I'll tell you when we get there."

Inside, he closed the front door, went to the low dining table, sat on a cushion and pulled out the ivory ball.

"What is that?" Kat said.

"I'm not sure. Hui made it for me, but I think it must open or something." He started to examine the surface, bending close. "Bring a lamp, would you?"

"Hello, I'm not your servant," Kat grumbled.

Zet rolled his eyes. "Do you want me to tell you what happened over there?"

"Yes."

"Then bring the lamp. Oh, forget it, I'll get it myself."

But Kat was already pulling it from a cubby. She filled it with oil. Meanwhile, Zet told her everything that had happened. About the spying slots, and the guards, and being searched, and how Hui was sweating when they emptied the bag of gifts.

With the lamp glowing brightly, she sank down beside him.

"So he's not possessed?"

"No," Zet said, laughing. He turned the ball over in his hands. "This thing is pretty heavy."

"Do you think there's something inside?" she asked.

"I don't know. The servant who searched the stuff tried to open it, but couldn't figure out how to do it." He held it up to the light. "But the shell is kind of sheer, and it looks like there's something in there."

He gave it a shake, holding it next to his right ear. It didn't rattle. Instead, a soft, shifting noise came from inside. Like something padded moving back and forth. He placed it on the table. Upon closer study, it became clear the ball had been crafted out of four separate pieces. The seams were so perfect, however, they were almost invisible.

Zet grasped it with both hands. Carefully, he tried twisting it this way and that. He tried pulling outward. He tried pushing on the seams, to see if that would pop it apart.

"I don't get it," he muttered.

Lifting the ball again, he studied the wadjet eye etched in the center.

"Try pushing on that," Kat said.

He did. Nothing happened.

"It doesn't open," he said.

"Maybe the eye is supposed to mean something?" she said, doubtful.

He scratched his head; he'd shaved it recently, and the stubble still felt strange and prickly. "This is so frustrating! I was there. I talked to Hui. And I still have no idea what's going on. But I know something's going on, Kat."

She fingered her jade kitten pendant. "Maybe."

"What are you thinking? What's that look?"

Kat bit her lip. "Well, I was just thinking, maybe something's going on, or maybe it has to do with the demon army that's—"

"Stop right there," Zet said. "This has nothing to do with some demon army. Hui's in trouble. And this ball isn't telling me anything. I need to talk to him. In private."

"I don't see how you're going to do that," Kat said.

Zet wrapped the ball back up and carefully stored it away.

"I do," Zet said. He went to the ladder that led to the roof, and clambered up the wooden rungs. Outside, the wind moved easily across the rooftops, cooling the evening air. A welcome breeze ruffled his tunic. Laundry rustled on a line, giving off the sharp, floral scent of natron mixed with lavender. From further off, he caught the faint, briny scent of the Nile, which flowed in the distance.

Turning his back on the Nile, he glanced toward the far away artisan quarter.

The sun god dipped toward the horizon.

"It's too early, still," he said, hearing Kat join him on the roof.

"Too early for what?"

"To pay Hui a visit."

"You don't mean—are you saying you're going to sneak in?" Kat gasped.

"Hui would do it for me."

Kat nodded. "All right. But we should eat something first. It's a long way, and you've already walked it once."

"We? You're not coming," Zet said.

"I am, and don't even think about trying to stop me. I'll just follow you. I can find my way there myself, anyway."

Zet groaned. Why had he said anything? The last thing he needed was Kat tagging along. An ebony colored cat met his eyes from a windowsill across the way. If he expected the cat to look sympathetic, he was disappointed. The cat flicked its tail and disappeared.

"You'll just get us in trouble," he said.

But there was no arguing with her, and he knew it.

14

UNDER A BLACK SKY

A sliver of moon cast an eerie glow through the window. Zet opened the front door. Overhead, stars twinkled like pinpricks in a thick, black cloak.

"Time to go," Zet.

"Wait," Kat said.

Zet turned. Kat stood knotting her hands.

"Changed your mind?" he asked.

"No, it's just—" She swallowed. "Well, you heard what that new vendor, Akar, said. About going out at night. What about the demon army?"

"Good point." He nodded, sagely. "You should definitely stay here, little sister."

She frowned at him. "Oh no, you won't get rid of me that easily."

Zet let out a frustrated noise. "Look, you'll never be able to climb over the wall. And you'll make too much noise."

She glared at him. Still, her voice shook a little. "I'm coming. If you're not afraid, I'm not either."

"Ugh. Fine. But if you can't keep up, I'm leaving you behind."

"I'll keep up. I'm as fast as you."

"We'll see about that," he said, frustrated beyond belief. He knew that if she couldn't keep up, he'd have to wait for her. He couldn't just leave her in the street in the middle of the night, even if that's exactly what he felt like doing right now.

They headed out the door and padded softly through the dead city.

It wasn't the first time they'd snuck through Thebes in the middle of the night, but that didn't make it any less eerie. The moon was only half full, so he had to squint just to see. In the narrower lanes, no light came in at all.

They'd walked in tense silence for at least twenty minutes when something small and soft brushed his ankle. A cat.

Kat let out a yelp. It must have brushed past her, too.

He yanked her behind a potted palm. She was shaking all over, and he knew it had nothing to do with fears of humankind.

"Quiet," he whispered. "Demons aren't furry. It was just a cat."

"Sorry," she said, trembling.

"Last thing we need is some adult finding us. There will be all sorts of questions about what we're doing and we'll never get there."

"Okay, I get it," she whispered back.

Together, they carried on. Zet had decided to follow the route the litter-bearers had taken. But now, he realized, that was a stupid idea. The first shortcut, Zet found easily. But now he was less certain of his surroundings. It felt like they'd been walking for over an hour. They probably had been.

"Are we almost there?" Kat whispered.

He groaned. "I knew I shouldn't have brought you."

"I'm just wondering because I'm lost."

"Well I'm not," he lied. Not completely.

"Didn't we pass that door before?" Kat said.

Zet walked faster. "The place is around here somewhere. Just come on. Hurry up!"

But the further they went, the more turned around he became. Soon, he was completely lost. He had no idea where they were.

"Okay stop. Stop for a second," he said.

Kat sank down against a wall.

He rubbed a hand over his face, trying to figure out which way the moon should be if they were going in the right direction. But of course the moon moved across the sky, and who knew how long they'd been walking?

Great. Some plan. Wander all night and never find the workshop because he'd decided he'd be clever and follow some stupid shortcuts. At least she didn't say anything, like how dumb he was. He sure felt it.

"What's that smell?" Kat said. "It reeks around here."

"Does it?" Zet sniffed. "It does, kind of, doesn't it?" Suddenly, he leapt to his feet. "The tannery! We must be near the tannery. We have to be close, then. Come on."

"It's stronger this way," Kat said.

Zet put a hand over his nose. "Phew, that's for sure."

"It stinks like old donkey urine," Kat said, giggling.

"You would know."

"Would not," Kat cried.

"Look, I recognize that water well." Zet pointed to its bucket, outlined in the moonlight. "We're almost there."

A few moments later, they reached it. They stopped in a shadow across the street.

Beside him, Kat studied the Kemet Workshop's locked, barbed gate.

"Creepy," she whispered.

He nodded, and whispered, "Still want to come in?"

Kat eyed him nervously. "Of course I'm coming in."

"Let's try to find a way in at the back of the complex," he said.

They skirted around the bakery, which stood to the right of the Kemet Workshop. He figured he'd find a wall all around the complex. Instead, what he found were dozens of tiny businesses. They'd grown up around the jeweler's complex, like thick bushes around the base of a giant tree. The tiny businesses blocked any passage to the workshop's wall.

Still, Zet stuck close as he made a circuit of the clump of buildings.

There had to be an opening somewhere.

There just had to be a way in.

FOUL ENTRY

"**What's** this?" Zet whispered. "Look, I think we found something."

It was a narrow alley filled with refuse. A wooden fence blocked the entrance to the alley. The alley looked like a long one, and he had no doubt it led all the way to the Kemet workshop.

He rattled the fence. Locked. Still, it looked easy to climb. Not that anyone in his right mind would. It was disgusting on the other side. Piled deep with meat bones, eggshells, old paintbrushes, broken tools, and slimy old vegetables. You name it. All decomposing in a mountainous, rotting heap.

"Gross," Kat said.

"Exactly. Do you want to wait?"

"You're going in there?"

"Yep." He looked at her face and grinned. "Guess you're not so heroic now, huh?"

She put her fists on her hips. "I didn't say that."

"Then come on."

Holding his breath, he gave her a leg over. Kat landed in the pile with a loud squelch. She sank into it up to her armpits, and made a noise like she was going to throw up.

"Shh," he said and hauled himself over the fence after her.

The squishy mess was soft, and he sank deep. He crawled for higher ground, and then buried his nose in one elbow. "Worm boogers! Start walking before I hurl my guts."

"Walking?" she said. "More like crawling."

She was right. They crawled, slipped and slid over and through the reeking pile.

"Just don't look down," he said.

"Ack!" She shook a long piece of vegetable peel from her hand.

"Quiet," Zet said.

"Sorry," she whispered, and slipped.

He caught her under the arms. The ground offered no footholds and they both went down. Slime oozed. His hand gooshed into who knew what. The stench clogged his nostrils. The pile made goopy noises as he righted himself. His stomach threatened to rebel. He swallowed. It took all his control not to throw up.

Struggling to his feet, he came face to face with a glassy eyeball, staring at him out of a rotting fish head.

"Ugh," he said.

"Help me up," Kat said in a trembling voice.

He pulled her upright. "Come on, let's get up on that roof before I toss my guts."

Her chin wobbled.

"Don't you dare start crying," he warned in a furious whisper.

She swallowed, balling her fists. "This is the dumbest idea you ever had."

"No," he whispered back. "You're coming with me was the dumbest idea I ever had."

They reached where the alley dead-ended at a wall. He gave her a leg up onto the roof above. Of course, she made way too much noise. Couldn't she move more quietly? They'd be killed!

Seconds later, he joined her. The roof spanned two human lengths. Then it ended at an open space.

"Let me go first," he whispered.

She nodded.

Belly down, he started forward. Hopefully he wasn't crawling over Snaggletooth's bedroom. The thought of the scary thug staring at his ceiling, wondering what was making that shuffling noise, set Zet's hair on end.

He reached the roof's opposite edge.

Instantly, he recognized the uncovered area that opened below him. It was the courtyard where he'd met Hui earlier. This was good. He knew where he was now. And the courtyard was deserted. The table where he'd sat with Hui was gone, but he was looking straight at where it had been. All was silent. Empty. No guards in sight.

He breathed a sigh of relief and motioned to Kat.

She crawled forward on hands and knees. Just as she reached the edge, however, her arm bumped a loose piece of tile. It skittered out of reach, too far to catch. Still, Zet lunged out, as if he could draw it back. He watched in horror as it fell to the ground.

The tile landed with a crunch.

Zet yanked her back out of sight.

Wormsnot and beetledung! He was a complete idiot to bring her here. How much more noise did she plan to make?

He lay on his back, unmoving, and she did the same. Together they listened for footsteps. Someone was bound to investigate.

Sure enough, the shuffle of sandals approached and stopped directly below their hiding spot.

16

FOUND

In the dead night air, Kat's fast breathing sounded like bellows. Zet squeezed her arm in warning, hard enough to hurt, and she stopped. He knew she was holding her breath. Any second she'd take a huge inhale. The guard would hear. They'd have to run for it. Back over the garbage pile. They'd never get out on time. The guard could dart out the front door and cut them off at the wooden gate.

Maybe it was Snaggletooth.

Zet's heart slammed in his ears. He stared at the sky and prayed to the gods for the guard to disappear.

Maybe the gods were listening. The footsteps died away down a corridor.

Beside him Kat gasped, like she'd been holding her breath too long.

"Stop it or he'll come back!" he said.

"I have to breathe," she hissed. "By the gods, Zet, this is crazy!"

"Stay here," he said.

"Why? What are you going to do?"

"What I came here to do. I'm going to find Hui."

"It's too dangerous."

"I didn't climb through all that garbage for nothing."

"We'll be caught." Kat's cheeks looked white with terror in the moonlight.

"Just stay flat. If anyone's going to get caught, it will be me." With that, he swung over the gutter and into the shadows of the courtyard.

Landing on silent feet, he crouched and looked both ways.

The sleeping chambers were to the right. He remembered their location from his visit. Inching slowly along, keeping his back to the wall, he reached the corridor. Zet knew he reeked. If a guard came this way, his smell alone would be enough to raise the alarm. He had to move fast.

The rooms weren't far now. He could see the dark openings.

Now all he needed was to remember which room belonged to Hui.

He counted the doors. There were a dozen on each side. Had it been the third one down? No, the fourth. Was it, though? He grimaced. He'd just have to pick one.

Aware of the tiniest sounds, he flinched at the sound of his bare feet against the paving stones. Holding his breath, he tiptoed through the third door. A tiny chink of moonlight followed him inside. A bed stood against either wall. The beds were full, the occupants breathing in a steady rhythm.

But something wasn't right.

Then he saw it. Hui's statue of his family god, Bes, was missing.

This wasn't Hui's room.

The boy on the right snorted and his arm went to his nose.

Zet stepped backward, preparing to sprint. The boy turned over and faced the wall. His breathing resumed a steady rhythm.

Back in the corridor, Zet's back prickled. He turned slowly. Someone was seated at the end of the corridor! A huge figure, with his back against the wall. Why didn't the man get up? Why didn't he say something? Zet's legs twitched, longing to flee. The man's head flopped slightly to the right and he let out a great snore.

Moonlight brushed his ugly face, turning it blue-gray.

Snaggletooth.

Cold sweat slid down Zet's ribs.

He had no choice but to try another door. Any tiny movement could wake the guard. He'd have to be smart, and fast. Moving silently, he padded to the next opening. Before entering, he squinted through the darkness and found it. Hui's statue. With a glance at Snaggletooth, he left the hallway and stepped inside.

Now he had a new problem. If he shook Hui awake, his best friend might call out. Or think he was being attacked and struggle. Snaggletooth would be there in two strides.

Zet could feel that big arm around his head, twisting until it disconnected with a sickening crunch.

Sweat prickled on his scalp.

He hadn't thought of this.

He stared at his best friend. They were several feet apart. But what could he do?

Hui solved the problem.

He sat up and stared hard at Zet. The faint light was on Hui's face. His friend looked shocked. He squinted, and Zet knew he had to be completely in shadow, silhouetted against the door. Despite that, Hui got quietly out of bed and crossed the short distance. He grabbed Zet's wrist and yanked him out the door.

With a glance at the sleeping Snaggletooth, Hui dragged him down several corridors in silence before he came to a stop.

"Are you crazy?" Hui whispered into his ear.

Zet nodded. Then he motioned for Hui to follow.

Hui put both hands over his face, as if in agony, but dropped them with a resigned groan and followed.

The boys made it to the courtyard. One after the other, they climbed onto the roof.

"Kat?" Hui whispered, seeing her there. "You, too? You're both mad. And you reek, by the way."

"We were worried," Kat said.

"It's too dangerous for you to be here."

OUT OF TIME

Despite Hui's joking, he looked totally freaked out.

"Move back," he whispered. "Out of sight."

The three of them crawled across the clay tiles, scraping their hands and knees. Some were loose, and made shifting, clinking noises that sounded loud in the silent night. Every sound made Zet cringe. He was reminded of old times back home, but this was no game.

For once, the danger was real.

Hui stopped and Zet banged into him. Despite everything, they grinned at one another. Then Hui made a face and covered his nose.

"I'm serious," Hui said, snorting with laughter, "You guys really reek."

"You think we reek? Try crawling through your garbage pile back there. Don't they ever clean that thing out?"

"Stop joking," Kat said. "What's going on here, Hui, are you in danger?"

"That's one way of putting it," he said. "Next time I get some dumb idea to become a jeweler's apprentice, pour hot oil on my fingers or something. If there is a next time."

"What's going on? What's Kemet doing in there? Is it Kemet, or someone else?"

Footsteps sounded in the courtyard.

"Shh," Hui whispered.

They lay there, waiting.

After a long moment, Hui whispered, "The place is full of guards. They patrol all night long. If they find me missing . . ." The words trailed off as he peered through the darkness, as if trying to see below. There was no trace of the joker in Hui now. He seemed genuinely terrified.

"What would they do?" Zet whispered.

"Look, there's going to be a shipment on the first day of the festival. If you want to help, bring medjay. Have the shipment searched."

"A shipment of what? What should I tell the medjay?"

Two sets of footsteps were heading their way.

Hui jolted to his knees. "Shoot. I have to go."

"No," Zet said. "Come with us! Right now. We'll hide you."

"I'm not going to spend my life hiding out. We have to stop them."

"We will. We'll take you to the medjay right now."

"And say what? No, we have to catch them at their game. It's the only way. Look, I have to go. I can't make Kemet suspicious of me. If I'm not careful, he'll make me disappear. I know that's what happened to his partner. I heard them talking."

"His partner? You mean the one who left?"

"Yes. I don't think he left. I think they got rid of him. He screwed up, big time, and that's why everything—" Hui broke off as the clank of armed guards approached.

"He's not in his bed," growled a man. Snaggletooth.

"D'you think he's made a run for it?" said the other.

"Take the right corridor." Snaggletooth cracked his knuckles. "If he's here, we'll find him."

Zet's stomach roiled.

"Show yourself, boy," Snaggletooth called.

Hui bought a tiny moment by creating one of his famous, voice-throwing diversions. He placed his hands around his mouth and made a strange choking noise that sounded like it came from a hall in the distance.

The guards ran off after it.

Hui turned to Zet. "Look at the ball. You'll figure it out!"

"The ivory ball? I did."

"Then look again," Hui rolled off the roof and ran.

A moment later, Zet heard the scuffle of footsteps and Hui struggling.

"Caught you," Snaggletooth growled.

"Let go!" Hui said. "Can't a kid use the bathroom?"

"The bathroom is the other way."

"Well, it's dark. I got lost."

Nudging Kat, Zet said, "Time to get moving."

Her eyes were focused in the direction of the voices, and her face was pale. She nodded slowly, and then dragged her attention away from their friend. "They won't hurt him, will they?"

"Don't worry, he can handle them," Zet whispered. He just hoped it was the truth. All he could do now was leave and try to figure things out before the first day of the festival.

The sight of the refuse pit was even less welcoming the second time around.

"Let's make this fast." He jumped down into it. He wanted out so badly that he stopped trying to be careful about what he touched. He just waded through the garbage. Clearly, Kat felt the same. He glanced over his shoulder to see her propelling herself through, using her hands to scramble along.

Almost there. The gate lay just a few feet up ahead.

And then Kat screamed.

Not a quiet scream, either.

It was like a high-pitched explosion. It tore through the silence. It echoed off the stones. It filled the night sky. It had to have woken every human within shrieking distance, because the effect was instant.

Bodies could be heard slamming out of beds. Doors banged open.

Footsteps hammered the ground. People were running to investigate. They'd be here in seconds.

Still, Kat kept screaming. She scrambled backward, fell under, and came up again.

Zet grabbed her and shook her hard. "Stop it. STOP IT!"

She choked into silence. Her eyes were wild.

"Move," he told her. "Quick."

She nodded. Somehow, he got her to the gate and forced her over it. He scrambled after her and landed in a crouch. Looking right, Zet spotted people coming down the street.

"There!" shouted a man who sounded a lot like Snaggletooth. "Down there, by the garbage gate."

"Run," Zet gasped. "Run or we're dead!"

White-faced, Kat turned and fled. Zet ran after her. He could hear men in close pursuit. Kat rounded a corner, black hair flying. Zet sprinted past her. He pulled her around another corner, and then another. She was starting to gasp.

"Keep going," he said.

Hauling her forward, they tore through alleys until he was completely lost. Suddenly, in a haze of horror, he saw the bakeshop. They'd made a full circle.

The gated front entryway to Kemet's Workshop gaped open, dark and menacing—like a black hole into the underworld.

Kat put her hands on her knees and bent to catch her breath. She started to sob.

"What are you doing? Don't stop!" he said.

18

DEMONS

Shouts sounded in the distance. Footsteps, getting closer.

"I can't—" Kat gasped, clutching her sides.

"You have to. Come on, you can do it. Run!"

Fastening on to his sister's wrist, Zet hauled her through the darkness. He was breathing hard. The sprint combined with the struggle through the dank garbage pit was taking its toll. Still, he couldn't stop. He had to get them out of there.

"That way." He pounded through the shadows, his lungs on fire.

How long they ran, Zet had no idea.

The moon hung large and yellow over the lower walls of a temple. It glistened in the shallow, rectangular pool of water that stretched before the temple doors. They skirted around the dark, holy water. Everyone knew the temple pools were doorways into the underworld. He glanced into it, and saw shadows moving in its depths.

"Keep going," he told Kat, spooked.

"Haven't we lost them yet?" she gasped.

"Just keep going, I'll tell you when to stop."

He didn't want to lead the men to their home. He needed to be sure they'd lost them. For a moment he had a crazy notion to hide in the temple, but it was too risky. He heard footsteps in the distance, and they pressed on.

Silence surrounded them as the world slept, oblivious to Zet and Kat's terror.

He turned into a narrow lane, and then another. Suddenly, something sparkled up ahead.

"The river," he cried. "Thank the gods."

Kat sprinted alongside him, somehow finding a second wind. They reached the edge at the same time.

"That way, under the stone ledge," he said, and slipped in.

Kat didn't hover around the edge like she usually did, wading to her ankles, looking this way and that for crocodiles, water snakes, and hippos. Instead, she slipped in after him, and ducked beneath the stone overhang.

Together, they floated in silence. No one came to investigate. Still they waited, until he was sure it was safe.

They'd done it. They'd lost the guards.

Desperate to be rid of the reeking stench, Zet dove under. The water closed overhead, blissfully ending the foul smell. He floated in the darkness, letting the world and its problems disappear.

When he finally surfaced for air, Kat was still clinging to the stone overhang, but her hair was completely drenched.

With the danger gone, he felt anger well up. "What were you doing, screaming back there?"

"I didn't do it on purpose."

"You almost got us killed! And what about Hui, don't you think they're going to connect it together? Him being out, and you screaming in the garbage pit?"

She went pale. "I hadn't thought of that."

He knew she'd never get Hui in trouble on purpose. Zet felt mean about what he said. But he was mad. "Well you should've thought of it, before you woke up the whole world."

"I'm sorry," she said. "I touched . . . something. Something horrible."

"Hello—we both touched something horrible. We were in a garbage pit!"

"Yes, but..."

"But what?"

She covered her face. "It was awful."

Zet stared at her. "What was it? What did you touch?"

"Hands."

A chill ripped down Zet's spine. "Hands? What do you mean, hands?"

"Fingers. Grabbing me. That's what it felt like."

"Did you see them?"

"No, but I felt them, I'm sure I did."

"Fingers grabbed you? Come on. Do you hear yourself?" He was furious. Her wild imagination had nearly cost them their lives.

Kat's chin trembled. "It's the truth. Maybe it wasn't human. Maybe it was—"

He held up a hand. "Wait, don't tell me. The evil spirit army. Hiding in the pit."

She made a face. "It could have been. I felt it!"

He snorted. "I've heard enough. That's the last time I bring you with me. Ever."

With that, he pulled himself out of the water onto the stone ledge and stomped off. From behind, he heard Kat do the same.

She hurried to keep up. "What time do you think it is?"

"I don't know. Almost morning."

They'd need to be at the stall soon to open up. But first, he wanted to examine the ivory ball. Hui was in big trouble. Zet knew that now. Hopefully he could figure out what Hui meant when he'd said Zet would figure it out.

A VISITOR

When they reached home, Zet was exhausted. Despite his urgent desire to study Hui's ball, he needed a rest. Just for a few moments. Then he'd get out the lamp and study it carefully until he knew what Hui meant.

He and Kat sank down on the cushions in the front room, too exhausted to even climb the ladder to their sleeping pallets on the roof.

He leaned back, determined not to fall fully asleep.

As soon as he closed his eyes, he drifted off.

Heat on his face made his eyes jerk open.

Sunlight streamed through the front windows.

"We're late for work," he shouted, shaking Kat awake.

Blue circles rimmed her eyes. Grotesquely colored stains splotched her tunic and her hair was matted. She was groggy, but only for a moment. In a frenzy, she tore upstairs to change. Meanwhile, Zet found himself a fresh kilt, yanked it on, and then grabbed the linen wrapped ivory ball. There was no time to find a sack. He simply carried it and ran.

"We're in trouble," Kat said. "The other vendors already think we're irresponsible."

"I know."

When they reached the market, it was in full swing. But as it turned out, Zet and Kat weren't missed. Instead, a crowd of people that included five, uniformed medjay surrounded the new amulet vendor's stall.

Akar's amulets clanked in a gentle breeze. If the man with the bulging eyes was surprised by the attention, he didn't show it. Instead, he wore a cheerful, spirited smile.

But the long established vendors weren't smiling. They were glaring. Salatis the old date-seller stood right in the middle of it all. He had his hands on his wiry hips. He and Akar seemed to be having some kind of showdown.

"We want this charlatan removed," Salatis crowed. "He's stirring up trouble for his own evil ends!"

"Not at all," said Akar. "I'm just a humble salesman, like the rest of you."

"Like the rest of us?" The fumes of some acrid potion sent Salatis into a coughing fit. He whacked his chest a few times. "Well someone knocked over all my date baskets. Right into the dirt, too. And the next thing I know, you're over at my stall telling me it was the demon army, and I should buy a protection amulet from you or it will happen again. It's fishy business!" He pointed a bony finger. "I think you knocked over my baskets, just so I'd buy something from you."

"Hold on now," boomed a familiar deep voice.

It was Merimose, the head medjay and Zet's old friend. Zet had helped him solve the case to save Pharaoh's life. Relief washed over him. He'd forgotten all about his plans to go visit the medjay. But maybe the important man could help.

Merimose was eyeing Salatis, weighing what the man said.

"You think Akar sabotaged your wares so you'd buy a magical protection device? That's a serious accusation," Merimose said. "Do you have proof?"

"No," said Salatis, "But I'm sure he did it."

"Being sure and having proof are two different things." Merimose turned to the man with the stall of magical devices. "Akar, that's your name, isn't it?"

"Yes, indeed," Akar said, grinning ear-to-ear. Clearly, the man wasn't afraid. He seemed to think all this attention was good for business. And maybe it was, because the rest of the market was empty, and crowds were pushing closer to see what was going on.

"Well, Akar, do you have papers to run this stall here?" Merimose said.

"I do indeed."

There was a lot of murmuring as the papers were studied. After a time, Merimose pronounced them good. "But I suggest you stay out of trouble," Merimose told him.

"Oh, I will, good sir. I most certainly will. Now, can I sell you a protection device of some sort? Being a police officer, you must face all sorts of terrible dangers."

Merimose laughed.

Meanwhile, Salatis and the other vendors dispersed, all of them grumbling. At the same time, the waiting crowd surged forward and started browsing Akar's stall.

"We're in the wrong business," Zet said, rolling his eyes. Then he called out, "Merimose!"

The big medjay turned. At the sight of Zet and Kat, the man's tanned, leathery face spread into a bright smile. "Thought I might see you here," he said.

"I wanted to talk to you," Zet said. "I was going to come looking for you before. Do you have a minute?"

Merimose said something to his armed men. They dispersed down various side streets, off to walk their beats.

"I better go open the stall," Kat said.

"Why don't I help you," Merimose said. "Come on, I'll give you two a hand."

One of the women who'd made special orders was waiting for them. At the sight of Merimose, she frowned.

"Well," she said, arching one brow with a satisfied look. "I'm certainly glad to see the police involved. I knew it would come to this."

Merimose shot Zet a puzzled look.

"Yes," Zet said, deciding not to correct the woman's misguided assumptions. "We're doing everything we can to track down the missing orders."

Kat led the woman away, whispering that it was best not to disturb the investigation, and that in the meantime the woman could pick a second set in case the order didn't arrive.

"Trouble?" Merimose asked Zet.

"Don't even ask."

"Very good. None of my business." Merimose picked up a clay urn. He had huge hands, like two big platters. He turned the urn around easily, even though it took Zet both arms and a few good grunts to lift it. "What's this for?"

"A beer brewing jug," Zet said.

"Huh. You learn something new every day."

He set it down with a heavy thud. His face turned serious. "Now what did you want to talk about? I've never seen you look so grim."

THE GOLDEN SCARABS

Zet wasted no time. "Is it true that golden scarabs are being stolen from all over town?"

Furrows appeared on Merimose's tanned forehead. He rubbed the spot between his thick brows. "Where did you hear that?"

Zet shrugged. "Akar."

"Why am I not surprised?" Merimose shot a look at the busy vendor. "Well, he got it partly right. They're being stolen, but not from all over town. Just the Khonsu district."

"The Khonsu district? Where the rich people live," Zet said. "So the thieves only want expensive ones."

"Thieves always want the expensive ones, when it comes to jewelry," Merimose said with a laugh. "I suppose that's the only stuff worth stealing."

Zet nodded. Three women walked past, baskets over their arms, chatting about what they planned to cook for the upcoming Opet feast days. They stopped at Salatis's date stall across the way.

Zet lowered his voice. "So you're sure it's thieves. You don't believe it's a demon army of dead Hyksos soldiers stealing the scarabs?"

"Akar's telling people that?" Merimose said.

"Yes."

"I'm a religious man," Merimose said. "But I'm also a medjay. And where there's trouble, we usually find a living person behind it."

Zet let out a breath of relief he didn't realize he'd been holding. "That's what I thought. Still, I could see how people might believe it. It's strange the thieves aren't stealing whole jewel boxes of stuff. Why pick out only the scarabs and leave the rest?"

"That's what puzzles me too," Merimose said.

"I mean, not that I believe in the demon army," Zet said, voicing a concern he'd never admit to Kat. "But scarabs protect long life and everything. Akar says the demons are swallowing the scarabs to weaken Egypt before the Opet Festival. So we'll be unable to fend them off when they come. And the demons will come when Pharaoh and the whole city is out celebrating."

Merimose looked grim. Quietly, he said, "That's why the first person I notified, after my men, was the Head Priest."

"You notified the Head Priest?" Zet whispered, shocked.

Hearing about the demons from Akar was one thing. But from Merimose? He took the threat seriously enough to involve the priests? That was more frightening than anything Zet could imagine.

A shadow seemed to pass over the square.

"How many scarabs have been stolen?" Zet asked.

"It's hard to say," the huge medjay replied. "We've gone door to door, investigating. You'd be surprised at some of these people we've interviewed. Some of them have so many jewels they don't know what they own. And then there are mothers and sisters who are away shopping, and half of them couldn't say what the other bought recently. It's an impossible task."

"Has anyone seen the thief? You know, like running out of the house or something?"

Merimose put his big, muscular hand on the sword hilt strapped to his waist. "Not exactly."

Zet gave the man a questioning look. Merimose glanced toward Kat's bent head. Her braided hair flashed black and blue in the chinks of light. She was on the far side, disappearing through the deep stacks of pottery, moving pieces here and there.

"Don't spread this around," Merimose said. "It's not a secret, but we don't want people to panic. Basically, a servant was attacked in Khonsu Street and almost killed. He was found unconscious, his head bleeding."

"Right in the middle of all those glittering mansions?"

Merimose nodded. "We patrol the area regularly. You can imagine how upset people are. Unfortunately, my men on duty that morning saw nothing."

Kat worked her way closer, cleaning and arranging. The clonk of dishes being shuffled around broke the stillness of the air.

"Why was the servant attacked?"

"Well, he was carrying a scarab amulet. How the attacker knew that is anyone's guess. Apparently the thing was made of solid gold and studded with rare precious jewels—rubies, emeralds, you name it."

"What was a servant doing with an expensive scarab amulet?"

"The jewelry had been sent out some weeks ago to be cleaned and repaired. The household received a letter saying the amulet was ready for pick up. So the servant went to pick it up, and was bringing it home."

Zet's skin prickled, and he was suddenly on alert. "From where? I mean, where was the amulet cleaned?"

"At a place called the Kemet Workshop."

Kat's head snapped up and she gasped.

THE MISSING AMULET

S omeone was attacked leaving the Kemet Workshop?" Kat asked, eyes wide.

"You have good ears," Merimose said.

Kat colored. Obviously, she'd been listening in the whole time.

Merimose said, "Apparently the Kemet Workshop has the best jewelers in Thebes. But it sounds to me like you've already heard of the place."

Zet and Kat glanced at one another.

"We have heard of it," Zet said.

"Something you want to tell me?" Merimose said, studying them both.

"I was there, yesterday," Zet said.

If the medjay was shocked or impressed, he hid it well. "Why?"

At that moment, a woman emerged from a dark alley and headed toward them. Clouds of perfume billowed around her as she approached. Kat's shoulders went around her ears.

"It's one of the women," she said in a tense voice. "I better go talk to her."

"Do you want my help?" Zet said.

"I can do it."

He nodded. "Tell her about mother going down river."

"I hope she tracked the missing orders down," Kat said.

"So do I." He desperately wanted the stall back to normal, with happy customers, and without the worry they'd be kicked out of the market and lose their business.

Merimose didn't pry.

"Thanks for giving me a few minutes with your brother," the medjay said. Then he followed Zet out of the hot sunlight, back to the shaded, private area at the rear of the stall.

Zet offered his uniformed friend a cushion.

"Ah, that feels good. I've been on my feet since before dawn," Merimose said. "So what were you doing at the workshop?"

"My best friend, Hui, took a position there as apprentice."

Zet told him about his run-in with Snaggletooth when he first tried to visit Hui. He went on to explain how he'd convinced Delilah to attend the semi-annual visit.

"So you got inside?"

"Not easily, but yes," Zet said.

"And what were your thoughts on the place? I know you've got a sharp pair of eyes."

"I thought it was creepy. There are spying slots everywhere. And they searched us on the way out. And everyone seemed to be acting really strange. Including my friend, Hui. And the owner was weird."

Merimose nodded, thoughtful. "We did notice the slots. I don't have a problem with them. Probably a good security measure. As for the rest, they're no doubt on guard given what's going on."

"Then you don't think it's suspicious?"

"In what way?" Merimose said.

"Maybe someone from the shop stole the jewels. They knew the servant had them."

"Unlikely," Merimose said. "Why would they do that? The place exudes wealth. Even if the piece were worth a lot, it wouldn't be worth risking the shop over. In fact, it would be bad business. Not only that, it's too obvious. It would just point right back to them if they stole a piece every time it left the workshop."

Zet nodded, thoughtful. "But was it worth a lot? Like a giant fortune?"

"It was worth a lot. But like I said, not enough to steal."

"Maybe they're in trouble? Maybe they need the money?"

"No. They're fully paid up with their creditors. In fact, Kemet pays early, I'm told. And if his servants' clothing is anything to go by, Kemet's rolling in wealth. That can't be it. He has a solid business going. I'm told he makes pieces for Pharaoh's wife and daughters. Maybe even some of the royal jewels."

"Humph." Zet scraped at the ground with his foot. "Did you at least search the place for it?"

Merimose grinned with that bright, flashing smile. "That's why I like you. We think alike. Yes, I searched for it. Of course, I searched for it. I don't care how things look, or how wealthy he is." His smile faded a little. "But no luck. It's not there. We tore the place apart."

Zet pictured the servant who'd searched his bag, and decided they'd gotten a taste of their own medicine. He smiled. "I bet they didn't like that."

"No, to put it mildly. We searched Kemet's residence as well."

"He doesn't live there?"

Merimose shook his shaved head. "Nope. Kemet's got a great mansion on the river. You've probably seen the place on your way to your friend Padus's papyrus plantation. It's the second to last house on the way out of town."

Zet stared off for a moment, imagining the road. "I think I know the one."

"The place is practically a palace. Statues leering down from every corner. Pillared hallways and courtyards. He welcomed me and my men in like a lord, and sat back drinking wine while we turned the place upside-down. That's what convinced me."

"Of what? His innocence?"

Merimose rubbed his neck. "Yep. I almost wanted him to be guilty. Smiling little beetle he is. Not my sort. But justice is justice, and I don't have to like all our citizens. I just have to protect them."

Through a gap in the curtained back area, Zet saw that the special orders woman had left. Kat was helping another customer, who'd chosen several dishes. Kat pulled an armful of reeds from a sack and stacked layers of them between the dishes. The dry plants crunched and crackled; their dry, fragrant scent filled the air.

"There's something else I need to tell you," Zet said.

"Oh?"

Zet itched his neck. He wasn't sure what Merimose thought about trespassing, but the man needed to know. "We snuck in there last night. I talked to my friend, and he pretty much told me something was going on."

The man's dark eyes sparked with interest. "What's going on, then?"

"Well—that's the thing. He couldn't tell me much, because guards showed up."

"Oh."

"I did learn one thing, though, he says Kemet's partner was gotten rid of somehow, because he'd made a big mistake."

"Gotten rid of? I don't like the sound of that."

"Not only that, Hui said Kemet's planning a shipment on the first day of the festival. And he said if we searched them, we could catch them."

"A search is not possible. Not without just cause. Kemet has proven himself innocent, we searched him completely. I'd need solid proof to do it again."

"But you have to!"

"Did Hui say what was in the shipment?"

"No, but does it matter?"

"Yes. As far as what you've told me, Kemet's done nothing wrong. He's bound to make shipments, it's a business after all. And if it eases your worries, my men are examining every ship before it leaves Thebes. They're looking for stolen scarabs, and any illegal shipment will be found, no matter what it is."

"But what about Kemet's partner disappearing?"

"Most likely apprentice gossip. People make up rumors. Especially when they're cooped up with each other for a long time. Look, like I said, I'm not a fan of Kemet. But he's wealthy. I don't think he'd sabotage his business over a few baubles."

What more could Zet say?

Still, he was sure Hui was in danger. Hui said so himself.

Merimose stood. "I need to get back to my office. As for you, just focus on your stall here. It's a good one."

22

CRACKED

Merimose was nearly out of the square, when Zet had a sudden brain flash.

"Merimose!" Zet shouted. He sprinted past the goat pen, and a stall selling cabbages and carrots. "Merimose, wait up!"

Merimose stopped at a pen of honking geese. He raised one brow, waiting.

Shoppers watched as if wondering what business a twelve-year-old, barefoot nobody could have with the head medjay. Merimose did look impressive, with his polished sword and breastplate gleaming in the sunlight. If you didn't know him, he might even frighten you. Zet realized then just how lucky he was to call such an important man his friend.

"Well?" Merimose asked.

"I had a question."

"I told you to stay out of this one," Merimose warned.

"I know. I was just wondering—" He blurted out, "You know the servant who was attacked? Whose house did he work at? You never said."

Merimose's face darkened. "And I don't plan to. Stay out of it,

Zet. Don't you dare go questioning people in the Khonsu District. That servant was almost killed. These are dangerous people."

"But I helped you before, on another case. Maybe I can help now."

"You lucked out last time."

"Ouch," Zet said, stung. "It was a bit more than luck."

"This isn't a game. People could die."

Zet shuffled his feet. Yes, people could die, maybe even Hui. But Merimose didn't seem to understand that. Zet glanced down at the honking geese. The closest bird ruffled its feathers and blinked hopefully. Zet wished he had a handful of grains.

How could he convince Merimose that Hui needed help?

Merimose cut in on his thoughts. "I need to get back to my office. If you hear from your friend, report it to me. Understood?"

Zet nodded.

Merimose studied him, his face suspicious. "I'm serious, Zet, this case is too dangerous for you to go meddling around."

"Zet," Kat called, saving him from answering. "I need you!"

"Gotta go," Zet said, glad to escape.

The mid-morning swarm had descended. Things got busy, and it wasn't until closing time that Zet remembered the ivory ball. When they'd finished packing up for the evening, he stuck it under his arm.

"Come on, let's go home, I'd rather look at it there," he told Kat.

They ran, headlong through the streets, enjoying the cool air and the shadowed paving stones against their bare feet.

Suddenly, a man stepped out of his doorway and slammed into Zet.

The linen-wrapped ball flew one way, Zet the other. Eyes on the flying package, Zet somersaulted and stretched as far as he could. The ball landed in his fingertips. But his relief was short lived. The man lost his footing. He took Zet and the ball down with him.

They landed in a heap.

The ball made a sickening crunch.

"Watch where you're going," the man grumbled.

"Sorry," Zet said. Gingerly, he lifted his package into his arms. Even without unwrapping it, he knew the ball was broken.

The man's face softened. "I hope it wasn't something important."

"It wasn't your fault," Zet said. "I'm sorry I knocked you down."

After that, Zet and Kat walked more slowly. Their route took them down a busy thoroughfare. People bumped up against Zet in their hurry to get home. With each jolt to the package, he could feel a loose piece of ivory moving around.

"Stop," Zet told Kat. "Let's go back there behind the temple of Maat. I want to see how badly it's broken."

She nodded and they padded quietly past the towering structure.

The sky was still blue, despite the late hour. A pointed obelisk stood in the distance, framed between the walls of the narrow alley. Hieroglyphs had been carved into the stone; the writing stretched up as far as he could see.

"Okay, Hui," he said. "This ball of yours better tell us something."

He removed the linen, and dropped the covering to the ground.

The globe was still in one piece. A crack, however, zigzagged across its milky surface. Zet pried the crack apart. It was hard to see inside, but there was definitely something in there. Something pale brown. It almost looked like . . . no, that couldn't be right.

"Here goes nothing." Crouching, he smashed the ball against the flagstones.

The crack widened.

"Zet!" Kat gasped, her voice a mixture of horror and curiosity.

"Hui said to look at it. Well, I'm looking at it." He smashed it again. This time, the ivory came apart in two jagged pieces. His mouth dropped wide when he saw what the ball contained. He'd been right.

Kat's brow creased. "Is that bread?"

"Yep."

"Is that for padding or something? Do they normally put bread in ivory carvings?"

Zet rolled his eyes.

"No," she said, coloring. "No, I guess that would be stupid. It must be a clue then."

Zet pondered the roll. One half of the ivory shell still clung to it.

"Did you talk about bread when you were there?" Kat asked.

"Not really. Well, I guess sort of. At lunch, we had bread from the bakery next door. It was good, and we talked about it being good. That's about it."

"Maybe he wants you to talk to the people at the bakery?" Kat said.

"But he could have just said so on the roof." Zet pried the remaining ivory shell from it, set the shell down and turned the bread roll over. "There's a hole in the bottom."

"Let's see!"

Zet wedged a finger into the crust. "I think there's something in there. Yes, I feel something."

"What is it?"

"Something metal."

"Pull it out!"

Zet ripped the bread in half. A gleaming object fell into his lap. He gasped.

"A golden scarab," Kat breathed.

23

A SCARAB OF GOLD

Zet stared at the object in his hand, unable to believe his eyes. The scarab had to be worth a fortune. Its jewels winked at him, and the polished gold seemed to give off a light of its own. A large red stone had been set in the middle, and the beetle itself was colored with crushed blue lapis.

"Don't let anyone see," Kat hissed.

Zet snatched the linen cover and partially wrapped it again. "This thing is crazy," he said. "It's like something Pharaoh would have."

"I know. But Zet, it's a scarab! Which means it's all connected."

"Yes, but how?" Zet frowned, trying to put himself in Hui's shoes.

What was Hui trying to say? Zet turned the scarab over, shielding it from prying eyes with the linen. When he saw the underside, his confusion grew.

"What in the name of the gods? Look at this."

The scarab beetle's belly was not gold, or bejeweled in any way. Instead, it was a dusty red color.

The bottom is made of . . ." He picked at it with one fingernail. "Clay?"

"Clay?" Kat said. "Let me see that." She took it from him.

"That is the strangest thing I've ever seen," Zet said. "It's the most expensive thing in the world if you look at the top, and the cheapest bauble known to mankind if you look at the bottom." He ran a hand over his scalp and let out a frustrated groan. "Hui," he said, speaking to the sky. "This would be a lot easier if you hid a note in there."

"He can't write," Kat said.

"I know."

"And neither can you."

"Okay, okay. Don't rub it in. Little Miss I-learned-hieratic-script-and-you-should-have-too."

"Well maybe now you see why it was a good idea. What did you want him to do, dictate a rescue note to Kemet's scribe?"

Zet rolled his eyes.

"But hold on," she said. "Let me see it again." Kat crouched down, holding the underside to face the dying light. "There's something here, scratched on the bottom."

Zet bent closer. She was right.

Two lines, side-by-side, with a connecting line at the bottom.

"It's the symbol for the number two," he said.

She nodded. "It must mean something. They're carefully drawn. It's obvious he put the symbol there for a reason."

But what reason?

Hui had done the best he could do by making this missive. It must have been dangerous; he would have had to make it in secret. But what was Hui trying to say? What did a strange, half gold, half clay scarab, with the number two on the bottom, embedded in a piece of bread mean? How was it connected to the scarab thefts? Or the shipment? Or Kemet's missing partner?

Feeling more frustrated than ever, they headed home. Once inside, Zet bee-lined for the kitchen and hid the scarab at the bottom of a basket of onions.

"No one will look for it here," he said.

"What are we going to do?" Kat asked.

"Tomorrow I'll go talk to the people at the bakery," he said.

Kat nodded. "They must know something." She let out a sigh of relief. "Maybe we don't know what the amulet means, but I feel like we're getting somewhere. I really do. And you know what, there's something else to look forward to."

"What's that?"

"Finally we're going to have an answer for those women. Mother comes home tomorrow."

"You're right. Thank the gods for that!"

With this cheerful thought, the two of them rummaged around the kitchen and put together a simple meal.

Kat carried bowls of food to the dining area; Zet set two lamps flickering on the table to chase away the darkness. They munched on thick slices of bread, heaps of spicy, chickpea stew, and garlicky, roasted vegetables. There was a jug of good, cold fermented barley water to wash it down. And for dessert, there was a pale yellow sweet cake. It was so delicious that they ate nearly half of it, drizzling their thick pieces with honey.

Finally, satisfied, Zet groaned and leaned back against the wall.

"What's that you're wearing around your neck?" Zet asked her.

Kat's hands went to it. "My pendant Hui made," she said in a high voice.

"Yeah, but beside it. The other thing on the chain."

She shrugged.

"Is that a protection amulet?" he said, squinting at the tiny roll of papyrus.

"Don't laugh."

"Am I laughing?"

"Yes."

"Please don't tell me you got that from Akar."

Kat colored.

"It's not demons. I'm telling you, it's something else. We have a scarab here from Hui. Obviously this whole thing has something to do with the workshop."

"Maybe," she squeaked. "Or maybe the demons will come here looking for that scarab, and we'll really be in trouble."

Zet tried hard not to laugh. He really did.

But he couldn't help it. Somehow, the thought of demons rushing in the door and searching the onion basket made him laugh until tears streamed down his face.

Kat punched his arm, but she was grinning. "Just help me clear the dishes, big brother."

A CONTEST

On the way to work the next morning, Zet was thoughtful.

"I just wish there was some way to question the people in Khonsu Street," he said.

"You mean to ask for information about the attack on the servant?" Kat said.

"Yes. Even if it's not the right house, people gossip, everyone over there must know about it. Maybe I could learn something useful. But it's not like I could just go knock on someone's door and say, 'Hi, I'm Zet. Would you tell me what you know about the servant who was attacked? And by the way, has anyone stolen your scarabs?'"

Kat giggled. "No. Probably not."

"Anyway, maybe I'll learn something from the bakers. You're sure you don't mind if I go over there after we open up?"

"I can manage the stall," she said. "We have to help Hui. We don't have a choice."

Kat chewed her lower lip as she walked. He knew that look. She was smart, even though he'd never actually tell her that, and she was onto something.

"What are you thinking?" Zet said.

"It's a long shot."

"What is?"

"We could have a contest."

Zet stared at her, completely baffled. This was the last thing he expected her to say. "A contest?"

She outlined her plan. "It might work, right?"

His heart leapt. "It's good. It's really good."

As Zet opened up, Kat disappeared into the back of the stall.

"How's it going?" he called. "Are you almost finished?"

"Almost."

He wandered back and found her kneeling on the ground, writing on a big piece of linen.

"There," she said, with a final flourish of her brush. She held it up. "What do you think? It says: Happy Opet Festival. Enter to win this bowl."

"It's perfect," Zet said.

"And this is the bowl." She held up a big, brightly colored serving bowl that was certain to stand out. Painted blue ibis birds flew gracefully around its rim.

"Don't forget to get their street addresses," Zet said.

"Like I would. I'm not stupid. In case you forgot, this was my idea." She went out front to hang up her sign. "Help me with this, and then go to the bakery."

Zet helped her hang the sign, but decided to hang around in the hopes they'd get lucky early. Dusty light filled the stone plaza. At the stall next door, Geb, the old herb-vendor, removed the lids from his wares and set them out on display. The scent of cardamom, cinnamon and cumin rose from the mounds of brightly colored spices. Across the way, Salatis piled fresh golden dates into his baskets.

Customers were flooding in, too. The jar of entries started filling up fast.

Everyone wanted a chance at winning the beautiful bowl.

"Anyone from the Khonsu Street area?" Zet asked, for the tenth time.

"Stop asking me!" Kat said. "Just go to the bakery, will you? You're driving me crazy."

"All right, all right," he said, grinning.

"But Zet?" she said, looking suddenly worried.

"Yeah?"

"Promise you won't let the Kemet workshop people see you in there."

He hadn't thought of that. What if one of the men from next door came to the bakery to buy bread? They'd recognize him as Hui's friend from visiting day. And then they might connect him with the disturbance from the night before. How would he explain his presence in the artisan quarter? It could be bad. Very bad.

Still, to Kat he said, "They wouldn't remember me. I'm just another kid."

"Okay," she said doubtfully.

With that, Zet took off at a run.

Hopefully he could get in and out, questions answered, without being seen by Kemet's henchmen.

25

INTO THE OVEN

Zet wound his way back to the artisan quarter. The route was beginning to feel familiar, and he made his way quickly through the streets. He passed the familiar stench of the tannery, covering his nose as he ran.

How could anyone spend his days working there?

But that was not his problem. Right now, he had bigger things to worry about. The block with the bakery and the Kemet workshop was right around the corner. As he neared, he hoped to lose himself in the crowds. But unlike near his market square, crowds in this part of Thebes were thin. If he'd been clever, he might have thought to disguise himself. Hui would have; that's for certain. He'd have pulled out his mother's face paints, like some black kohl, to draw a crazy beard on his face or something.

Too late now.

Zet reached the familiar block and paused in the shadow of a doorway to survey the scene. To his relief, the locked gate was deserted. Not that Kemet would bother posting a guard. His henchmen wouldn't be expecting Zet to return. Especially in broad daylight. Only someone stupid would do that.

Right?

But Zet wasn't stupid. He was just determined to save his best friend.

He took a step out of the shadows when the barbed gate to the Kemet workshop slammed open. Zet ducked back. Snaggletooth and an equally large thug stepped out.

Frantic that he'd been seen, Zet tried the door handle behind him. It turned, and he opened the door a fraction and slipped inside. Heart thumping, he waited, expecting Snaggletooth to barge in and strangle him.

A moment passed. He risked a peek and saw Snaggletooth and the other man pass by. Zet sagged against the door in relief. He glanced around the room he was in. There were shelves full of what appeared to be woven sandal soles. A table held tools, and half a dozen sandals midway through construction.

He heard the sound of someone whistling in the adjoining room.

With a quick glance to make sure the coast was clear, Zet hurried back out into the street.

A moment later, he was standing in the warm front room of the bakery. The most delicious scents filled the air. Cinnamon and dates and the yeasty smell of rising dough.

The reception room was really just a small cubicle with a counter down the middle. Behind the counter, a rack with various breads on display rose to the ceiling. Next to the rack, a curtained doorway led to an area beyond.

On the counter sat a little bell. It was beautifully made, and he wondered if they'd got it from the Kemet workshop next door.

Zet picked it up and rang it.

A moment later, a woman thrust the curtain aside and stepped out. She was stooped and wrinkled, her skin dark from the sun. A puckered scar ruined whatever beauty she may have once had.

Before the curtain closed, Zet caught a glimpse of the baking courtyard beyond. The roof was open to the sky and on the ground were several pits loaded with hot coals. He'd seen bread being baked before, and knew bakers did it by placing lidded clay pots full of dough directly into the coals. He sold bread-baking pots himself. He wondered if they used his pots here.

"Can I help you?" the scarred woman said in a warbling voice.

"Yes. At least I hope so."

She wiped her hands on a spotless towel that hung from her waist. "What can I get you? A bread round, like this? Or something sweet perhaps?"

Zet fumbled in a small pouch. He'd brought a few deben to barter for bread, sure that he'd get better information if he bought something. "Two sweet rolls, please."

She smiled and fetched two plump buns from a basket. Zet handed over the deben, and she gave him several copper kite in return.

"I was wondering if I could ask you some questions?" Zet said.

At this, she stiffened. "What sort of questions?"

"About the workshop, next door. The Kemet Workshop?"

Her face hardened. "I don't have time."

"It would only take a minute. I have a friend over there. He's an apprentice, and I'm worried that—"

The curtain was thrust aside, and a second woman stepped out. She had no disfiguring scar, but apart from that, she looked identical to the first. Zet realized they were twins.

"What do you want, boy?" the second woman asked. "What's going on, Kissa?"

"Nothing," said Kissa, shooting Zet a warning glance. "He's just leaving. Aren't you, young man."

"No. Wait, listen, please! I think my friend wanted me to talk to you. He gave me some bread and . . ." Some sense of caution made him stop talking. Maybe this wasn't what Hui wanted him to do.

Kissa had her hands around the towel, and her knuckles were white with tension. "And what? He gave you some bread and what did he say?"

"Just—" He looked from one dark, wrinkled face to the other. Several months ago, he would have trusted these women without question. But he'd begun to learn that people weren't always what they seemed. Still, why had Hui sent him the bread to begin with?

The baker-twins were waiting.

"Just," Zet began, "My friend said I should ask you if you have a message for me."

"A message? Why would we have a message?" Kissa said, her hand going to her old scar.

"We wouldn't," snapped her sister. "We don't carry messages. If he had a message, he should have told you himself." Her voice had risen, and her eyes flashed.

"You have your bread," said Kissa in a gentler tone. She glanced out the door, and back at Zet again. "Now quick. Go."

"Maybe we shouldn't let him."

"Don't be a fool, Kakra," Kissa said. "I smell bread burning. Please, go back inside."

Kakra looked furious, but the fear of burned bread won out. She left.

Turning to Zet, Kissa said, "Now go, run, and keep away. Understand?"

"No, I don't," Zet said.

She was trembling. "We don't like nosy children. Please don't make me force you to leave."

HOME SILENT HOME

Zet was more confused that ever as he headed back to his market stall. He hurried there, almost in a daze, barely noticing the people around him. Crowds bumped him this way and that. All he could think about was getting back to Kat and telling her about the strange reactions of the women.

What could have made them act that way? Were they afraid of Kemet? Had something happened to put them on guard? Had they, perhaps, witnessed the murders somehow, and now they were terrified to speak in case Kemet set his henchmen on them? Finally, he reached the square. He saw Kat up ahead, haggling with a pair of men over a large clay urn, used to store wine.

Zet waited until the men left, and then told her all about the strange sisters.

She looked completely baffled. "That is so strange. I was sure Hui wanted you to go there. What else could the bread mean?"

"I have no idea." Zet handed over a sweet bun. They munched in silence.

The bakery had been a dead end.

Their only lead now was Khonsu Street. He desperately hoped

they'd find a winner for the bowl soon. They were running out of time.

The festival was in two days!

That left only tomorrow. Because the following day, the shipment had to be stopped. According to Hui, it was the only way to help him escape alive.

Until Zet could figure out a better plan, there was nothing left but to focus on work. He moved about, polishing plates and vases. He helped customers sort through all the beautiful choices to find just the right thing. He wrapped packages, and did his best to smile and say all the right things. Kat was also going through the motions, but it was clear that her mind, like his, was elsewhere.

The day inched forward. No one from Khonsu Street entered to win the bowl. Zet and Kat headed home in silence.

The thought of seeing his mother and baby brother, however, lifted his mood somewhat. Zet could hardly wait to see them.

When they reached their street, however, Zet frowned.

The windows were dark.

He ran up the steps and pushed open the door.

"Hello?" he called.

Nothing.

Kat wrapped her arms around herself. "Where are they?"

"I don't know! She should have been back, hours ago."

Kat looked frightened.

"I'm going to the boat dock," Zet said.

"I'm coming with you."

But when they reached the boat dock, it was deserted. Finally, they found a familiar looking man who'd helped them unload goods in the past.

"Nope," the man said, "I haven't seen your mother. Or the potters' boat for that matter. I've been here all day. Now don't look so worried, children," he added. "She probably just got held up. She'll be here tomorrow. Go on home and have your dinner."

They wandered away from the man.

The river lapped gently against the water's edge. The night air felt humid and heavy, pressing down, making it hard to breathe.

"I'm sure she's fine," Kat burst out, but didn't sound sure.

"You're right," Zet said. "I'm sure she is."

Three men sat in a circle of lamplight, two of them playing a game of Senet. One started to shout that the other was cheating. The other man leapt up, balling his fists. Kat watched in horror as they shouted at each other, and Zet was sure they were going to start a fistfight.

"Let's get out of here," he said. He walked quickly, his own anger bubbling up. Nothing in his life was working right. He felt trapped. He had to do something. He turned to Kat. "I'm going to Kemet's mansion to look around."

"When?" Kat asked. This time, she didn't say she wanted to come along. She didn't argue that it was dangerous, either. Clearly, she knew they were running out of choices as well as he did.

"I'm going tonight. I'll walk you home first."

"I can walk home by myself," she said.

And so, Zet set off at a run for the edge of town.

Kemet's mansion was just as Merimose had described it. Huge and looming, and surrounded by high, white walls. A pair of towering statues presided over the front entry, with bodies of giants and faces molded to look like Kemet himself. Music drifted from somewhere inside, along with the burble of chatter and laughter.

It sounded like Kemet was hosting a large dinner party.

This could be good. It could provide the cover Zet needed.

He searched the wall for a spot to climb in. A cluster of date palms towered over the rear of the complex, leaned up against the walls. He made it quickly up the trunks, and dropped down onto the manicured grounds on the other side.

A dog snarled.

Zet's head snapped up. Three large hounds crouched at the open door to the house. The snarling dog bared its teeth. Then it shot toward Zet, barking. In a flash of fur, the other two dogs followed. They bore down on him in a flash of teeth and fur.

Zet turned and threw himself at the wall. There were no toeholds.

Frantic, he made for a birdbath, jumped onto it, and leapt for the top of the wall. He missed. The dogs were nearly on him. And men were shouting now, too. Desperate, he leapt onto the birdbath a second time.

Teeth caught hold of his ankle.

He felt skin tear.

He wrenched his leg free. Threw himself at the wall. His fingers latched onto the top of it. Holding on in a death grip, he pushed off with his toes and cartwheeled over. He landed on all fours.

Then he sprinted.

Fast.

The doors were opening, and the dogs were shooting out.

Zet found a palm grove near the river, climbed the nearest tree, and stayed there until the coast was clear.

27

A WINNER!

A strange mood gripped the little market square the next morning. Sales were up at Akar's stall; the line to buy magical devices wound out and down one of the side alleys. Some people were terrified of the demon army.

Others, in contrast, spoke in excited voices about the Opet Festival opening ceremonies on the following day. There was to be a chariot race down the Avenue of the Sphinxes.

"I heard the Royal sons organized it," a man told Geb.

The herb-seller said, "I heard that, too. And I heard the sons will be racing, with Pharaoh, the Royal wife, and Pharaoh's royal mother in attendance."

Zet was listening to this discussion, but his mind was elsewhere. All he could think of was that the clock was ticking down. He only had today left. Tomorrow morning, the shipment would be leaving the Kemet workshop. And he was no closer to stopping it. Maybe he should talk to Merimose. And say what?

Suddenly, Kat jolted him back to the present.

"Zet," she gasped, grabbing his arm. Her face was alight. "We have a winner for the serving bowl!"

His heart seemed to stop. "You mean we have an entry from Khonsu Street?"

Kat nodded furiously, her cheeks red with excitement. "I told the woman you'd bring it to her house later today. She seemed happy, and she said that servants manned the house all day, and that they would accept the bowl for her if she hadn't returned."

He leaped into the air with a shout.

Geb and his customer turned in surprise.

"Er, just excited about the chariot race," Zet said.

He ran after Kat, who had disappeared into the back to wrap it.

"Don't bother, there's no time," he said, taking the bowl. "What's the address?"

Kat took out a scrap of old broken pottery, on which she'd written it down. "Okay. Her house is on the corner of Khonsu and Temple Way. The delivery entrance is a wooden double-door, with a brass knocker in the shape of a cow's head."

"I'm there," Zet said.

"You should try to beat her home," Kat said. "It'll be a lot easier to talk to her servants. I bet every servant in Khonsu Street has gossiped about it, since they're probably friends with the man who was attacked. I bet they know more than anyone."

Zet grinned. "I can't believe the contest worked! For once, little sister, you really used those smarts of yours."

"For once?" she cried.

"Gotta go," he said with a grin. Then he gave her braids a tug and took off with the bowl through the crowds for Khonsu Street.

The further Zet got from the market district, the quieter the streets became. Large walls hid expensive homes. Shade trees, heavy with fruits, hung over the wall tops. The scent of hidden flower gardens filled the air. Someone had swept the streets, and the stones felt smooth, hot and dry under Zet's bare feet.

He found his way to Temple Street, and followed it west a few blocks. The sound of voices carried to him from the distance. It sounded like a crowd had gathered, with many people talking at once. Several voices rose in excitement, and were lost in the chatter.

Zet turned into Khonsu Street and saw that it was full of people.

Gripping the bowl tightly in both arms, he slowed his walk and approached.

To his right, he spotted a pair of double doors with a knocker in the shape of a cow's head. Instead of stopping, however, he kept walking toward the crowd.

He could see several men dressed in medjay uniforms. One turned, as if sensing Zet's eyes on him. Zet saw it was his friend, Merimose.

Zet grinned, but the head medjay looked less than pleased to see him. The big man excused himself from the two men he was speaking with, and broke away from the crowd.

"What's going on?" Zet asked.

"A better question might be, what are you doing here?" Merimose said.

Zet indicated the bowl. "Bringing the winner their prize. We held a contest. Someone from Khonsu Street won it."

"Uh huh." Merimose looked skeptical. "Funny coincidence, someone winning the bowl from this area."

Zet rubbed his neck.

The big medjay crossed his arms over his polished chest-plate. "I don't suppose this contest has anything to do with you coming to investigate?"

"Why would you say that?" Zet asked, trying to look innocent.

"Zet, I told you to stay out of it. People have been attacked. It's not a game."

Zet shuffled his feet. He indicated the crowd. "Has someone else been mugged?"

With a snort, Merimose looked skyward. "Do you ever give up?"

"Look, the only reason I care is because I'm worried about my best friend. I'm sure you can understand that."

Sighing, Merimose met Zet's eyes. He nodded. "I can. But you're not a trained fighter. And these people are dangerous."

"So what happened? Why are all those people standing in the street?"

"A house was robbed."

"Oh."

"They stole a casket of jewels."

"Scarabs?"

"Must have been looking for them, that's my guess." Merimose glanced over his shoulder at the crowd. "I don't even know why I'm telling you this, but we found the casket abandoned on the next block over. Nothing was taken. It's all still in there."

Zet let out a frustrated breath. "I don't get it. Why do they only want scarabs?"

"That's the puzzle, isn't it?" Merimose said. "And since I know you're going to ask, the owner has never purchased services from the Kemet Workshop."

"Oh." Zet wondered if he should tell Merimose about the half clay, half golden scarab Hui had given him. But it wasn't proof of any kind.

"Merimose!" shouted a uniformed man. He looked hot and irritated, as did the two wealthy looking people standing with him.

"Be right there," Merimose called back. To Zet he said, "Deliver your bowl, but don't let me catch you hanging around. Got it?"

"Why would I hang around?"

Merimose gave him a dark look. "Really, my friend. I mean it."

"All right, all right," Zet said.

KHONSU STREET

Delivering the bowl turned out to be harder than Zet had hoped. No one answered the door, despite his repeated banging. He was starting to grow worried, when a slim young girl detached from the crowd and approached at a fast walk.

She was dressed simply in a long, white dress, and her feet were bare. But she had the prettiest face Zet had ever seen.

"You are looking for someone?" she asked.

"The bowl. I mean, I'm bringing this bowl. To the house," Zet said. For some reason, his face was turning hot and he was having trouble getting his words out.

"I can take it," she said with a smirk.

"Who are you?" Zet asked, annoyed by her self-satisfied expression.

"I work here. That's who. And who are you?"

Zet drew himself up to his full height. "I own the stall that raffled this bowl off to the winner. And your owner won it. That's who."

If she was impressed, she didn't show it. "Then I shall give it to my owner. Hand it over." She held out her slender arms to receive it.

Zet stood there a moment, unsure why this pretty girl was so unsettling. Finally, still holding the bowl, he said, "Do you know anything about what's going on over there?"

"Of course," she scoffed. "Some box of jewelry was stolen, and the thief didn't like any of it, so they tossed it on the next street over."

"But the jewelry must have been worth something."

She shrugged her delicate shoulders. "I suppose so. Although I had a look just now and it was all terrible stuff. Big and clunky and really old-fashioned. Probably they realized they could never sell it."

"They could melt it down, though, couldn't they? And sell the gold?" Zet asked.

"I suppose. I hadn't thought of that."

"What's everyone saying about it over there?"

She laughed. "That it's the work of the demon army. That they were looking for scarabs to eat, and didn't find any. You should see some of them, I swear, they're terrified out of their minds. *We're all cursed!* You know, that sort of gibberish."

"And you don't believe it?"

She considered this a moment. "If you want my honest opinion, no. If a demon army had bothered to come here, to this street, I think we'd know about it."

Zet didn't bother to ask how they'd know. Instead, he said, "Then what is going on?"

Her face took on a focused look, as if she were trying to see something, or maybe put it all together. "Here's what I think. It's not just any scarab the thief wants. He's looking for one scarab in specific. Obviously, he's desperate to get it. He's taking a lot of risks, coming back to Khonsu Street again and again."

It was an interesting idea.

"But could one piece of jewelry be that important to someone?" he said.

She frowned at him. "Look, I don't feel like standing here arguing with you. Are you going to give me the bowl or not?"

He handed it over, thinking it a shame such a pretty girl could have such a sharp temper. She cradled the bowl tightly, and her eyes seemed to soften as she studied the design along its rim.

"The water-birds are pretty," she said.

"Thanks. We get our things from a pottery guild down river."

"I know," she said without looking him. "That was my village, once. I'll take good care of it," she said, and disappeared inside.

Zet stared after her, surprised at this turn of events. But there was no time to wonder about the girl and what had brought her away from her family. The afternoon shadows were growing longer. He needed to get back to his stall.

He left the well-swept streets of the Khonsu district behind.

Still, her theory about the jewels was a good one. Could Kemet be looking for a specific piece of jewelry? Trying to get it back, maybe? How did it all tie together?

So many questions swirled in his mind that his head hurt.

By the time he spotted the familiar tented awnings of the marketplace, the wooden slats of the goat pen, and the baskets of produce up ahead, he had a pounding headache.

FAKES

Zet rubbed his face as he wound behind the stacks of pottery. A group of women stood chattering away to Kat, all of them laughing in the afternoon sunlight. It was hard to imagine Hui, trapped in the gloomy workshop with its big guards and spying slots when Ra, the sun god, stood brightly overhead.

Zet caught snatches of the women's conversation.

"What do you think the Royal Wife will be wearing?"

"Something glorious. Do you remember that gown she wore last year?"

"The one made of solid gold?"

"It wasn't solid gold. Don't be silly."

"It was. I heard it was constructed all out of gold beads, held together with gold thread."

"Well I just acquired a copy of the Royal Wife's wedding necklace to wear," said a tall woman, changing the subject. She had her hair all done up on top of her head.

At her words, something sparked in Zet's mind. The hairs stood up on his neck.

"A copy?" he asked, joining the woman.

"You got it today? Is it in your bag? Let's see," said another.

The tall woman's face brightened, clearly enjoying the fuss. "It's right here."

"Zet," Kat said, trying to pull him aside. He saw by the set of her shoulders that something was wrong, and that her smiles and chatter had been nothing more than forced politeness. She was worried.

Still, he said, "Just a minute. I want to see them."

"But Zet!"

"Hold on."

The woman unwrapped the necklace and held it to the light.

Zet had never paid much attention to jewelry before, but now he found himself examining the glittering beads.

"Pretty, isn't it?" she said.

"Do lots of jewelers make copies of things?" he asked, trying to sound more casual than he felt.

"Certainly. Not many can afford the real thing. It's still expensive, but the beads are wooden instead of solid gold. They're painted with real gold leaf."

A chill ran through him. "And the other beads? The clear ones? They must be real."

"Some are colored glass, some are semi-precious stones that look similar to their more expensive cousins."

"You'd never guess," Zet said.

Is that what Hui was trying say with his scarab? That some of the jewels made at the Kemet workshop were fakes? Still, if lots of jewelers did it, then the fact Kemet's jewels were fake shouldn't be a problem.

As long as he told the truth.

What if he lied to people? Was it possible to make copies of jewels so well that people couldn't tell the difference?

If a person was skilled enough, Zet bet they could.

"Zet, you've seen it. Now can I please talk to you?" Kat whispered. Louder, she apologized to the woman for dragging her brother away.

When they reached the back of the stall her smile faltered. She was shaking all over.

"What's the matter?" Zet said quickly.

"Men came here," she gasped.

"What kind of men?"

"Horrible looking men. Like the ones from the workshop. I think it was the same people who chased us."

His heart slammed in his ears. "What did you do?"

Her face was pale. "Nothing. Fortunately, it was crowded. They asked for you, though. By name."

Zet swallowed. "I told Kemet I owned a pottery stall."

"Oh, Zet, It's all my fault! You know what this means, don't you? They've put it all together—the fact that Hui was out of his room, and me screaming in the garbage pit. They know it's connected."

"Well by that reasoning, it's my fault for going to see Hui in the first place. Forget it, okay? We're not going to get anywhere by blaming ourselves. So we made mistakes. We both did. We have to get Hui out. That's all."

"That's not all! The men will probably come back here."

"What did you say to them?"

"I told them I'd never heard of you," she said.

"Well, at least there's that." He grinned. "Most of the time, you probably wish it was true."

"Stop joking," she said, but still a whisper of a smile touched her lips.

The women had dispersed, and the crowds were beginning to thin.

"We should go home," Zet said. "There's no point in risking staying here any longer."

"I agree. But you should leave right now," Kat said, "Before they come back. I'll close up myself and meet you at home."

Zet decided not to argue. It was a good idea to distance himself from the stall. No point in getting them both in trouble.

"But I'm not going home until you're in the clear. I'll make myself scarce, but I'll keep an eye on you from a distance. I don't want them coming back and trying to drag you away for questioning."

The color drained from her face. "I hadn't thought of that."

Zet went to the back of the stall where he'd hid the scarab. It occurred to him then that if the thugs had managed to search the stall, and had found this piece, it would point straight to Hui.

He wrapped the scarab and snuck out the back, into the adjoining stall.

30

FRIENDS

Geb, the grizzled herb-seller, glanced up and shot him a look. His white brows were thick and tufted; he looked like a serious, old bird. He was covering up his baskets of spices, herbs, clothing dyes and pounded wheat grain.

"Happy Opet Festival," Zet said.

Geb nodded. "And to you and your family."

Zet hurried into the nearest alley. It was deserted and dark in shadow. He looked both ways, and then scaled the wall. On the roof, he lay belly down and inched forward until he could see Kat far below across the square.

So far, so good.

She lifted stacks of plates and piled them against the rear of the stall. She dragged the big vase backward. She took out the thick sheets and tied them down. Geb said something to her. Kat replied with a smile.

Hurry up, Zet thought, and glanced toward one of the streets that led into the little square. His body went rigid. Two large, powerful looking men appeared.

Snaggletooth! And his henchman.

Zet looked back at Kat, unable to breath as he willed her to hurry up. She was still talking to Geb. What could be so important? He wanted to shout a warning, but that would draw the thugs' attention. His fists clenched, and sweat prickled on his neck.

Go! *Hurry up.*

Finally, she started to move off.

Across the square, the thugs were drawing closer. Kat kept moving, ducking through a stall hung with scarves, and then heading around the goat pen. The thugs had reached the stall. They looked this way and that.

Kat, however, had reached the entrance to an alley that would take her into the maze of streets. Zet allowed himself a small breath of relief. They weren't out of the clear yet. The thugs started to poke around their closed stall.

Then, to Zet's shock, Salatis, the grumpy date-seller, yelled, "Get away from there."

Snaggletooth turned and glared at the wiry, sun-wrinkled man.

"You heard me," Salatis crowed.

Geb joined in. "Move off. That stall's closed."

Zet could hardly believe it. Zet thought the two vendors wanted him kicked out. And there they were defending his wares? He wanted to cheer the pair of brave old men on. Snaggletooth marched at them with a menacing look, however, and Zet grew worried.

The thug could snap Salatis and Geb in half singlehanded.

"Move off, I say," came a third voice, speaking in a slow, spooky tone. It was Akar, the strange new vendor. He was waving some kind of wand. "Move off, I tell you!" he chanted, waving at Snaggletooth. "Be gone, big man."

Snaggletooth looked momentarily surprised. "What's it to you?"

"I shall curse you with horrible boils. Be gone!"

Zet didn't know whether to laugh or whoop with joy at the sight.

"What Akar here is trying to say," Salatis explained, "Is we protect our own."

"Really?" Snaggletooth said.

"Really." Salatis crossed his arms, his skinny legs planted like wishbones.

"And how are you going to do that, stork-legs?"

"This is how," came a fourth voice. The soft-spoken woman sold scarves. She stepped forward with a dozen other stall owners.

Then the rest appeared. They came out from under their awnings, one after the other. Skinny, fat, young and old.

Zet's heart swelled. He blinked back a few embarrassed tears.

Snaggletooth could never fight them all.

Zet had never felt so honored, so proud to be called a member of that group.

Snaggletooth swore under his breath. Clearly, he realized he'd been beaten. Without another word, the pair of scary men walked away. Just before Snaggletooth exited the square, however, he glanced around.

Zet ducked low against the roof. But he caught the look on the man's ugly face. Snaggletooth wore an expression so murderous, the hair stood up on Zet's arms.

If Zet wanted to stay among the living, he'd have to make sure they never crossed paths again. But that wasn't going to be easy. Not if he wanted to help Hui.

When the coast was clear, he slid to the ground and sprinted for home.

Kat met him at the door, her face a mask of fright.

"Mother's not back," she said.

The words hit him like a stone. He turned and ran for the wharf.

Kat pounded along behind, matching his strides.

At the wharf, they found the man they'd met the night before.

"Nope, still haven't seen her," he said. This time there was worry in his voice, too. Still, he added, "Now children, I'm sure there's a good reason."

"I want to hire a boat," Zet said. "Right now."

"Not possible. Do you see any boats here? They're all rented out for the festival ceremonies tomorrow. People hired 'em out so they could watch the chariot race along the Avenue of the Sphinx from the comfort of a boat. Can't say I blame 'em. There's going to be a lot of pushing and shoving to get good seats along the Avenue."

Zet was too dazed to answer.

Had something awful happened to their mother and Apu?

He and Kat stumbled home.

UNDERSTANDING

Back home, Zet went straight to the household shrine. He knelt in front of the statue of Bastet. The cat goddess regarded him with her gold-rimmed eyes. He lit a cone of incense for her and stroked her smooth, ebony head.

"Please bring Mother and Apu home safe," he whispered. "And Hui, too."

Kat joined him, her face red and tearstained in the lamplight.

"What are we going to do?" she asked.

His stomach turned with fear. How could his mother be two whole days late? What if something happened? What if she never came back? The vision opened like a shadowy abyss. He hung on the edge of a future so black and horrible that he tore his mind away.

"I don't know, Kat," he said quietly.

They sat like that until the incense burned away to nothing.

Zet rubbed his face, and then looked at his little sister. "Maybe I can't help Mother right now. But I can still try to help Hui. I have to. There's no point in me sitting here any longer, it won't bring her home."

Kat wiped away her tears and blew her nose. "What are you going to do?"

"Remember those women talking about fake jewels?"

She nodded. "Kemet's making fakes and telling people they're real, isn't he. That's the meaning behind Hui's scarab."

"Yes. But I think it's more than that. There has to be a reason for the thefts. They don't fit into the puzzle. Why make fakes and sell them, and steal them back? I want to have another look at Hui's scarab."

In the kitchen, he pulled the package from its hiding place in the onion basket. He unwrapped it.

"What do you think this number two means?" he said. "Why did he put that there?"

Kat twisted her braid in her fist. "You know when we get pottery pieces from the guild, and there's more than one in the same style?"

"Yes."

"Well, on the bottom, the artist marks the matching pieces with a number. One, two, three, and so on. It makes it easier for me to keep records. If five matching plates come in, I mark that down. Then, when we barter one, I cross it off my list and I know how many we have left."

"Okay," he said, wondering where she was going with this.

"What if he's trying to say there are two fake scarabs? Could that be possible?"

Zet froze. "That's it. That's exactly it!"

"It is?"

"Yes! You're brilliant. Don't you see? There are two fake scarabs! Kemet got one of the fakes back when he attacked that servant in Khonsu Street last week. But there's still one more out there."

"What are you talking about? Why bother stealing something after he just sent it out the door?"

"Because he made a mistake."

Kat looked even more confused.

"Think about it—two scarabs went in for cleaning. Right? And maybe, instead of cleaning them, Kemet made two copies to send back, so he could keep the good ones for himself."

"Yes . . ."

"But when his partner made the two copies, he screwed them up. He switched the stones around by mistake!"

"You mean, like he gave one scarab a yellow stone for a head, and the other one got a blue head, when they were supposed to be the opposite?"

"Exactly. And any owner would spot the difference instantly."

"But how would Kemet know, if his partner's the one who made them?"

"The partner must have realized his mistake after. Maybe he picked up the real ones to put them away for safekeeping. And then it struck him the stones weren't right. And then he knew. So, he warned Kemet, who sent Snaggletooth after the servants. Except they only stopped one scarab from getting to its owner."

"Which means one scarab is still out there, like a ticking time bomb, waiting for the owner to look at it," Kat gasped.

Zet nodded. "I guess Kemet was mad enough that he got rid of the partner. Whatever that means." He shuddered. "And now he's forced Hui to do the man's dirty work. He's forced Hui into making his fakes."

The lamp guttered, casting creepy shadows dancing along the walls.

"That's where Hui was going in the boat that day," Kat said softly. "To the private workshop at Kemet's house. This is awful, Zet. I see why Hui said he can't escape. If Kemet had his partner killed, he'll kill Hui too for ratting him out." She held her stomach and groaned. "I feel sick."

"Well, I don't. I feel mad. The shipment must be all the real jewels. Kemet must ship them upriver to sell in another city. He's probably been doing it for years. No wonder he's so rich! But I'm going to bust him, and show everyone he's been replacing his repairs with fakes, and stealing the real things."

"Zet, if all this is true, then it's going to work out. Kemet will get caught eventually. The person with the mixed up scarab will take it out and look at it, and he'll raise the alarm. And the medjay will be brought in."

"I don't think Kemet plans to wait around."

"What do you mean?"

"My guess is he's going to escape, along with tomorrow's shipment, and disappear forever. The stolen gold and jewels will pay to keep him alive, wherever he goes. Even if he has to abandon his mansion and business here." Zet paced back and forth, running a hand over his scalp.

"You should go to the medjay. Right now," Kat said.

"And say what? They won't believe me, not without proof. I have to do it myself."

"How? Alone? You're just a kid!"

"I'll figure it out when I get there," Zet said.

32

ACTION

In the kitchen, faint moonlight strobed through the straw roof overhead.

"I want to come—" Kat began.

"No." Zet's voice was flat. "Not after last time. Let me do this my way Kat. I don't want you screwing this up."

She looked upset, but said nothing.

Going to the stove, he took out some coals and blackened his face, arms, hands and feet. This time, he'd be going to the workshop in disguise. He needed every edge he could get. He smeared the coals around until he was dark and filthy.

Kat found a rough sack that once held emmer wheat grains. She cut holes for his neck and arms. "Wear this. Kemet's men will never recognize you dressed like a beggar."

He slid the rough outfit over his head. It was scratchy, and he knew he looked terrible. Which was great. She handed him a coil of twine. He wound it around his waist like a belt.

"It's a costume worthy of Hui," Kat said.

"It is, isn't it? He'd love it. No one's going to notice a filthy beggar like me now."

She wished him luck and he stepped into the night, wearing the biggest grin in the world. This was going to work.

He headed for the artisan quarter, but at the last moment, he switched directions. He'd give Merimose one last shot. Maybe the head medjay would believe him, if Zet told him the whole story. Stopping Kemet would be easy with a band of policemen to help.

He soon reached the police station.

The surrounding streets were deserted. Lamps flickered in sconces on either side of the station door. He hurried up the steps. Light spilled from the interior. The whitewashed office was like an oasis of bright safety in the dark night.

An officer stood just inside the front door.

"Whoa there, boy. Lost your way?"

"No, I'm looking for Merimose. The head medjay."

The big man look amused. "Are you now? Well, he's not here."

"I know I look strange," Zet said, "but, well, I'm in costume."

"Little late for a boy to be out in a party costume," said the big man.

The doorman's partner, who sat behind a desk, laughed. "That's your idea of a party costume?"

Zet recognized the deskman from earlier visits, but couldn't think of his name. "I wasn't at a party," Zet said. "I need help. I know who's behind the scarab thefts, and we have to stop them."

Both men looked sharply at him. "Stop who?"

"The people at the Kemet Workshop. They're planning a big shipment in the morning. You have to stop it."

Silence fell. A breeze crept through the front door, causing the lamps to flicker.

Zet shuffled his feet, waiting.

"What kind of shipment?" the deskman asked.

"Stolen jewels."

The officers shot him skeptic looks. Clearly, his appearance wasn't helping any. His sackcloth outfit was itchy beyond belief. He rubbed his belly, where the scratchiness was the worst. Both men watched, their mouths turning down at the corners.

"That's a story, if I've ever heard one," the doorman said.

"Boy," said the deskman, "If I was even inclined to believe you, which I'm not, no shipment leaves town without a search. Security has been stepped way up. And with the Royal Family out in full force tomorrow morning, every officer will be on duty."

Zet said, "But the thieves must know that. I'm sure they have a plan. Please—"

"Wait." The doorman grinned and stuck his head outside. "Someone's pulling a joke on us here, aren't they? I get it, Festival First Day station humor for us guys stuck here all night."

The deskman laughed. "Has to be Paneb. Was it Paneb?" he asked Zet. "An officer with an Eye of Horus tattoo on his right bicep? How much did he pay you?" He glanced outside too, as if expecting to see their friend laughing in the street.

"No one paid me," Zet said. "It's the truth."

"You're good," the deskman said. "Beggar-boy, I think you've got a career as an actor in your future."

"I'm not acting. Don't you recognize me? I helped Merimose before!"

"You're bringing the station chief into it? That's going too far." The doorman took Zet by his collar, lifted him with one burly arm and deposited him outside. "Joke's over."

"But it's not a joke. I'm telling you—"

"Clear out," the doorman said. He wasn't smiling.

Zet knew when to stop. He left before they decided to throw him in a cell overnight. He couldn't afford to get trapped behind bars.

Outside, a hush had fallen over the streets.

It was as if everyone were waiting with baited breath for what tomorrow would hold. The beginning of the Opus Festival, chariot race down the Avenue of the Sphinxes, and if the rumors were true, an attack from a demon army of dead Hyksos soldiers.

Zet knew now that the scarab-eating demons weren't real.

At least, he hoped so.

Something brushed his ankle. He leapt into the air with a yelp.

Yellow kitten-eyes gleamed at him in the velvet dark.

"You scared me," Zet whispered.

The ebony colored kitten reminded him of Bastet, their family goddess, back home. He breathed a sigh of relief. He bent and she let him scratch her ears.

Then she scampered off into a curtained doorway and was gone.

33

BROKEN GOD

If the Kemet Workshop had anything special going on, you couldn't tell from the street. Zet stared at the blackened iron gate, with its knife like bars sharpened to points at the top. No lamps were lit. Apart from the partial moon, the whole area was pitch black and silent.

Zet guessed he had four hours to wait until sunrise.

He decided to make use of his time by doing a full circuit of the workshop. He wanted to make sure the gated entry was the only exit through which the stolen shipment would come.

Halfway around, Zet reached the notorious, foul garbage pit.

Zet paused to peer through the wooden gate. His jaw dropped. Someone had cleaned the whole thing out. It was empty, from end to end. He thought of Kat screaming, sure there had been fingers grabbing her. But maybe there were other clues Kemet was worried might get found if the pit was examined.

He felt stupid for not thinking of it earlier.

But it was too late to worry about that now.

Still, Zet climbed over, wanting to get a closer look. The long, dark walls were stained with remains. A faint, foul odor still hung in the air. He turned fully, looking in all directions, when something caught his eye.

Some kind of small statue leaned up against the gate.

Like it had been placed there on purpose.

Zet crouched down. A shudder of terror shot from the base of his neck to his ankles.

It was Hui's family god, Bes!

He'd recognize the cheerful statue Hui kept by his bedside anywhere.

The little dwarf god looked up at him with his happy face of stone. Except the dwarf wasn't quite himself. His right ear, which stuck out in a comical fashion, had been broken off. As had one of his legs. The sight of Bes so destroyed was like finding his best friend Hui, all smashed to pieces.

Was this a message? Was Kemet trying to say something, by leaving Hui's protective statue out here like this? Had he known Zet would return? Or worse, had Kemet just throwing Bes away because Hui was no longer . . .

Zet wouldn't finish the thought.

Hui was alive. He had to be. It couldn't be too late. It just couldn't!

In confused desperation, Zet searched for the little guy's arm. And then his ear. He held the god and his broken pieces to his chest, as if doing so could somehow keep his friend safe.

Zet's fear soon turned to fury.

He had to know if Hui was alive. He didn't care if what he was about to do was stupid. He was going in for a look.

"I'll come back for you," he told Bes.

Climbing onto the roof was harder this time, without the tall pile to climb over. Still, he found handholds in the rough walls, and hauled himself up. Taking less care than he should have, he dropped into the Kemet Workshop courtyard. On silent feet, he sprinted for Hui's room.

The door stood open. One boy slept on the bed to the left.

Zet's heart dropped to his toes.

Hui's bed was empty. Completely stripped to its frame. Not a shred of Hui's things remained. No clothing. No hippo's tooth.

Hui was gone.

In a daze, Zet backed out into the hall.

He heard voices heading his way. He wanted to run toward them. To shout at them, to demand what they'd done with his best friend. But what use would that be? None. He hated himself for leaving, but he had no choice.

He turned his back on Hui's empty bed and left.

Back in the garbage alley, Zet scooped Bes into his arms and clambered out. He cradled the broken god, as if it were his best friend himself. As if by keeping the god together, he could somehow bring Hui back.

He felt beaten down as he shuffled along the gritty street. The humidity made the air thick and hard to breathe. Partway along the block, someone had tried to grow a few potted plants. The stems, however, were straggly and dead. Zet pulled the pots out a little ways, and set Bes behind them. It was as good a hiding spot as any, and he couldn't carry the little god around if he wanted to confront Kemet and his shipment.

If nothing else, he'd confirmed there was only one way out of Kemet's workshop.

He found a dark alcove across the street and sank down to post up for the night.

If anything or anyone came out that door, he'd be on his feet in an instant.

It was time to end this nightmare.

34

AND THEY'RE OFF

The mutter of voices made Zet start upright. He must have fallen asleep.

Dawn had begun to filter down into the humid, dusty murk. He cursed silently. All those big words to Kat about doing things himself—and here he'd fallen asleep?

Panic and a sickening feeling gripped him. What had he missed? How long had he been out? He rubbed his eyes hard and stared across the street.

Had someone come out the gate, while he dozed like a fool?

There was no way to tell.

Suddenly, the bakeshop's curtained doorway was thrust aside. A large wooden cart emerged into the street. Kissa, the kinder of the two twins—the one with the puckered scar—was pushing it.

Round loaves of bread had been piled high in the shape of a pyramid. The wheels creaked and groaned under the weight.

Kakra, the second twin, emerged. She took hold of the opposite side of the cart and helped push.

Zet ducked lower. Kissa and Kakra, however, didn't look around. Grim-faced, perhaps unhappy at having to work on a holiday, they trudged forward. Grit crunched under the turning wheels, and the cart took up a rhythm, rolling and grinding off down the street.

Zet let his head fall back against the wall behind him.

What should he do now?

Keep waiting?

He thought about the festival getting underway. Despite the early hour, the streets were probably already lined with people. Maybe he could find a medjay and report Hui missing. But there would be no pulling a man away now. Not with the events going on in town.

He was still pondering what to do when the gate to the workshop whispered open. Zet flattened himself against the wall.

Snaggletooth stepped out. The thug glanced over one muscled shoulder, into the workshop's dark alley entrance. He growled something. A second man replied, then emerged onto the street.

Clearly the two thugs were headed somewhere.

Strangely enough, they were dressed as if they were going to watch the chariot race. They wore festive clothing—clean kilts, some simple jewelry, and Snaggletooth had a red sash around his waist. Cleaned up as he was, he almost looked normal. Almost—but Zet doubted a man with a face like that would ever look normal or fit in anywhere. He was too scary looking.

The thugs were armed with nasty looking weapons. Snaggletooth had a long knife strapped to his waist. He'd polished the scabbard, so it looked somewhat decorative.

His partner had a club studded with nails. At a comment from Snaggletooth, the man laughed. He had a strip of linen in one hand, and he proceeded to wind it around the club as they walked.

Zet realized it would be concealed, but equally deadly. The nails could still harm a person—even kill them—cloth or not. A few strikes from a man that size would knock Zet down, he had no doubt of that.

But the more important issue was, where were they going? The fighters set off, their eyes looking into the distance as if seeing something they planned to do.

Should he follow, or stay and watch the workshop?

Where was the shipment?

He thought back to the way Hui had told him the answer was inside the ball.

Then his mind roamed to the bread. It seemed like a lot of work to get the roll and hollow it out, just to use as stuffing. With a frown, he glanced in the direction the twin bakers pushed the loaded cart. Snaggletooth and the thug had gone the same way.

A thought started to form, but he couldn't quite grasp it.

Then, with a cry of understanding, he leaped to his feet.

He ran.

He tore along the first few blocks. Snaggletooth and his buddy came into view. The heavily muscled fighters had nearly caught up with the bakers' cart. Zet slowed and watched.

The two thugs slowed as well, keeping pace with the bakers. They didn't quite catch up, but remained close enough to be next to the sisters in a few paces. To an outsider, it looked like they had nothing to do with one another.

But Zet knew differently.

Snaggletooth and the huge man with the concealed, barbed club were guarding that cart with their lives.

The bakers merged into the growing trickle of crowds. Zet pushed closer, joining a group of people as they exited a door. They glanced at him strangely, noting his filthy outfit. One of them fiddled in a pouch, produced a copper kite and offered it to him.

Zet shook his head. "Thank you."

The man shrugged. "Happy Opet Festival to you."

This could be a problem; Zet didn't want people noticing him, even if he knew the man was being kind. Still, he stuck near his group and watched the cart ahead. Two well-dressed ladies approached the bakers' cart. Zet could tell the ladies wanted to buy bread. The bakers, however, shook their heads no in a sharp voice.

The elegant ladies, surprised, walked on.

They were approaching an intersection. Medjay had taken up

posts on either side of the roadway, and stood in full battle gear. The bakers wheeled their cart toward the road that led left.

The medjay blocked them with his long, wooden spear. "Halt!"

35

PILES OF BREAD

"We need to turn here," came the sharp voice of Kakra.

"Road's closed. Go straight, please," the medjay told the twin bakers.

"The road's closed?" Kissa gasped, looking frightened.

"Festival precautions, madam."

"Where can we turn?" Kakra demanded. "We're working here. We need to make a delivery. This bread has been ordered for a special party. We need to get to the Nile!"

"The main road goes to the Nile, madam."

"Yes, but not where I need to be. I need to get farther down!"

"You'll have to carry on straight like everyone else until you get to the Avenue of the Sphinxes." He waved his fiber shield at the main road. "When you get to the waterfront, you can follow the Nile to your party."

Kakra's mouth tightened in a hard line. Kissa paled.

"Fine," Kakra said.

Then she glanced back at Snaggletooth. Under her anger, Zet read dismay mixed with fear. Snaggletooth nodded at Kakra. She wheeled the cart back into the main roadway and carried on.

They had just confirmed every one of Zet's suspicions.

The stolen jewels were hidden in the loaves of bread! The sisters must have baked them right inside so no hole in the bottom would give them away. That's how they planned to get past being searched.

No medjay would give the bread cart a second glance.

Kissa and Kakra simply had to deliver the goods to a boat. A boat, where Kemet would obviously be waiting to make his escape. The bread would be loaded. Right under everyone's noses.

Then Kemet would happily sail away with his load of stolen goods.

Clever Hui, Zet thought. In the end, the ivory ball had told Zet everything. He wondered what his best friend had had to risk getting that information. Hui must have been living in terror, between sneaking around and constructing the fake scarab and ball.

It was up to Zet now to stop that cart.

Snaggletooth glanced over his shoulder.

Zet dodged behind a noisy family. Panic gripped him, but he forced himself to calm down. Snaggletooth must not have seen him; otherwise, he'd be on him right now.

He needed to do something, but what?

Ahead of him, the kids from the family were joking around. One boy jabbed his older brother from behind with a toy sword, and then darted away.

"Quit it," the older brother said.

"What?" said the boy with sword. "Wasn't me. Must have been the evil spirit."

"Mom!"

"Stop it, both of you, that's not funny," the mother whispered in a nervous voice.

Until that moment, Zet had forgotten all about the demon army.

Zet knew the demon army didn't exist. But no one else did. He had an idea. Maybe it was time to create a demon of his own.

He followed the crowd a little further, looking for an unguarded alcove where he could slip away. He needed to get to his market square.

With the medjay blocking every side street, he needed a different route. The medjay would never let him through. He'd just have to take to the rooftops.

Fortunately, he was getting his climbing skills back. He hadn't spent this much time clambering around since Hui left home.

Music drifted from up ahead. A small band had taken up residence along the side of the street. They pounded on drums, plucked lutes, and sang about the war in Hyksos. People had stopped, and some were kicking up their heels to dance. Zet thought of his father, away fighting, and his heart swelled hearing the song.

Perfumed incense drifted thick on the morning air. He had to push now to keep the cart in sight. Men and women were approaching the bakers, trying to barter for a loaf. It was slow going. Still, he'd have to be quick.

Then he saw his chance. A dead end alley, unguarded, opened to his right. He slipped down it, blending into the dark shadows. Without pause, he ran for the farthest wall. The stones were rough, pressed into mud. His fingers and toes found handholds, and he scrambled upward. When he reached the rooftop, he bent low and sprinted over the loose tiles to the far side.

The street below was full of people, all moving toward the broader avenue he'd left behind. He glanced right and left, and saw he'd have to travel further along the roof to get a clear spot to drop back down. He climbed up another story onto a high patio full of potted plants. He had to sprint across half a dozen private terraces before he found a quiet place to climb down.

Silence met him. He recognized the lane. Usually full of people, today it was still as a Pharaoh's tomb. He ran onward. He ran until he was breathless.

He gasped in triumph when his familiar market square opened before him.

Everything was bound up tight. It was strange to see it so still.

"I hope you don't kill me for this, Geb," he said as he hurried to the herb vendor's stall. With a glance both ways, he got down on hands and knees and crawled under the tightly wrapped stall covers.

It was dark, and he had to squint to see. The smells of cumin and cardamom, cinnamon and myrrh bombarded him in the confined space. It was heady and overpowering, jarring his senses to life.

DEMON BOY

Head spinning, Zet waited for his eyes to adjust to the darkness. The colored pyramids of herbs and spices, flours, clothing dye and crushed incense came slowly into focus. He crawled forward. A clay urn leaned up against a wood pillar. The outside was cool and damp to the touch. He pulled the cork and sniffed. Cooking oil. And, thank the gods, it was full.

He poured some slick oil out, coating himself by the handful as best he could.

"I promise, I'll repay you Geb, wherever you are," he muttered, as he reached for the flour. Then he dumped some over his head.

Next came streaks of bright blue woad, yellow cumin, and crushed red madder root. He crisscrossed his face, arms and legs with crazy, bright marks. Then it was time to go.

He only hoped he could cut off the cart on time.

After slipping out, he went to his own stall and found a length of old linen, worn paper-thin. Once folded, it made a half decent robe. Well-covered, he headed into the maze of deserted streets.

Birds dozed on the hot stones. They flew up in annoyance as he ran past.

Zet cut left and right, weaving his way closer and closer to the broad road that lead to the Avenue of the Sphinx. The sounds of the crowd grew louder. People shouting, laughing, singing.

He was nearly there.

Ahead, a medjay stood with his back to Zet, watching over the crowd.

Zet paused.

If he'd timed it right, the cart should be passing soon.

Several tense moments went by.

No cart.

What if he'd missed it? Sweat poured down his sides. Should he stay? Should he wait? Should he run ahead? His stomach clenched as his mind tore him in opposite directions.

Then, as if by a miracle, the cart wheeled into view. Kissa and Kakra were red-faced with the heat and the effort of maneuvering through the people. Snaggletooth and his henchman still tracked them, several paces behind.

Under his makeshift robe, Zet started to sweat. The sackcloth tunic felt like a thousand nails scratching at him. He went to wipe his brow, but stopped himself. It would be no good ruining all that crazy paint. Instead he let it drip, stinging his eyes.

Time to go.

Just as he started forward, Kissa stumbled. Snaggletooth gave up pretending to be separate from the women. He strode forward and grabbed the left cart handle. The other henchmen motioned Kakra aside, and took hold of the right cart handle. Together, the big men began to push.

Zet groaned at this unexpected development. Still, he slid past the medjay, who took no notice. There were too many other distractions to keep an eye on.

Zet shoved forward into the crowd.

People propelled him past, just to get him out from underfoot.

The cart came up quickly.

Now only four people separated Zet from Snaggletooth. The thug pushed onward, deftly maneuvering the cart with its pyramid-shaped mound of bread.

With a shout, Zet threw off his robe. He leapt into the air, screaming in a high-pitched yowl. Like a demon, he tore at his hair. Eyes wild, he threw his arms around. Shouted. Howled. Screamed.

People fell back in shock.

In the heat, the oil had mixed with his sweat, and the streaks of color melted down his face, arms and legs. The scratchy burlap sack made him look even more crazed. Judging from their faces, he looked like a fiend straight from the underworld.

"The demon," a woman screamed. "It's the demon!"

"Run!" shouted another.

"We're trapped!" shouted a third.

Zet rushed this way and that, flinging his arms around, clearing a path to the cart. Only the four people guarding the bread stood their ground. Snaggletooth dove for Zet, but Zet was faster. He circled around the other side of the wheels. The henchman met him there with a swing of his deadly club.

Zet darted left. The club smashed into the cart's side. The cart shuddered under the impact. Zet skirted past the man.

Kakra lunged forward, arms outstretched. Her arms closed around air as Zet jumped onto the wooden contraption. He landed on the pyramid of bread, sending loaves scattering.

"Get him," Kakra screeched, her eyes wide with fear.

Kissa fell back, her puckered scar red against her frightened face.

Snaggletooth grimaced. The huge man snatched Zet's ankle. Meaty fingers took hold of Zet's oiled skin. Zet wrenched backward, and his oily foot slid free. He scrabbled left, and saw the club coming down. More loaves scattered as he dodged the club's blow.

"Get him!" the crowd was screaming.

"Help," shouted others. "Help, medjay!"

"Come here, boy," Snaggletooth growled.

Zet scrabbled backwards to the far end of the cart, keeping his eyes on the weapons. Someone shoved him hard. Kakra. He flew forward.

As if in slow motion, he saw Snaggletooth's sword chop down. Desperate to stop himself, Zet plunged his hands deep into the mound of bread. He landed belly first, eye-to-eye with cold, hard steel. But under his fingers, he felt something strange.

Not bread. Something warm and soft and covered in fabric.

JEWELS

Zet somersaulted backward. Snaggletooth's blade hissed past.
"There's nowhere to go, boy," Snaggletooth hissed.
"Get down from the cart," Kakra said.
The crowd had gone quiet, watching the strange spectacle.
Zet turned slowly. He could kick the bread away and reveal what lay in the bottom of the cart, if what lay there was who he thought it was. But the sides came up too high. Only the top loaves would fall away, and the bottom would still be covered. There was only one thing to do. He hoped he guessed right.
"Beware," he shouted. "This cart is cursed!" Then he grabbed a loaf and tore the bread in half.
It was empty.
Some people laughed, nervously.
The four lunged for him. He kicked and bit and got his hands around another loaf. Zet tore it open. Empty again.
The henchman landed a glancing blow against Zet's leg with his club. Nails scraped down his shin. If it had been any closer, it would have broken Zet's leg. He was starting to tire. Desperate, he got his hands on another loaf. His fingers were so greasy with sweat and oil that it flew free.

He took up a fourth one. A long, oddly shaped one.

It was heavy.

Very heavy.

He jumped down from the cart, dodging past Kakra. But Kakra caught him. She got her gnarled fingers around the loaf. Zet wouldn't let go. Their eyes met. Hers were enraged.

Zet wedged his fingers down through the crust.

He felt the bread tear.

Kakra tried to hold it together. "Stop it," she gasped.

In one swift yank, he ripped the bread in two.

From the center, a large golden collar, glittering with precious gems, fell to the paving stones. Zet dove for it. He raised it, victorious, high above his head.

"It's full of stolen jewels," he told the crowd.

"The demon turned bread into jewels!" someone shouted.

"There are jewels hidden in the bread!" shouted another.

Frenzied, people pushed forward and started pulling the loaves from the cart and tearing them open. Gold pieces were held high in triumph.

"I found one, too," shouted someone.

"Look at mine! It's a festival trick!"

Snaggletooth, his henchman, and the twins, watched in horror. They started running this way and that, trying to recover the treasure. The looting went on; people grew wild. They shouted and cheered, like it was the best party trick ever.

Then, a woman next to the cart screamed.

She clutched at her chest, looking down into the depths of it, and kept screaming.

Zet felt sick. He knew what that scream meant.

Still, he had to see, had to know for himself.

Medjay approached from all avenues, weapons raised. Trying to control the chaos.

"Put down the jewels," the nearest medjay bellowed. "All of you! I order you to put down the jewels."

Zet ignored them. He pushed his way forward. He shoved people out of the way. He didn't care about the lost jewels. He didn't care that Snaggletooth and the others were clearing off, dispersing, leaving. Getting away.

He stumbled ahead, as if in a daze.

Then his hands were on the sturdy wooden sides of the cart. He looked down into it. Most of the bread had been removed, but a layer still covered the bottom. At the far end, the tips of two small bare feet jutted up between two loaves.

"Get away from the cart," bellowed the nearest medjay.

Zet threw himself into it anyway. He started up at the top end where it was deeper. He tossed loaves out, left and right, wild, desperate. Made a hole. His head was spinning in terror. He pulled two clear, and suddenly he was looking down into the face of his best friend.

Hui's mouth was bound with a thick, wadded strip of cloth.

But his eyes were wide open. Staring.

He was dead. It was too late. Zet thought of Hui's mother Delilah, with her curls and ready smile. His heart clenched, and he let out a muffled cry of despair. How could this be? It wasn't fair. Not Hui. Not his best friend.

"Hui," Zet said. "No."

Then, as if by a miracle, Hui's eyes blinked.

They opened slowly. Hui looked confused, groggy. He focused on Zet and registered disbelief. Then his eyes crinkled into a grin.

From behind, the medjay grabbed Zet by his burlap tunic. "I told you to . . . what's this?" he gasped, staring down at Hui.

"Help me get him out," Zet said.

It was the doorman from the night before. Together, he and Zet tossed away the last of the bread. Hui's arms and legs were bound tightly to his side. The medjay whipped out his blade and cut the bindings free.

Hui winced and lurched upright, looking left and right. "Where are they? Don't let them get away!"

"You mean these four?" a medjay said. He and several officers hauled Snaggletooth, his henchman, and the baker twins forward.

"We're innocent," Kakra cried. "I didn't know the boy was in there."

"Explain that to the courts."

"We were just following orders," she said.

"Some orders," Hui said with a laugh, leaping out of the cart to stand beside his best friend.

Snaggletooth said nothing. He knew he'd been beaten. Half of Thebes had witnessed him trying to cut Zet into pieces.

A man with a polished breastplate strode toward them. Merimose.

"Zet? Is that you under all that paint? What's going on?"

"Long story," Zet said, and quickly filled him in.

Hui rubbed his wrists. "The coast isn't clear. We still need to stop Kemet."

KEMET

Merimose turned to Kakra. "Where were you taking this cart?"

Kakra glared at him and said nothing.

Then Kissa spoke up. "To a boat."

"Stop it," Kakra snarled at her twin sister.

"No, Kakra, I won't hold my tongue any longer." Her cheeks were flushed. "I blame myself for letting it go this far. But I won't be a part of it any longer." To Merimose, she said, "We were taking it to Kemet's boat on the Nile. It has red and gold sails, and is docked at the farthest end of the Avenue of the Sphinx."

"Show us."

"They'll have lookouts posted," Kissa said. "They'll bolt if they see medjay coming."

The officers, Zet and Hui stood there, stumped.

Zet spoke up. "I have an idea."

And so, three big medjay piled into the cart and lay on the bottom. Over them, Zet, Hui and Merimose repacked the cart with as many loaves as they could gather.

"You six," Merimose said, retrieve whatever jewels from the crowd you can. "The rest of you, fan out down the side streets and make your way to the end of the Avenue of the Sphinx. Hang back in the shadows until I give the signal."

"What about these two?" asked the medjay Zet had met the night before.

"Secure them, and take them to the station." Merimose turned to the sisters. "Kissa and Kakra, you'll push the cart to the boat. Just like you're supposed to."

Kakra glared at her twin sister. Kissa glared back.

"And don't try anything funny," Merimose said.

And so, the procession started up once again.

The Avenue of the Sphinx gleamed up ahead, its statues polished white in the hot sunshine. Meanwhile, the crowd went back to enjoying the festival. Vendors selling every type of sweetmeat lined the road, shouting and calling out to people. Thebans pushed and shoved, intent on getting to the chariot race.

Bordering the broad Avenue of the Sphinx, the Nile glimmered. Ahead, boats bobbed in the smooth band of water.

The group followed the bread cart away from the action.

A big hand clamped around Zet's forearm. Zet jumped.

"It's just me," Merimose said. "Stay back. I don't want you seen."

"I don't think they'll recognize me like this," Zet said.

"It's too dangerous."

Zet and Hui exchanged a glance. No way were they staying back. Still, Zet nodded. He and Hui let the others get ahead.

"We'll just keep low, right?" Zet said.

"Right," Hui agreed.

They crept forward, using the crowd as cover. But as the crowd thinned, that became more and more difficult.

Hui put a hand on Zet's arm. "Look, the red and gold sail."

They ducked behind a stone sphinx and watched the baker twins push the cart closer. On board the boat, a curtain flickered. No one, however, stepped out onto the deck.

"They suspect something," Zet said.

Then a boy appeared. He started to untie the ropes. They were preparing to cast off. They were going to get away!

"Why doesn't Merimose do something?" Hui said.

"How? He can't search Kemet without proof of wrongdoing. Kemet has no stolen jewels on board either. He can deny it all. He can say he didn't know what was going on."

"I'll get them out of there," Hui said. Then, in a perfect imitation of Snaggletooth, he called out, "Kemet!"

Nothing happened for a moment.

Kissa spoke up, and called, "We've brought your bread, Kemet!"

A hatch opened, and someone came on deck. It was Kemet himself. The hobbled man hurried over the boards to the rail. He looked angry.

"You're late," he called the bakers. "I thought something was wrong."

"We had some trouble," Kissa said.

"But it's all there?"

"All of it," Kissa said.

Merimose raised the whistle that hung around his neck and blew. Sharp, short and loud. Instantly, bread loaves flew everywhere. The medjay leaped out of the cart. They swarmed on board, while others swarmed out of side streets and joined them.

Kemet had given them all the proof they needed.

Kemet and his band were done.

The crooked jeweler glanced down and saw Zet and Hui on the wharf. His face darkened. He looked ready to hiss curses at them. But as Merimose bound Kemet's wrists, the jeweler's shoulders sagged. His reign as a powerful smuggler had come to a bitter end.

ALL IS WELL

"Do you realize how great it is to be standing out here?" Hui cried. "I'm a free kid again."

Zet nodded. All would have been well, if only their mother was home safe.

And then, from the corner of his eye, he saw someone waving from an approaching boat. The boat was tiny, barely large enough to fit the three people seated in it. And it was piled high with pottery.

"Zet?" cried his mother. "Is that you?"

The relief at seeing her and Apu was so overwhelming that tears stung his eyes. At least no one could tell, between the sweat and the crazy face paint.

It was only moments before he and Hui were helping her on shore, and hearing how the potters' delivery boat had sprouted a hole, and how strange things had been going on in the village itself.

"The family who usually does the orders has left the village, and no one knows why," she said. "But I was able to find someone else to do the work. It was all very last minute. And finding the boat wasn't easy. But we need to get these orders delivered, and fast."

"I think I know just the way to do it," Zet said.

He and Hui commandeered the bakers' cart. They loaded it high with pottery.

"I could have some men deliver a set, too," Merimose said, when he'd heard the story.

"And I'll deliver these two serving bowls," Zet's mother said. "It's only two pieces, and the house isn't far from here."

By mid-morning, the deliveries were complete. All of the women were happy to finally have their special dishes. Even the angry one was impressed when she heard why the pottery hadn't come, and what lengths Zet's family had gone through to get them.

"Now want to go watch the races?" Zet said.

"Hey, I'll do anything with you dressed like a demon."

He hadn't bothered to change; there wasn't time. "I thought the women would be scared, but they all loved it," Zet said.

"Go figure," Hui said, grinning. "Next thing you know, they'll be hosting demon dress up parties." They'd reached the edge of the chariot races. "Look, I think the Royal Mother likes it, too," he said, pointing to a golden pavilion whose curtains fluttered in the faint breeze.

In it, the Royal Mother was indeed staring at Zet. So was Pharaoh himself.

The ground shook, as a chariot roared past.

Then came a second, and third.

Wheels glinted in the light, and the riders looked glorious in their uniforms.

Hui wore a huge grin. "This is like old times. Except better. We just had an adventure for real."

"You're not kidding, talk about adventure. I thought you were dead," Zet said.

"It's not that easy to kill me. And speaking of which, now that I'm out of work, maybe I can help you with your side business."

"Side business? What side business."

"You know, the whole Secret Agent Zet thing."

"Secret Agent Zet, huh?"

"It has a catchy ring, doesn't it?"

"Uh, not really," Zet said, laughing. "I'm not exactly a secret agent."

Hui ignored him. "And everyone knows a secret agent needs a side-kick." He waggled his eyebrows and elbowed Zet. "How about it? You and me? Solving crimes in the city?"

Zet groaned and rolled his eyes.

But Hui's attention was elsewhere. He grabbed Zet's arm and pointed. "Over there. A girl calling for help. Quick, we need to save her!"

In a panic, Zet turned to look.

It was Kat. But she wasn't in trouble. She was waving her arms at them, laughing and screaming and jumping up and down.

Zet groaned. He couldn't believe he fell for it.

"I'm throwing you in the river," Zet said.

"You'll have to catch me first," Hui replied.

Together, they took off into the bright, Theban afternoon.

SCOTT'S HISTORICAL NOTE

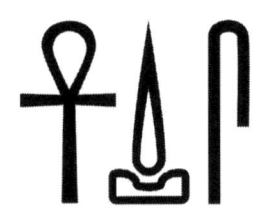

Can you imagine going to school in a workshop instead of a regular classroom? That's how things used to be done in ancient Egypt! Workshops, such as the Kemet workshop, were a popular way to teach skills to the next generation of craftsmen. A workshop educated pupils in a specific craft. That craft could be making sandals, or pottery, or like Hui, making jewelry.

It seems odd to us today. However, by learning from such a young age, the students were able to excel at their work. The jewelry that people created during this era is still marveled at today. Be sure and Google ancient Egyptian jewelry. I think you'll be amazed.

Here's another fun fact: Most families kept a household shrine. Bes was a popular household god as he was considered a protector of families, particularly mothers and children. He was known as a trickster and he loved to make babies laugh.

How do we know all of this? Ancient Egyptians loved to write things down. They kept excellent notes! Which is a great thing because it allows writers like me to craft fun stories about these amazing people for you.

MYSTERY OF THE EGYPTIAN TEMPLE

ZET'S THIRD CASE

BY SCOTT PETERS

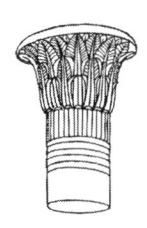

1

STRANGE VISITORS

Twelve-year-old Zet grabbed at the pair of lean arms that tightened around his neck. He tried to yell, but his yell came out as a gasp. He lurched forward, pulling the boy with him. The two of them fell to the ground. They rolled several times across the sun-scorched paving stones.

With a holler of triumph, Zet yanked himself free.

"I won!" Zet said.

"It's not over yet," shouted his best friend, Hui.

Hui lunged again. The boys were equally matched. Hui usually had some trick up his sleeve but Zet was fast on his toes. He sprinted to the edge of Hui's rooftop. He was two-stories high.

Zet glanced back over his shoulder and then jumped.

He cleared the gap and landed on all fours on the neighbor's roof, just a hand's width from the drop. Behind him, Hui charged and took his own flying leap. Zet headed for the next roof, and then another.

Four rooftops down, he threw a glance backward. Not watching where he was going, he let out an *oof* as he slammed into a tall, soft figure. It was old Teni.

She screeched. The basket of laundry in her arms flew one way, Zet went the other. He landed on his behind and winced.

"What, by the gods, are you doing up here?" she cried. Her cheeks were bright red and her forehead was sweaty under her braided wool wig. She glanced at the top of the neighboring house and spotted Hui, who looked like a guilty dog.

"And you, too!" Teni cried. "Your mothers will hear about this!"

"Sorry," Zet said, and scrambled to his feet. He quickly started gathering Teni's laundry.

"Leave it! Your hands are filthy! Hui, get over here now. Both of you are going back onto the street where you belong."

Shamefaced, Hui came across. Teni ordered them down the hatch. At the bottom of her ladder, she grabbed them by their ears, dragged them through her house, thrust them outside, and slammed her door.

"Oops," Zet said, unable to suppress a grin.

"You can say that again," Hui said. "My mother is going to kill me."

"Well, my mother is baking right now. I say we go to my house and eat cake before she finds out. Because after that, I probably won't be eating cake for weeks."

Hui's eyes lit up. "Cake! Race you!"

Together, they sprinted down the narrow streets of Thebes, laughing. Late afternoon sunlight burned down. Hot, bright rays gave way to cool shadows as they turned into a side street.

It had been weeks since Zet had saved Hui from the whole cursed scarab mystery. The upside was that Zet had his best friend back. Ever since their fathers went to war, life had seemed far too serious. Zet ran the family pottery stall with his younger sister, Kat, while their mother took care of the baby at home. Now, with Hui around, the days the market was closed had become a lot more fun.

The downside was that Hui was out of work. An incredibly skilled novice jeweler, Hui had been the star apprentice at the Kemet workshop. The other downside was that Hui and Zet's sister Kat had huge crushes on each other, which for some weird reason meant that Hui and Kat spent a lot of time arguing—with Zet stuck in the middle.

Go figure.

"Wait till Kat hears about Teni." Hui's grin was a near perfect imitation of his family's household god—Bes—the ancient trickster himself.

"Kat will not want to hear about Teni," Zet said.

"What? Kat will think it's hilarious. She'll love it!"

Zet groaned. He could just picture his younger sister's face. She might only be eleven, but she had a no-nonsense, logical side when it came to anything that might hurt sales at their pottery stall. He could feel a Kat-Hui argument coming on.

"Kat will not love it," he tried to explain. "She thinks upsetting the neighbors is bad for business."

"She'll think it's worth it when I tell her about the look on Teni's face—" Hui paused, staring ahead. "What's going on up there?"

They had just rounded the corner into Zet's street. Two-story, mud brick houses with brightly painted doors lined the well-swept, narrow lane. At the far end, standing in single file before Zet's front steps, stood six uniformed guards.

At first, Zet thought the men were medjay, the city police. But then he saw the heavy weapons on their hips, and the medals that gleamed at their shoulders. Most carried fiber shields, and several wore helmets. Soldiers.

"What are they doing at your place?" Hui said.

Zet walked faster. "I don't know." He broke into a run. Was it possible? Had the thing he wanted most finally come true?

Hui matched him stride for stride. "What do you think they want?"

"Father," Zet gasped, running. "My father must be home! Back from fighting the Hyksos invaders!"

Hui latched onto Zet's arm. He yanked him to a stop. "Wait."

Zet tried to shake him off. "Let go! What are you doing! I haven't seen my father in over a year."

"If your father was home, others would be too. Mine would be, and . . . well . . ."

Zet's expression faltered. A sick feeling grabbed him. He glanced at the soldiers. They stood, arms crossed over their breastplates, and stared stiffly straight ahead.

No, Hui was right. This was no welcome home party. If Father was back, the war would be over, and the whole town would be celebrating.

"That's true." Still, he started forward, a lump in his throat.

"Maybe your father won a medal," Hui said, trying to grin, but his expression was shaky. "And they've come to tell you about it."

Zet nodded, not saying what they both really thought. Medals that arrived like this were bleak things.

"Whatever the reason, I have to know." He approached his door.

Please let father still be alive.

The closest soldier raised a thick arm to bar his way. "Name?"

"Zet, son of Nefer. This is my friend Hui. Why are you here?"

"I am not authorized to say. Please, go inside. They're waiting."

Fearing the worst, Zet stepped through the door. Hui followed and the soldier shut it firmly behind them.

For some reason, the windows had all been fastened tightly shut. After the fierce brightness outside, it took a moment for his eyes to adjust. Not only was the front room unbearably hot, it was crammed with more soldiers.

Kat appeared, maneuvering her way clear of the adults. Zet's sister grabbed his wrist.

"Thank Ra you're here. I was going to come looking for you!" Kat's cheeks were bright. "She's back!"

Zet frowned. "Who's back? Why are the soldiers here?"

"Come on." She dragged him forward.

Zet glanced back at Hui, who looked equally mystified. The soldiers parted to let the three of them through.

Zet spotted his mother first.

"Zet!" she said, sounding relieved.

A cloaked figure sat next to his mother on one of their comfortably worn pillows. The hood fell back when the figure glanced up, revealing a wrinkled, familiar face. The old visitor did not meet his eyes. She couldn't. She was blind.

Hui elbowed Zet hard. "That's the Queen Mother!" he whispered in awe.

"I know," Zet said, grinning.

He breathed a shaky sigh of relief. His father was safe. But why had Pharaoh's mother come?

2

MISSING

This wasn't the first time the Queen Mother had visited Zet's house. Her appearance amazed him nonetheless.

It was shocking to see a royal figure here, in their front room.

Meanwhile, certainty that this visit had nothing to do with his father caused his heart to stop hammering. The knot in his stomach loosened. He knelt and bowed low.

"Hello, Your Highness," Zet said.

The Queen Mother smiled, focusing her blind gaze where he knelt. "Is that you, my friend?"

"Yes," he said, beaming.

"Please, no kneeling," she said.

How could she tell?

"We know each other too well for that," she said.

Zet rose, but Hui stayed plastered to the floor. The Queen Mother cocked her head to one side as if listening.

"Is someone with you?" she asked.

"My friend, Hui."

"Well, Hui, it's a pleasure to meet you," she said.

Hui jolted as if shocked by the sound of the famous Mother of Egypt's Pharaoh speaking his name. He stuttered out a garbled reply.

"All of you, come sit beside me. I'd like to hear your news. I hear so little of life outside the palace. It's a treat for an old woman like me."

"Come on," Zet whispered, pulling Hui to his feet.

"Sit there?" Hui whispered. "Beside the Queen Mother?"

"She won't bite," Kat whispered, at Hui's elbow.

"I might, unless you hurry," the Queen Mother said. She had sharp ears.

Hui winced. "Sorry, Your Highness."

It was easy for Zet and Kat to act nonchalant. They'd helped her in the past, and she'd rewarded them with a huge chest of gold deben. Still, Zet's nonchalant attitude was partly an act. He remained in as much awe as Hui, but it was fun watching Hui's reaction.

The Queen Mother reached forward blindly, found a cushion and patted it. "Here. Come. Tell me how you've been. And then I'll explain why I'm here."

At first, Zet couldn't help feeling formal. But soon, they were talking and laughing about things that had happened since they'd last seen one another. Zet told her about the pottery he had purchased with her reward to restock his family stall.

The Queen Mother told him that everyone in the palace was now regularly eating the chickpea salad recipe she'd gotten from Zet's mother.

"It is wonderful to come here, away from the palace and its busy intrigues," the Queen Mother said. "You are blessed in this home."

Zet nodded. He knew the time had come for the truth of her visit. "Highness, why are you here? What's happened?"

In her lap, her bony fingers tightened around an object fastened to a golden chain. The color drained from her frail cheeks. She looked afraid and suddenly fragile. Something was wrong. Very wrong.

"Zet, I'd like to speak to you alone," she said.

Kat and Hui scrambled to their feet. Meanwhile, she raised her blind eyes to the soldiers in the room. "My good men, please, give us some space."

"But My Lady!" said the closest soldier, one hand on his gilded sword hilt. "Do you know where we are?"

"Yes," she said drily. "I know exactly where we are. As I recall, I provided the directions."

Zet and Hui grinned at each other.

"Of course you did, what I mean is—well, Madam, the neighborhood, it's not safe for you!"

"I trust you will protect me should any harm arise," she said with an amused smile.

"She's been in worse places," Zet couldn't help adding.

At this, the Queen Mother laughed out loud. "Indeed I have."

After the soldiers left, and Kat and Hui had retreated to the kitchen, she turned to Zet.

"What I'm about to share, you must not tell anyone," she said.

"I understand."

Worry lines creased her face. "You're familiar with my oldest granddaughter?"

He nodded. "Princess Meritamon."

"And you know her birthday is coming up?"

"Yes," Zet said, wondering where this was leading. "Definitely. I hear it's going to be amazing. The whole city is looking forward to the celebration."

"There may not be one," the Queen Mother said.

"What? Why not?"

"Princess Meritamon is missing."

3

A ROYAL SPY

Zet stared at the Queen Mother in shock.

Missing? He'd never met the Princess, despite his friendship with Pharaoh's famous mother. Like the rest of Thebes, he'd only glimpsed her from a distance. His mind flew back to the last time he'd seen her—at the Opet Festival, just over three weeks ago. There had been a chariot race, with crowds lining the Boulevard of the Sphinx.

Princess Meritamon sat in the large royal booth; like Hui had pointed out, it was hard *not* to notice her. She was thirteen, going on fourteen. One year older than Zet. She'd been seated next to her half-sister, Sitamun.

The half-sisters were the same age, but nothing alike.

Sitamun was pale and quiet, like her nickname—daughter of the moon.

When Zet thought of Meritamon, he pictured a girl who practically sparkled when she laughed. She had this bubbling energy that drew your attention. When a chariot rider nearly crashed during a daring play to pass his opponent, instead of shrinking back, she'd actually shouted with delight.

Kat said Princess Meritamon was the prettiest girl in Egypt. The

Princess seemed almost unconscious of the fact. Mostly she seemed interested in people. She'd tilt her head to listen when someone spoke to her, and her eyes would light up when she was talking. Zet couldn't help wondering what it would be like to meet face to face.

Apparently, he wasn't alone. Pharaoh's guests had seemed more interested in having the Princess include them in her circle than watching the chariot race. As did the people in the streets. They'd shout her name, which would make her laugh in apparent surprise, and then she'd wave.

Zet came back to the present, his mind spinning.

Missing?

But she must have been guarded; the royal family was under constant protection!

"How can she be missing?" he asked.

"It's the same question I've been asking myself. And it's the reason I'm here." The Queen Mother squared her shoulders to face him. "I need you to help me find out what happened. I need you to help bring my granddaughter home."

Zet stared at her in disbelief. "Me?"

"Oh, we have medjay police working on the case, but you have something unique. You can get into places others can't. Many adults don't believe children know much." She smiled, looking rueful. "They're willing to let their guard down, and say things they wouldn't dare tell a man in uniform."

"That's true," Zet said with a laugh. "You wouldn't believe some of the things people discuss in front of us at the stall. Like we're not even there."

"They were children once. You'd think they'd remember how it was."

Footsteps moved across the upper floor. His mother was busy doing some chores.

Zet shifted on his cushion, wanting to ask something but worried about offending her. "This might sound crazy, but—"

"Tell me."

"Well, is it possible she went off on her own? For a day or two?"

"Meritamon is certainly capable of such mischief. She enjoys raising a little trouble now and then—not that I didn't at her age! But no. First, she wasn't in Thebes. And second, we have proof she was kidnapped."

"Kidnapped." Shock ran through him. "Where was she?"

"At Abydos. Pharaoh's building a new temple there. Merit went seven days ago by boat for a small vacation," the Queen Mother said, using the princess's shortened name. "She was to tour the project, and then meet with her father as he came south from the battlefront." Her voice became quiet. "They planned to travel back here together for her birthday celebration."

Zet swallowed. The darkness and heat of the room felt suffocating. "If Princess Merit was kidnapped, is there a ransom?"

"A terrible one. But there's no time to go into it now. You'll hear it soon enough."

Zet frowned, wondering what she meant by that.

"Only a few people know, that's why I sent my soldiers out of the room. Merit went to Abydos disguised as a priestess. She is Pharaoh's heir. We are at war. If word spreads of her disappearance, fear would spread with it. It would be seen as a terrible omen."

"Can't you just pay the ransom?" he said, wondering why the Queen Mother would do anything besides that.

"Gladly! If it were gold. The kidnappers don't want gold. They want our army to give up the battle and let the invading forces take over our country. My granddaughter has been kidnapped by the Hyksos. She's become a piece in a game of war."

It was the worst blow Zet could ever imagine. "What is Pharaoh doing? He must be tearing Abydos apart."

"No, he can't."

Zet stared at her in shock.

"We've been warned by the kidnappers that if Pharaoh launches a full scale military search, my granddaughter will be killed immediately. That's why I sent only a small contingent of medjay." Her voice faltered. All her steely reserve threatened to break, and a glimpse of complete and utter despair showed through. She was simply a grandmother whose granddaughter has been snatched away. "We must find her. We can't let them win. Not now."

"She'll be found," Zet said, even though he had no idea if it were true.

The Queen Mother reached for his hand and squeezed it. Her fingers looked frail, but there was strength in them.

"I'll do anything," Zet said. "Tell me what you want me to do."

"I want you to go to Abydos."

Abydos. Zet's heart leapt at the thought. It was a far off place he'd only heard about in stories. A place Pharaoh Ahmose had chosen as his eternal burial site. Remote and far from any village or town, it would be unlike anything he could imagine.

Of course he wanted to go. It was his duty. But what about the pottery stall? Taking care of his family was his duty, too. His mother and Kat needed him here. He couldn't just leave.

"I know you run a good business, and I'm asking a lot of you. I've already talked to your mother," the Queen Mother said. "I offered to have my own people help out at your stall. She told me she would work things out."

"Then, yes. Of course. I'll do it."

"Just be my eyes and ears up there. I've assigned you to work for the head architect as a runner. Keep watch, and report what you see to him. Anything you learn will be passed on to the men leading the investigation."

"I can do that."

"Good. Remember, watch and listen, nothing more. I have no intention of putting you at risk. Any questions?"

"I have a request."

"Name it."

"I want Hui to go with me."

4

ROYAL TOKENS

Zet watched the Queen Mother's face. Would she let Hui go with him? Would she trust a second person, someone she didn't know? He pictured traveling all that way without a friend to run ideas with, with no one at his back. He didn't like it. With Hui, he stood a chance of succeeding. Without him, he wasn't so sure.

Finally, she said, "This is a dangerous mission, I have no right to ask even you to go."

"I want to." And he did. Either way, he'd go.

"All right." Her face looked fierce and full of hope. "I think bringing Hui is a good idea. You'll have someone to rely on. If he's able, I'm in favor. It's safer than you being alone. But we need to act quickly. The boat's waiting."

Zet stood. "I'll tell him."

At that moment, Zet's mother came down the steps from their sleeping quarters—which for Kat and Zet was usually the roof. They liked to sleep up there on hot nights, under the winking stars.

She held a sack. "I hope I've put enough things in here."

"I promise, whatever's missing can be provided at Abydos," the Queen Mother said. "But I must trouble you with another request."

After the Queen Mother explained, Zet's mother nodded.

"I think I can convince Hui's mother, Delilah, without giving too much away. Even still, she's no gossip. She'd never tell a soul. And she'll probably be glad to see Hui busy."

"It's a lot to ask, to put your son and hers in danger," the Queen Mother said.

"These are dangerous times," she said softly.

Zet flashed on his future. He'd rarely slept away from home. And never without his family. The few times he'd traveled had been to buy pottery at the potter's village downriver. Despite the seriousness of his task, and his fear for the Princess, he felt suddenly alive. More alive than he'd ever felt.

Bastet's whiskers!

This was going to be an adventure.

Moments later, a confused looking Hui was called out of the kitchen where he'd been waiting with Kat. He stammered out his goodbyes to the Queen Mother, still clueless as to what was going on. How Zet hoped he could come!

"Meet you at the harbor," Zet's mother said, leaving with Kat, Hui and Zet's baby brother.

The Queen Mother turned to Zet. "I have some things for you." She rummaged in a soft, calfskin satchel stamped with the royal insignia and pulled out a leather tube. "These are your work papers. Show them to Senna, the architect, when you arrive."

He took the small, leather tube and pulled off its cap.

A scroll lay nestled inside. He tipped it out into his palm. A wax blob sealed the smooth, finely burnished papyrus. Stamped into the blob was a fancy cartouche. He moved his fingers over the raised hieroglyphics, awed to be holding such a thing.

"That's my personal seal. It reads, Tetisheri—my birth name. Don't let anyone see it, except the architect. Otherwise, your cover will be blown and the game will be up."

"I won't."

"The other thing I want to give you is this." She opened her frail right hand and Zet saw what she'd been holding all this time. The golden chain held a ring. She found Zet's hand and pressed it into his palm. "Guard it carefully."

The ring felt warm. Made of thick gold, it looked ancient. "Wait. Is this . . .?"

"My coronation ring."

"But Your Highness—" His head spun with the enormity of this thing in his fingers. "With respect, don't ask me to take this."

"You're going as my spy. Only one person at Abydos knows this, and that's Senna the architect. Should anything happen to him, you'll be on your own. In a situation like this, things could turn bad quickly. If you need to demand passage home—or if your actions raise too many questions with the medjay, this is your safeguard. Use it only if you need to! And hide it wisely."

He didn't move. "Highness, I can't take it."

"I won't send you without it. Put the chain around your neck."

Stiffly, he did as he was told. It felt heavy against his chest. Filled with a worry he couldn't define, he tucked the royal coronation symbol into the front of his tunic. The ring felt like it held the power of the gods. And in a way it did, for the Queen Mother was a living god on earth.

She touched his head. "May the hidden powers of Egypt keep you safe."

In the street, Zet set off at a run.

An hour ago, he'd been worried about old Teni getting him in trouble for charging across her rooftop. Now, he was being sent on a quest to find a missing princess. Fresh excitement surged through him.

It struck him suddenly that he'd forgotten all about the honey cakes his mother had been baking. His stomach roared. He hadn't eaten since breakfast, and they were his favorite. No doubt Hui had eaten half a dozen while he was in the kitchen with Kat.

Too bad he hadn't stuffed one in his bag!

Zet reached the dock out of breath.

Numerous ships bobbed nearby. Kat, his mother and baby Apu stood at the appointed location. And with them, stood Hui.

Zet whooped and pumped his arm in the air. "Yes!"

"Adventure twins!" Hui said, and raised both hands.

They fist bumped each other.

Zet glanced at Kat, who looked considerably less excited. In fact, she looked downright glum.

"What's wrong?" Zet asked her. "Is it because you're not coming?"

Hui winced. "Kat, I didn't mean—"

Kat crossed her arms and her cheeks turned bright red. She made a point of ignoring him, and said to Zet, "I could care less about coming. Not when you're going to save *'the most beautiful girl in the world'*, like Hui said."

Hui had his hands clutched in his hair. "The most beautiful *princess* in the world," he said in a whisper.

Kat glared.

Zet choked back a laugh. Hui was just digging himself deeper.

Looking frantic, Hui said, "She's probably all looks. She's probably nowhere near as smart as you, Kat."

"That's what you have to say? That I'm smart?"

Zet groaned. Usually Kat liked being called smart. But clearly right now that was not the case. Girls were weird. Then again, so were boys, according to the ridiculous expression on Hui's face. Zet's best friend looked confused and desperate.

Trying to save him, Zet said, "Is that our boat?"

5

ALL ABOARD

Birds screeched and dove over the Nile's broad expanse. A breeze whipped across the shimmering surface, ruffling the moving currents. Nearby, fishermen offloaded nets of silver perch. The air smelled of seafood and wood-sealing pitch.

Zet and the others stood on the wharf, surveying the lineup of boats. Zet's mother ignored the argument between Kat and Hui. Instead, she was reading a set of instructions.

"I believe it's the furthest one down. Come on."

Clearly glad for the change of subject, Hui said. "Wow, we're going on that boat?"

"It's huge," Zet said. "Has to be longer than eight cows standing nose to tail!"

"Acacia wood construction. See that, Kat?" Hui said, looking hopefully at her. "They make wood bricks and glue them together with reeds and sap."

Kat looked at the boat but said nothing.

On board, men moved everywhere on deck. Some tied down crates. Others fitted jutting oars into place. Still others tightened down the square sail that flew from the center mast. Tattoos covered their thick arms, and their sun-darkened faces were like leather. It was clear everyone spent day and night outside. The only structure was a small cabin mid-ship, which was surely reserved for the Captain.

Already Zet's heart was leaping with the thrill of adventure.

The last two times he'd been involved in a mystery, Kat had helped. She must be feeling left out. He would be.

"Kat." He grabbed her elbow. "Thanks for managing the stall. It might be the boring part of this job, but it's just as important. I couldn't go without you here."

Kat let out the breath she'd been holding, and beamed for real. "Thanks."

Hui approached Kat. "You won't forget me, will you?"

Zet couldn't help snorting. "We're only going for a few days, we're not coming back as graybeards."

Meanwhile, Kat seemed to have softened somewhat. Zet thought she might be preparing to throw her arms around Hui's neck in a farewell hug.

"Please tell me you're not still mad," Hui said.

Kat twined her fingers together.

"She might be beautiful," Hui said in sudden earnest. "But your braids are longer. Much longer!"

At this, Kat's forehead scrunched up and her mouth opened. The color started to rise in her cheeks again and she dropped her arms to her sides. She never managed to get out what she was about to say, because Zet cut in.

"We have to go!"

"Zet's right," their mother agreed.

Hui, however, was busy leaping about and making funny faces at Kat, trying to make her laugh. She wouldn't have any of it.

From the ship's rail above, a deep voice boomed, "What's going on? You boys boarding today or not?"

Zet looked up to see a man who had to be the Captain. His eyes were hard, like two black onyx stones. The man gripped the rail with meaty fingers and glared down at them.

"Yes!" Zet called. "We're coming up. Right now."

"Maybe you should leave your buddy behind. He looks thick in the head."

Hui stopped capering and put his fists on his hips. "I am not thick in the head."

"Are too," Kat said.

Zet's mother said, "My apologies, Captain. We didn't mean to keep you waiting." She herded the boys toward the gangplank. "Now, watch your manners and everything will be fine. And don't forget to bundle up at night. It can be cold this time of year. I've packed several tunics, along with a pair of your father's old sandals in case—"

"Don't worry, Mother. We'll manage," Zet said, hugging her and grinning.

A moment later, he and Hui hopped off the gangplank onto the warm deck.

Deeply tanned sailors started pulling in ropes.

Zet glanced around and saw that he and Hui weren't the only guests on board. A small crowd of passengers was also headed for Abydos. To one side stood an ominous looking priest. His shaved head glistened with oil and dark energy seemed to swirl around him; probably because he was murmuring strange words and staring with glazed eyes at the horizon.

Nearby—but keeping their distance from the daunting holy man —sat a dozen or so construction workers. Zet knew they were construction workers by their toolboxes, which most men were using as seats. On one box, a big man sat sharpening a bronze chisel. He looked hot and impatient.

The Captain's wide torso cut off the view. Zet looked up into the man's creased face.

"State your names," the Captain growled.

They did.

"Well, Zet and Hui. We're late. I had to hold my boat." One thumb tucked into his waistband, he eyed them with distaste. "I'd like to know why."

Zet hadn't expected this. Was the man suspicious about holding the ship for two kids, or just annoyed? The Queen Mother's ring on its chain felt suddenly heavy and huge against Zet's chest, as though it were visible through his tunic.

"We're replacing someone," Zet said quickly.

"We just found out," Hui added. "We came right away."

The Captain's dark eyes swept over them as if he knew something wasn't quite right. His lip curled in a snort. Abruptly, he turned and shouted, "Prepare to cast off." To the boys, he said, "Move to the aft deck."

"Will do," Zet said, glad to be relieved of the Captain's scrutiny.

As soon as the Captain left, Hui whispered. "Uh, which way is the aft deck?"

"No idea. Let's just get out of here."

NO TURNING BACK

Zet and Hui clambered over ropes, past the central cabin, and headed as far from the gruff Captain as they could get. Only when they reached the curving prow did Zet stop. A trickle of sweat ran down his ribs. He held his pack closer, thinking of the scroll inside, and then of the valuable coronation ring around his neck. He felt like a walking booby trap. Any moment, someone could find either.

In a low voice, Zet said, "We need to put up a good front if we're going to stay undercover."

But Hui wasn't listening. He was belly up to the rail, giving Kat the most pathetic look ever. "She's never going to speak to me again."

"Good," Zet said. "Then I won't have to listen to you fight anymore." He waved at his family. "Anyway, we have more important things to think about right now."

Sailors let out the sail. Wind caught the giant square of linen with a snap. It bowed outward, and the boat jumped away from shore. Zet grabbed the boat's side for support. The wake sent dark ripples weaving across the river's smooth surface.

To Hui, he said, "We need to keep our wits about us. Starting right now."

Hui finally focused on him. "Of course we're keeping our wits."

"What I mean is, we have to act like we're going to Abydos to work. We need to get our story straight. So when people ask what we're doing, we have something to say."

"Right. Of course—putting on my Secret Agent Assistant Hat now," Hui said.

"Don't even say that word."

"What, secret agent?"

"I'm serious!" Zet whispered. "Quit it or I'm dumping you in the Nile right now while you can still swim to shore."

"Oh, great friend you are. Ditch me at the first sign of trouble." But Hui was laughing. "Fine. I like it, having a story. Always good to have a story. So what's ours?"

"We're going as runners for the Head Architect."

"How did we get the job?" Hui asked.

"Through my father. They're old friends, and the architect wants to help my family by giving me work. You're coming because he needed two boys, and I suggested you."

"Wait, your father knows the architect?"

Zet gave Hui a playful punch and laughed. "No!"

"Oh! Right, of course not," Hui said. "Pretty convincing, you were right then. I believed you." He leapt up. "Now that's settled, I'm going to have a look around this ship."

Zet wrapped a protective arm over his satchel and nodded. "I'll catch up with you. I need to sort something out first."

Before turning to go, Hui shot one last longing glance at the shore. Zet followed his best friend's gaze. From this distance, Kat, Zet's mother and baby Apu looked like three tiny grains of wheat. Like the wind could blow them away into nothing.

Zet felt his stomach tighten. He realized it was the first time he'd left them home alone. What if something happened? What if something happened to the pottery stall? He'd sworn to his father he'd protect them, and here he was leaving to solve someone else's problem. Yet it was Pharaoh's problem—the Great Bull, the living god himself. What choice did he have?

Zet wiped the sweat from his palms on his kilt. His family would be fine. He'd see them in a week. What could possibly happen to them in Thebes?

From amid ship, a rowdy bark of laughter issued from the seated workers.

"Well, see you over there," Hui said. Still looking glum about Kat, he tore himself from the rail and headed for the men.

Zet untied his satchel and dug through it until he saw the scroll nestled in the bottom. It seemed unlikely anyone on board would search his bag. They'd never suspect he had anything worth stealing. Still, to have it just lying in there seemed incredibly risky. Better to hide it someplace. Worst case, if it was found, no one could tie the Queen Mother's letter to him, and he'd still have a chance of doing his job.

But if the scroll were found in his personal possession, it would all be over.

His thoughts shifted to the sailors. If this boat went back and forth often—ferrying workmen to the building site—could any of the sailors be involved in the kidnapping? If they were and they found the scroll, not only would the ruse be over, something worse could happen. He and Hui might end up as crocodile food.

Zet glanced around the deck.

The smell of oiled wood and the creak of the sail filled his senses. This boat was a foreign world. Ropes that lay coiled now probably wouldn't stay that way for long, so they wouldn't make a good hiding place.

Would any place be safe?

Butted up against the cabin lay a rowboat made of reeds all lashed together. The boat was upside down. Zet peered under it, and decided it wouldn't do. What if someone used it partway through the journey to ferry someone to shore? Or go fishing?

He moved on, and stopped next to a large wooden crate. Lifting the lid, the earthy smell of onions rose to greet him. The box was heavily loaded. They'd only be on the boat until tomorrow. They'd never eat all these.

A glance told him the coast was clear. The center cabin blocked his view of the men. Still, he'd have to act fast. Heart pounding, he dug deep and fast, shoving onions aside until he could see the crate's bottom. Zet thrust the scroll inside.

His fingers went to the front of his tunic where the Queen Mother's ring lay concealed. The chain felt like a noose around his neck. He began to remove it, but something stopped him. He couldn't shove something so holy in this crate.

Reluctantly, he let go, and then piled the vegetables over the scroll. Soon the leather tube disappeared from view, buried deep. Zet dropped the lid.

The sense of being watched made him jolt upright.

He peered both ways, but saw no one. Heart slamming, he stood. Not a soul in sight. He backed up and wiped sweat from his brow.

The boat rocked under his feet as he set off to find Hui.

The oars had been pulled in, and the oarsmen seats were empty. A steady breeze had caught the square sail, pulling it tight. The powerful ship leaned into the wind and picked up speed. Wood groaned and water churned alongside. The shores reeled past as the boat began its journey northward.

On the left riverbank he could see lush farms close to shore, bordered by desert and a backdrop of steep, rocky mountains. On the right bank, the city gleamed with sparkling monuments and crawled with people going about their business.

It felt refreshing to be detached from it all, flying north in a swift, modern ship.

Zet decided to forget the scroll and his worries and enjoy himself.

There was nothing he could do about the Princess's disappearance right now. Who knew when he'd get to relax again? Tomorrow they'd be landing at Abydos, and then the chase would be on.

7

A FAMILIAR FACE

Zet edged along deck past the cabin, holding the rail to keep steady. The ship's sway would take getting used to. He headed for the knot of construction workers. They were laughing—deep throated rumbles and guffaws.

Hui stood between the men, dwarfed by their size.

Hui turned and the workers did the same. Zet was pinpointed with a dozen stares. The men were all huge and scarred from work—and maybe fighting, too. Puckered burn marks ran down one man's muscled forearms. Another had poorly healed gashes. All had calloused hands with bruised, blackened fingernails. At least half looked to be the kind that turned from laughter to brawling at the first sign of offense.

"Zet, look who's here, can you believe it?"

Zet glanced at the man, but didn't recognize him.

"It's Jafar!" Hui said, "From the Kemet workshop. Jafar, this is my best friend, Zet."

The Kemet Workshop? Instantly, Zet went on alert. Thoughts of the events that had nearly killed Hui flashed through his mind.

"Nice to meet you," Zet said, feeling wary.

"Same." Jafar stuck out a thick hand and they shook. He was

missing his little finger. His right eyelid drooped, which made him look like he was winking. But he wasn't, and probably never had. "A pal of Hui's is a pal of mine."

The circle closed around Zet.

"So . . ." Jafar said in a way that suggested he was sizing Zet up. "I hear you two are on a big job."

Inwardly, Zet winced. What was Hui telling them? He tried to keep his face neutral as he shot Hui a look.

"You know, working for the head architect," Hui said. "We're going to be pretty important."

"You couldn't make me give up my craft to be a runner," Jafar said with a snort.

Hui colored. "No," he said quietly. "Well, you take what you can get. Beggars can't be choosy."

Jafar nodded. "Now that's the truth, isn't it? I've been out of work since that whole cursed amulet business."

"Jafar was one of Kemet's master jewelers," Hui told Zet.

"You, my friend, weren't so bad yourself," Jafar said. "Yep. Kemet was worried some jealous apprentice would slit your throat in your sleep and kill his upcoming star! Turns out it was all pointless. We all ended up on the street, didn't we?" He cracked his knuckles and grinned. "But things are looking up."

Zet frowned at the master jeweler. "I don't understand, you'll be making jewelry at the temple?"

The men all barked with laughter.

"No. Hinges and door handles, decorative ornamentation and the like," Jafar said.

"Oh. Right," Zet said, and laughed.

Jafar scratched his chin, then tapped Zet's chest with a thick finger. "You aren't that kid who helped the medjay, are you?"

Another man spoke up. "You sayin' this boy here works with the medjay?"

To Zet's horror, Hui gave a broad grin of acknowledgment, looking ridiculously proud and important. "My buddy Zet here, he's—"

"Way too dumb for something like that," Zet said with a weak laugh. "Me, work with the medjay? That's crazy. Right Hui?"

"Er, right."

Zet managed to pull Hui aside.

"By the gods, Hui, you almost gave us away!" he said.

Hui frowned. "What are you talking about? Don't worry. These men are friends."

"The only friends on this boat are you and me. Everyone else is either a suspect, or a potential danger."

"How? They weren't at the temple. How could they be suspects?"

"All right. Maybe not, but the sailors could be. And the Captain. They've been up and down the Nile ferrying workers."

"That grumpy old Captain, I wouldn't put it past him," Hui said. "Have you seen his smile? I think he's part crocodile."

At this, Zet broke out laughing. "Yes! I think you're right!"

Hui pointed toward shore. "Look at that!" Thebes was fading into the distance and an enormous stone structure had come into view. "The Karnak Temple complex."

The boys leaned on the rail, elbow to elbow, and watched it drift past. At their backs, the sun hung low in the sky. The sun god's slanting rays colored the Karnak temples and monuments with a wash of deep red.

The colossal structures gave way to tilled farmland. Hui settled down and opened his bag. He laid out various pieces of wood, including a bunch of small pegs and two long slats. On one slat, three mischievous faces had been carved in a row. With deft strokes of his knife, Hui began forming a fourth face. It was amazing to watch it appear out of nothing.

"My little brothers," Hui said, grinning as he worked.

"What are you making?"

"It's a lock," Hui said.

"A lock?" Zet had heard of locks, but had never actually seen one.

"It's for mother, for our front door. Look, I'll show you how it works."

The strange priest seated nearby inched closer. "Where did you learn this art?"

"At a jeweler's workshop," Hui said. Kneeling forward, he laid two long slats of wood on deck. Crosswise, he placed several small, duck-bone sized pegs. "These pegs will be the teeth inside, also known as tumblers, which will be inserted right here. To open the lock, a person will need a wooden rod, specially shaped to fit inside and lift the tumblers. It's very secure."

Despite his narrow, haughty face, the priest looked impressed.

Zet was. "Maybe you can make one for my stall, and I can lock up some of our pottery at night. Instead of just covering it with linen like we do now."

Hui nodded. "Done." His face colored. "If I do that, do you think Kat will forgive me?"

PLAYING WITH FIRE

It was dusk when the Captain guided the boat toward shore. Rushes slid against the wooden hull. Sailors jumped out, splashing through the marshy shallows and then hauling on ropes until the boat came to rest against the soft sand. Stars had begun to wink overhead, and cool air settled on Zet's shoulders.

"Out 'o my way," a man grumbled at Zet, who'd been leaning protectively against the vegetable crate where he'd hidden the scroll.

Zet jumped aside, panic stricken when the man raised the lid. The man took out an armful of onions, let the lid slam down and made for land. Breathing a sigh of relief, he and Hui went onshore to find dinner. Zet, for one, was starving.

They pounded down the gangplank toward the fire flickering on the beach.

It was pitch dark by the time food was handed out. Bowls of hot stew and bread. Silence fell as everyone set to eating.

"It's really good," Zet said, after his first few pangs of hunger had been sated.

The cook looked up from his dinner and shot him a toothy grin.

"That it is," said the Captain, raising a thick slice of bread in a toast. "Here's to the cook who keeps my men from jumping ship."

"Hear, hear!" shouted the sailors with a roar of laughter.

In a low voice, Jafar said to Hui, "Ah, but the bread's not as good as our old baker friends', now is it?"

Zet caught a strange expression on Jafar's face. Again, he got that unsettling feeling about Hui's old workmate.

Hui sounded uncomfortable as he said, "Those bakers sure had a way with dough."

Jafar guffawed.

On the circle's far side, the Captain stoked the fire with a long branch. Sparks flew, crackling high into the night sky. The red, dancing flames threw shadows and light wavering over the scarred, dark faces of the men. Zet wondered what Kat would think of such a sight. She'd probably cower in terror. He grinned.

Feeling suddenly brave, he got to his feet.

Now was as good a time as any to question the Captain. Maybe the man knew something about Princess Merit's disappearance.

"Going somewhere?" Jafar asked.

Zet shrugged. "Just want to thank the Captain for his hospitality."

Jafar raised one brow.

Trying to look nonchalant, Zet made his way round the fire pit. The closer he got to the Captain, the weaker his legs felt. *Get it together,* he told himself. The Queen Mother hired him for a reason. It was time to start working.

The Captain stiffened as Zet approached. Between his bushy brows, the V-shaped crease deepened and the corners of his mouth turned down.

"I don't brook complaints after hours," he growled.

"I didn't come to complain, I wanted to say sorry for making you wait earlier. Thanks again." He nodded at the big vessel. "That's a really nice boat."

He grunted. "Best on the river."

"How does it compare to the royal barges?" Zet said.

"What kind of question is that?"

Zet raised his hands. "Just asking. I don't know much about boats."

The Captain's shoulders relaxed a little. "I've never been on a royal barge. But mine's the latest in shipbuilding."

It struck Zet that it must have cost a small fortune to build. Did he really make that much as a ferryman? "I guess you ferry a lot of people."

He nodded. "I do."

"Mostly to Abydos, then?"

"Right now, yes."

"How's it going up there?" Zet tried to lead the conversation around to the Princess. "Any trouble we should know about?"

The Captain's eyes narrowed. "What are you getting at?"

Zet shrugged. "They just hired us last minute. It seemed strange. I'm wondering what kind of work I'm headed for, that's all."

The Captain nodded, slowly. "I see. Want a piece of advice?"

Zet opened his mouth to answer, but paused at the look on the Captain's face.

"Stop asking questions," the Captain said.

"But I just—"

The Captain got to his feet, gripping his mug of beer in his meaty fist. "Kontar!"

The nearest sailor cracked his knuckles. "Problem, Captain?"

"There will be, Kontar, unless you take care of this kid."

"Gladly." Kontar grabbed Zet roughly by the neck and towed him away. "My Captain don't like you."

"I was only—"

"Shut it, kid."

Kontar's fingers tightened around Zet's throat. He shoved him along in front of him. The further they got from the fire, the more Zet started to panic.

"Let go," Zet managed, choking and trying to wrench free.

The man's circling grip narrowed like a rope being pulled tight. Zet couldn't believe it—this was crazy. Was the sailor strangling him?

"Stop!"

"I ain't done with you, yet."

Blackness crept around the edge of Zet's vision. He clawed at

Kontar's fingers and arms. This was no joke. If Kontar didn't let go soon—

"Let 'im go," came Jafar's voice.

Kontar spun, keeping his hold on Zet. Jafar strode toward them with Hui sprinting alongside. Kontar's grip didn't loosen. Zet was losing consciousness.

"I said let 'im go," Jafar growled.

Kontar laughed. "Says who?"

"Says me and my brothers," Jafar snarled. "We stick together."

As if to prove it, two more construction workers moseyed toward them.

Kontar snorted. "I wasn't hurting the little brat. Just giving him a fright."

He boxed Zet's ear hard. Then Zet was stumbling free. His hands flew to his windpipe. He gasped, sucking in deep breaths. A fright? If Jafar hadn't shown up, Kontar could have killed him! For what? Asking questions?

Kontar hooked one thumb into his knife-belt. "Have a nice night," he sneered, nodding at Zet.

Zet knew then that the danger wasn't over—just postponed. He kept his face blank, hiding his fear, but knew he'd made a dangerous enemy. Why? What were they up to?

When Kontar left, Jafar fastened his drooping eye on Zet. "What's going on?"

"Nothing," Zet said, too quickly.

"Brothers don't keep secrets," Jafar said in a menacing voice.

"No secrets here," Zet lied, rubbing his throat.

"Look at his face," Hui said, grinning. "You think he has a secret worth keeping? Zet? Most boring kid around. He'd be nowhere without me."

"Er . . . Right," Zet said, deciding Hui was laying it on a bit thick.

Jafar laughed, but his droopy eye wasn't smiling. Studying Zet's face, he grunted.

As they made their way on ship, Zet felt the weight of the

mystery looming over him, dark and horribly complicated. He needed to know more about Kontar and the Captain. But how?

He felt like an idiot for accepting the Queen Mother's request. He'd been all puffed up with pride. Sure he'd solved a crime or two before, but he'd been lucky. It was easy to solve crimes back home where he knew people, knew the streets, and knew the medjay. Here, he knew no one.

Except Hui, of course.

A glance at his best friend lifted Zet's spirits. He wasn't alone. Thank the gods he had Hui along. Still, they couldn't talk with Jafar between them.

Until they could talk, he'd just have to puzzle things out on his own. Questions ran through his mind. What had made the Captain and Kontar so angry? What were they hiding? He ran a hand over his throat. There was something shifty going on.

And what about this expensive boat?

How had the Captain paid for it? With Hyksos bribes?

Still, if the Captain was the kidnapper, where would he be hiding the Princess?

NORTHWARD

Zet, Hui and Jafar had only been on board several moments when raucous voices filled the air. Both craftsmen and sailors were returning. Their footsteps shook the gangway and the boat rocked under their weight.

Hui sat in the prow. "Do you think Kat's still mad at me?"

"Are we back on that subject?" Zet smothered a grin. Hui looked miserable and Zet's heart went out to him.

"It's not funny," Hui said in a glum voice. "Just wait until you like a girl. Then we'll see who's laughing."

"Ha! After watching you two, I probably never will."

Jafar belched and rubbed his belly. "Girls are trouble."

The rest of the construction crew joined them on the forward deck. Zet suddenly felt glad of their presence. At least with them nearby, Kontar would have a hard time getting Zet and Hui alone.

"I'm beat," Jafar announced. He made for the overturned rowboat, raised it with his four-fingered right hand and peered underneath. "Looks like I found a bedroom."

Zet said a silent prayer of thanks that he hadn't hidden the scroll there.

Meanwhile, the other workmen staked out spots against the bulwarks and the Captain's cabin wall. The air had grown chill. Blankets were tugged out of packs. Zet found the neatly folded cover his mother had provided. It smelled of home—of his mother's soap. He held it tight around him and lay down with his back to the crate that hid the scroll. Despite his worries, he soon slipped off into a deep, dreamless sleep.

The sound of gently lapping water woke him.

Grey dawn stretched overhead. He stared up at the sky. This wasn't his rooftop. He frowned, momentarily confused. His neck hurt.

Then it all came rushing back. The Queen Mother's visit, the boat, the run-in with the Captain and Kontar. He sat up and touched his throat. It felt sore and tender. Around him the construction workers snored away.

Elsewhere, however, sailors were moving about the boat.

Zet thought about Princess Merit, hidden away somewhere. Were her kidnappers hurting her? Treating her how Kontar had treated him? The idea made him furious.

Glancing at the horizon, he watched the sun god, Ra, crest over the edge of the world. Feeling the warm rays on his skin, Zet closed his eyes and prayed.

Until I find her, keep Princess Merit safe!

"You have a funny look on your face," came Hui's voice.

Zet's eyes flew open. "Do I?" He grinned. "It's because my head's still ringing from you snoring in my ear all night."

Hui stretched. "Keeps the flies away."

"What's that? I think I've gone deaf."

Hui cupped his hands and shouted into Zet's ear. "Keeps the flies away!"

"In your mouth, more like," Zet said, imitating a snore that involved sucking down a large fly and swallowing it.

"Very funny." Hui stood and rubbed his belly. "What's for breakfast? I'm starved."

Zet's own stomach growled. Being on the river gave him an appetite. He leapt up. "I think I smell bread toasting. Come on. Race you!"

Together, they made their way on shore. Zet kept an eye out for Kontar, but the sailor was nowhere in sight. Neither was the Captain.

The cook handed out loaded plates. Fried goose eggs with golden yolks. Toasted bread, dripping with sweet honey. Roasted, shredded waterfowl that was deliciously greasy and melted in your mouth. A sailor's breakfast, through and through. Meant to feed men who labored hard all day.

Zet and Hui leaned back and groaned, deliciously full.

"I can't move," Hui said.

"Me neither," Zet said. "Which is bad, because I think the boat's leaving."

"What?" Hui cried, leaping to his feet.

"Kidding!"

"No, I think you're right! Come on!" Hui gasped.

They sprinted on board as the sailors prepared to push off.

The cabin door opened, and the Captain emerged along with Kontar. Kontar wore an angry expression. Zet craned to see inside the cabin before the door closed, but it was too dark in there. Both men were arguing in low voices. They didn't notice Zet watching.

He wondered if he could sneak into the cabin. What was so important in there? Why were they arguing? Could they be hiding the Princess in the cabin?

A sailor gave Zet a shove.

"Forward deck or aft deck—move it," the sailor barked. "No passengers mid-ship when we're under sail."

The morning passed with no chance to investigate the cabin further. But there were plenty of things to distract him. A strong wind carried them swiftly north, the prow cutting knife-like through the glistening water. Zet and Hui sat with the breeze in their faces. Pelicans, herons and egrets played in the reeds by the banks. A crocodile surfaced, raced alongside, then swished its leathery tail and dove out of sight. Dragonflies dipped and glittered.

Onward they flew. Despite everything, Zet felt sure he'd never grow tired of this view. As morning wore into afternoon, however, the wind began to die.

The sail flapped noisily, sagging overhead.

Hot air descended. The Captain barked out orders. Sailors took up the oars. The boat began moving once again, but nowhere near the pace they'd made under sail. Everywhere, faces gleamed with sweat. Kontar pulled the lead oar, glaring at Zet through narrowed eyes.

Then, over it all, came an eerie chant.

Zet had forgotten about the priest. Now, without the wind to carry the priest's voice away, he could hear the man muttering. The rowers rowed in rhythm to his song—if it could be called a song. In the heavy heat, it sounded more like a death march.

"Creepy," Hui whispered.

Even the construction workers seemed spooked. They glanced at one another, exchanging uneasy looks.

Hours passed. The Captain shouted a command. They'd reached a small canal, which cut sideways off the Nile. The rowers leaned into their oars, pivoting the big boat. Zet watched, impressed, as they nosed it into the smaller canal. Lush greenery brushed the hull, surrounding the waterway on either side. The dip and splash of oars propelled them slowly up it.

They lost sight of the Nile as the canal snaked around a bend. There the canal widened again.

Zet and Hui stared out over the bow. Flies buzzed and swarmed. The air smelled of marsh reeds and verdant overgrowth. Ahead, far inland, desert hills rose steeply skyward, turning dark shades of blue and purple in the dusk.

Evening had fallen by the time the winding canal finally opened into a large, circular lake—a harbor, Zet realized. The lamps of bobbing boats glowed here and there. Some boats floated at anchor. Others were tied to watersteps against the shore. More lamps flickered on land, revealing a large, busy camp.

Hui whistled softly. "Look at this place."

"It's a small city."

Somehow he'd stupidly pictured Abydos as a tiny, quaint place, with a group of tight-knit workers that would be easy to investigate. Not this huge, sprawling camp! Way further off, he could see even more lights glowing. A second camp? No wonder the Queen Mother's people couldn't find the Princess. They needed a full-on military search, which was not an option given the kidnappers would retaliate by killing her on the spot.

Zet recalled the Queen Mother's despair, which she had so quickly hidden. He'd sworn to himself then that he'd find Princess Merit.

Now with Abydos spread before him that promise seemed like some childish wish. He'd been arrogant, picturing this as some big adventure. This was no adventure—a girl's life was at stake.

His heart slammed and his fingers tightened on the rail.

As for questions about what was in the Captain's cabin, and why the two men were arguing, he had no clue. The voyage was nearly over. Time was running out.

He watched the makeshift city grow ever closer as the Captain maneuvered their boat toward shore.

BROTHERS IN THE DARK

The boat hummed with commotion as sailors unfurled ropes and made ready to dock.

"Hui," Zet said in a low voice. "Whoever kidnapped the Princess has a lot to lose if they're caught. You know that, right?"

Hui glanced sideways, meeting Zet's eyes. "I do, now that you bring it up."

"They'd kill us in a flash."

"Right. I see what you mean," Hui said.

"You still with me?"

"All the way."

The Captain steered the boat into an open berth between a dozen other vessels. As they glided sideways against the watersteps, sailors tossed lines to men onshore. Everywhere, people moved and chattered in the flickering lamplight.

Zet's eyes swept left and right, searching for the temple. He expected to see pillars rising in the darkness, the shadows of colossal statues, dark and undefined, looming over vast temple grounds. All he saw were tents and people.

He smelled meat roasting and his stomach grumbled.

"I wonder where we're going to stay?" Hui said.

"I guess we'll find out when we talk to Senna, the architect."

Hopefully not with Jafar. He might have helped Zet, but Zet still didn't trust him. Jafar seemed to have his own agenda, and Zet had no idea what that agenda was.

Hui shouldered his pack. "Ready?"

Zet still needed to get his hidden scroll. But Kontar was leaned up against the captain's cabin door, as if making sure everyone cleared the deck before he did the same. Zet pulled Hui out of view.

"I need to grab our papers. But I don't see how, Kontar is watching like a jackal."

Hui cracked his knuckles. "Good thing I'm a fast runner." With that, Hui shouldered his bag and sauntered around the corner.

Zet risked a peek.

Hui reached Kontar's side. He crooked a finger at the sailor. The man frowned and bent closer. Hui cupped his hands and said something to him. The man's face turned a bloody shade of red. He lunged at Hui, but Hui danced out of the way.

Hui raised his right hand high. In it, he held Kontar's dagger.

"Fetch," Hui shouted, and sent it flying toward shore.

Zet could just see the dagger's point drive its way into the dirt. Then Hui and Kontar were running. With a roar that made Zet's hair stand on end, Kontar retrieved his prized possession and sprinted after Hui. *The man would kill him!*

Zet needed to act fast.

Quickly, he crouched and dug in the vegetable crate for his scroll.

"Are you still here?" came the Captain's voice.

Zet flinched.

He whipped around, expecting to meet the Captain's eyes. But the Captain was facing the gangplank, a good twenty steps away. Zet let out a soft breath, realizing the man was speaking to someone else. Heavy footsteps sounded on the swaying walkway. Someone was coming aboard.

Zet closed the crate's lid. Getting the scroll had to wait. He knew he should get back into the shadows as far as he could. But maybe he could learn something. He crouched lower.

"Still here? Of course I'm still here," came the jolly reply. "Exactly where you left me."

"I didn't leave you," the Captain said, sounding annoyed. "You do what you want. Like always. So don't pull me into it."

This caused a bark of laughter. "So I do. Good to see you too, brother."

"Why are you hanging around this camp?" the Captain said.

"I like it here."

"You like it when there's something to be had," the Captain said.

"You're always down on me, aren't you? My big, impressive, firstborn brother. Once in a while, you could say something nice."

There was a heavy pause.

"I'm sorry," the Captain growled. "I'd like to see you settled, is all."

"Worried about your reputation is how I see it," the brother said.

Zet could feel the tension, even without seeing them.

"I offered you a sailor's position."

"Work for you? Forget it," came the younger brother's voice. "But I'd take another duck hunting trip. How about it? You and me, up to the marshes in your big boat? The camp's still buzzing about the last feast we supplied."

"Not this time. I have some troubles I have to get back and deal with. But Darius—" He lowered his voice, and Zet strained to hear. "What's the word on the Princess?"

Zet perked up, instantly alert.

"They're not going to find her," Darius said.

"Wipe that grin off your face. It's a good thing we were duck hunting when she was kidnapped, or I'd think you were involved."

"Me?"

"It's your kind of game, isn't it? Fast money?"

"Like you said," snarled Darius, "We were duck hunting. And this is what I get? Accusations? Some family reunion."

The Captain said nothing.

Darius laughed as if trying to ease the tension. "I hope you're not leaving without saying hi to Nan."

The Captain blew out a breath. "If I see her tonight, good. If not, give my little sister my regards."

"How about leaving me your rowboat 'till you get back?"

At this, Zet twisted toward the small boat several feet behind him. His hands went slick with fear. He tensed, preparing to bolt for new cover.

"Are you serious? Leave you my skiff?" The Captain let out an explosive snort. "It's always about what you can get out of me. Well, I've given you plenty. And it all ends up broken. I'm tired of playing father."

"As if you could."

"Get a life, Darius. And stay out of mine."

"Gladly."

Footsteps tromped down the gangway. Zet waited for the Captain to follow, but the man stayed on deck. Hui must be frantic by now, wondering what was going on. That is, if Kontar hadn't caught him— Hui could be hurt. What if the Captain didn't bother to go to dinner and stayed here all night?

Zet sank into a sitting position. At least he'd learned something. Whatever the Captain was hiding had nothing to do with the kidnapping. He could cross the Captain and Kontar off his suspect list. He realized he'd scored his first point. Unfortunately, it meant he was back to having no real suspects.

It seemed like forever, but finally the Captain made his way off the boat.

Zet yanked up the crate's lid. He dug deep, grabbed his scroll, and stuffed it in his pack. Then he stood and ran for shore, glad for the cover of darkness.

SENNA

A desert wind was blowing, kicking up sand. Zet glanced along the wharf, blinking in the dust, but saw no sign of Hui. Worry gripped him. The area was deserted. Hitching his pack over his shoulder, he hurried for the lights and noise.

A giant, dusty tent proved to be the mess area. He reached the flap and pulled it open.

Inside, there had to be a hundred workmen. Again, Zet felt overwhelmed at the thought of investigating so many people. They sat in makeshift circles on the ground. Everyone was eating and talking, and the noise was deafening.

Zet heard a familiar shout.

He spotted Hui, sitting beside Jafar. Relief washed over him. With them were construction workers from the boat, along with half a dozen unfamiliar faces.

"Over here!" Hui shouted, jumping up and waving his arms. "Come on, what took you so long?" His face was flushed, and he was grinning. So much for being worried. Clearly, Hui was having the time of his life.

A smile creased Zet's face, and again he felt glad to have Hui there.

Zet weaved through the crowd.

When he reached Hui, several men made room. Zet smiled and thanked them, sinking down gratefully. Large bowls in the center of the group had clearly been piled with food but were now mostly empty. Zet grabbed a dish and scavenged what he could. He cursed himself for being delayed. He was starving. Two dates, a burnt bread crust and a few slices of zucchini would never fill him up.

"What did you say to Kontar?" Zet asked with a grin.

Hui looked impish. "Something about his mother and baboons."

Laughing, Zet made quick work of his meal. "Thanks. I guess we better check in with Senna."

Standing, he glanced both ways for Kontar. Even though the scary sailor was no longer a suspect, Zet was glad the man was leaving tomorrow. He took one final look and saw no sign of him. Kontar must have headed back to the ferry.

At the exit, a tall, narrow-faced man stopped Zet. "You are the new boy?"

"We just got here, if that's what you mean," Hui said.

The man looked from one to the other. "The architect informed me to expect only a single runner."

"I brought a friend," Zet said.

The man raised one thin brow. "Indeed. Follow me."

The man, who informed them his name was Ari, led them back down to the wharf's edge. They passed the big boat Zet and Hui had arrived on, and several others.

Ahead, tied up near a statue of Ra, lay a small, sleek vessel. The boat was painted with curling designs in gold leaf. In the rear, a sun canopy with open sides roofed in the deck. Under the canopy, plump cushions lay scattered in an inviting, messy jumble. From there, a long, polished wood cabin stretched down the vessel's middle. Talk about luxurious.

"Here we are," Ari said, and motioned them up the walkway.

On deck, the ship smelled of oiled acacia. Here and there, glints of gold gleamed in the twinkling lamplight. A carved falcon's head guarded the cabin door.

Zet felt like everyone here must speak in hallowed whispers.

The illusion broke when the cabin door slammed open.

A scrawny, white-haired man stood on the threshold. His eyebrows jutted out like giant white feathers. His sparse hair was surprisingly long. It stood mostly on end, flying this way and that in the gentle breeze. With his skinny arms and legs and jutting belly, he looked like a scrawny water bird.

The man's face broke into a toothy smile. "What's the hold up, Ari?"

The man bowed. "Master, I came as quickly as . . ."

"Yes, yes." Senna waved a bony hand at Ari. "Never mind, they're here. Go away. No, on second thought, bring us refreshments. Chamomile tea, sweet cakes, almonds, whatever you can drum up from that stingy cook of mine."

"But the boys just ate!" Ari said.

The architect ignored him. He motioned to Zet and Hui, his tunic flapping around his limbs. "Come in. This breeze is giving me arthritis."

Zet and Hui glanced at one another. Zet struggled with a terrible desire to laugh, which he definitely did not want to do. He could see Hui felt the same, because Hui pressed his lips together and made a wide-eyed face.

The cabin was long, all shifting shadows and flickering light. Piles of scrolls lay everywhere. Some were filed neatly in holes in the wall, but most were heaped on low tables or overflowed from baskets. A desk held writing implements: cakes of ink, drawing brushes and tools. The white-haired man maneuvered between the chaos. He made his way to a low table, surrounded by cushions.

"This way," he called, sweeping the table's contents into an already full basket. "And close that door behind you!"

"Yes, sir," Zet said.

"And don't call me sir! I'm ancient enough already without being called sir. It's Senna. And if Ari tells you otherwise, ignore him. Stiff bird, that one."

Zet glanced back and saw Ari had returned.

"Master," Ari said, "I've roused the cook. She's taking care of your order."

Senna was easing himself onto a cushion. He looked up and beamed. "Excellent! Probably complaining, too, the old tyrant. But I have to show some muscle once in awhile. Isn't that right, boys?"

"Er . . ." Zet said.

"Definitely," Hui agreed. "Tell her what's what!"

"My thoughts exactly," Senna said. "Wait. What's this? Two boys? Why am I seeing double?"

Ari said, "If there's anything else?"

"No, no, go away. Close the door," Senna said.

Zet said, "It's my fault. When the Queen Mother came to me for help, I asked if I could bring a friend. She agreed. This is Hui, and I'm Zet by the way."

The architect narrowed his eyes. "The Queen Mother, you say? Who said anything about the Queen Mother?"

12

THE PRIESTESS

In the dimly lit cabin Zet stared at Senna, thrown off guard. The dancing light made Senna's jutting brows look eerily like goat horns.

"I thought—" Zet began, and broke off.

Senna's eyes glittered, fixed on his face.

Zet swallowed. Was Senna testing him? "Wait." He dug through his pack and produced the tube. "Here, my papers."

Senna took the tube, opened the lid and tipped the scroll into his gnarled hand. He broke the seal and unrolled the document. He could read quickly, that was obvious. Under his strange exterior was an aura of intelligence. Maybe that's what made him a good architect—a crazy mix of wisdom and eccentricity.

Still looking at the page, Senna spoke in a non-committal voice. "Interesting."

"I also have this," Zet said, pulling the cord with the Queen Mother's ring from around his neck.

Hui gasped. "Where did you get that?"

A smile lit Senna's wrinkled features. "Well now. I'd say the chase is on!"

Zet blew out a huge sigh of relief. "Good. I hope it's okay if we get right to it? I have a lot of questions. Mostly, I want to know how Princess Meritamon disappeared. Wasn't she guarded?"

"Hush!" Senna said, waving his arms wildly. "Don't say her name!"

"Sorry," Zet said, wincing.

"Sound carries over water," Senna said.

"Who else knows besides us?" Hui asked.

"Ari, of course," Senna said. "Her closest servants, and one or two medjay. As for the rest of the medjay, they think they're searching for a priestess. So does everyone in the camp. And it's vital we keep it that way."

"What about the Captain of the boat we came here on?" Zet asked. "Does he know who she is?"

"Definitely not."

Zet frowned. His mind flashed back to the conversation he'd overheard between the Captain and his brother. The Captain had asked about the *Princess*. But maybe Zet had heard wrong. Maybe he'd said *Priestess*. The words sounded similar, and they'd been whispering.

"Got something to say, spit it out," Senna said.

"It's nothing. Go on," Zet said.

At that moment, a ruddy-faced woman entered bearing a tray of delicious scented sweetmeats and a large cake. She set the tray down, left and returned with a steaming pot of tea. Then she fussed around, serving out generous slices of cake to Zet and Hui. Zet, who was starving, took his plate gratefully.

"Need some meat on those bones," she told him, her cheeks dimpling as he dug in.

"What about me?" Senna crowed.

She set a plate down in front of the scrawny architect. "You'll get indigestion eating this late."

"Oh good," Senna said. "Some excitement to look forward to."

She ignored him. To Zet and Hui, she said, "Try my glazed apricots. They're delicious."

"We will," they assured her as she bustled out the door, humming a tune.

"Indigestion, indeed," Senna said. "Now. Where were we?"

"You were telling us what happened when the . . . *Priestess* got here."

"Excellent. Yes. Thoroughness, that's what we need. A top to bottom telling of events. Let's see, she arrived by boat six days ago with half a dozen servants. She docked three boats down." He pointed to the wall, as if they could see through it. "I wanted her next to me, but others had arrived first, and since no one knew who she was, she couldn't claim precedence. But that's no matter." He waved his hand. "After she got settled, she came right here. A bright girl! And interested, too. We went over the drawings of her father's temple. She wanted to know what had been done, and what was still left to do. Of course, we're only early in the temple construction." He rambled on about columns and mud bricks, and how they'd moved blocks to the site for use, which had taken nearly a year in itself.

Zet finished his cake. Hoping it wouldn't be rude to take another slice, he did.

"But you don't want to hear about all that," Senna scolded, "Why are you letting me ramble?"

"Er—sorry!" Zet said, glancing at Hui.

"We're interested in all of it!" Hui cried. Being an artist, he clearly meant it.

Zet, however, did his best to shift topics. "Where was she kidnapped from? Her boat?"

"No." Senna took a long sip of tea. "Since you've just arrived, I should explain the layout here. To get to the temple, you must walk inland fifteen minutes. That's why I need a runner. I work from my boat. Doctor's orders." He toyed with his cake. "For three days in a row, she set out on a little mule to visit my construction site. The distance is too far for her."

"But it's only a fifteen minute walk," Zet said. Princess Merit, with her bright, laughing face, didn't seem like the type to insist on some old mule to get around.

"Why would she ride an old donkey?" Hui said.

Senna said, "How the healthy scorn the weak!"

"Weak? What's weak about her?"

Senna drummed his bony fingers. Then he cleared his throat. "Here's a little known secret, so keep it to yourselves. That bright young girl has a deformed spine. She was born with a back that curves like a disobedient old tree." He nodded, watching their faces. "Not only is she in continual pain, it affects her health greatly."

Zet's jaw dropped. "But that's—"

"Impossible!" Hui said, finishing Zet's thought.

"Oh, she takes great pains to hide it. You never see it in her face. She's livelier than anyone. Maybe that's why. She doesn't want people to know. And if you care for her, you'll keep it to yourselves. I only tell you for the sake of this investigation."

"You don't need to worry," Zet said. "Her secret's safe."

"So now you see why she went by mule."

"She must be in agony, wherever they're keeping her," Hui said, looking as furious as Zet felt.

"How long have they had her?" Zet said, fists clenched.

"Four days." Senna smoothed his brows with a shaking hand. "I told her to take more attendants. Stubborn girl. *A priestess is not surrounded by attendants, Senna. People will wonder!* Her words. She didn't take one man with her. Just two girls. I should have insisted."

Zet wanted to say it wasn't Senna's fault, but was it?

Senna stared at his barely touched piece of cake. He sighed and pushed it away.

CONSEQUENCES

Questions raced through Zet's head as he stared across the table at the architect.

"Where was she kidnapped from, exactly?"

"A partially constructed chapel."

"With so many workers, someone must have seen *something*," Hui said.

"We're not working on the chapel at present, and it backs onto unused land. Shrubs and tall grasses. It's easy to go there without being seen."

"Whose idea was it to go there?" Zet said.

"Hers, I assume."

Zet wasn't so sure. "What about her attendants? The girls? What happened to them?"

"One was kidnapped. The other's here."

"Here? How did she get away?" Zet said, stunned.

"By pure luck. The Priestess had sent the girl to investigate a loud crash. While the handmaiden was gone, the kidnappers moved in."

"A crash?"

"There was a construction accident. The girl returned to the chapel, found them missing and raised the alarm."

"And that was four days ago?"

"Yes."

Zet rubbed his face. "Four days. She could be anywhere by now."

"Well, don't forget the ransom, and the agreement. If there's to be a handover, she can't be too far away."

"True."

Hui said, "What exactly do the Hyksos want?"

"They want Pharaoh to remove our army's blockade at Avaris. We're winning by preventing the Hyksos from getting reinforcements."

"How did the kidnappers even know the Priestess was you-know-who?"

"Khamudi, the rebel leader, must have spies here."

The cake in Zet's stomach felt heavy. "Would Pharaoh remove the blockade?"

"Canaan warriors would more than double the Hyksos army. We'd be sorely outnumbered. Everything we've fought for the last twenty years would be lost."

"Then that's not going to happen. We'll find her," Zet said.

"Don't make promises you can't keep." Senna unfolded his ancient limbs and got to his feet with a grimace. "It's late. Ari is constructing a tent for you boys. As to whether he's capable, I'll let you find out."

Zet still had questions, but it was obvious the interview was over.

He and Hui scrambled up.

"Be here first thing tomorrow," Senna said.

"Wait," Zet said, "I was wondering, what happened to your original runner? The one who worked for you before we got here?"

Senna put his bony fists on his hips. "Ill."

Zet frowned. "He's ill?"

"That's what I said. Now good night."

Outside, Hui said. "Ill? I don't believe it for a minute. What a strange thing to say."

"What do you think happened to him?"

Hui made a slicing motion across his throat.

"Don't be stupid," Zet said with a nervous laugh.

The cook appeared on deck and told them where to find Ari.

The tent was leaning ominously to one side when Zet and Hui reached it. A roar came from inside. A long arm shot out, and then a foot, and then the whole thing tumbled into a heap.

"Flea dung!" shouted Ari from inside.

Zet and Hui hurried to rescue him. Ari appeared from the folds, his face red and his hair damp with sweat.

"Hey," said Hui. "Should be easy with three of us."

Fifteen minutes later, they stared at their lopsided creation scratching their heads.

"I thought you said this would be easy," Zet said.

"Yeah, well." Hui raised his shoulder, sheepish. "It's a roof. It's windy out here and calm in there. I'm beat, and I'm going to sleep."

"Good idea."

"Excellent idea," Ari said. "Allow me to bid you good night." The tall man bowed and made a hasty retreat. Clearly, he didn't want any more to do this evening.

Neither did Zet.

Yawning, he crawled inside with his pack. Bedding had been provided. Zet barely registered the soft coverings. He lay down, rested his head in the crook of his elbow, and dozed off.

The next morning, Zet woke later than planned. He shook Hui. "Wake up!"

Hui fought him off with a few slugs.

Ducking, Zet said. "Quit it, it's me!"

Hui rubbed his eyes. "So it is." He grinned. "Nothing like a bad dream to get me out of bed."

"Thanks. Speaking of bad dreams, you have drool on your face."

"Explains why I'm so thirsty," Hui replied. "I must have drooled myself dry."

"Gross." Zet grinned and crawled out of their crooked tent.

In broad daylight, the mysterious shadows of night had disappeared. He went still, taking in the spectacular view.

Rosy dawn splashed the circular bay with sparkles and streaks of colored light. The water undulated with soft movement. Boats rocked here and there. Their tie ropes, dripping with water, rose and fell with the creaking vessels. In the distant shallows, ibis birds poked around where the bay met a sandy shore.

"We're not in Thebes any more," Hui said.

"That's for sure." Zet's family and home seemed an impossible distance away. "I wonder how my mother and Kat are doing?"

"I wonder if Kat's still mad at me. Do you think she's still mad?"

"She's probably found another boy to crush on," Zet said.

Hui's mouth dropped open. "What? Really? No! Do you think so?"

Zet groaned. "It was a joke. Not to change the subject, but it's late. Let's split up—grab us breakfast and I'll find out what Senna wants us to do."

"Good idea," Hui said, rubbing his belly. "I'm starved." With that, he took off for the mess tent.

Back on board the architect's boat, Ari and Zet bid each other good morning.

"He's waiting for you," Ari said.

Zet crossed the sun-warmed planks and let himself through the door.

Senna sat at his desk, buried up to his elbows in scrolls. The old man looked up. He wore a beaded wig, which might have made him look more dignified. Except that the wig was slightly off kilter. His white brows were feather-like as ever, and shot up at the sight of Zet.

"There's no explanation for it," Senna said. "It's a waste!"

TROUBLE

Zet hovered in the architect's doorway. "Er . . . can I help, sir?" He remembered belatedly that Senna asked him not to call him sir, but Senna seemed too distressed to notice.

"Not unless you can make me a new obelisk!" He glared at Zet. "It'll take weeks to bring a new stone here. And have it carved and . . . oh, never mind!" He waved a hand as if to bat the subject away.

Zet shuffled his feet. Finally, he said, "I came for my orders?"

"Of course you have." Senna scrubbed his forehead, shoving the wig further back. He blew out a sigh. "Can you draw?"

"Not well."

Senna's lips curled down. "That's unfortunate." He shuffled through the piles on his desk. Then he moved to the baskets. Finally, he pulled out a scroll, held it aloft and shouted, "Ha! Here it is. My original drawing plan. Well, don't just stand there with your mouth hanging, come!" Senna spread the scroll across the low table. "Hold that corner down."

Zet put his fist on it.

"Here," Senna said, tapping the drawing with a bony finger. "The spot where she disappeared. When I'm done, that chapel will house a great shrine, and only the High Priest will be allowed to enter."

"I'll go there right now," Zet said.

"Yes. Good. The medjay have searched it, of course, but it's best if you see the sight for yourself."

"Definitely. Can I take this with me?"

"Take it, mark it. Clues and all that. Anything unusual, mark it down for me. Then bring it back."

"All right." Zet doubted there would be any clues left at this point. What he wanted to do was start asking people questions. "What should I mark it with?"

Senna produced a stick of charcoal. "Can you manage with this?"

"I can't write, but I'll do my best."

"Good enough." Senna frowned, as if noticing something. "Where's your partner?"

"Fetching breakfast."

"Late rising, hey? Go outside and find Ari. He has your uniform. Get changed, drag your friend from the old feeding trough and have him report in."

"No disrespect, but I can tell Hui our instructions on our way to the site."

"Hui won't be joining you. I still need a proper runner. Hui's it."

Zet tried to mask his disappointment. He saw no point arguing. Hui could still ask questions while running messages to and fro, couldn't he? In fact, spread out, he and Hui could cover more ground.

On deck, Ari handed him a tunic with the architect's mark stitched across the chest and back. Over the tunic went a belt with loops and pouches. Zet buckled it and tucked the drawing plans into one loop. Then he went to find Hui.

There was no sign of him on shore. Zet headed for the mess tent, wondering what could have held him up.

"Let go of me!" shouted a voice.

"Hui," Zet groaned. What in the name of the gods was he up to?

He soon caught sight of the scuffle. Three medjay were jumping around a small, struggling figure. One medjay got a kick in the shins; another pinned the boy's arms back.

A crowd had formed. It grew larger by the minute. Zet sprinted toward them.

"Stop struggling!" shouted one medjay.

"I found it," Hui said fiercely. "Tell the stupid girl it was there already!"

The girl in question was probably Zet's age. Her thin arms clutched a large, leather bag. The bag was wet, and drops pooled at her beaded sandals. Clearly she didn't enjoy being called stupid. Her cheeks were red, offsetting the deep black color of her hair. Her eyes were striking, large and lined with kohl. Despite her anger, she was very pretty.

"He was stealing them!" she shouted. "He's a thief!"

"I am not a thief!" Hui shouted back.

"Then what were you doing with this bag?"

"Don't worry, miss," a medjay said, fastening Hui's wrists with rope. "He'll be dealt with."

Zet stared, stunned as the medjay hauled Hui off. Hui kept struggling and hadn't spotted Zet in the crowd.

Flea dung! This was the last thing they needed.

"What happened?" Zet demanded, turning to face the scowling girl.

Her flashing eyes raked over him. "It's none of your business."

Hui might be a joker, but he would never steal someone's stupid bag. The idea was ridiculous. Not that she'd understand.

"We both work for the architect. I'll have to explain to my boss why he's lost a runner. Could you please at least give me an idea of what happened?"

Patches of color appeared in her cheeks. "I found him crouched along the river, holding the bag."

"Maybe he was just washing his hands?"

She put her fists on her slim hips and leaned forward. "He wasn't. I saw him with it!"

"Maybe he found it?"

"Found it?" Her cheeks flushed deeper and she stomped her foot. "Just like a boy to not believe me! He was tying the bag to a branch so it wouldn't float away. I caught him doing it! I saw him! Do you have any idea of the value of what's in here? No, of course you don't. That's why you don't understand."

"You're right, I don't," he said stiffly so as not to laugh. Which was ridiculous, because this was horribly serious. She reminded him of his favorite cat, clutching some feline prize.

She held the bag tighter. "They're my mistress's jewels."

"Jewels?" His throat constricted. "Uh, and who, exactly, is your mistress?"

"The Priestess who was kidnapped four days ago."

Zet felt like he'd been crushed flat by a giant boulder. This girl was Princess Merit's handmaiden. And Hui had been found with a bag of royal jewels.

"This is terrible," he choked out.

She sat down on a weathered stone. "You have no idea."

Zet sank down beside her. "Why, by the toes of Bastet, did she bring something so valuable here?"

It was more of a lament than an actual question. The girl, however, said, "She wanted to wear them to a special event. After we left."

Zet nodded, thinking that one minute the Princess had been looking forward to her fourteenth birthday party, and the next she was caged in some horrible place, wondering if she was going to die.

The girl sighed. "Sometimes life has a way of taking us by surprise," she said quietly.

He followed her gaze across the lush soil and into the dry hills beyond. The swaying palms marked the edge of the humid earth. Once you passed those shady guardians, the world became all blinding heat. A waterless desert filled with deadly scorpions, snakes, hyenas and lions, waiting to claim your life. If thirst didn't kill you first.

Where could they have taken the princess?

"Is there any news from the medjay? They're looking for her, aren't they?" he said.

"Yes. Not that it's done any good."

"I'm sorry," he said, realizing she and Princess Merit must be close friends.

She said, "Without that runner, will you have to do double the work?"

Hui. He had to get Hui free. They'd have to let him go!

She watched his face. "It's good the boy was caught."

"Well—"

"You don't want to be working with a thief, do you?"

"Right. I mean, no." Zet felt horrible at pretending Hui was a thief. He couldn't tell her Hui was his best friend. She seemed nice and he hated deceiving her, but he had a job to do. This was an opportunity to find out first hand what happened to the Princess. Anyway, she wanted the same thing, right?

"I guess I better go," she said.

Seeing his chance slipping away, he blurted, "Look, I'm just a messenger boy, but I want to help find your priestess."

She stiffened. "I don't see how you could."

"I don't know either."

Her shoulders relaxed and she sighed. "Thanks for offering."

"What's your name?"

"Naunet. What's yours, messenger boy?"

"Zet."

"Well, Zet, I have to go put this away." She rose. "Perhaps I'll see you again."

He sat there dumbly, watching her flit off like a little bird with her white dress fanning out behind and wondered why he enjoyed hearing her say his name so much.

Speaking of names, why did hers sound so familiar? *Naunet.* Had the Queen Mother mentioned it? No. Nothing came to him.

Hui flashed into his mind and he felt suddenly sick.

How were they going to get out of this?

It was time to go help Hui. Zet ran in the direction the medjay had taken him.

15

ARRESTED

Blue sky arched overhead, rich as royal turquoise. Palm fronds cast jagged shadows over the warm earth underfoot. A scorpion scuttled across Zet's path, its tail curved in the familiar, deadly arch. Zet skidded to a halt. The creature paid him no notice. It went on its way, scuffling into the dry grass. If Zet had been running any faster, he'd have stepped on it. Probably puncturing his foot in the process.

He could be brave about a lot of things, but poison wasn't one of them. What a horrible, terrifying death that would be. He shuddered.

From now on, he'd have to be more careful where he stepped out here.

Moments later, he spotted Hui far along the wharf. Shoulders sunburnt after their two days on the boat, Hui sat on a stone block looking sullen. Two medjay stood there, one on either side. Behind them, an official medjay police boat was tied up securely. The medjay's symbol was painted on its hull and sewn into a flag that fluttered atop the mast.

Hui glanced up as Zet neared. His eyes brightened and he scrambled to his feet.

"Sit down!" one medjay barked.

Hui sat. He crossed his arms, grumbling about stuck up girls who were too stupid to see he was telling the truth.

Nerves clenched Zet's belly. "I'm sure we can explain this. It was just a big mistake."

"And who might you be?" one medjay asked.

"We work together."

"Not anymore. Now clear off."

Zet's hands were sweating. "If you come with me and talk to our boss—"

"I'll do no such thing!" roared the closest medjay. "This is official business. If you don't leave immediately, I'll arrest you too."

"But sir—"

"And still you keep talking! One more word and I swear you'll be thrown in shackles for the rest of your short life."

Hui leaped to his feet. "You have no right!"

The medjay grabbed Hui, and was about to deal him a heavy blow when a deep voice boomed, "What's all this, then?"

"Commander, you're here, thank the gods," said the nearest medjay.

He snorted. "You called me back to deal with two boys?"

Zet stared at the commander's face in disbelief. As of yet, the commander hadn't looked at him. The man stood taller than the rest. His chest was broad and muscled, and he had hands the size of platters. A wide belt circled his muscled midsection, and a sword hung from a loop. His brows were thick, and his square jaw was shadowed with a faint hint of stubble. He turned his eyes on Zet. His mouth opened in surprise.

"Zet?" he said in disbelief.

Zet grinned, so glad to see his old friend Merimose that he wanted to shout with joy.

Merimose shifted to squint at Hui. His disbelief turned to outrage. "Hui, too? By every god, what in Ra's name are you boys doing here?"

Despite the big man's tone, Zet felt relieved. He and Merimose had had their share of run-ins back in Thebes—most of them good.

Even if Merimose did have a way of forgetting how helpful Zet had been in past cases, he'd get Hui free. Zet felt sure of it.

To the men, Merimose said. "You're dismissed." To Zet and Hui, he said, "On board. Both of you. We need to have a little chat."

The nearest medjay protested. "Commander, I'd like to report what this boy was doing."

"I'll get a full explanation. Don't you worry." He glared at Zet and Hui.

The medjay shrugged. Then, with fresh orders from Merimose, he and the other man marched off with their weapons jingling at their sides.

This was the third boat Zet had been on in as many days. It was as different as the other two. Everything about it seemed ship-shape and official. More sparkling clean than his mother's kitchen, the deck practically squeaked underfoot. Merimose ushered them into the central cabin. It was like a miniature version of the office in Thebes. Cubbyholes held neatly rolled scrolls. The place gleamed with efficiency. At present, it was empty.

Merimose shut the door.

"Explain yourselves," he growled.

Zet and Hui started in at once, both talking over each other.

"Stop!" Merimose said, raising a hand. "Zet, you first. Don't you have a pottery stall to run? If I hear you've come because—no, that's not possible. No one knows except myself and a few others." He rubbed his head. "Why are you here?"

"Well . . . " Zet began. "It's not true, exactly, that no one knows about—"

"This is outrageous!" Merimose said. "If you tell me you're here because of some rhino-brained idea that you're an investigator . . . oh, by the beard of Osiris, I can read it in your face! That *is* why you're here. How did you possibly find out? Of all the ridiculous things a boy could do!"

"It wasn't my idea," Zet said quickly. He glanced at Hui for help.

Hui's mouth dropped open. "Don't look at me, I'm in enough trouble."

"Yes," Merimose said drily. "We'll get to that."

"Look." Zet lowered his voice to a whisper. "The Queen Mother came to me. She figured I could help, just ask questions, that's all."

"She did, did she?"

"I'll prove it!" Zet pulled out the Queen Mother's ring.

Merimose waved his huge right hand. "Put it away. Whatever you might be, you're not a liar. Not about something like that. But Queen Mother or not, I can't have you running all over, upsetting my investigation and getting underfoot!"

"We're working for the architect as runners. We won't be!"

Merimose rubbed his face and sighed. "You already are. Want to explain what happened out there?"

Hui said, "It was a simple mix up. Honest. I'm making a lock, and I needed a piece of wood to make a pin. I saw the bush along the river's edge, and was going to cut off a piece. There was a rope dangling from the bush into the water. I was curious, so I pulled on it, the bag came up, and then that girl showed up and started screaming at me. I didn't even know that some jewels were in there until later!"

Merimose said, "You found a bag of jewels? Great. Just great. Who was the girl?"

"Naunet is her name," Zet said.

Hui glanced at him like he was a traitor. "You talked to her?"

"Naunet?" Merimose said. "It gets even better! Not only did you find jewels, they're royal jewels."

Zet and Hui were silent. Zet didn't like the look on Merimose's face.

"I can't let you go, Hui. I'm going to have to lock you up."

"What?" Hui gasped. "But I'm innocent!"

Merimose grimaced. "I believe you. But others won't. You'll have to stand trial."

"Stand trial?" Hui blanched. "Are you serious?"

"Unless we find out who put that bag in the river, I'm afraid I am."

Sweat broke out on Zet's forehead. "You're the Commander, the head medjay."

"Yes. Which means I have to uphold the law. I'm sorry boys, my hands are tied."

"This can't be happening." Zet stared at Hui's pale face. "Don't worry. There's no way I'm letting you stand trial. I brought you here. I'm going to find out who did this."

"No," Merimose said. "You're going to leave things to me and my men."

Zet's mouth opened. He glared at the commander.

"If you want to keep working for the architect, I can't stop you. As for this case, drop it. If you start poking around, you put not only you, me and my men at danger, you might get the Princess killed."

Hands in fists, Zet stared at the scrubbed wooden floor.

"Do you understand me?" Merimose asked.

Zet nodded.

"I mean it. These people are vicious. They've kidnapped *Pharaoh's* daughter. They plan on winning their battle against Egypt with this move. If they suspect you're snooping around, you're dead." He paused. "And as for that ring you're wearing? I advise you to find a spot and bury it. One look and they'll know you're the Queen Mother's spy."

Hui shot Zet a frightened look.

"It's time you went back to shore," Merimose said.

A PRIEST'S WORK

Zet stood on the wharf, wondering how things had turned so badly.

Hui was going to have to face trial. If they found him guilty, he'd be put to death. The image was so bleak, his legs felt numb. He sat heavily on a stone block and stared blankly ahead.

Hui, dead?

Zet couldn't give in to panic. If he did, Hui would be lost for certain.

He tried to summon his courage. There was only one way to save him. Unravel the mystery, fast.

Back at Senna's boat, he gave Ari the news. Then he left quickly. Back on shore, Zet's skin prickled with a sense of being watched. He glanced at the gently rocking boats, but saw no one. His fingers went to the ring hidden on the chain around his neck.

He needed to hide it, but not in broad daylight. He'd wait until night.

His stomach grumbled loudly. He cursed at it, but knew he needed food. He took one last glance at the medjays' boat. Then he skirted by the dining tent like a dog looking for stray scraps.

"Meal's over!" said a woman clearing away the last of the empty platters.

"I don't suppose you have leftovers? I missed it."

"Wake up earlier, next time!"

He went outside. Behind the tent lay the cooking area with a giant fire pit and huge pots for making meals to feed a crowd. He spotted a basket with a heel of bread. It would have to do.

"Oho, no you don't!" shouted the cook. "You're the one whose been nibbling at my stores! You already got a cooked meat pie last night!"

"That wasn't me," Zet said.

She relented. "All right then. Can't have you fainting. Grab a handful of dates while you're at it. In the sack behind the beer jug."

He grabbed the bread and dates. "Thank you!"

He headed for the temple in the distance, chewing as he went.

"Boy, hey!" came a man's voice. "You there, stop!"

Zet turned. It was the priest from the boat. The man stood in the shade of a palm tree. His linen kilt was so white it was nearly blinding. How did he manage to keep it so clean in a place like this?

"Hurry," the priest said. "How dare you keep me waiting?"

Zet frowned. "Whoever you're waiting for, it's not me. I'm on business for the architect. And I have to get going."

The priest eyed Zet sharply. "The architect's business can wait. I am the High Priest of Osiris. You will do my bidding."

At this, Zet gulped. High Priest to Osiris, God of the Underworld? So that's why the man had such dark energy. A chill ran down Zet's spine. He definitely didn't want to risk stirring up the wrath of the mighty God of the Dead.

"What do you need me to do?" Zet asked.

The priest motioned to the large wooden chest at his feet. The sides were inlaid with gold and jewels. The top looked extremely strange, like it was made out of the wings of some large bird. A falcon perhaps.

"Carry this and follow me," the priest said. He set off in the direction of the half-constructed temple of Pharaoh Ahmose.

Zet hurried to get the rectangular box. He had to stretch his arms wide to grasp the rope handles on either end. It took two tries to heft it off the ground. Now, with the strange feather lid so close to his face, he saw that it was definitely wings. Four of them, all stitched together and held in place with leather hinges on one side.

Chills rippled along Zet's forearms where they touched the thing. Eerie.

What was in there that was so heavy? Zet was wiry, but strong for his size given that he spent most days hefting heavy pottery jugs, urns and stacks of plates around his stall back home. Lean muscles stood out on his arms. He tightened his handhold and hurried to catch up.

"I guess you know about the missing priestess?"

The man didn't answer.

A thought struck. "Wait, is that why you've come?"

The man walked faster.

Was it possible the Queen Mother had sent the priest, too? If so, they were working for the same cause. "Are you here to help?"

The priest paused. "Her disappearance has placed a stain on this holy ground."

What was that supposed to mean? It wasn't her fault she was kidnapped.

The priest sped up.

Zet decided to try again. "The architect asked me to go to the chapel where she was taken. He wants to start building there soon. I know it's none of my business, but I was thinking—maybe you want to come with me? Being a holy man, you'd be able to spot anything out of place."

The priest turned and snapped, "The matter has nothing to do with you. Remember your place, serving boy."

Zet felt his cheeks turn hot.

He swallowed, thinking of the Queen Mother who'd sent him with so much trust. He had no business trying to solve this case! What was he doing here? Everything was all messed up.

Time was slipping away. Hui was facing a death trial. Zet had learned nothing about the Princess's hostage location. Pharaoh would be here in a few days. Panic rose and he shoved it down.

The priest began to chant. More like a stream of low sounds than actual words. He marched to the creepy tune.

In Zet's arms, the box shuddered of its own accord. His eyes flicked to the priest, and back to the flimsy feather lid. Sweat stood out on his chest and arms.

What was in there?

Ahead, stone pillars and half built walls rose to the sky. They were nearing the construction site. Men moved in teams, building, carving, painting. Before Zet could breathe a sigh of relief, however, the priest kept going.

Whatever was inside the box shifted again.

Zet kept his eyes on the lid, trying to see between the feathers.

"Stop and kneel," the priest said.

"What?" Zet glanced up. He'd been so focused on the chest he hadn't noticed anything else.

He sucked in a shocked breath.

He stood at the base of a huge triangle. The building tapered in and up on all four sides, and came to a single point on top. A pyramid! He'd heard of such things, but never dreamed he'd see one. The angled walls shone in the sunlight, so smooth you wanted to run up to them and glide your hand over the surface.

Instead, Zet set the chest down and sank to his knees.

"This will be the burial place of Pharaoh," the priest said. "If you value your life and your health, you will pray now to be forgiven for setting your eyes upon it."

Zet never asked to set his eyes upon it. Still, he thought it best to take the High Priest's advice, and whispered every fervent prayer he could think of.

THE BOX

"Now," the priest said, rising, "Attend me to the entrance."

Zet rose, hefted the box up again and headed for the pyramid's arched entryway.

"That is a false door. Only spirits may pass through it."

The priest marched around the pyramid's far side. Zet struggled after him with the monstrous box. When he rounded the corner, he spotted several medjay. They stood guard at the entrance to the giant structure. Something about this suddenly felt very official. The medjay were obviously waiting.

Was it because they needed to get inside, but didn't dare?

Zet gasped. "Do you think the kidnappers are hiding the priestess in there?" He was horrified, but saw how it could make a good hiding spot. No Egyptian would risk the curses for entering the pyramid. Maybe the Hyksos believed they were immune to the wrath of Egypt's gods.

"We shall see."

At the entrance, the medjay gave the priest a wide berth. Even they seemed to fear his spooky presence. A sudden tune issued from the priest's lips. It echoed sharply off the hot, slanted wall. It rose to an alarming pitch.

Zet felt his cargo thrash. Jarred by the terrifying movement, he carefully lowered the box to the ground.

As he did, the feather lid began to rise.

Startled, he crouched motionless.

The lid continued to open. A sleek, scale-covered head snaked up from the opening. The serpent's body moved and writhed, pushing itself higher, weaving back and forth. Its eyes were like glass, black and shining. Zet stared into its cold, hypnotizing gaze.

Clammy terror made his insides turn to liquid. A king cobra.

The cobra's hood opened, wide and muscled. Its colored patterns dazzled him. With a hiss, the serpent's tongue flicked out. Gaze fixed on Zet's gaping face, it reared back, revealing dagger-like fangs.

Death had come.

In a flash, the cobra shot forward.

Zet rolled onto one shoulder and tumbled away. As he scrambled to get clear, he flinched, waiting for the bite.

He heard the snake come at him through the dirt and he twisted in horror.

Then the priest was there, his hand snapping forward to catch the snake from behind. The man's sinewy fingers closed just below the cobra's head. He pulled it to his chest as if it were a pet. Meanwhile the snake hissed and spat, eyes glued to Zet.

"We have work to do," the priest told it. He turned and entered the pyramid, leaving Zet gasping in the dust.

"That was close," called one of the medjay.

Zet's heart was practically banging out of his chest. "He had me carry that box from the harbor! The lid wasn't even fastened."

"Ha! I wouldn't want to get on his bad side."

The second medjay laughed. "If we hear shouts from inside, we'll know someone has."

"Let's just hope he doesn't kill the missing priestess by mistake," said the first.

"He'd better not," Zet said in a harsh voice. Would the cobra know the difference between friend and foe? What if it killed the

Princess in her father's own burial tomb? But the priest wouldn't be so careless. Would he?

Then again, the priest had called her disappearance *a stain on this holy ground*.

Zet thought back to a time in Thebes when he'd had a run in with the High Priest of Amenemopet. Not every man was who he seemed. Not everyone could be trusted. He hoped for the Princess's sake that this man was on her side.

He stood for a long time with the two medjay, but no sounds came from inside.

"Don't you have work to do, messenger boy?" a medjay asked.

With no excuse, he had to agree. He bid them goodbye and set off for the temple construction site. As he drew near, the sounds of ringing hammers against stone filled the air. The maze of half built walls looked daunting. Everywhere, men chanted in rhythm as they worked. Some were dragging a heavy stone into place. Farther off, a tall young man led a pair of donkeys weighted down with sacks of supplies. In a wide-open area, dozens of men were bending and scooping a muddy, wet substance into molds. Brick-makers, Zet realized.

He paused on the path and pulled out the architect's scroll. Time to find the partially built chapel.

Zet studied the complex drawing. He wished Hui were here to help make sense of it! The thought of his best friend sent fresh worry coursing through him. Zet had to figure out who'd stolen those jewels.

A thought struck. *Was it possible the kidnapping and the jewel theft were connected?*

He pondered this for some time. If there was an enemy spy in the camp like Senna suggested, that spy knew the Princess. He'd be close enough to steal her jewels. And if Zet found him, he'd save Hui and Princess Meritamon in one blow.

No more time to wait. He had to find that chapel. Studying the scroll, he tried to puzzle out the diagram. The lines had to be walls.

And the breaks? Maybe they were doors? But what about the circles, and those small squares?

Finally, he just started walking.

Senna said the chapel was on the outer edge. Zet walked the worksite's perimeter. Glancing through the labyrinth of walls, he saw pillars and pylons reaching skyward. Heavy foliage forced him to turn into the site. He came across a wall painted end-to-end with a giant war scene. The mural showed Pharaoh leading his men against the Hyksos invaders. There were thousands of soldiers.

One had to be Zet's own father. Even though the faces were small and only representations of the fighting men, Zet reached out and ran his fingers over them.

"Come home safe," he whispered.

Footsteps sounded nearby. He glimpsed a medjay and started walking, quickly. He didn't want to rouse any suspicions, especially if Merimose was on site. Merimose would demand to know what he was doing. Friend or not the Commander would put a stop to Zet's investigation if he caught him disobeying his direct orders to do so.

He spotted a doorway barred off by a length of dusty fabric. The fabric was marked with the medjay's official symbol.

This was it. The site where the kidnapping had taken place.

Zet gulped and glanced around. Now or never. He raised the linen strip and ducked under.

The chapel was long and narrow. There was no roof yet, so the dirt floor was a mix of shadow and hot sunshine. Someday, this would all be decorated with spells and elaborate carvings. Even without them, it felt strange to be inside. Not just because the Princess had been kidnapped here. A mystical power seemed to grip the room with breathless silence.

Carefully, he combed the space for clues, all the while glancing back at the door.

Unfortunately, there wasn't much to see. A few dusty footprints, but that was all.

He should have figured as much.

Zet rubbed his head and blew out a frustrated breath.

THE SECRET WADI

Zet peered into the undergrowth that led away from the chapel.

The medjay must have searched for tracks. Still, it wouldn't hurt to take another quick look. He couldn't think what else to do, and time was running out.

Low scratchy bushes raked his shins. He zigzagged through them, searching for footprints or donkey hoofmarks.

Nothing.

He crouched in the shade of some waving bulrushes and pulled out the temple plans. Should he keep going?

Senna had shown him where the chapel lay. Now Zet began to understand the drawing better. He rotated it until the chapel on the page matched the chapel in the distance. Senna had only sketched a bit of the grassy area where Zet sat now.

He tried to think like the kidnappers. Which way would they go?

There were several choices. Hide here until dark, and then circle the temple perimeter, enter the mountains and hole up in a cave. It would be nearly impossible to find them.

But if they hadn't? If they'd gone straight away from the worksite, where would that take them? Zet decided to keep walking. Maybe he'd be lucky. Maybe he'd find a clue the medjay overlooked.

Standing, he glanced both ways. If someone spotted him—medjay or kidnappers—he'd be in trouble. A runner had no business combing the area for clues. As far as he could tell, no one was watching.

Stuffing the scroll in his waistband, he set off.

The scruffy bushes grew thicker the further he walked. Soon the undergrowth grew so thick that he had to stop and choose a new route. Backing up, he found a clearer way and kept going.

He was ready to give up when he noticed something. A bush crushed on one side. His heart began to race. He ran forward and discovered that the ground ahead sloped into a wadi, a marshy gorge.

He clambered down and slipped on fresh mud. When he landed on his butt, he nearly whooped at what he saw.

Hoofmarks.

There were hoofmarks! Fresh ones. A donkey had come through here. A number of them, by the look of it. *Was this the way they'd come?*

The wadi grew wider and deeper and the bluffs rose higher. Anyone could be up there and he wouldn't see them until it was too late. A wind whooshed over him, rattling dry bushes that clung to the slopes.

He began to run.

Feeling alone and exposed, he forced himself to keep going. How he wished Hui were with him. Glancing this way and that, he wound downward.

A forest of gnarled brush blocked the gulch's far end. Carefully, he approached. Holding his breath, he pried the brush apart. He had no idea what he expected to see. A hut perhaps, surrounded by guards. A cave with a guarded entryway. But he saw none of those things.

He stared in disbelief.

It was the canal.

The wadi had led him to the canal that ran between the Nile and Abydos harbor.

Disappointment flooded through him. All hope gone, Zet shoved his way through the bushes and out onto the red, sandy bank. He ran a hand over his head. He'd been so certain he was on the right track. This was nothing but a dead end.

His shoulders sagged. Finally, he turned and plodded back the way he'd come.

The hike seemed harder now. It seemed to take forever.

By the time he reached the worksite, his stomach was making fierce complaints. Judging by the sun's angle, noon and lunch had long since passed. Feeling hollow, he pushed through the last of the undergrowth.

As he emerged in front of the chapel, a man shouted at him.

"Hey! What do you think you're doing?"

Zet stood frozen, startled by the man's angry tone.

Two huge workers thrust their way toward him. The men were bare to the waist. Stone dust colored their skin, blending with their sweat. One wore leather wrist-guards that came halfway to his elbows. They made his bulging forearms look impossibly huge. The other had a soft belly, as if he'd only been doing construction for a short time. His arms were lean and patchy with fresh sunburns.

One grabbed Zet by his arm and dragged him toward the chapel.

"What's going on?" Zet said, glancing around for help. Now, when he actually wanted to see a medjay, none were in sight. His heart drummed in panic.

"Shut up." The guard thrust Zet under the linen that blocked the chapel door.

Zet sprawled in the dirt. He flipped over and leaped up as the two men followed him inside.

"What were you doing out there?" asked the sunburnt man. His voice was strangely familiar.

"I work for the architect," Zet said, stumbling back.

They kept coming at him until he was pressed against the wall.

"Out in the bushes?" The sunburnt man laughed. "What kind of work do you do in the bushes?"

"None! I came to check on the chapel," Zet said quickly. "He asked me to look for damage, and, well, I drank a lot of tea this morning. When I got here, I had to go. You know, nature calls." He swallowed and tried to look defiant. "Is there a crime against it?"

The sunburnt man eyed him closely. "The architect's a dangerous man to work for."

"Oh yeah?" Zet said. "Why's that?"

"Look what happened to his last runner-boy who came snooping."

Zet shrugged, although he felt sick with fear. "I got his job, that's all I care about."

"Is that so?"

"Why, what happened to him?" Zet asked.

The sunburnt man leaned down, right into Zet's face. His breath stank. "A horrible curse."

A warning told Zet to keep silent. Instead, he wrinkled his nose and said, "Did this curse have your name on it?"

The sunburnt man went still as death.

Big mistake, Zet decided. The Queen Mother's seal ring suddenly felt heavy against his chest. Merimose's warning came to him. He stared into the sunburnt man's eyes, wondering if he was staring into the face of Princess Merit's kidnapper. If they found it he was dead.

He needed to backtrack, fast.

Clenching his fists, he dropped his gaze to the ground. "Sorry," he muttered. "It's just, I'm new here, and I've been getting flack all day from my master."

He could feel their eyes drilling into the top of his skull.

"Hey! What's all this?" came a man's voice from the door.

All three turned. A man stood there, hands on his hips. He wore a medallion on one shoulder, and looked official. "What are you men doing? Get back to work."

The sunburnt man took a step back from Zet. Muscles worked in his jaw. "Watch yourself, boy," he said quietly

The thugs left. Zet followed. At the door, the official stopped him.

"This area is off limits. Why are you here?"

"The architect sent me," Zet said.

"I'm the Overseer—if he wants to send his servants poking around, he'd better talk to me first. Got it? Or maybe you want to talk to the medjay."

"No! No—I'm going."

19

THE PRISONER

Back outside, Zet's heart was still racing. *What was that about?* He looked both ways. The two men were gone.

Was it possible they were Princess Merit's kidnappers? What other explanation could there be? And why were they worried about him snooping in the bushes? All he'd found was a dead end. If they'd taken the Princess that way, they'd put her in a boat and had sailed off where no one could follow. Everyone knew it was impossible to track a boat, so why would the two men be worried about him being in the brush?

Even more puzzling, why did the sunburnt man's voice seem so familiar? Where had Zet heard it before?

Part of him wanted to report his attackers to Merimose. But if Merimose questioned the men, they could deny it. They could say they caught Zet snooping. Merimose would be furious. Worse.

He could send Zet home.

The chilling realization shook him to his core.

Stumped, he headed back toward the harbor. It was time he checked in with Senna.

Small birds wheeled in the cloudless sky. Zet reached the road. He felt eyes on his back and turned. At the temple, hundreds of men still labored under the waning sun. He squinted, but saw no sign of his attackers. The sunburnt man's warning flashed through his mind—that the last runner had suffered a 'curse'.

Zet gulped, picturing a deadly visit from them to his tent in the middle of the night.

Hopefully, they believed what he told them—that he was just a clueless messenger.

His mind roamed to Hui, and his spirits sank even further. Nearly a whole day had passed, and what had Zet learned? Nothing. Fear for his best friend gnawed at him.

He felt dizzy, and realized it was more than fear. He'd eaten nothing since his meager breakfast, and the day was nearly over.

Deciding to risk the cook's anger, he angled off the road so he could come up behind the mess tent. Maybe he could beg a few scraps before dinner.

The smell of animal dung drifted on the soft breeze. He looked right and saw donkeys clustered in an open-air pen. Next to the donkeys lay a long, low, mud-brick building. A barn. Zet thought of the wadi and the donkey prints.

This was worth investigating.

As he neared the mud-brick building, a man stepped out. The man shielded his eyes from the slanting sun and watched Zet approach. His gnarled hands were calloused and stained with dirt. Straw dusted his tunic. He held a grooming brush. The stable master.

The man eyed Zet's uniform. "You're the other runner."

"The architect's runner? Yes."

"I suppose you've come to talk to the prisoner?"

Zet tried to hide his surprise. He glanced at the building. This is where they were holding Hui? "Yes," he said quickly. "Er, the architect wanted me to ask him something."

The man nodded. "Go in. Stall at the end. But don't be long."

Zet could hardly believe his luck! Until that moment, he didn't realize how completely alone he'd felt. Hui was here. They'd think of a plan out of this mess together.

It was dark inside. He squinted and made out a narrow pathway with animal stalls on either side. No doubt at night the stable master herded the donkeys in here to protect them from prowling lions and hyenas. The sound of soft breathing came from his right. He approached a stall door made of sturdy bamboo rods, and peered through.

Expecting to see Hui, he jolted in shock.

The figure curled on the ground, eyes closed, was a woman! Around his mother's age. The sight made him uncomfortable. Why was she locked up in here? He wrapped his fingers around the bars, working up the courage to wake her. He had to know.

Someone was coming. Zet wrenched himself away.

A tall man clad in pristine white robes appeared out of the gloom. He smelled of incense and temple oils. The priest.

"Hello," Zet said.

"Good evening." The priest kept walking, and soon disappeared.

How strange!

When Zet finally found Hui's stall, his best friend leaped up with a shout of joy.

"Tell me you've come to let me out."

"I wish," Zet said.

Hui's shoulders sagged. He pressed his forehead to the bamboo rods in despair.

"But I'm going to get you out," Zet said. "I swear it." They stood a moment in shared fright. "Are those your tools? And that lock you were carving? They let you bring those in here?"

Hui nodded. "Yes, the priest ordered them to."

"That priest? He almost killed me. What does he want from you?"

"Never mind that. What's important is that I'm going to break out." He pointed to the wall behind him. "I've been digging out the mortar between the bricks. It's slow work, but if you went around back of this place, you could help from the other side!"

"And then what, run for the rest of your life? It's like saying you're guilty."

"Either way, I'm dead."

"I told you I'm going to get you out."

"How?"

"Listen, the thief had to be a Hyksos spy. All I have to do is find him and unmask him for who he is."

Hui went silent. Finally, he said, "Do you have any leads?"

"Maybe." Zet told him about the hoofmarks in the wadi. And the attack in the chapel.

"Sounds like they're protecting something. But what?" Hui said.

"I don't know."

"Remind me what Senna said about that day. What time did she disappear?"

"I'm not sure. But I just thought of something. Remember that accident the girl went off to investigate? You know, when she left the chapel and came back to find it empty? Well, this morning Senna was in a horrible mood because of some obelisk that fell over at the worksite. That must have been the accident. I wonder if it's important to the mystery?"

Hui's eyes lit up. "It might be. I heard people talking about it at breakfast!"

"What did they say?"

"Some men told Jafar that it's a big hassle because the stone is expensive and the carvings will have to be redone."

"Did they say why it fell?" Zet said.

"No. The obelisk was a four-sided needle shape, with a pointed top and carvings up and down its surface. Straight as an arrow, which is extremely hard to do. It would kill me if a piece of jewelry I'd spent months making was smashed like that."

"I wonder if someone sabotaged it?"

"That would be so evil," Hui said, blanching. "If it was close to the chapel, maybe they thought she'd walk out just as . . .?"

Zet pulled out the building plans. He handed the scroll through the bars.

Hui pored over it. "I see Senna marked the chapel for you." He moved his finger across the giant page, over the lines that represented walls, the breaks that symbolized door openings and the circles for pillars. He tapped a square shape. "This small square is the obelisk. Look, Senna made a note beside it."

Zet eyed the scrawl. "That's a note?"

"I can't read too well, but I'm pretty sure that says *Obelisk*." He ran a finger back to the tiny chapel room. "They're pretty far apart. Too far."

20

NAUNET

After Zet and Hui had talked awhile longer, Zet said, "Who's the lady in the other cell?"

"I was wondering that, too. I asked the stable master. He told me to mind my own business."

Out of nowhere, something jolted Zet's memory. "I just figured out where I heard the sunburnt man's voice!"

"Where?"

"Talking to our boat Captain! The sunburnt man is the Captain's brother! Darius, that's his name." Zet quickly told him about the conversation he'd overheard.

"Sounds like they're not exactly close."

"I'd say. Still, they did go duck hunting together."

"And you said they have a sister here?" Hui said. "I wonder who she is?"

"Good question. But I just thought of something awful." He knocked his forehead against the bars. "Darius was on that duck hunting trip—he couldn't be the kidnapper."

From down the hall, the stable master bellowed, "Boy! What are you doin'?"

"*Beetle dung!*" Zet said.

"Can you come back later?" Hui said.

"I'll try!"

"Boy, didn't you hear me?" The stable master marched down the hall. "I thought you had a message to deliver, not a speech. This ain't no social club in here. You'll get me in trouble. Now go on, get out."

"Sorry, I'm going," Zet said.

Hui looked desperate as Zet said goodbye.

Zet felt equally so. Both of his leads had turned out false—the prints in the wadi led nowhere, and Darius had an alibi. He grabbed his head, his thoughts racing. He had to do something. But what?

"Why are you hanging 'round my door?" the stable master said, emerging from the barn. He looked like he was normally a nice guy, but really wanted to stay out of trouble.

"Sorry," Zet said, apologizing for the second time. "I wanted to ask you about these donkeys. Who uses them?"

"The workmen. Who do you think?"

"Was anyone using them the day the Priestess disappeared?"

"You ain't the first to wonder that. As it happens, one went missing all night. But it was back the following morning."

"Where was it?"

"Boy, donkeys can't speak. If we knew that, we knew where she'd got to, wouldn't we? Now I gotta get these donkeys in for the night."

"Thanks." Zet nodded and trudged off.

His feet carried him to the dinner tent. Lost in thought, he followed the line through the door. The crowd chattered and laughed, talking in loud voices about their day. He reached a long table from which the food was being served. A woman ladled vegetable stew into a clay bowl and handed it to Zet. Next, a second woman sliced a piece of meat from a roasted haunch and laid it on top of his stew. Further along, a deep basket held thick slices of warm bread. Zet grabbed two. The food smelled delicious, and his mouth watered.

He glanced around, looking for a place to sit.

The workmen sat in groups, filling the tent to capacity. He spotted Jafar and hesitated. If he sat there, he'd have to answer questions about Hui.

"Zet!" called a girl's voice.

He turned. He grinned when he spotted Naunet, and his heart raced a little. He was glad to see a friendly face, that's all. She had two other girls in tow, and was just leaving the food table.

"Hi," he said, approaching. "Can I sit with you?"

The two girls laughed, as if this were the funniest thing they'd ever heard.

Naunet, meanwhile, simply said, "We take our food back to the boat."

"Oh. Right. Of course."

"Come on," one of the girls said, frowning at her.

Naunet colored. "Hold on! I'm coming." Brushing her dark hair from her eyes she turned to Zet. "What happened to that boy?"

"He's going to have to stand trial."

"Well, he's definitely guilty. I couldn't believe it when I saw him with that bag! I almost fainted. Where is he? Where are they keeping him?"

"In a cell. By the way, do you know anything about a woman who's being held there?"

"A woman?" she said, her eyes widening.

"I saw a woman in a cell near his." Then, realizing she might wonder why he was visiting the prisoner, he added, "I had to check on the runner, so that I could make a report to my master."

She was watching his face, as if waiting for him to go on.

"And that's when I saw her. It was kind of creepy. Seeing a lady in there like that."

The other two girls with Naunet shifted nervously from foot to foot.

"You don't have to wait for me," she told them. "I'll catch up. I just want to talk to my friend for a minute."

The girls shot dubious looks at Zet, but they left.

"Sorry, we're supposed to keep to ourselves," she said.

"I don't want to get you in trouble."

"I think it's probably too late for that," she said with a small smile. "What I wanted to tell you is that we know her. The lady."

This staggered him. "You do? How, who is she?"

"She's a healer. Or was." Naunet paused. "She and her daughter helped care for the Priestess. The Priestess has some health issues."

Zet thought of what Senna told him. Again, he felt a shudder of unease roll through him at the thought of the Princess being sick and out somewhere locked up in the desert.

"The woman's daughter, Kissa, was with my mistress the day she disappeared. So was I."

"Wait, you *were there?*"

Naunet nodded. "Yes. Terrible isn't it?"

Zet wondered if she was going to start crying, so he stared into his dish of stew and waited for her to go on. "What happened?" he finally prompted, unable to contain his curiosity any longer. He couldn't believe he was about to get a first hand account.

"Everything was fine. It was a lovely day, and we were looking around in a little chapel that's being built near the edge of the site. But then we heard a loud crash. A great explosion, really. My mistress sent me to see what it was. I ran through the construction site. All the way to the courtyard. An obelisk had fallen. Pieces had flown everywhere. Clouds of dust filled the air, people were screaming and shouting."

He and Hui had been thinking the obelisk was meant to kill someone.

But wait—could it have been used as a distraction?

Naunet clutched her dinner bowl so tightly that her fingers were white. "I ran back to the chapel to tell her. She and Kissa were gone." Raising her chin, she looked Zet in the eye. "At first, I thought they left without me and headed back here. But they hadn't."

Her face was stoic. Zet wondered if she blamed herself. Or if others blamed her.

"Why did they lock Kissa's mother up?"

Naunet's face turned dark. "Kissa is a Hyksos!"

Zet's mouth dropped open.

"Yes," Naunet said, shaking. "She's a Hyksos, our sworn enemy. The very people our army has been fighting against to take back our lands! All this time they've been hiding the truth, but they were found out. They were spies. They were in on it!"

Zet's mind reeled. Why hadn't Senna told him this?

Naunet stared at the ground. Softly, she said, "You just never know who to trust, do you?"

"No," Zet murmured.

"I wish I could sit here and eat with you," she said suddenly. "I really do. I feel like I can talk to you. Even though we've barely met, I feel like you're the first friend I've had in a long time."

At this, Zet grinned. "I don't think the other girls would like that too much!"

She laughed. "That's for sure. There are a lot of rules. And everyone's always maneuvering for control. It's . . . competitive. You never know who's being nice and who's just trying to get something."

"Sounds awful," he said, feeling guilty for trying to pick her brains. He really did like her though. "Why don't you quit?"

Her eyes twinkled. "I just might. But I'd better get back to my boat. I'm probably in big trouble already."

"Maybe I should come and tell them to leave you alone?" Zet said, beaming.

"Probably not a good idea!" But she was laughing.

DISASTER

Outside the tent, Zet took a deep draught of stew. It was delicious. Hunger took over, and he shoveled more into his mouth with his bread. He was halfway finished, and wondering if they'd give him seconds if he went back inside, when he spotted Ari.

Senna's tall servant made a beeline for him.

"You're safe," Ari said, obviously relieved.

"Why wouldn't I be?" Zet asked.

"You need to come with me."

Zet wasn't leaving until he'd downed his dinner. He did so, and then darted inside to return the bowl. He looked longingly at the food. Men were lined up for seconds. Then Ari was at his elbow pulling him outside.

"Senna's boat was ransacked," Ari said in a low voice. "While Senna was away reporting to the medjay. They found the scroll you brought from Thebes."

"Uh oh."

"Your cover's not blown, yet. That scroll didn't mention you by name. The Queen Mother's spy could be any of the men who came on the boat with you."

"Yes, but I'm Senna's new runner. They'll suspect me first."

"That's why you're to sleep on Senna's boat tonight. It's safer. Medjay Commander's orders."

Zet spotted Senna's boat, bobbing against the wharf. "No. It will look too suspicious."

Ari raised one eyebrow. "You can't be thinking of sleeping in your tent."

"I'll take my chances."

"Talk to Senna. He's waiting for you."

When Zet entered Senna's cabin, he found the man looking flustered and irritated. Scrolls and shards of ostraca lay scattered across the room. It had been messy before, but now it was a disaster.

"Why didn't you tell me about the Hyksos woman?" Zet blurted.

Senna looked up, arms full, white brows jutting like bird feathers. "I forgot."

"You forgot? That's she's Hyksos? The enemy?"

"Since she's locked up, she's no threat now. Anyway, she denies it."

"Still, why didn't you tell me? I need to know these things!"

"And now you do," he snapped.

Fury rose in Zet and he forced it back down. No good would come of arguing with Senna. He pulled the building plans from his belt and handed them over.

"Thank you. Now unless you have anything useful to report, I need to get back to work." Not waiting for an answer, he turned away.

"I'll be sleeping in my tent," Zet told him.

"As you wish," Senna said in a sour tone.

The tent felt incredibly empty without his best friend. He and Hui had set out on this together, thinking it would be an adventure. How had everything gone so wrong?

Zet's mind wandered back to Thebes. Home seemed so far away, like another world.

Kat would be sick with worry if she knew Hui was going to stand trial for stealing the royal jewels. As would Hui's mother Delilah, and his four younger brothers. With good reason. Hui would be killed for it. Unless Zet cleared his name.

Thank the gods they didn't know.

Zet's mind flew from one thing to the next. He'd forgotten to ask Hui what the priest wanted. Then he thought of the bag of jewels. Maybe Kissa's mother hid them in the river, tied to that branch? Before she got caught?

Around and around he went, thinking of the wadi and the arrest, the priest and Hui in his cell, the missing donkey, and the break-in at Senna's boat. He lay back, flopping one arm over his eyes. As he drifted off to sleep, his last thought was that he needed to hide the seal ring.

He woke with a start. It was pitch black.

Sweat broke out across his chest. Was someone outside?

He crept on all fours and pressed one eye to the door. The dark world was silent, apart from the gentle swish of water slapping against the harbor and the creak of boats.

Wide awake, he crawled through the flap.

Not a soul in sight.

When his stomach growled, he jumped at the noise. Then he almost laughed. The noise seemed to be the theme song of his life right now. According to the cook, he wasn't the only hungry person in camp. Zet thought of the cook's missing meat pie.

Wait—could that be a clue?

Was it possible the kidnappers were taking food to some hideout? Little bits here and there, but not enough to rouse suspicion?

Zet caught his breath.

They could be hiding out across the river. That's why Darius wanted the skiff! To ferry food across the canal! But there, his theory fell apart. Darius never got the skiff. His brother refused to lend it to him. And Darius had an alibi, anyway.

Still, he couldn't shake the idea that Darius was involved.

An idea began to form. That duck hunting trip—Darius had

access to the rowboat. He probably snuck off with it after dark, when his brother was asleep.

He could have rowed up the canal to the wadi, where his accomplices were keeping the Princess waiting. Then they forced the Princess into the boat and ferried her away. Maybe there was a hut on the canal's opposite bank. Or a cave. A place where they were keeping her. And they were stealing food and bringing it out there.

Excitement snaked along Zet's spine.

Could that be it?

He started walking toward the outdoor kitchen area. When he reached the dark mess tent, not a single shadow moved. He crossed back behind, toward the kitchen area and kept going. A thick date palm, fringed by tall grass, made a good hiding spot. He melted into the shadows to wait.

His gaze drifted to the barn. The long, low stable loomed black as ink. Stars and a partial moon gave just enough light to see that the door was unmanned. He pictured Hui inside. It must be locked up tight.

Then, to Zet's surprise, the door slowly opened.

A boy emerged, dressed in a cloak that covered him from head to toe.

Osiris's beard! Hui was escaping!

He had a donkey by a rope bridle, and was leading it out the door.

Zet was about to shout Hui's name. Something stopped him.

Where would Hui get that cloak from? And Hui was bigger than that. Zet saw that now. The boy was coming closer. Zet flattened himself against the tree as the boy glanced his way.

The donkey was loaded down with saddlebags. Clearly the boy rode often, because he leaped onto the donkey's back with practiced ease. Where was he going at this hour? The boy pulled the bridle and turned the animal around. He kicked the donkey's flanks, and the animal took off.

The food, this boy was taking food! That had to be it!

Heart in his mouth, Zet sprinted after him.

NIGHT TREK

Away from the barn, the world was gray-black. Lizards scuttled through the dry grasses. At least, he hoped they were lizards. He remembered the scorpion he'd seen the other day, and his toes cringed as he ran. His household god, Bastet, the ebony cat, was far from this dark place. Still he sent out a silent prayer, asking for her protection.

Zet was a fast runner. The donkey and its rider were faster.

Breathing hard, Zet pushed himself until his heart hammered in his chest.

There would be no catching them. That grew painfully obvious.

Zet was pretty sure they were headed for the wadi. Maybe the kidnappers stole a boat from someone else. If the boy on the donkey planned to meet the kidnappers, it would take awhile to transfer the goods. And the men might want a report from him, too.

Zet might just make it in time.

With fresh hope, he ran on.

He knew he must have bypassed the construction site by now. He'd been running for at least twenty minutes, trying to follow the angle the donkey had taken. Tall brush rose around him. The wadi had to be close. He slowed and sniffed the air, hoping to catch the brackish scent of the river.

The air smelled of dirt and sunburnt leaves.

He was lost.

Bearing left, the undergrowth grew thicker and thicker. Turning backwards grew difficult. Thorny plants grabbed at his bare legs. Jabbed into the soles of his feet. For all he knew, he was going in circles. With a shout of frustration, he ripped at the branches and sprinted, thorns cutting into him, his jaw tight with agony.

Finally, he burst free.

Sitting down, he plucked barbs from his toes and heels.

Too much time had passed. He'd never catch them at the river now, even if he did know the way. This trek had been completely useless. There was no point in going on. He only hoped he could find his way home.

The moon had risen higher, just enough to cast a glow on the outline of the desert mountains. Using them as a guide, he began to walk, keeping them to his left. After a long time, the pyramid came into view, jutting up to touch the stars.

He breathed out a sigh of relief.

By the time he reached the harbor, he was dragging his injured feet in exhaustion. He approached his tent. Even in his tired state, he knew it looked more crooked than how he'd left it. A sixth sense made the hairs on his forearms stand straight.

He swerved before he reached it, and softly padded for Senna's boat.

A medjay dozed at the end of the gangplank. The man came to with a start.

"Oh, it's just you," the medjay said, recognizing Zet. "Go on up."

On the forward deck, Senna had an outdoor sitting area. Cushions lay under a broad sunroof made of thick fabric. The feathered pillows fluffed up around him as he sank deeply into the luxurious mass. An instant later, he was fast asleep.

The following morning before dawn, footsteps woke him. Someone was running onto the ship.

A moment later, Senna could be heard grumbling. "By the snout of Anubis, what's the emergency?"

Ari murmured a reply that Zet couldn't quite catch.

Zet propped himself up on one elbow and rubbed his face.

What was going on?

He got to his feet and headed for the door to Senna's cabin. When he reached it, a boy not much older than Zet came out. He shot Zet an apologetic look. The next moment, Zet knew why. Senna was making angry noises, slamming things around.

"Zet!" Senna shouted.

Gulping, Zet went in.

"What happened?" Zet asked.

"This!" Senna held up a scroll in his fist and shook it. "This message is what happened!"

As the architect turned it over, the huge seal became visible. Anyone would recognize the marking stamped in thick wax. Pharaoh had written to Senna in the night.

Senna nodded, seeing Zet's face. "Yes, the Mighty Bull himself." Then he wrung the paper between his hands with a look of despair. "He's coming tomorrow morning!"

"Tomorrow! But . . . he wasn't supposed to be here for three more days!"

"Pharaoh does what he wants. And if that's arriving early, he'll do so."

"We have no idea where she is. That's not enough time." Zet's skin prickled with cold sweat.

"It will have to be. We've kept the secret from Pharaoh this long. But there will be no keeping it from him when he arrives."

"Wait, he doesn't know? How can he not know?"

Senna grimaced. "Queen Mother's orders."

"Can she do that? He'll be furious!"

"I never should have listened to her! He'll have to be told. He'll say it's my fault!" Senna swallowed, looking pale. "It'll be my neck. I might be Pharaoh's favorite architect, but Princess Merit is his favorite daughter. And then there are the Hyksos demands. He won't like it. He won't like it at all!" Senna sank down into a heavy slump and put his face in his hands. "He's coming early, because they've won a great battle. Imagine what he's going to say when he gets here and learns . . ."

"That the Hyksos want the barricade removed," Zet murmured.

"Yes. If Pharaoh does this, everything he's won will be lost. The Hyksos will continue south. Soon, they'll be fighting in Thebes."

The image of battle in Zet's hometown struck such fear into him that he felt sick. His wonderful town, with his family and their house, and their bright, happy stall in the market, it would all be destroyed.

What would Pharaoh do? Give up his daughter for the peace of Egypt? Let the Hyksos kill her so the rest of Egypt's people could live? Or save her and fight a losing battle? It was a horrible choice to face.

Zet had to do something, fast. Time had almost run out.

"I need to talk to Merimose," Zet said.

"Do what you will. I fear it will make little difference."

Outside, the deck was still cool and damp with dew. He pounded down the gangway and sprinted along the shore. Moments later, he reached the medjays' sturdy vessel. A broad-shouldered man stood on the watersteps, barring his entrance.

"I need to talk to Commander Merimose," Zet said, breathless.

"He's not—" he paused. "Hold on, I know you!"

In that instant Zet, recognized him, too. "You're the desk officer from the main office at Thebes!"

"And you're the pottery boy who won that big reward some months back," the man said with a grin. "But you can't talk to the Commander. He's not here."

23

THE LADY PRISONER

Zet should have figured Merimose wouldn't be there. He had to find him, fast. Before he could speak, the medjay leaned forward.

"Good news, though." The man's eyes flickered. "I think they found our missing Priestess."

Was it possible? "Where?"

"Can't say. But they'll be back in a few hours."

Zet let the news sink in. Was it possible they'd really found her? It was too much to be believed. Too much to hope for.

Cautiously, he said, "That's great."

"I'll relax when they get back," the medjay said, as if reading Zet's mind.

Zet knew he should report the news to Senna. Instead, he headed for the barn. He wanted to tell Hui first.

What had Merimose learned last night that had tipped the medjay off? He pondered this as he walked. And would finding the kidnappers get Hui off the hook? That wasn't guaranteed.

When he neared the pasture, a pair of floppy-eared donkeys milled about. One was gray, the other brown. They both had wide eyes, rimmed with thick lashes. As Zet passed, the brown one trotted over and stuck his nose over the bamboo enclosure.

"Hello," Zet said, laughing. He stroked the animal's soft nose. The other donkey approached, looking hopeful. "Sorry, I don't have a snack for you guys. Maybe next time."

Turning away, he made for the barn door. It was deserted. The stable master was probably still at breakfast. Zet pushed at the door and found it unlocked. He stepped inside, into the dusty gloom. Straw crunched as he walked, perfuming the still air.

Movement caught his attention.

He glanced left, through the bamboo bars. It was the cell with the Hyksos woman. She sat against the far wall, looking wide-awake and cautious.

Their eyes met.

Zet's first thought was that she didn't look Hyksos. She looked like any normal Egyptian. Dark hair and intelligent, almond shaped eyes.

"Good morning," the woman said, with no trace of foreign accent.

"Hello," Zet replied. He was tempted to question her, but kept walking.

"Wait," the woman called after him. She rose and hurried to the bars. Worried lines creased her forehead. "Has there been any news?"

"Of the Priestess?" Zet said.

"Yes, and the girl who was with her."

"Your daughter?"

Her proud shoulders sagged. "Ah. So you know."

"I do." He studied her face. "I never would have guessed you're Hyksos. I'm not surprised people were fooled."

"I am not Hyksos. Whoever told you that is a liar. But I suppose the whole camp believes it now."

Zet frowned. "There's no point in keeping up your story. The medjay know."

"That's where you're wrong. They know the truth. I told them I could prove it, and begged them not to smear my name. They gave me their word. I guess their word means nothing!"

Zet was completely confused. "Well, if you're not Hyksos, what are you?"

"I'm Egyptian!" she cried. Her cheeks had turned a deep shade of red. With apparent effort, she seemed to calm herself. "I'm Egyptian," she repeated quietly.

"And your daughter?"

"We're innocent!" she said, and then clammed up.

"My friend is being held in another cell. He's tied up in all of this. They think he stole something, and he might have to stand trial. If you've already told the medjay, and if you're innocent like you say, what's the harm in telling me the truth? If you're not Hyksos spies, and you didn't hatch this kidnapping plot, surely you'd want to help me?"

The woman was silent for a long time.

Zet was growing antsy. He thought she was going to refuse, to send him on his way. He was about to leave when she nodded.

"All right," she said. "I grew up in a village in the North of Egypt. Next to the Hyksos border. In my fifteenth year, Hyksos warriors invaded our village. I was kidnapped, taken from everyone and everything I loved."

Zet watched her face. Her cheeks were flushed and her breathing had increased. She looked frightened, as if she were living it all over again.

She let go of the bars and wiped her hands on her linen skirt. "Still, I survived. Things could have been worse. I'd been learning the healing arts. I saved a dying man, and that earned me a little respect with my captors. But when a Hyksos warrior took me as his bride, I was desperate to escape. I tried and failed many times. Things grew worse when we had a daughter. Seeing her tiny face, I knew I had to get away or die." Her face was hard. "I refused to let her be raised as Hyksos, sworn enemies of my people!"

"What did you do?"

"I didn't run, like the other times. I secretly sold one of my husband's jeweled daggers and bartered for passage south. Traders smuggled me and my daughter aboard a trading vessel, hidden in rolls of carpets! We went all the way to Thebes, as far as we could get."

The story was too fantastic to be a lie. He suspected she spoke the truth.

"How did you go from being runaways to working with—"

He almost said Princess Meritamon. But it was too late. Her eyes widened. She knew.

Out loud, she said, "The Priestess was born with an illness. Her back is curved, and it affects her terribly. Meanwhile, my reputation as a healer was growing." She smiled sadly. "Her father heard about me, and the rest is history. My daughter and I went to live in her household. Kissa was learning my skills. But she's not just a healer, they're close friends."

"So you never told them your daughter is part Hyksos?"

Her cheeks colored. "No. Not even Kissa knows."

Zet's jaw dropped.

"She was a baby!" the woman said. "She didn't choose her father. She's loyal and honest and wouldn't hurt a mosquito."

"Then why did you tell the medjay about her now?"

"I didn't. Two men from my old village did. They saw me and recognized me, and remembered," she said with a miserable laugh. "Manu and Darius."

"Darius," Zet repeated.

She drew away. "You know him?"

"A tall, sunburnt man with a round belly? We're not friends. He attacked me at the construction site."

Zet's thoughts were racing. Darius grew up on the border with the Hyksos. Understanding fell into place. Darius would do anything for quick profit. Even his own brother, the boat Captain, said so. Had Darius approached the Hyksos, or had they approached him? How much were they paying him to be their spy? How many other evil acts had Darius committed for the enemy against his own people?

Did Merimose and the other medjay know Darius was guilty?

Zet wanted to ask more questions, but the entrance creaked open.

A shaft of light illuminated the straw dust that floated in the warm air.

The stable master entered, carrying what appeared to be breakfast. He paused at the sight of Zet, and his brow furrowed in a dark line.

"What are you doing in here?" he demanded.

"I came to talk to the runner."

"My fault," the woman added. " I stopped him to see if there's news. Is there?"

"No," the man growled. "And the runner's not here. You need to leave. Now."

"The runner's not here? Where is he?" Zet said.

"That priest came for him this morning. That's all I know."

GLIMMERS OF FEAR

When Zet stumbled back out into the sunlight, he stared across the paddock in confusion.

Why had the Priest of Osiris taken Hui away? *And on whose authority?*

Maybe Senna would know. He headed for the architect's boat. Then he realized he'd better hurry. He hadn't reported in with the news that Merimose had a lead on the Princess. Senna would still be worried out of his mind.

As he ran however, he couldn't help pondering what he'd learned from the woman. Darius had gone to the medjay about her. If the medjay trusted him, they were wrong. Was it possible Darius would do something to stop the men? What if he'd set a trap?

The hopeful feeling he'd felt earlier started to fade.

A small voice inside warned him something was off. He wished he could talk to Merimose. But he had no way of learning where the medjay had gone.

A calm had fallen over the waterfront. Far overhead, tiny birds circled in the vast blue sky. In the bay, several fish broke the surface, flashing into the air. They skimmed across the water, appearing and disappearing. A bird swooped down and snapped one up in its beak. The harbor surface turned dead calm.

Senna hadn't yet heard the news. The wrinkled old architect listened to Zet with eyes that were more wary than hopeful.

"Do you know what the priest wanted with Hui?" Zet asked.

"No idea." He shoved a basket of ostraca Zet's way.

"What are these?" Zet said, staring down at the white, pottery shards covered in Senna's scribbled hieratic.

"Messages for my workers. Now that you're no longer the Queen Mother's spy, it's time you got to work."

"But they haven't actually found her—"

"That's no longer your concern. The temple construction will go on! And until you're excused from duty, you work for me."

"But I could still—"

"This one here is for Hori," Senna said, picking out a shard. "You'll know him by his red belt." He went on and on. There were so many shards, Zet had no idea how he'd keep them straight.

"Put the strap over your head," Senna advised, "There you go. Excellent."

With the leather shoulder strap slung across his chest, Zet had to lean sideways not to fall over. He couldn't believe he was going to do this, when the case wasn't yet solved! Then again, at least he'd be out running around. He'd run out of leads. Sure, he could ignore Senna's orders and take off, but with what purpose?

He set out to find Hori.

It turned out Hori had a message to take back to Senna. To Zet's dismay, so did everyone who received one of Zet's shards. Even worse, most he just had to memorize, because few of the men bothered to write them down. And every single person he asked about the missing priestess stared at him blankly.

"I don't know nothing about that!" said one.

"Don't involve me, I got my job to think about," said another.

By the time he'd made his fourth trip, he climbed on board Senna's boat, he was sweaty, frustrated and bordering on furious. "Wouldn't it be easier to go there and set up camp for the day?"

"Do you realize how hot it is outside?" Senna cried, raising his fluffy brows.

Zet mopped sweat from his face and arms. Senna handed him another basket.

"Now hurry!" Senna said. "These are important. They've put the wrong foundation stones down. The wall is liable to fall over."

And so Zet dashed out into the blazing heat.

Lunch came and still the medjay hadn't returned. The fissure of worry he'd felt that morning was growing. He'd managed to detour by the barn and learn from the annoyed stable master that *'no, Hui was not back yet'*.

Somehow he managed to choke down some food, but his stomach felt jittery.

By late afternoon, patches of ground that had burned his feet earlier grew dark with shadow. An unusual coolness settled over the valley. His sweat turned chill. Zet shivered.

Back on the waterfront, he glanced toward the medjay's boat. The same man who'd been there in the morning still stood at the foot of the gangplank.

Otherwise, it was deserted.

Ra, the sun god, hovered on the horizon.

What could have happened? What could be taking them so long?

Was it possible the medjay had been led into a trap? Or on a wild goose chase?

When dinner came and went, Zet's stomach began to cramp with fear. Something had definitely gone wrong.

Merimose and his men could be in real trouble right now. Hyksos could have ambushed them. Maybe Merimose was somewhere in the desert, fighting for his life.

And what of Hui?

Zet swallowed down a horrible dizzy feeling.

It was his fault Hui had come here. If something happened to Hui, the guilt and horror of losing his best friend would kill him.

Workers were filing toward the dinner tent, laughing and talking like everything was normal. For them, it was. Zet couldn't even think about eating. When he spotted Jafar, Zet turned away and slunk into the shadows. He ran straight into Naunet.

She smiled, but her smile quickly faded. "Are you all right?"

Suddenly, he wanted to tell her everything. He needed to talk to someone, and he felt sure she'd understand. Then he remembered—she thought Hui was a thief.

He nodded. "Yes, everything's okay."

"I wanted to ask if you want to bring your dinner and eat at the watersteps by our boat?" she said, coloring.

"Really?" To his dismay, he felt his own face growing hot. What was the matter with him? Anyway, he couldn't. He had to find Hui. Right now. "Thanks, I really want to. But I can't."

"Another time," she said, sounding disappointed.

Running on silent feet, he ran for the barn. When it came into view, he slowed. The stable master stood chatting with a few workers out front. Zet skirted through the tall grass, making his way around back.

He went to the end of the building, feeling pretty sure he'd reached Hui's cell wall. Then he picked up a loose stone and tapped it against the mud bricks.

"Come on, Hui," he whispered. *"Be in there!"*

Crickets hummed. Distant chatter and the smell of roast game wafted on the breeze.

Zet knocked again, harder this time.

"Hui! It's me!" he whispered.

There was a short pause. Then, a soft chink of metal against stone rang out from the opposite side of the wall.

Zet's breath caught.

Hui was there!

The tapping came again, several hand-widths away from where Zet stood. Zet moved toward the sound. He knew Hui had been digging the mortar from between the stones in his cell. This must be the place. He tapped the rock to be sure, and an excited tapping came from the other side.

Zet found a sharper stone. He started digging at the sun-dried mud that sealed the bricks together. Hui was clearly doing the same. Together they worked hard and fast. Zet was terrified they'd be caught. Still, he kept working.

No way was he letting Hui stay in there any longer.

Suddenly, the tip of a blade shot through to Zet's side. It glimmered in the moonlight, and disappeared back between the bricks.

"I'm through, aren't I!" Hui whispered.

"Yes! Don't stop," Zet whispered back.

Soon Hui's blade appeared more easily, stabbing out in various spots along the wall.

"Start kicking," Hui said.

"Stand back," Zet whispered.

25

RUN!

Zet glanced both ways. Then he delivered a hard kick to the wall.

The bricks held firm.

"*Come on!*" He slammed into it with a second kick. His bare foot stung with the force of the blow. He kicked it a third time. The wall shook a little, but didn't break.

"*Harder!*" Hui whispered.

Zet backed twenty steps away. He sprinted forward and launched a kick so powerful that the force of his strike sent him flying onto his behind.

The bricks shuddered. And cracked inward. Hui's hands appeared, and then his face. He grinned at Zet through the hole.

"*Lying down on the job, I see,*" he whispered.

"Ow?" Zet said, half laughing, half groaning as he rubbed his foot.

Hui broke his way through and stretched his arms. "Freedom!"

"Not yet," Zet said, "But I'm pretty sure Darius stole those jewels. And I think he's sent the medjay into an ambush. And come to think of it, I haven't seen him all day."

They talked quickly. Zet told him about the donkey with the food supplies, and how he felt sure it had gone to the canal last night.

"Their camp must be on the opposite bank," Zet said.

"Do you think the rider will bring food there again tonight?"

"Possibly. Food and messages. I suspect the kidnappers are still over there with her, and whatever trap the medjay have fallen into is as far as you can get from that place. On this side of the water, in the mountains or something."

"We could wait here," Hui said. "Until the rider comes for a donkey. But that might be dangerous."

"Agreed. What if we go to the wadi and hide out? And if the boy doesn't come, we'll find a way across the canal before dawn and start searching."

"How wide is it?" Hui said.

In the big ferry, it had seemed narrow. But standing on the bank had been a different story. "You don't want to know."

They crept around the far end of the barn and paused. The stable master still stood talking with his friends near the door. Despite the darkness, he and Hui would have to move carefully not to be seen.

In the far distance stood the hulking mountains. The Traveler—the moon god Khonsu—rested between the peaks. Soon Khonsu would forge his way through the shimmering stars.

"We'll have to go around the paddock," Zet whispered. "Make a run for it on the far side."

Hui nodded.

Ducking low, they skirted along the enclosure. A furry cluster of donkeys nosed at the ground, looking for grass. Zet and Hui reached the far side, when Zet noticed gate access into the donkey pen.

On impulse, he tried the handle. It lifted easily.

"Come on," he whispered, opening it and squeezing through.

"I'm liking this idea," Hui whispered.

"Why walk when you can ride?" Zet said, pulse racing.

He spotted the brown donkey he'd seen earlier that day. "Hey, Brownie," he said, taking hold of its rope. To his relief, the soft-nosed creature followed him out the gate. Zet scrambled up onto its back.

Meanwhile, Hui was still dodging amongst the pack. He yelped, barely missing a kick from a big donkey. Another almost took a chomp of his fingers.

"Quit playing around. Let's go!" Zet hissed.

"What do you think I'm doing?"

Zet was growing more nervous. "The stable master's going to bring them inside any minute. Hurry up!"

"Tell that to my gray-eared friend here!" Hui said, waving a handful of grass under a small donkey's nose. The donkey took the bait and trotted after him. Hui shut the gate and clambered on top.

Zet gave his animal a nudge. "Come on Brownie. Let's get away from here."

Brownie started into a happy trot. But when Zet looked back, he saw Hui's animal hadn't budged. Shouts came from the barn. *Flea dung!*

"A little help?" Hui said.

Zet trotted back to Hui. "Toss me your rope!"

Hui did. "Wake up, Gray Ears! It's adventure time!"

After Zet gave Gray Ears' rope a few tugs, it reluctantly started forward. And then they were off. Zet headed for the construction site. He didn't want to risk getting lost like the night before. He kept turning back to peer into the darkness, sure he'd see the stable master coming after them.

Soon, it became clear they'd gotten away.

Zet shot a grin at Hui. His best friend's wide grin shone back at him in the moonlight. It felt great to be back on the chase together!

Hui whooped. Zet did the same.

Riding made everything go so much faster. He hadn't spent much time on a donkey, his animal was tame and required little direction. Hui's seemed happy to follow, as long as Zet had hold of the rope. They reached the chapel in no time. From there, Zet was able to find the wadi without too much trouble. Being higher up on the donkey's back had advantages. He could see farther.

They reached the broad, ink-black canal and stopped.

The surface flowed quickly, making sucking, gurgling sounds where it rushed against the shore.

"*Sobek's fangs*, I hope we don't have to swim across that," Hui said.

They sat for a long moment, staring.

"The boy will come," Zet said, trying to convince himself as much as Hui.

"You're not going to like this, but—maybe the rider's just a boy stealing food for his family."

They looked at one another. Zet pondered this horrible possibility.

"We better find someplace to hide," Hui said.

A stand of rushes far down the bank provided the only spot. But there was nowhere to tie the animals. Hui, master of all things trickster-like, came up with the idea to tie each animal's lead rope around its two front legs. They could move, but couldn't take off.

"Not that Gray Ears will run anywhere," Hui said with a grin, patting his donkey.

Then they hurried back to the river to wait.

And wait . . .

Khonsu, the moon god, reached his zenith in the sky, and still no one had come. The chill air was making Zet stiff. He wanted to get up and stretch. And he was getting worried.

Suddenly, he heard something.

"Someone's coming," he whispered and ducked lower.

THE BOY AND HIS DONKEY

The small boy approached, riding quickly.

Zet wanted to jump up and tackle him. Good sense won out.

The boy's hood hid his face. Still, it was clear he didn't expect to be followed. He didn't even bother to look around. He simply led his donkey to the water's edge.

Zet frowned. There was no boat in sight.

Then the boy did something strange. He tucked the long sides of his cloak up underneath himself until he was sitting on them. Then he settled back in place.

With a kick of his pale heels, he urged the animal forward down the riverbank. Soon water rushed over the donkey's front hooves. Again, the boy kicked the beast. He made a clicking noise with his tongue, urging the donkey on. Finally it gave in.

In amazement, Zet watched it wade up to its flanks.

And then the donkey began moving across the wide canal.

Swimming.

The donkey was swimming. That's how they got across. No wonder Darius wanted that skiff! It would be a lot better than this.

"Come on," Zet said.

Hui was already on his feet.

They ran for their animals. Getting them into the canal was another matter. Zet and Hui pushed and pulled. Finally they managed to do it. Despite the struggle, the donkeys were strong swimmers. But the delay had lost precious time.

The boy was just a small figure in the darkness when Zet and Hui reached the far side. The donkeys waded out and shook, sending water in all directions.

"Good boy, Brownie," Zet cried. "Now hurry, before we lose him!"

The partial moon rose steadily higher, but the foliage was thick.

The boy vanished in the tall, weaving grasses. They spotted him again, far up ahead. Together, they followed the boy for close to an hour. Zet thanked the gods they had the donkeys. Brownie plodded steadily onward. Zet patted its neck in gratitude.

In the distance, the boy never bothered to turn around. Again, Zet wondered if the boy was simply a thief stealing food for his family.

A dark mass of trees blotted out the starry sky. They passed into the grove. Thick trunks broke the scrubby undergrowth. Date palms swayed overhead. The palm leaves made shush-shush sounds in the gentle wind. The air smelled sweet. Clusters of heavy fruit hung from reedy stalks.

Soon, the flowery scent mixed with the smell of brackish water.

He heard a rushing river. The Nile. After they left the canal, they must have cut across land at an angle to meet up with it.

A faint light glowed ahead. Then he saw a mud brick building. It looked like some kind of old storage facility. Maybe shippers used it to store goods on their way up and down the river. Whatever the case, the cloaked boy headed straight for it.

"Stop," Zet whispered.

Hui nodded his chin at the date palms. "We can tie up back there."

They did so, and then snuck as close to the building as they dared.

It was smaller than Zet first thought. Just a shack. Down on their bellies, they crawled around the perimeter. A poorly constructed lean-to came into view. It was set up to guard the front door. Zet spotted sleeping pallets under the makeshift shelter. Lamplight flickered. The air was smoky.

They crawled further and spotted a smoldering fire. Three men stood around it, talking to the boy. Someone laughed.

The boy's donkey was tethered next to two others.

One man went to unload the saddlebags and Zet saw his face. *Darius.*

"I hope you brought something good!" Darius said. "This calls for a celebration."

"We'll be rich," said the man who still wore his leather wristguards over his thick forearms. Manu, the other traitor from the border village.

"That we will," Darius agreed. "The medjay are dead, so we're in the clear. I guarantee they weren't expecting to meet a band of Hyksos in the mountains."

Zet listened to the news in horror. Merimose, dead? He wouldn't think about it now, he couldn't.

While Darius unloaded the supplies, the third man stoked the fire.

Since the kidnappers only had three donkeys tied up—the boy's and two others—Zet guessed the third man stayed all day to guard the prisoners. Then Darius and Manu came here straight from the worksite, after spending the day keeping their eyes on Senna and the medjay for signs of trouble. As for the boy, they had him pack up food when people went to sleep and steal out here to feed them.

At the thought of the prisoners, Zet's heart began to slam. Princess Meritamon was inside that shack! Just yards away.

The man by the fire emptied the contents of one sack into a cook pot. Then he stuck the cook pot right into the smoking coals.

"Three men," Hui whispered, his mouth close to Zet's head. "And we don't have weapons."

Zet stared grimly at the little group. He motioned Hui backwards.

"We have to get them away from there," he whispered.

Hui nodded, mischief beginning to flicker in his eyes. "Distraction time."

They snuck back to the date grove and worked out a plan.

"Poor chumps," Hui said. "They're in for a surprise."

It was easy to joke around, but they both knew the danger they were in. If things went wrong, this would turn deadly. Smart or not, Zet and Hui were just boys. If it came to a fight, they'd never win against full-grown men. They'd be killed, and no one would ever know what had happened to them.

In the dark, Zet and Hui did their old secret handshake for good luck. Then Hui darted away. Zet headed back for the shack. He lay on his belly in the dark. Insects crawled over him, tickling any bare flesh they could find. Finally, from far in the distance came the sound of splashing.

Hui had reached the Nile.

At the hut, all heads turned.

"What was that?" muttered Manu.

A soft, higher voice spoke. The boy. "Someone's coming from the river!"

"Shut up and let me listen," Darius snapped.

The splashing came again. Then a voice boomed, "Who's over there? At my shack?"

A second voice said, "Wait, it might be thieves!"

Hui sounded so convincing, even Zet was almost fooled.

Darius leaped to his feet. He grabbed his knife and stuffed it in his waistband. The others did the same. They squinted in the direction of the Nile. It was impossible to see. A papyrus forest, twice as high as any man, stood along its edge.

From the papyrus's depths, the deep voice spoke again. It was a forced whisper, but one designed to carry.

"Into the boat," the voice said. "We'll head back and get the others."

The splashing came again.

When Zet saw the way Darius bared his teeth in a grin, Zet felt sick. The yellow stumps shone in the moonlight.

Darius waved the other two men forward. "Quietly," he said. Then, to the boy, "Stay and keep an eye out."

At this Zet scowled. Just what he needed. If Zet tackled him, the boy could shout a warning.

The boy moved closer to the shack's barricaded door. As for the three men, they left the circle of light and made for the river.

And for Hui.

THE SHACK

The underbrush swallowed the three men to their chests. It would take another few minutes to reach the tall papyrus. When they got there, Hui would lead them further up river. Still, Zet had to act fast.

The boy stared off, watching the thugs.

Silently, Zet approached. At the last moment, the boy must have sensed him because he began to whirl. Zet grabbed him from behind and clamped his hand over the boy's mouth. The boy stiffened in shock. Then he began to struggle. He was smaller than Zet but wiry.

"Shut up or you're dead," Zet hissed, panicked they'd be heard.

The boy kept struggling. His hood fell over his face, almost to his chin. He wrenched forward and managed a muffled cry before Zet's hand clamped back in place.

Zet's heart pounded in terror. "I swear I'll kill you!"

He'd never do such a thing, but he hoped he sounded convincing. To his relief, the boy stopped struggling and went limp.

A shout from the Nile sent tremors of fear shooting through him.

"Pull out your swords, men!" shouted a deep voice. Hui's.

What was he doing? He was going to get himself killed!

Sweating in fear, Zet kept hold of him. He had to free the prisoners. Now. He forced the kid around to face the door to the hut. A long wooden bar blocked it from the outside. The boy tried to bite Zet's palm, but Zet had been expecting something like that. He squeezed the boy's cheeks on either side with his thumb and forefinger.

The wild kid bit down on empty air. Then he started struggling again.

With one arm around the boy's neck and the other over his mouth, Zet kicked at the wooden bar. It rose slightly from its housing, but not enough to open the door. He kicked again, a second and a third time. With every kick, he felt sure the men would hear. The fourth time, the bar came up and over the wooden support that held it in place.

The door eased outward a fraction.

Zet drove his adversary up against the wall beside it and wrenched the door open with one hand. The boy nearly got away, but Zet quickly grabbed him and pushed him forward. Together, they tumbled into the little room.

Inside, the boy stood panting like a wild animal.

Zet didn't dare let go. He reached back and yanked the door shut.

A lamp burned on the floor. Two grimy girls sat against the wall, watching. They were on a sleeping pallet. The girls were wide-eyed. One looked terrified. The other uncertain but hopeful.

Despite their grime, and the fact that Zet had never seen her up close, he immediately recognized the second one as Princess Meritamon. She wasn't smiling like the girl at the royal festivals, but neither did she cower in fear. Her eyes, shaped like almonds, curved up slightly at the corners. She gave Zet a fast, frank assessment, with a confidence that could only come from being the daughter of Pharaoh himself.

"What's going on?" she demanded.

"Help me," Zet said, still holding the struggling boy. "Find something to tie him up!"

The other girl—Kissa—shrank against the wall.

"Him?" Princess Meritamon said. "Gladly. But that's no boy."

"What are you talking about?" Zet said.

"See for yourself."

Zet grabbed at the boy's hood, and his struggles increased. When he yanked the rough cloth down, a mass of hair tumbled free. Familiar eyes flashed as they met his. Zet felt like he'd been punched in the stomach.

"Naunet?" he said.

She gazed at him. "Why did you have to get in the middle of this, Zet?" Her voice was soft but heart-wrenching.

He stared at her in confusion. This had to be a mistake!

Tears appeared at the corner of her eyes.

Then she opened her mouth to scream. Shocked and devastated, he covered her mouth just in time.

Naunet's warning scream turned into a muffled cry.

Meanwhile, Kissa and Princess Meritamon ripped the sheet that covered their sleeping palette into several strips. As the Princess moved, Zet suddenly saw how curved her back was. It looked painful, and the thought of her trapped like this made him sick.

How could Naunet have done this? Zet had believed she was his friend. He'd trusted her.

"Tie her up," the Princess told Kissa. "Hurry."

Naunet kicked and bit, but Zet managed to tie a strip around her face. He felt horrible.

Once they'd tied Naunet's hands and feet, they lay her on the sleeping palette. Zet opened the door. The coast was clear.

"Come on," Zet said.

Princess Meritamon said, "Why should I trust you?"

"Why? I just helped tie up one of your kidnappers! Now come on!"

"You tied her up, yes. But you're certainly not a medjay. Or a palace guard. *She* seemed to know you well enough. Who are you working for?"

"You think I risked my life against those men because I'm a kidnapper, too?"

Kissa looked panicked. "Highness, we'd better go!"

"Not until he tells me why we should trust him. I have no intention of trading one group of kidnappers for another."

The men would be back any moment. Zet hadn't planned on this. He felt ill! If they didn't hurry . . . Then he remembered something—all those times he'd been warned to bury the coronation ring, and he hadn't. He reached into his tunic and pulled it out. He thrust it before her eyes.

"Grandmother's ring!" she gasped.

"She gave it to me, and sent me to find you."

Her eyes narrowed. "Tell me your name."

"Zet."

At this she nodded. "Help me up. She told me about you. Let's get out of here."

Outside, the fire still smoldered, casting off a wide pool of light. The three of them stepped through the door. He bolted it shut on Naunet. One arm circling the Princess's waist, he led her toward the darkness. Then he heard a shout across the broad expanse of scrubby fields.

"Faster, they're coming," the Princess said.

"I don't want to hurt you," he replied.

"Better hurt than dead," she gasped.

He broke into a run and dragged her with him. "Our donkeys are tied to the date trees," he shouted to Kissa. "Run and untie them!"

Kissa came to life, sprinting into the gloom. Zet glanced back. He should have untied the kidnappers' donkeys. He could have scattered them! Too late now.

Where was Hui?

From behind, the kidnappers' shouts grew louder.

ANSWERS IN THE NIGHT

Zet's breath was growing ragged. Still he kept running, half-carrying Princess Meritamon with him.

He heard Manu shout, "They're headed for the trees!"

"Stop them!" shouted Darius.

The men were gaining.

Then, from up ahead, their two donkeys burst from the grove. Hui was leading Brownie at a run, and Kissa was riding Gray Ears. Thank the gods! Zet tightened his hold around Princess Meritamon's waist, lifting her almost off the ground, and sprinted.

"Get them!" Darius roared, enraged. He sounded just yards away.

Hui threw Brownie's bridle rope toward Zet.

Zet caught it. Taking hold of the Princess with both hands, he lifted her with a strength he didn't know he had. She landed astride the donkey. Zet leaped up in front of her.

Darius was only three strides away.

The princess screamed as Darius latched onto her leg. Zet crooked his elbow, and putting all of his weight into it, slammed it in Darius's face. Darius fell back just long enough for Zet to kick his donkey into action. Brownie, clearly spooked, took off like a shot toward Hui.

Manu had reached them now, too. The huge man lunged at Hui and Kissa, but Gray Ears skittered sideways.

Zet scooped up Gray Ears' bridle rope. And then they were charging together through the date grove. Princess Meritamon tightened her arms around his waist. With sudden clarity, he realized just how amazing this was. He was riding on a donkey with a princess clinging to him.

But they weren't out of danger yet.

The men were doubling back for their own mounts. Zet angled left.

"Stick to the trees for as long as we can," Zet called back to Hui.

Hui nodded. He and Kissa were bent forward, giving Gray Ears its head.

The group stayed within the grove's cover until finally they were forced into the open. But it wasn't exactly open. Thorny branches tore at their legs. Zet's donkey slowed. Painfully, they picked their way forward.

Soon, overgrown bushes closed behind them.

"I think we lost them," Zet said softly.

"Agreed," Hui said in a low voice. "But we still have to cross the canal."

Zet glanced back at the Princess. "Are you all right?"

She nodded, but her cheeks were pinched and her eyes looked dark with pain.

Kissa spoke up. "I have my satchel. I can mix some herbs. It would only take..."

"No," Princess Meritamon said. Then in a parched sounding voice she added, "I'm fine. Unless someone has water?"

Zet wished he could help her. "Sorry. We didn't bring any."

She nodded. "But you came and got us. That's more than enough."

The journey was far from over, he thought. *And the danger.* To distract himself from his worry, he let his thoughts wander to Naunet. Her betrayal had left a painful spot in the middle of his chest. He guessed it would be there for a long time.

As he rode and thought of her, another piece of the mystery fell together. He recalled that conversation he'd overheard between Darius and the boat Captain.

"I hope you're not leaving without saying hello to Nan," Darius had said.

"If I see her tonight, good," the Captain had replied. *"If not, give my little sister my regards".*

Nan was a nickname. They'd been talking about Naunet. Darius, the Captain and Naunet were siblings. It seemed obvious now. How could he have missed it? How could he have trusted her?

With heavy heart, he imagined Naunet and Darius plotting the kidnapping.

He knew exactly how they'd done it.

First, Darius went upriver with the Captain on a 'hunting trip'.

Then, Manu and the other man weakened the obelisk by chiseling at the base during the night. The next morning, Naunet convinced the Princess to visit the chapel. When the obelisk crashed, Naunet ran to 'investigate'. In truth, she went to inform Manu that the Princess was alone in the chapel as planned.

While everyone was distracted, Manu moved in and snatched the Princess and Kissa. Naunet rushed back to the harbor, screaming that the Priestess had disappeared—but only after she'd given the men plenty of time to escape.

Darius was upriver. He snuck off with the skiff and rowed to the wadi. There he ferried the two girls across the canal.

How could Naunet have betrayed her own people like that? And him, too.

Zet's shoulders sagged. Never had he been so completely fooled. It was like he'd been blind, because he'd wanted to believe her. He realized then that he'd liked her. This was the worst blow of all.

The donkeys were walking side-by-side.

Zet glanced at Kissa, remembering she was half-Hyksos and didn't even know it. What would she say when she learned the truth? Would she feel betrayed by her mother?

Had that been part of Darius's plan? Had he seen Kissa's mother with Naunet, and decided she'd make the perfect decoy? Or had it been a fluke?

When they finally reached the canal, the sky was turning a pale shade of gray. Dawn would be here soon. The four paused at the reedy bank, and stared at one another in the growing light. They were a long way down from their earlier crossing.

"Better get this over with," Hui said, trying to urge Gray Ears forward.

"Wait," Zet said.

Hui glanced at him.

"I don't know if they can swim with two of us riding."

"I take it you have a plan?"

Zet nodded. "The girls ride. We swim alongside."

Hui looked at the river, as if seeing it with fresh eyes. Zet did the same. It churned and swirled, gurgling and spitting as it passed rocks and reeds on its way downstream. And who knew what lay under the burbling surface? Poisonous snakes. Crocodiles. Hippos.

"Come on," Zet said, not wanting to spend another moment thinking about it.

"I can't swim," Kissa blurted. "What if we fall off? The Princess can't either—"

"Look!" Princess Meritamon said. "Down there!"

The three kidnappers had just emerged onto the bank. They were tiny from this distance. Still, they turned and their shouts of triumph could be heard.

"Can you manage?" she asked Zet.

"Yes." Zet wound Brownie's bridle rope around his waist and tied it into a knot. Hui followed suit. Zet plunged in, pulling Brownie and the animal's precious cargo forward. Gray Ears clearly didn't want to be left behind. He responded to Hui's urging and got into the water.

The bank dropped off quickly. The current grabbed hold of Zet.

Only the bridle rope kept him from being carried away.

The swim was long and hard. Even the donkeys were being carried sideways. The current was much stronger here. No wonder Darius and Manu had chosen the other spot to cross. Zet could see them, along with the third man, on their donkeys swimming their way to the far bank.

But then the current ripped Zet and the others even faster. He went under.

The Princess pulled him, spluttering, to the surface. Moments later, the wild flow threw them against the bank. Zet stumbled for his footing, and then he was standing on land. Hui was right beside him. Up river, the men were still crossing.

"Which way is the harbor?" Princess Meritamon asked.

He pointed right.

"We have to cross their path?" she gasped. "They'll cut us off!"

"We'll try to skirt around them. They're still swimming, we'll make it."

29

A LAST STAND

Zet led Brownie by the rope into the towering rushes. Soon, the canal was lost from view. He stroked the donkey's matted fur. The animal was clearly exhausted.

"Just a little further." Feeling horrible, he climbed onto its back.

The Princess wrapped her arms around Zet's waist. It was clear escape was taking its toll. He could tell by her ragged breath she was in extreme pain.

"How much further?" she gasped.

"Not far," Zet lied.

When they burst out of the towering rushes, Zet's hopes fell. They were much further from the harbor than he ever expected. The pyramid rose, toy-sized, in the distance. They still had to pass by the construction site on the way.

The three men were sure to cut them off.

He prayed that medjay would appear out of the shadows, brandishing swords. Then he remembered what Darius had said, about the Hyksos trap.

As if to confirm his worst fears, none appeared.

A crazy idea came to him. A way to buy time. Maybe they'd have a chance.

"Head for the hill!" Zet told Hui.

"The pyramid," Hui said, clearly understanding Zet's plan.

Zet spoke into Brownie's ear, urging it forward. The animal was winded, snorting and shaking its furry head. But then, Brownie began to trot. Zet glanced back at Gray Ears. Reluctantly, the donkey started into a trot as well.

They rode for the giant structure. A cliff rose directly in front, forcing them left along the road. They reached the hairpin turn at the rear of the monument and the valley was momentarily lost from view. By the time they reached the front door and could see the kidnappers once again, the men were much closer.

Zet leaped to the ground and ran to open the giant door.

"Don't bother," Hui said. It's locked."

"Locked? You put your lock on this?"

Hui shrugged. "A priest of Osiris tells you to do something, you do it."

"Right. Fine. But can you open it?"

"What do I look like, an idiot?" Hui had dismounted and was moving his hands across the pyramid wall, counting the stones. He counted twelve to the right, and then three up. Then he dug his fingers into an all but invisible hole and pulled out a long, thin wooden rod. "Here it is. The key." He held it up.

"Just open it!" Princess Meritamon gasped.

"She's right, hurry."

On the broad plane below, the kidnappers were moments away. Zet could see their evil faces clearly in the moonlight.

Hui opened the door.

"Everyone inside," Zet said.

"But whose going for help?" Princess Meritamon cried.

"No one," Zet replied. "Close the door."

"I don't understand!" she gasped. "What are you doing?"

Hui said, "Yes, what are we doing?"

"Trust me. Just wait."

The four of them stood in the pitch-black entrance. Fear shuddered up Zet's spine. And not just because of Darius and Manu.

They were in a sacred pyramid. Who knew what the gods would do?

He had to time it just right. The men must have reached the switchback by now.

"Get ready," Zet whispered. "Princess Merit and Kissa, on my command, run out the door, in the opposite direction of the road. We'll all hide on the far side. Can you do it?"

"Yes," Princess Meritamon whispered in the dark.

"Now!" Zet whispered. He slid open the door softly. All four snuck out. The donkeys huddled a few yards away. Otherwise, the area was deserted. The four made it around the corner just as the three men approached from the far trail.

"I'm not going in there," Manu growled.

The second man agreed.

"You'll do what I tell you," Darius said.

A short argument ensued. Darius won.

Zet held his breath, listening as the door creaked open. He and the others had their backs pressed to the wall. Zet was breathing hard. He'd wait long enough for the men to get several yards inside. Then, he'd lock them in.

"Now!" he whispered to Hui.

They ran for the big door.

At that instant, one of the kidnappers emerged. Darius.

Zet's only weapon was surprise. He threw himself at Darius, who rocked unsteadily on his feet.

"Lock it!" Zet shouted.

Hui dodged a punch from Darius. From inside the pyramid, the other two men shouted. Their voices echoed up the dark passage and out through the gap. Zet tried to reach the open door, but Darius swung a meaty fist at his head. Zet ducked. Not fast enough. It clipped him and sent him sprawling.

Hui slammed the door and jammed the stick into the lock. Darius lunged at him as Hui pulled the stick out. Just before Darius got hold of him, Hui rolled sideways.

"Give me that stick!" shouted Darius.

Hui threw it to Zet. He caught it and rolled, sending Brownie and Gray Ears skittering backwards. Darius pounced on Hui and fastened him in a headlock. Zet's best friend cried out in pain.

Meanwhile, from inside, huge fists pounded the thick wood door.

Darius wrenched Hui around to face Zet and shouted, "Give me that stick or your friend's dead!"

"Pharaoh's soldiers are coming," Zet gasped, trying to call his bluff.

Darius laughed. "Nice try. Now give it to me!"

Hui was choking, his face crimson. Still, he gasped, "Run!"

"Run and I'll snap his neck," Darius snarled.

"No!" Zet cried, bargaining for time. "Wait, I'll do what you want."

"Open the door. NOW!"

"All right," Zet said. "Let him go and I'll open it."

"DO IT!" Darius barked. "You have until the count of three. One ... two ..."

Running forward, Zet made for the door. But before he got there, he tucked into a shoulder roll, flying head over heels. As he rolled over, he shot out his foot in a jarring kick. Darius had been ready, and jumped sideways.

The kick landed, but the force wasn't enough to knock him down.

Still, it was enough to make him loosen his grip on Hui.

Hui bit down on Darius's forearm. The big man yowled like an animal. He tried to shake Hui loose, but Hui wouldn't let go. Zet grabbed a stone and pelted it at Darius's head. The stone bounced off, but a trickle of blood started behind the man's ear. Darius ripped his forearm away from Hui and landed a punch on Hui's jaw.

The force sent Hui flying.

Zet sent a second stone winging toward Darius's head. Darius turned, and the rock hit him full in the face. Blood rushed from Darius's nose. Meanwhile, inside the pyramid, the two men kept pounding at the door, trying to break free. Darius staggered a moment. He regained his balance, and his dark eyes looked deadly.

"I'll kill you," he growled.

The third stone in Zet's hand never made it into the air. Darius was on him. The man knocked him down, and together they fell. Zet kicked and punched, but Darius was too big. The man's huge fist laid into Zet's stomach, knocking the wind out of him. A second blow slammed into Zet's jaw. Darius pulled his fist back a third time, but then his expression changed.

A shocked look came over his sunburnt face.

His eyes rolled up into his head.

He slumped onto Zet, as heavy as a bag of wet sand.

30

TRIUMPHANT DAWN

Zet tried to struggle out from under Darius. He wiggled sideways, far enough to see Hui standing over the limp kidnapper with a big rock in both hands.

"Should I hit him again?" Hui said.

"Uh, no, I think once was enough."

"And he thought he could beat us."

"Well, he's still beating me, I can't move," Zet said with a groan.

"Oh, right, hold on." Hui was smiling, even though he had a fat lip and his left eye was swollen almost shut.

Together, they got Darius onto his back. Then, deciding the man might choke from his nosebleed, they rolled him onto his side. Hui ran for some rope from the donkeys while Zet stood over Darius with the rock, just in case the thug came to.

Moments later, the kidnapper was trussed up like a duck ready for the cook pot.

The other two men still slammed against the pyramid door. They shouted now in more than just anger. They sounded terrified.

"Can they break that door down, do you think?" Zet said.

"No way. Not a chance. That door's as thick as a man's arm. They're not going anywhere."

"It's safe!" Zet called.

Princess Meritamon and Kissa peeked around the corner. A smile brightened Princess Merit's face. On the ground, Darius moaned. His eyes fluttered open. He tried to struggle upright, and then realized he was completely bound. Zet thought the Princess might shrink back, fearful of meeting her kidnapper face-to-face.

Even if he was all trussed up.

Instead, she cheered. A wonderful, loud cheer that echoed across the plains. Kissa joined in with a laugh that lit up her face. Watching the two of them celebrate was the best reward he could ever wish for.

Then to everyone's surprise, the donkeys brayed as if in agreement and they all started to laugh.

Finally, Hui sobered.

"We're not in the clear yet. At least, I'm not. I'm an escaped criminal."

"I don't think there will be a problem," Zet said. "Obviously Naunet hid the jewels in the river herself."

"Jewels?" Princess Merit asked.

"It's complicated."

"Well, on my honor as a Princess, I swear no harm will come to you. You saved me. You and Zet are heroes."

This cheered Hui up considerably.

"Come on, let's head back," Zet said.

"Good idea," Kissa said. "The Princess needs rest and water."

"You worry too much," she said with a laugh.

Zet said, "Actually, speaking of worrying, we need to approach the harbor carefully. We still don't know what happened to the medjay." His chest clenched, thinking of Merimose, the big Commander. What would they find?

He started toward Brownie, who flicked his tail and trotted over. He hoped the animals were up for another ride. It had been a long night.

"Looks like you've made a friend," Princess Merit said.

Zet stroked Brownie's nose. "We'd be dead without these guys."

The Princess let him help her up onto Brownie's back. She was so easy to be around that he'd nearly forgotten who she was. But then a wave of awe swept over him and he shook his head in amazement.

The sturdy donkey set out, with Zet walking alongside. The group wound back down toward the harbor, sticking to the shadows. They stayed off the road, and took the long way around.

Princess Merit insisted on hearing the whole story, so Zet and Hui talked in low voices, telling her and Kissa everything, from the Queen Mother's visit, to the boat ride, to Hui's discovery of the jewels, and breaking him out of prison.

The girls listened in amazement, laughing quietly and asking questions. The only thing Zet kept to himself was Kissa's story, and the truth about her birth. It wasn't his to tell.

Zet and Hui left the girls hidden near some date trees and covered the last distance alone. If Hyksos soldiers had attacked, who knew what they'd find.

Pharaoh's boat stood at anchor, white sails fluttering in the gentle breeze. In front of the boat, clustered along the harbor, stood a band of strange looking men. They wore foreign clothes, and their broad shoulders and arms were bloodied and bruised. Hui grabbed Zet's arm, his fingers like pincers. A bolt of horror shot down Zet's spine.

Hyksos warriors.

Then his eyes went to their sword belts.

They were empty.

He frowned. Suddenly, he noticed how close together the men stood. Realization dawned. This wasn't an attack. They hadn't taken control of Pharaoh's boat. The men were tied together by ropes.

They were prisoners.

The dark head of Merimose became visible on the far side of the group. Zet's heart leaped. The captain was alive. Still, his arm was bandaged from wrist to shoulder. He looked haggard with worry.

"We're safe!" Zet gasped, sending a prayer of thanks to the gods.

He and Hui ran back for the girls. When they returned, Merimose spun at the donkeys' approach. When he saw the four of them, he looked like he almost sagged with relief. Then his eyes lit up with joy.

But before either Zet or Merimose could speak, there came a loud roar of delight.

The Mighty Bull appeared from between a pack of medjay. He shouted with undisguised relief at the sight of his favorite daughter. Striding forward, he lifted her from Brownie's back and held her in his big arms as if she were a child of five, and not a grown girl.

"All right, I'm safe! Let go!" she scolded, but she was laughing.

While Pharaoh rejoiced, Zet learned from Merimose that the medjay had tracked the band of Hyksos. They'd been lying in wait for the handover. If things went wrong, they planned to kill Pharaoh, and Princess Meritamon as well. There had been a long, drawn out skirmish, and the medjay won by the skin of their teeth.

"You were wise to approach with caution. Things could have turned out much differently," Merimose said.

Zet let this sink in. They might still be running. "Then I guess we make a good team," he said.

At this, Merimose looked chagrined, but laughed.

Zet told Merimose about Darius and the others, still back at the pyramid.

Men were dispatched to round them up.

"And take the priest," Merimose told the men. "Being Pharaoh's holy burial place, I'm sure he'll want to be involved in purging it from the likes of those three."

"There's someone else," Zet said.

Merimose gave him a quizzical look. "This is quite the morning."

Zet felt a pang of sadness as he described the shed where they'd left Naunet. Beside him Hui was fidgeting nervously, despite the Princess's earlier assurances.

Zet said, "She was the one who stole the jewels."

"She deserves what she gets," Hui said. "Trying to frame me for her theft!"

"We'll find her," Merimose said.

"Thank you," Zet said.

Merimose patted him with his good arm. "You did well." And then he was gone.

Morning light spread warm fingers through the camp, filling it with golden light. Everyone had come out to see Pharaoh. It wasn't often one got to stand in the presence of a living god. The camp stood at a respectful distance, watching in breathless silence.

People were talking about Princess Meritamon, too.

"Can you believe it was her all along? She visited our mess tent three times before she was kidnapped. I stood behind her in line!"

"I knew it was the Princess!" someone whispered.

"You did not, you dolt," whispered another.

Glancing around, Zet wondered where the architect was. Then he spotted Senna in conversation with a formally dressed man. Pharaoh's personal scribe, no doubt. Did Senna ever stop working?

"Come on," Zet said to Hui.

They headed over.

"Ah, my runners," Senna said. "Now, I have plenty of messages to go out today. Seeing that the Princess is found, it's time you got to work."

Hui opened his mouth. Nothing came out.

"Er—" Zet began, "We'd love to, but we have to get going. Home and all that."

"Home!" Senna cried, his feathery brows waving in the breeze. "Ridiculous! Do you have any idea how much—"

Zet said, "I think I hear Commander Merimose calling us!"

He grabbed Hui's arm and took off.

"I was joking, boys!" Senna shouted.

Zet glanced back. Senna, the old trickster, wore a toothy grin.

HOMEWARD

The morning celebration continued into breakfast. Entering the mess tent and seeing the camp's happy faces, Zet realized he'd had no idea how unhappy and concerned people had been about the kidnapping. It would have been worse if they'd known then the Priestess was the Princess.

They were a transformed group. It was as if a hidden weight had been lifted.

"I knew you were pulling one over on me!" shouted Jafar, laughing and grabbing Zet around his shoulders and scuffing up Zet's hair. "Not a friend of the medjay, huh?"

Hui grinned—fat-lip and all—and was bursting with pride. With his swollen eye, he looked like a scruffy, heroic dog.

"And you, too!" Jafar shouted. "Kemet's best young jeweler, the architect's *runner*? Ha!"

They finally stumbled outside, grinning, their backs sore from so many construction workers pounding them with congratulations.

"This has been crazy. Fun, scary, exciting," Zet said. "But you know what? I'm suddenly really looking forward to getting home."

"Me, too," Hui said. "Speaking of that, how exactly *do* we get home?"

"Good question. But before we find out, we need to visit Brownie and Gray Ears." He pulled a handful of honeyed apricots from his pocket and grinned.

Later, they were wandering along the wharf toward their crooked tent, when the flap was thrust aside. A man in a gold embroidered tunic had Zet and Hui's packs in his arms.

"You will follow me," the man said. "We embark shortly."

"I guess that's our ride," Zet said, glancing at Hui.

But when the man in the gold embroidered tunic led them to Pharaoh's gangplank, bowed and motioned them on board, Zet and Hui shot each other looks of disbelief.

"Is this really happening?" Hui whispered.

"We're sailing into Thebes on the royal barge?" Zet whispered back.

Hui whooped, they performed their secret handshake, and Zet was about to do some completely ridiculous happy dance when he noticed Princess Meritamon on deck.

"Tell me you'll teach me how to do that!" she said, laughing.

Zet was suddenly reminded of the day he'd seen her at the Opet festival, surrounded by people vying for her attention. He thought of her grandmother, too, and felt a rush of happiness. The Princess would be home for her party, and the world would be whole.

"All right," Zet said, laughing.

"I'll show it to my handmaidens. They're always far too serious."

"Maybe I could teach them a few magic tricks," Hui added. "That would definitely lighten them up."

The three of them glanced at the Princess's boat, which was getting ready to set sail and follow them south. A woman stood on deck with her arm around Kissa. It was Kissa's mother, the woman from the cell.

She spotted Zet and a grateful smile lit her eyes.

Had she told Kissa, yet? They'd have a lot to talk about.

"Kissa's my dearest friend. I don't want her mother to tell her," Princess Meritamon said suddenly. "As far as I'm concerned, she's Egyptian. But I suppose she deserves the truth."

Lunch and dinner on board were royal affairs. They ate on plates trimmed with gold and drank from cups made of real glass. Every food imaginable appeared, and all of it delicious. Zet was eating too fast to taste it!

"So," Pharaoh said. "You hid in my pyramid?" Living god that he was, he laughed like any human. "I'll be thinking of that when I go off into eternity!"

"Did you know donkeys can swim?" Princess Merit asked.

"Brownie and Gray Ears deserve medals," Zet said.

Princess Meritamon and Hui agreed.

"I think that's a grand idea," Pharaoh said. "Medals, and we'll make sure they get the best life a donkey could ever wish for!"

Later, the Great Bull pulled Zet and Hui aside. "You saved my daughter. For that, I and the gods are eternally grateful."

Zet knew those words of praise would stay with him for the rest of his life.

That evening, he stood by the rail and watched the water trail behind them. He was thinking of Naunet. *Why had she done it?*

The princess appeared, walking slowly. Her limp was barely visible. She leaned on her elbows beside him.

"All this time," she said, "I've been racking my brain, wondering if I'd treated Naunet poorly."

Zet rubbed his thumb against the polished rail, staring down at it. "I don't believe that for a minute."

She was silent.

"I just wish I knew why she did it," he said.

Stars sparkled in the dark water.

"We were friends," she said. "I thought we were. But I knew there was a lot of tension between her and the others. Naunet had a way of treating everything like a competition. One thing I must tell you—

she was the one who insisted Kissa be there on the day we were kidnapped. And she insisted Kissa bring her healing herbs. So I suppose she did care a little."

Zet sighed. "I was thinking about Darius. Maybe he threatened her?"

"That's possible," the Princess said. "I'll be sure it's raised when she faces trial."

It was the only bitter drop in the wonderful outcome. The Princess was safe. They'd averted a new war. Zet was determined to be happy.

Once they reached Thebes, the sight of his familiar city lightened his spirits.

No one knew of the kidnapping plot, but as Pharaoh's boat neared shore, people spotted the white and gold sails. They began to gather, running along the watersteps, appearing out of nearby streets and buildings. Soon, a crowd of cheering citizens stood to welcome their Pharaoh and his daughter.

"I can't forget to give you this," Zet said, pulling the golden cord with the Queen Mother's ring over his neck and handing it to Princess Meritamon.

She cradled it in her hands, her eyes shining. "She was right about you. I am forever in your debt for saving my life."

Zet didn't know how to answer. Instead, he just bowed low.

After bidding goodbye to Pharaoh, Zet and Hui ran down the gangplank. They sprinted through the familiar streets, glad to be back. When they reached their own block, the street was quiet.

It was as if nothing had happened.

Except a lot had. And now, to Zet, the city seemed smaller. Still wonderful, but different. It was amazing how a few days could change you. He grinned when he spotted his front door, and saw movement through the open window.

"We're home!" Zet shouted.

The front door flew open.

Everyone was hugging and laughing.

Hui and Kat had a tearful reunion—on Kat's part—Hui was too busy showing off his bruised face to be tearful.

Zet's mother ran to fetch Hui's family from their house a block away. Everyone piled into Zet's house. Their story was told over a huge brunch. The only part Zet left out was the part about Naunet. He'd never told Hui about her, and he never would.

When a knock sounded on the door, Zet ran to answer.

A royal courier stood there, a boy around Zet's age. The courier eyed Zet strangely, obviously surprised to be delivering news to a place like this.

Kat appeared. "What is it?"

"A message," the courier said, holding out a leather bound scroll. He looked doubtful. "Should I read it for you?"

"No. Thank you." Kat took it. "I can read it on my own."

The courier's brows shot up. Then he left.

"What does it say?" Zet said.

"Hold on! Let me open it," Kat replied.

Hui squeezed between them. "Who's it from?"

Kat scanned the contents, and her eyes widened. "The palace! We're invited to the palace, next week. To see the Queen Mother!"

"Us?" Zet said. "That's crazy!"

"She wants to thank you in person. Wait, and there's a note from the Princess—she hopes we'll sit with her in her royal box at her birthday celebration." Now, it was Kat's turn to freak out. "What will I wear?" she practically screamed.

Zet covered his ears and rolled his eyes.

Hui grinned. "I told you I saw a future in this! Didn't I? Secret Agent Zet and his trusty partner Hui win again!"

"By the way," Zet's mother interjected, "Old Teni came by, said something about her roof?"

"Uh oh," Zet said, glancing at his best friend. But then he started to laugh.

Already the sights and smells and dangers of Abydos were fading. They were home. With their families, the people they cared about most. Everything was back to normal.

They really had won.

SCOTT'S HISTORICAL NOTE

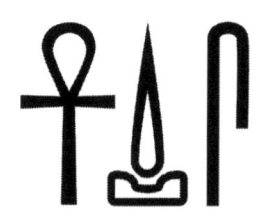

Although this is a story, Zet, Kat, and their friends' world is much as it would have been. Egyptians loved to write things down. Using ancient records, we can picture their clothing, the houses they lived in, their boats, and their methods of building big structures.

I want to mention the story's writing and dialogue style: it's common to imagine that people spoke more formally in ancient times, but we have no evidence of that. In fact, ancient Egyptians loved parties and games, they faced social struggles, and were even known to paint graffiti! Keeping in mind that the English language didn't exist, neither formal nor casual English would be correct. Because of this, I veered away from the formal to make the story more accessible.

Abydos is one of the most important archaeological sites in Egypt. King Narmer (also thought to be Menes), Egypt's first pharaoh, was buried there. The pyramid of Ahmose the First was the only pyramid built at Abydos. Although it has mostly crumbled away, its remains can still be visited today.

MYSTERY OF THE EGYPTIAN MUMMY

ZET'S LAST CASE

BY SCOTT PETERS

THE MUMMY

"*OOoooooooooooo...*"

The ghostly moan filled the night air.

Twelve-year-old Zet bolted upright on his sleeping mat. What was that strange noise?

"*OOOoooooooooooo...*"

There it came again, like a man in groaning agony. Where was it coming from?

From overhead the yellow moon god, Khonsu, peered down. Sweat stood out on Zet's forehead. He and his eleven-year-old sister Kat were camped out on the rooftop to try and escape the heat. They disagreed on a lot of things—but when it came to keeping cool at night, they were united. The roof was their domain.

Zet spun to check on Kat. Her sleeping pallet lay on the roof's far side.

He gasped. It was empty.

"Kat?" he whispered.

No answer.

By the gods, where was she?

"*OOOoooooooooooo...*"

The moan sounded close. Creepy close. But that was impossible.

How would a moaning man get up here? Zet leaped to his feet. Where was his sister?

He clambered down the steep ladder to the front room.

"Kat?" he whisper-shouted.

He found her clinging to their mother. The two of them were staring out the open front door. His sister's shoulders were scrunched around her ears in terror.

Still, she shot him a reproachful glance and hissed, *"Shush!"*

Good old Kat.

"What's out there?" Zet demanded, trying to see past them.

"Stay back," his mother said, blocking the door. "Both of you."

"Let me see," he said, standing on tiptoe.

From outside, fresh moans made Zet's short hair prickle. He pushed forward. "Mother, let me see!"

Kat elbowed her brother as Zet gained a foothold in the doorway.

"It's not safe!" his mother cried. "Close the door. Quickly!"

But Zet was already on the front stoop.

The moon painted their street in shades of grey and blue. The eerie colors only heightened the terror that shot through him when he saw the monster.

A bandaged figure.

It looked as horrifying as the ancient stories described: a creature of death come to life. And it was making its way along their street.

The man—or what had once been a man when he'd been alive—was entirely wrapped in tattered cloth strips. His head. His arms. His torso. His legs.

The creepy figure walked with jerky motions. Slow and monotonous, arms outstretched. Ready to throttle any human in its path.

"A mummy," Zet whispered.

His worst dream had come to life, right here in front of his house. A body risen from the dead. How had this mummy escaped its tomb to wander the land of the living? How was that even possible?

What evil had been cast upon it to keep it from eternal peace?

As if sensing Zet's presence, the mummy paused, its face shadowed in darkness. It raised one bandaged arm and pointed a bony finger at Zet. An eerie whisper issued from the mummy's bandaged mouth. A horrible chant.

Awoahaoh huhshhhhh ooohamamima awoahaoh huhshhhhh.

Zet gulped in terror.

Get a hold of yourself! Mummies don't come to life!

Awoahaoh huhshhhhh ooohamamima awoahaoh huhshhhhh.

Was this some kind of joke?

Up and down the street, oil lamps were being lit. The blood-drained faces of horror-stricken neighbors stared at the bandaged creature from windows and doorways. Worried eyes darted from Zet to the mummy and back again.

The mummy kept up its harsh chant.

Finally, it fell silent. Then the mummy resumed its jerking walk.

Without thinking, Zet launched himself toward the street. An enormous jackal, the largest he'd ever seen, leaped from the shadows. Tall, pointed ears jutted from a sleek head and dark, golden fur covered its muscled body. Snarling, it bared its gnashing fangs.

Zet jerked back.

Drool dripped from the animal's jaws. It began to bark, vicious and fast and loud.

It was as if Anubis himself, the jackal-headed God of the Underworld, had come to life in his earthly form and was preparing to launch up their front steps.

Zet edged backward. Every part of him wanted to bolt the door shut. But a small voice inside argued that none of this could be real. It just couldn't. That jackal wasn't a god. And mummies didn't come to life. He needed to find out who or what was behind this. He refused to let this trickery terrorize his family.

The mummy kept on its slow pace down the street.

Zet had to go after it. He needed to see where it was going. The wild beast, however, barred his way. The jackal gnashed its jaws.

Kat's trembling voice cried it, "It's Anubis, come to protect the dead."

The jackal's eyes gleamed. Then it turned and loped after the mummy.

Zet launched after them. Before his feet could hit the street, a hand caught his arm. His mother's.

"Oh no you don't," she commanded.

"Mother, let go!"

"Not even if the gods command it."

"But it's getting away!" he pleaded as the mummy neared the street corner. "Look!"

At that moment, the creature's spooky profile became visible.

Zet choked back a strangled cry. Under the yellow moon, the linen wrappings that covered the monster's face glistened oily black. They were tattered and scorched as though his head had been burned. Where the eyes should have been lay two gaping holes.

Zet's stomach roiled. Kat let out a sharp gasp.

Their mother's arms wrapped tighter around them both, pulling them against her as if to ward off the creature.

From the distant corner, the mummy seemed to glare straight at Zet. It remained frozen, locked in an awful stare.

And then it walked on, moving in its jerky fashion.

The jackal let out a gruesome howl. *Aooooooooh!*

A moment later, the two spooky figures disappeared from view.

Silence reigned for a long, terrible moment. Whispers rose as the neighborhood stirred to life. Across the street, the old sandal-maker hobbled outside. Others joined him.

The sandal-maker pointed a gnarled finger at Zet. "The boy's cursed!" he crowed. "The boy and his family. Cursed!"

The others stared, open-mouthed, at Zet, Kat, and his mother. And it wasn't a good stare. He read fear in their eyes. Not just fear of the mummy, but fear of them.

"We're not," Zet scoffed. "No, we're not!"

The sandal-maker said, "We all saw it point at you. We all heard it whisper that awful curse."

"It wasn't a curse. It was just mumbling!"

The sandal-maker looked ready to argue when a scream pierced the night.

It came from somewhere down the street—a woman's scream. The horrific scream was so loud and awful that Kat clapped her hands over her ears.

The sandal-maker and the other neighbors turned their backs on Zet and ran toward the frightening cries. Zet broke free from his mother and sprinted after them.

Frantic, the crowd scoured the streets for the shrieking woman but her cries had died away.

Despite turning the neighborhood upside down, she was nowhere to be found.

2

DAYLIGHT FRIGHT

The sun god, Ra, inched his fingers across the rooftop in rosy hues. All night, Zet had lain on his sleeping pallet, eyes wide, replaying the memory of the mummy lurching its way down his street.

It couldn't be real. It just couldn't!

A mummy?

Come back from the dead?

How? Priests had clearly wrapped it in the bandages of eternity. They'd entombed the body. So how had it gotten loose?

Zet was as god-fearing as any Egyptian in Thebes, yet such things didn't happen. Walking mummies belonged in scary stories, whispered over lamplight to frighten your friends and kid sister.

Stories were different. They were fun.

There was nothing fun about last night.

And what were those evil words it had chanted?

Zet rubbed his face. He might be a kid, but he'd made a promise to his father to keep his family safe until the war was over and his father returned. Zet and Kat both had. Together, the siblings worked hard to keep the family's pottery stall running in the marketplace. Their mother and their new baby brother were finally growing stronger, but Zet and Kat couldn't let down their guard.

And now this had happened?

What if the mummy came back? He had to keep that monster away. Even if it meant fighting the creature of death barehanded.

. . . if it *was* a creature of death.

In the light of day, he was finding it hard to believe it was anything more than an awful trick. But who would do such a thing? And why?

He'd get to the bottom of this mystery. Starting now.

He found Kat in the kitchen. She stood lost in thought, a half-peeled orange in one hand. Zet snagged it from her and she started.

"Hey!" she said, "I was about to eat that."

"This month or next? Listen, we need to talk."

She eyed him warily and grabbed another orange from the dish. "Why do I have a bad feeling about this?"

"You know exactly what we have to do."

"No, I don't."

"We're going to investigate, sis."

"Are you crazy? No way," she said. "Not this time—*no way!*"

"Look, come on. That mummy couldn't have been real. We both know mummies don't come back from the dead. They don't walk around in the land of the living. Someone's playing an evil prank. We need to find out why."

"It was no prank. I saw it. That monster's face was half burned off."

"Yeah . . . well." Uneasily, Zet recalled how the monster had stared at him from that singed mask of tattered linen.

"And what about that huge jackal?" Kat demanded.

In the next room, their baby brother Apu wailed. Their mother made cooing noises, trying to settle him.

Kat stepped closer and spoke in a whisper. "Remember Aziza?"

"Aziza?" Zet frowned. "You mean that cousin of Pharaoh?"

"Shh! Yes, of course I mean that cousin of Pharaoh. Who else would I be talking about?"

"Well then, yeah."

Aziza's house was the largest in the neighborhood. Back when Aziza had been alive, the man had bullied everyone. He'd talked behind people's backs. Complained about even the smallest noise. And he'd hated kids.

"Aziza was mummified," Kat whispered.

"So?"

"Only because he could afford it," she said in a low voice. "And because he was Pharaoh's cousin."

"Distant cousin. But still related. A fact he never got tired of reminding people. But yes, he was mummified. What's your point?"

Bending closer she said, "Do you think *Aziza* could have come back to haunt us?" Worry pinched Kat's dark brows. "You know . . . for what happened?"

"Don't be silly," Zet scoffed, warding off a shiver. He grabbed a date bun and took a huge bite.

"*Silly?*" Kat glared at him.

Their mother's graceful shadow fell across the doorway. Little Apu sat on her hip, sucking his thumb and looking from Zet to Kat with watery, earnest eyes. His face was red from bawling.

"What's all this whispering?" their mother said.

"Whispering?" Zet said. "We weren't whispering."

Kat quickly said, "Just getting ready to leave for the pottery stall."

"Speaking of which, we better go." Zet reached for the linen-wrapped bowl his mother always prepared with his lunch. "Don't want to be late!"

Their mother eyed the rising sun through the window. It struck Zet that she looked fearful. He could see from the dusky shadows beneath her eyes that she hadn't slept. When she spoke, her voice was strained. "Wait a moment. I want to speak with you, children."

She set Apu on his woven mat. He let out a howl.

"What's got into you, little one?" she asked, sticking a wooden rattle in his chubby fist. "You're usually such a happy monkey."

It was true, Apu was always grinning his drooly grin. But strangely,

Apu had cried all night. Zet and Kat exchanged a glance. *Had the mummy's apparition affected him somehow?*

"I suppose it's growing pains." Their mother watched Apu hammer his rattle against the floor. Then she raised her worried gaze to Zet and Kat. "You're to come right home after closing time. Understand? No loitering around town."

Kat said, "We will."

"Are you two all right?" she asked, reaching to place a cool, soothing hand on their shoulders.

It would be easy for Zet to act like a little kid again. Back when mother made everything better. When he could hide behind her linen skirts from the scary world outside. Yet that boy had disappeared when his father went to war.

He cracked a smile. "Someone's just playing a trick."

"A *trick?*" Kat said. "Stop saying that! The mummy had no face! It's come back from the dead, it's a cursed thing, an unholy thing, and it was in our street. In front of our house. Right out there."

"Shush, you'll scare Apu," Mother said.

Apu threw the rattle and it bounced across the floor.

"Apu has no idea what we're talking about." Zet picked him up and spun him around. Kat darted out of their way. He wheeled his brother around until Apu's wails turned into hiccups and then a reluctant grin. Setting him down, Zet said. "I wish you'd let me go after that mummy last night."

"*Zet,*" their mother cautioned.

"At least then we'd know where it went."

"That's for the medjay police to find out," she said.

"Or the priests," Kat said. "Some poor, cursed soul has left his tomb. And he's found his way here. They need to put him back in his sarcophagus. Fast."

"Yes, and they will," their mother said. "They'll sort it out." She shot Zet a stern look. "Without *your* help."

"Who said anything about me helping?"

"You think I don't know my own son?"

"I only want to protect us."

"You'll protect us by doing what you and Kat have already been doing so well. Watching over the pottery stall. Making sales. Keeping the business going while I've been ill." Still holding Kat in one arm, she pulled Zet close. "I don't thank you two enough. You've kept this family alive. Your father will be so proud when he comes home. I'm proud. Promise me you won't get involved in this mummy business."

Zet shuffled his feet. How could he make such a promise?

"Zet?" she asked.

"I'll take care of the stall, don't worry." At least that was true. As to the rest . . .

"Thank you," she said.

Guilt slid over him. Clearly, she thought he meant he'd leave the matter to the police. He glanced at Kat, who pursed her lips in exasperation. Nothing got past her.

Well, guilt or not, he couldn't let this mystery go.

"We better get to the pottery stall." He wiggled out of his mother's embrace. Quickly, he patted his baby brother on the head, waved his mother goodbye and headed for the door.

MARKET MADNESS

The usual crowds filled Thebes' narrow, dusty streets, growing thicker as they neared the city center.

Today, however, people seemed different. They seemed scared. Three women in gold-trimmed linen sheaths stood with their heads close together, whispering in frantic voices. A street-sweeper scanned this way and that with wide, frightened eyes, clutching his broom like a weapon.

The siblings neared a temple. Out front, several medjay police questioned a priest in urgent voices. Zet slowed, trying to eavesdrop. The air was thick with incense.

Kat yanked his elbow. "Come on! It's late. We have to get to the stall."

"Shh, let's listen," he whispered. "They're obviously talking about the mummy."

But the medjay had sharp ears. He turned and glared.

Zet had friends in the police force, having helped them solve several crimes. Unfortunately this officer, clad in a leopard-skin kilt with a club fastened at his waist, was a stranger.

"Move along," the medjay warned, hand on his club. "The pair of you."

"But we—"

"This is official business," the medjay said. "Keep walking."

"Come on," Kat said. "Let's go."

"We should tell him about last night. We should tell him that we saw the mummy. It might be helpful," Zet hissed. Plus, he wouldn't mind getting in a few questions of his own.

"No. We have customers waiting. You promised Mother. Besides, we can't afford to set tongues wagging again for opening late. This time, the market owner will kick us out for sure. And then we'll be in serious trouble. You know we can't afford to lose our stall."

She was right. He groaned out loud.

Then he took off at a run, sandals slapping the hot earth.

"Last one there is a rotten goose egg," he shouted.

He knew without glancing back that she was rolling her eyes. Still, she got there nearly as fast as he did.

"Only because you had a head start," she panted, hands on both knees.

Together they opened the stall's tent doors and lifted protective sheets from their wares. Inside, dishes of every size gleamed in the early light. There were bowls and cooking pots, vases and decorative pottery. The swish of curtains sent up puffs of dust as Zet tied them back.

From all around, other vendors' stalls clattered to life.

Spicy smells rose from a food takeaway nearby. Across the way, spices of every color were mounded in baskets. Fruits and vegetables shone brightly. Goats bleated and fishmongers laid out their catches. Shoppers filtered in, poking and prodding and haggling.

"Pots for sale!" Zet shouted, adding to the din. "Clay pots! Come and get your pots!"

But nothing could banish the mummy from his thoughts—the mummy and the strange chant and the way he'd pointed directly at their door. At *him*.

"Is it just me, or are people avoiding us?" Kat said.

It was true. To their dismay, not a single person came to buy their wares all morning. At midday, they sat in the shade behind stacks of pottery to eat lunch.

Zet shoveled chickpea salad into his mouth. Worried or not, nothing ever dampened his appetite. "People are definitely avoiding us."

"Why?" Kat said. "This is awful! Even with the Wag Festival coming, I'm not expecting a rush on fancy plates. It's not that sort of event. But we've never gone a single morning without selling a few cooking pots. They break all the time. Water jugs do, too. And clay bread loaf pans. What's going on?"

"I don't know. Could it have to do with the mummy?"

Kat's forehead wrinkled under her dark bangs. "Wait." Her face paled. *"Do you think the mummy actually cursed us?* Oh by the gods, I knew it was Aziza. I just knew it!"

"Nah," he muttered. He tried to push all thoughts of Pharaoh's cousin—bitter, vengeful Aziza—from his mind. "It's probably just a coincidence. We did *nothing* to him! That whole business wasn't our fault. Look, forget I said anything. Let's get back to work."

Lunch over, they returned to the front of the tent. As soon as they had, Kat grabbed Zet's arm and her fingers dug in hard.

"Ow!" Zet said.

"Look!" She pointed. "At that stack of plates."

Zet did as she said, seeing the pile of pottery that hadn't been there earlier.

"Someone's returned all of their dinnerware," she gasped.

Zet stared in shock. "Strange. They paid for them. Don't they want them anymore?"

As if in answer, a frantic-looking couple scuttled up with armloads of pottery. The man wore his wig low to cover his eyes. The woman hid her face behind a clay jug. She'd bought that jug only last week. Zet remembered selling it to her.

"You're bringing those back?" Zet asked, baffled. "Is something wrong?"

They made no reply. Instead, they set the pottery down and scurried off.

"Wait!" Zet called after them. "Let me give you some deben coins!"

The couple ignored his calls.

Zet sat heavily on an upside-down urn. He grabbed his head in both hands. "I have a bad feeling about this."

Kat said, "I was right! We are cursed! And everyone knows!"

"We're not cursed," Zet tried to insist.

At that moment, a woman inched up to the tent. She crouched down to abandon a beautiful serving dish. Before she got away, Kat caught the woman by her shawl.

"Please," Kat begged. "Don't leave."

"I must. Let go of me!"

"At least tell me why you're returning that dish," Kat begged.

The woman's face flushed scarlet. "My husband says it's unsafe to keep your platter in our house."

"Why?"

"Because of Aziza." She tried to disentangle her shawl from Kat's fingers.

Kat was nearly in tears. She held the woman fast. "But what does Aziza have to do with your platter?"

"Don't play coy. We both know Aziza never forgave you for that time your brother tripped him—in this very stall—and broke his nose on that jug."

"My brother didn't trip him, it was an accident! Why does no one believe that it was an accident?"

"Aziza was very particular about his looks. He used to be a handsome man, but after that? With everyone calling him Jugnose?"

"I never called him Jugnose," Kat said.

"Maybe not, but the rest of Thebes did. Is it any wonder he's come back from the dead to curse you?"

"I'm very sorry about his nose," Kat said earnestly. "But it was an accident!"

"As to that, I can't say," the woman sniffed.

"My lady," Zet said, "There's no reason to return your platter. Trust me, we're not cursed."

She scoffed. "Aziza was haunting your doorstep last night. With Anubis, snarling God of the Underworld, at his heels! And I have no intention of crossing either of them." The woman yanked her shawl free from Kat's hand.

"But—that doesn't make sense!" Zet protested, "Aziza can't return from the dead. That's not how it works!"

The woman hurried off.

"Wait," Zet called after her. "Let us at least refund your platter!" If they had to refund everyone's returns, they'd soon be poor. But what choice did he have? It was the right thing to do.

The woman ignored him and disappeared into the crowd.

Kat moaned. "Oh Zet, we're in huge trouble."

"This makes no sense," Zet said. "Aziza either made it to the Underworld, or the gods destroyed him at his judgment trial. He couldn't return to haunt us. No one can."

Kat looked at Zet. "I don't know."

He set his jaw. "I'm right and you know it. So let's hide away these returns. Because when this blows over, everyone's going to want their stuff back."

Kat blinked away tears. "We're cursed, Zet. Curses don't blow over."

Zet ignored wary stares from market-goers. "This is a mystery," he insisted. "And like any mystery, it can be solved." He picked up the abandoned platter. "Hey, don't worry. We'll figure it out. Now do you see why I need to investigate?"

Her tears turned to annoyance. She rubbed her face and finally blew out a sigh. "All right, yes. You win. We investigate. *Together.*"

TROUBLE ON THE NILE

For two days, Zet and Kat scoured their street for clues. They tried to question the neighbors, but all ran away, shouting that they didn't want Aziza cursing them, too. At night the siblings slept in shifts, watching in vain for the mummy's return.

The mummy hadn't paid a second visit. The pottery returns kept piling up, though. And Apu kept crying and pointing out the front window like he was being haunted.

Today the market was closed. Zet and Kat were meeting up with their two best friends.

Hui, whom they'd known since birth, was a joker who loved getting into trouble. But he was also a highly skilled jewelers' apprentice who now worked in the royal foundry. Princess Meritamen, who they'd met on an earlier adventure, had become a fast friend. She loved sneaking out of the palace and pretending she was a normal kid. Still, caution forced her to wear a cloak that shadowed her face.

Maybe together they could come up with answers.

All four friends were gathered on a small river raft. Zet stood with both feet planted and shoved his bamboo pole into the Nile's rushing waters. Carefully, he guided them around a rock. Hui jabbed a fishing net into the water and came up empty. Ibis birds floated alongside, white feathers gleaming. Kat kicked her feet in the current as she chatted earnestly with Princess Meritamen, or Merit as she liked to be called.

Zet was working hard to keep the raft straight but found it hard to concentrate. He was too worried.

Hui lunged with the net. "Aw, missed again!" he cried.

"Uh huh," Zet agreed in a flat voice. "Hey, Merit, you don't believe we're cursed, do you?"

If anyone knew about curses, mummies, and burial secrets, Merit would. She was Pharaoh's daughter after all.

She scrunched her eyes in thought.

"We're in real trouble," Kat said. "If people keep returning their pottery, we'll be ruined."

"I'm so sorry. This is terrible," Merit said.

The raft flew downstream with the current.

Zet said, "Well, I don't believe the mummy was Aziza. There's no way he's come back from the dead. Not after facing the goddess, Maat at his judgment trial. You know what? I bet he used a scarab spell. So that his black heart weighed less than Maat's feather of truth. It's the only way grumpy old Jugnose could make it into the Great Beyond."

"Zet!" Kat hissed, "Don't call him that."

Hui said, "Maybe he didn't make it to the Great Beyond." In a spooky voice, he added, "Maybe Maat's tossed his rotten heart to Ammit. *Devourer of the Dead.* They say it has the legs of a hippo, the front paws of a lion, and the head of a crocodile. And when you fail the judgment test, it snatches your heart, chews it up and swallows it. *Poof*, it's all over. No afterlife for you. I bet *that's* what happened to Aziza."

Kat made a face. "Gruesome."

Hui waggled his brows at her. "Really? Are you scared?"

She crossed her arms. "Of course I'm not scared. I don't have a wicked heart. Not like some people I know."

Hui looked wildly offended. "What's that supposed to mean?"

Zet rolled his eyes. Merit snickered. But Hui had a point.

"Either way, whether he passed the test or if Ammit finished him off," Zet said, "He couldn't be haunting us."

"True." Hui rubbed his shaved scalp.

"Right, Merit?" Zet said.

For the second time that morning, she simply squinted away at some sunny spot downriver. Water lapped at the raft's edges. Zet pushed off the bottom again with the paddle. He stayed close to shore, keeping an eye out for dangers like crocodiles and hippos.

"Right, Merit?" Zet prompted.

She pulled her knees up and turned to face them. "I shouldn't tell you this because it's secret knowledge."

Hui sat forward, his eyes wide. "Really? Now you have to!"

She trailed her feet in the water in silence.

Finally, she said, "I'm only speaking of this because I feel you have a right to know. Priests have created certain spells that can be written on tomb walls. They . . ."

Hui sat further forward. "They what?"

"They awaken the mummy. So that he can haunt and kill his enemies."

Kat let out a small cry.

Shaken, Zet shouted, "We weren't Aziza's enemies."

"Awaken the mummy," Hui cried, dropping his net and scanning the riverbank. "What does the spell say? Tell me exactly what it says."

Merit recited it in a low, clear voice, ending with the final, awful verse: "*I shall seize his neck like that of a goose. I shall make him miserable. I shall make him die from hunger and thirst.*"

A spooked silence fell.

Kat had turned pale.

Zet spoke up. "But we didn't do anything to him! It was an accident."

Making a face, Hui said. "Aziza didn't see it that way."

Merit spoke up. "There's another problem."

"Another problem?" Kat asked in a high, worried voice.

"You said a jackal was guarding the mummy. So Anubis, God of the Underworld, has taken his earthly form. That doesn't bode well, I'm afraid."

Zet tried to swallow the lump in his throat. "Oh?"

"If this mummy has returned to the living, it has done so with the blessing of Anubis. If the God of the Underworld has appeared in the form of a jackal . . ."

Hui got unsteadily to his bare feet as if he could sit still no longer. The raft had drifted into a fast-moving current. It rocked under him as they sped along. "So what are you saying?"

"The God of Death walks amongst us," Merit whispered. "People are right to be afraid. Egypt is in danger. We cannot forget that we're at war in the north. The army is the only thing holding back the Hyksos invaders. We need the gods on our side."

Zet thought of his father, a soldier on the front lines. His chest tightened. Hui's father was up there fighting, too.

Merit's ringed fingers tugged at one another in turn.

Their raft had sailed far from the noisy watersteps, where fishermen unloaded their catches. Here in a lonely river bend, reeds grew tall along the shore. The dashing current gurgled and slapped the plants.

A mud-brick wall came into view. It barricaded the right bank. Beyond the wall, city buildings loomed in the sun's glare. The nearest one, the Royal Treasury, rose higher than the rest.

Merit nodded at the Treasury. "Wars are expensive. I'm afraid I overheard my father say funds are running low. Without funds, we can't get supplies to our troops."

Everyone followed her gaze.

"If Anubis has come to Thebes," Merit said. "If he's angry, the God of Death could plunge us into terrible trouble. Our soldiers are the only thing holding off the invaders."

Zet struggled to find his voice. "Merit, you need to stay away from us. We need to turn around! If you get cursed because of us—if—"

"Stay away?" Her eyes flashed. "I am a royal daughter. I would never stand down when Egypt's people are in trouble. Let alone abandon my best friends."

Zet started to argue.

The raft slammed into some unmoving object.

The force threw Hui flat on his face next to Kat. Hui's hands shot out and Kat grabbed them. They held on to keep from falling over the edge.

The jarring halt sent Zet flying. He shouted in horror as Princess Meritamen tumbled off the raft.

With an awful splash, Merit hit the water. A hundred things flashed through Zet's mind. Most of all, he was thinking of the hippopotamus, the river's deadliest animal. If its massive jaws didn't crush you, it would drown you underfoot.

Merit's eyes met his for one brief, awful moment.

Then, she was sucked beneath the brown, swirling surface.

5

A STRANGE PAIR

"Merit!" Zet shouted.

He jumped in, his feet striking the murky bottom. The Nile waters rose to his chest. He plunged under, searching desperately for the Princess in the silty brown current.

Nothing.

"Merit!" Kat shrieked.

Suddenly there came a splash as Merit popped up a dozen paces away. She coughed and sputtered and stood unsteadily in the rushing current.

Zet plunged toward her. Crocodiles lurked in shallow places like this. They'd lie in wait, with only their eyes and snouts jutting into the air. And they pounced fast.

"Quick, back on the raft!" Zet shouted, pushing her forward.

"Give us your hands," Kat cried.

She and Hui hauled Zet and Merit back aboard. The four stood dripping and breathing hard.

Zet said, "We better get moving, we're like sitting ducks."

He pushed off with the pole. The raft wouldn't budge.

"What's happening?" Kat demanded.

Hui reached a cautious hand into the water. "We're stuck on a rock."

Merit said, "This is odd. I boated here last week in the royal barge and the Nile was deep. It shouldn't be shallow. Look at that sandbank, where did all that sand come from?"

"I don't know." Zet glanced around, feeling uneasy. It was a great responsibility to have Merit out here. "Let's free the raft and get back. I don't like this."

None of them did. They exchanged spooked glances.

Warily, the four children slid into the river. They shoved hard, but the raft was waterlogged and heavy. The lashings were stuck firm.

Movement on the riverbank made Zet turn and look.

On shore stood a rough-skinned woman with long hair and narrowed eyes. Tall grasses swayed up to her strong shoulders. She leaned out, holding a fishing net, and threw it onto the water.

"Hey!" Zet called. "Hello—my lady!"

The woman gave him the evil eye and waved the children away.

"We're stuck," Zet called, ignoring her glares. "Can you help us push off?"

That's when he noticed a small hut, partially hidden in the lush overgrowth. The door flew open and a huge man thrust his way outside. His muscular arms held a heavy-looking bucket. An enormous blade gleamed at his waist. It looked sharp and deadly.

"Here now," growled the man. "What's all this shouting?"

"It's those noisy children." The woman made a sour face. "Get rid of them."

"What's the trouble?" the man thundered.

Zet, Kat, Hui, and Merit exchanged worried glances. Water surged around their legs.

"We're stuck on a rock," Zet called back. "We need some help."

The man set down his basket. He wiped his hands on his barrel chest and waded into the Nile. "This is men's work. Outta my way, girls," he sneered. But then his eyes fastened on Merit and he studied her face as if trying to place the Princess.

Kat quickly whispered, "Pull your hood over your head."

Zet had to get Merit away from him. "I better walk the girls to shore. We're crocodile bait out here. I'll be back."

The man grunted but watched them go. Had he recognized Merit? Even though he'd agreed to help, this couple seemed strange. Merit had already been kidnapped once before.

As the three children sloshed on shore, Zet was dismayed when Kat and Merit restarted their earlier conversation about the mummy, for the woman's ears perked up.

"What's all this about a mummy?" she asked sharply.

"Oh . . ." Kat said, stopping short. "You . . . haven't heard?"

Zet elbowed her.

"Tell me," the woman cooed.

Kat bit her lip, glancing at Zet.

"Come now, don't leave me in the dark," the woman complained. "A mummy is cursing people? You'd better tell me. I'm a citizen, too. And my good husband is helping you, after all."

Reluctantly, Kat described the haunting. The woman clucked her tongue. As Kat spoke, Zet's eyes fell on what looked like an old stone building block that looked like part of a foundation. Odd.

Was that hieroglyphic writing carved on its surface?

Why would a fancy rock be lying here by the river?

Zet edged closer for a better look. The woman, however, pushed in front of him and sat heavily on the stone block. She spread her dirty linen skirt around her, covering the hieroglyphics. Was she hiding them? Or did it just seem that way?

He opened his mouth to ask about the stone when a great roar from the river made him spin around. The huge man had lifted the raft halfway out of the water.

"There!" the man shouted. "Now get lost, you kids. Stop bothering us poor fisher-folk."

Hui waved frantically. "Let's go!"

Zet and the girls were happy to comply. Before leaving the shore, Zet uprooted two sturdy reeds and lugged them onto the raft.

"Lucky you didn't get eaten by a crocodile, lots of 'em down here," the man told Merit in a sneering tone.

"Yes, very lucky, thank you," she said.

He helped her roughly onto the raft, giving her a small shove. "The river's a bad place for a bunch of pampered kids. Stay away if you know what's good for you."

Zet feared setting the man off, so he tried for an even tone. "Thanks for your help."

"Yes," the others chimed in. "Thank you."

Using the extra reeds as poles, the children worked together to make their way back upstream.

Zet said, "Last time you boated here, Merit, did you see that couple?"

"No." She shook her head. "But fishermen come and go. I still wonder what made that sandbank in the middle of the river, though."

They finally reached the shore from where they'd first set out. Together, the children beached the raft. Using an old rope, they tied it to a gnarled acacia tree.

"Mother will be worried," Kat said, glancing at the darkening sky. "It's late. Getting unstuck took a long time."

"I'll accompany Merit back to the palace," Zet said. "You two go home and tell everyone we're fine."

Hui nodded. "All right."

The four made none of their usual noisy goodbyes. Too many worries hung over them. Zet and Merit watched Kat and Hui melt into the shadows, then headed for the palace.

As they hurried through the nightfall, stars winked to life. Zet couldn't help worrying about his father and the warning the Princess had issued earlier that day.

He turned to her. "So treasury funds are really running low?"

"I'm afraid so," Merit said.

"Will you have enough to support the army? My father is up there. Hui's is, too."

"I know. Fortunately, when we gather the taxes from the coming harvest, they should replenish some of our funds. But if something happens to destroy the harvest . . ."

"You mean, like an angry Anubis?" Zet said.

"Exactly."

"The medjay police are out questioning priests about the jackal and the mummy. They must be worried, too."

Merit nodded. "The medjay police are on alert. But getting to the bottom of this problem is the Royal Guard's duty. The mummy falls under religious disturbances—which fall under the realm of Pharaoh the Living God."

"The Royal Guard! But if they're busy investigating the mummy, who's protecting the Treasury? Isn't that their job?"

"It would be near impossible to break into that building. Only a few Royal Guards are needed to protect the Treasury."

Zet breathed a sigh of relief. At least the Treasury was safe. He didn't need to worry about things he couldn't control. He needed to focus on two things: putting an end to the problems at the pottery stall and stopping that mummy from haunting Thebes.

They reached the palace wall. Here, they'd have to say goodbye, for he wasn't supposed to enter the Royal Grounds without Pharaoh's permission. He'd help Merit over the wall, but she'd have to run across the lawns and sneak back into the palace on her own.

Merit brushed her dark hair from her eyes. Jewels glowed on her ringed fingers in the moonlight. "I want you to climb over with me."

He hid his surprise, but then understood. "Of course. Your people must know you're missing by now. It's my fault. We never should have convinced you to come out on the raft. I'll talk to your father." Even if the threat of Pharaoh's anger made his short hair stand on end.

She grinned. "Thanks, but no—I'll have to face my father myself. And it's certainly not your fault. There *is* someone else I'd like you to talk to, though."

"Who?"

"You'll see. Will it be all right if you stay out a little longer?"

He laughed. "If you're going to be in trouble, I might as well be, too."

6

MUMMIFICATION SECRETS

Together, Zet and Merit clambered over the wall and dropped onto the palace grounds. They were in a quiet grove of citrus trees. In the distance, lamps twinkled in the palace.

"Who goes there?" came a sentry's voice.

"Stand down," Merit called. "It's me. Princess Meritamen."

The sentry approached. Bowing low, he said, "Your Highness."

She smiled. "There's no trouble here. Have a good evening."

The sentry moved out of earshot.

"Seems I haven't been missed." She sighed with obvious relief. "I suppose my ruse worked. Which means we still have time."

He didn't ask about her ruse. "Time for what?"

"Answers." Instead of heading for the palace, she guided him around a small lake. A temple stood in the distance. "Hurry."

Merit broke into a run. Zet fell into step beside her willowy form. Soon, the temple loomed over them. Rather than entering, Merit skirted past the temple. She kept going until they reached a small stone building around back. The cane door was shut. Lamplight spilled through narrow cracks. Merit made to knock and then paused.

Inside, a man chanted. Gooseflesh rose on Zet's arms. *A prayer? Or a spell?*

Merit pressed her eye to a crack. Zet did the same. He nearly gasped out loud. Clapping a hand over his mouth, he stared at the shadowy form inside.

The figure towered almost to the ceiling. He had a man's body, but his head . . . by the gods! He had the head of a *jackal!*

Pointy ears. A long snout. Canine teeth. Sleek fur over a muscled jaw.

"Anubis!" Zet hissed, unable to help himself.

The divine figure stiffened. He turned and stared at the door. "Who DARES disturb me?" boomed the God of Death. Anubis took three giant strides and threw the door open.

Zet cringed and fell at Anubis's feet. He covered his face with both hands.

By the wings of Isis, this was it. They were dead. It was all over!

The deep voice boomed, "Princess Meritamen?"

Face still pressed to the dirt, Zet's brow wrinkled. Anubis knew Merit's name?

"High Priest," she said. "I'm sorry to disturb your work."

High Priest?

Zet risked a glance upward. The figure untied a chinstrap and removed the jackal's head. This was no god. He was a man in a mask. Thank Ra!

"You should not see me like this." Angered, the High Priest set the mask aside. "Even if you are the Daughter of a Living God. And that boy should be punished!"

"I brought him," Merit said. "I'm responsible. He's under my protection."

The priest pinned Zet with a cold stare. To Merit, he said, "Why have you come?"

"It's an emergency."

"Indeed?" The priest frowned.

Zet, unable to hold his tongue, blurted, "Why were you dressed like Anubis?"

The priest shot Zet a sour look. "You've seen me. I suppose there's no point in keeping it secret. I am the Royal Mummifier. When I make a mummy, I wear the mask of Anubis. That way, the Jackal-Headed God's magic works through me to preserve the dead for the Afterlife."

"But no one has died." Merit's hand went to her mouth. "Have they?"

"Rest easy, Princess. It was a sacred temple cat. I'm sending her on to Bastet, the Cat Goddess who watches over home and hearth. Now, what's this emergency?"

"We need to learn about mummies," she said.

He drew himself up and towered over them. "That's priest's knowledge!"

Now it was her turn to straighten to her full height. Her eyes flashed. "I am Princess Meritamen. Royal Daughter. Child of the Lord of the Two Lands, Descendant of the High Priest of Every Temple, Daughter of the Living God himself! Will you defy me?"

Zet's eyes widened. He'd never seen her this way. For the first time, he truly realized that she was more than just his friend.

Lamplight flickered behind the Mummifier.

Finally, the priest said, "This boy is not royal. I cannot speak in front of him."

Zet smiled awkwardly.

Merit said, "His name is Zet. He's the famous boy who came to my rescue once before. He's saved Pharaoh, too. He's solved many crimes. And I've asked him to help solve the mummy mystery that's haunting all of Thebes."

Zet couldn't help thinking it sounded pretty good when she said it like that. He practically glowed.

"Doesn't look like much of a hero to me," the priest said.

Zet's glow turned to embarrassment.

Merit said, "He has my royal blessing. So will you help us? I'm sure you don't want me to trouble my father. But I could wake my Royal Grandmother and bring her down here."

Now it was the priest's turn to look awkward. Zet stifled a laugh.

"Oh, very well," the priest said. "But come inside and shut the door. The sacred Wag Festival of the Dead approaches. With it, the veil between life and death grows thin. Restless spirits draw near when a mummy is being made. Even the mummy of a small cat."

As they squeezed inside the hut, Zet's mind went to last year's Wag Festival. Like always, the people of Thebes had lined up along the Nile. They'd brought tiny paper boats, hundreds and hundreds of them. Each boat was a tribute to Osiris, the Mummified God who was Egypt's first mummy. People also made tributes to those who'd passed into the Afterlife. The boats had floated in a bright flotilla. Kat had called them pretty. Now, however, with a mummy on the loose, the coming Wag Festival of the Dead unsettled him.

Zet quickly closed the door.

Inside, smoke drifted from the lamp. It cast a haze over the assembled tools, worktables, and containers. Zet shuddered. Merit did the same.

"Now." The priest tapped his gnarled index finger on his worktable. "How will sharing my secret arts help you solve this mystery?"

Merit said, "Zet? Please go ahead and ask what you need."

"I'm grateful for anything you can tell me," Zet said.

The priest's deep-set eyes were like two black hollows. "I will tell you," he said. "But you must promise to never repeat what you hear tonight."

"I promise," Zet and Merit said at once.

Shadows played in the creases of the priest's lined face. "Then I will begin."

Zet and Merit stood spellbound as the priest lifted a mummified object from the table. It was tubular, around a foot long, and wrapped neatly from end to end. On closer inspection, it was almost doll-like. The priest had given the tiny mummy pointy cat ears made from linen strips. He'd drawn a cat's face, too.

Instead of being scary, the mummy was almost cute.

Zet's thoughts went to their family shrine honoring Bastet. He loved their Cat Goddess statue. He often rubbed its glossy black head and spoke to it when worried. Now, he couldn't help making a silent prayer to Bastet to keep this temple cat safe until she reached the playful fields of the Afterlife.

Perhaps the High Priest noticed, for he paused a moment before clearing his throat. "This mummy, like all mummies, took seventy days to create. There are many steps. I will explain."

Zet and Merit nodded in earnest.

"First, the body is carefully washed and purified. Second . . . " He paused, eyeing Zet and Merit as if daring them not to faint. "We cut out the organs. The lungs, the intestines, the stomach, the liver. Of course, we're not butchers. We do try to keep the body looking whole."

"That sounds hard," Zet said, ignoring his churning stomach.

"It is." From a tray, the priest lifted a hooked stick. "We push this long instrument up the nose and stir it around." He demonstrated in the air, gyrating the stick with great force. "Do you know why?"

Wincing, Zet and Merit shook their heads.

"To mash up the brain and pick it out of the nostrils."

"Eeeew," Merit said.

Zet leaned in. "What do you do with the brain?"

The High Priest leaned forward, too. "We throw it away."

"Throw it away?" Zet asked. "Where?"

"The garbage. The brain has no purpose."

Merit crossed her arms. "And then what do you do?"

He seemed almost disappointed at being unable to spook them. "The stomach, lungs, liver, and intestines are stored in what we call canopic jars. Each jar is guarded by a god whose head is carved on the lid. Next, when the body's empty, we stuff it with linen. That's to keep it plumped up. We then soak it in natron salts for forty days."

"Why?" Merit asked.

"We want to dry it out, to prevent rot. Now, when the body is dry, we wrap the mummy in yards of bandages—it's a long process. Partly because we tuck magic-spell amulets into the linen strips." He made tucking motion.

"Magic amulets?" Zet said, sharing a glance with Merit.

"Indeed. Each one must be activated by chanting a prayer. Then the mummy is placed in a sarcophagus and we fasten a carved death mask over the mummy's face." He seemed enraptured by his own words, as though this was the first time he'd ever had anyone to tell them to.

Zet said, "Did you perform the honorable Aziza's mummification?"

The priest looked startled. A shadow fell over his hawk-like eyes. "Why do you ask?"

"You must've heard what people are saying—that the haunted mummy is Pharaoh's cousin returned from the dead."

"I don't listen to gossip." He fussed with his tools.

Merit spoke up. "You said magic amulets are tucked into a mummy's wrappings. Could Aziza's amulets help him curse his enemies?"

The priest stroked the cat mummy's ears in silence.

"Could he have come back from the dead?" Merit prodded. "Like everyone's saying?"

In a clipped voice, the priest said, "I did not preside over Aziza's mummification. I was not told what spells were used."

"But is it possible?" Merit said.

"Do you dare question the powers of Anubis? Of course it's possible. But would it be done? That, I cannot tell you, Princess."

Zet said, "Why not? Why won't you say?"

"I humbly ask that you leave so I may get back to my work." Instead of humble, however, his words sounded almost threatening.

Was the priest hiding something? Did he honestly know nothing of Aziza's royal burial? Even though it had happened only recently?

The priest donned his frightening Anubis mask. The huge jackal's head with its gleaming teeth caused Merit and Zet to back away. Zet had nearly forgotten that this man was a servant of Anubis, God of Death. That was a frightening thought.

"My thanks, priest," Merit said. "We will leave you. My blessings are upon you." She took Zet's arm and they hurried back outside.

A chill gripped the night. Or maybe the sinister priest's presence had turned Zet cold.

Merit kept going until they reached the lake's far side as if trying to distance themselves from the servant of Anubis.

Yet the black, starlit water seemed poor protection from the ominous mysteries swirling around them.

NO MORE SECRETS

Merit sat down by the water, breathing hard. "I hope my father doesn't hear about this!"

"But you said—"

"If he found out I was grilling the High Priest of Mummification for sacred secrets, he'd double my attendants. And I wouldn't be climbing over any more walls!" She rubbed her shins. "He's told me to act more regal. Awful, isn't it? You heard that there's a statue of me going up outside the Temple of Isis next week?"

"Yes."

She grimaced. "Everyone in Thebes will recognize my face after that. I won't be able to go anywhere."

Zet sank down next to her. "I wish I could do something to help."

"You can't. That's just how life is."

Zet glanced at the temple from where they'd come. In the light of the half-moon, the lake waters looked black.

"Do you think that priest was hiding something? About Aziza?" he asked.

"I'm not sure. I doubt it."

Zet scratched his neck. The priest had been so abrupt when he'd asked whether Aziza's mummy could come back to life. He shivered, recalling the mummy on his doorstep, the way it pointed at him with its bony finger, and that awful whispered incantation. And how Apu hadn't stopped crying since.

By the gods, he should have asked how to get rid of a mummy's curse!

He turned to tell Merit that he needed to go back and demand more answers. But Merit spoke first.

"I need to get back," she said. Worry seemed to lie heavily on her regal shoulders. And responsibility.

He was again reminded that Merit was more than a friend. She was a royal daughter.

He nodded. "Good night, Princess."

"Good night, Zet. Go safely."

Zet ran toward home.

All throughout Thebes, doors and windows were shut tight. Fear hung in the air.

Unlike most people, however, Zet longed for a glimpse of the mummy. He wanted to chase the monster down. He wanted answers.

Zet reached his street, panting, and sped up the steps to his house. At the door, he paused. *Mother was going to be furious!*

From outside, Apu could be heard crying. Zet took a big breath and pushed open the door. His mother rushed from the kitchen. Kat, who held the wailing Apu, followed.

"Where were you?" his mother cried. "Kat said you went to the palace hours ago! What happened? Did you see the mummy again?"

"No," he said. "Merit asked me to help her with something and—" He broke off. Now was probably as good a time as any to tell her about the stall. "Mother, I have bad news."

"If you're talking about the pottery returns, I know all about it."

Zet glanced at Kat. "You told her?"

Kat looked equally surprised. "Not me!"

"Children, did you really think you could keep it from me? What were you thinking, hiding such a thing?"

"We—" Zet said, but she cut him off.

"I know that after I had Apu, I was unwell. With your father away, I had no choice but to let you manage the stall."

"And you said we were doing a good job!" Kat said.

"Yes, but now I see it's foolish to let you continue."

"But mother!" Zet said. "We're good at it."

"You are hiding things from me. I had to find out about the pottery from a neighbor. Do you have any idea how embarrassing that was?"

"We would have told you," Zet said, "But we didn't want you to be worried!"

"Enough." She turned and swept Apu from Kat's arms. "Tomorrow, we'll all go to the market. We'll bring the pottery returns home and close up shop until this . . . this cursed mummy . . . is sorted out by the medjay police."

Zet said, "Princess Meritamen asked me to help solve the mystery."

His mother's sharp intake of breath seemed to suck the air from the room. In the silence that followed, only Apu's soft sniffles could be heard.

Finally, his mother said, "I wish she hadn't done that."

"But she's the Princess, mother! I can't say no." And he didn't want to. "Besides, all of Thebes is saying we're cursed." He glanced at the sniffling Apu, worried but not wanting to say anything. Apu, red-cheeked, seemed to gasp for breath before making another sob. "We have to do something."

His mother walked away and could be heard setting Apu on his kitchen play mat.

Zet and Kat shared a glance.

Their mother returned wearing a resigned expression. With a sigh, she put a gentle hand on Zet's shoulder. "You are my oldest son. And like your fearless father, I worry you're too brave for your own good."

"How about me?" Kat asked. "What am I?"

Their mother's brows went up and she shook her head. "Oh children, what am I to do with you?"

"If I'm not brave, what am I?" Kat wanted to know.

Zet rolled his eyes.

"Kat, you are my beautiful daughter. And sometimes I fear you're too smart for your own good. And I love you both very much. That's why I worry."

The scent of dinner wafted from the kitchen in the back. Zet's stomach growled. He realized he hadn't eaten in hours. He was starving.

"Now come, let's eat," she said.

In the kitchen's cozy glow, the family pulled up cushions. They sat in a small circle. The simple act made Zet feel safe. Kat's shoulders relaxed. Their mother steered their chatter to comforting topics. Zet wolfed down warm, savory stew and thick slices of freshly baked bread, refusing to think about the threat of hungrier days ahead. Even Apu seemed slightly mollified as he chewed on a piece of cucumber.

After dinner, their mother laid out a game of senet. They took turns rolling the bones, trying to best each other and even laughing. For a time, their fears were banished to the shadows outside.

But when their mother kissed them good night, the fearsome shadows came creeping back. As Zet climbed the ladder to the roof, he noticed a mummy-shaped outline in one corner, causing him to look twice. It was just the old vase.

Kat paused on the bottom step. "Mother, what if we really are cursed? I'm scared."

"Come here." She hugged Kat. "Who could ever curse you, my perfect daughter?"

Until tonight, Zet would have agreed. The idea had seemed crazy. But meeting the Mummifier had shaken him.

Aziza could, Zet thought. *Aziza could have cursed us all.*

8

A GROUP EFFORT

The following day dawned bright and hot. The sun god, Ra, shone over the market. The mountains of returned pottery gleamed in the light.

Sounds of chaos soon filled the stall. For the first time in days, however, this chaos was of their own making.

Zet, Kat, their mother, and Apu were there. Hui, unfortunately, was busy at the royal foundry but his mother Delilah, had come to help. And she'd brought Hui's four rowdy little brothers.

The small boys raced around, shouting. Some tried to stand on their heads. Others dangled from tent poles. Hui's mother, meanwhile, was a whirlwind herself: she yelled at her children, packed pottery, and scolded customers who dared approach with more returns.

All day long, the two families carted pottery back to Zet and Kat's house and stored it in the front room. By mid-afternoon, their house was overflowing, and Zet and Kat were exhausted. Still, they headed to the market for another run.

"Hey, you know what?" Zet said as they passed what he realized was Aziza's street. "We should detour past Aziza's old house."

Kat paled. "Don't you think it's been sold?"

"Maybe not. We should have thought of this before. We might find some clues."

Kat frowned. "What kind of clues?"

Zet said, "I'm not sure. Let's sneak in and look around."

"Break in? Are you crazy?" Kat swiped the bangs from her eyes. "What if Mother finds out? She's just forgiven us. No, don't be stupid."

"Stupid? Well, sorr-ee, Miss Perfect, but do you want to solve this or not?"

Kat glared. "Of course I want to solve this. But what if it's haunted? I bet you didn't think of that."

"That would be bad," Zet admitted. "Oh, come on, we're out of options."

"I don't know."

"Unless you have a better idea?"

"Fine. A quick look," she said. "Let's hurry before we're missed."

They started running.

Suddenly, Kat slowed and her voice went up an octave. "What if we find Aziza's mummy asleep in his house? What if he's staying there and only comes out at night?"

Zet halted, picturing Aziza's mummy in a death-sleep with a massive jackal stretched out at his feet. Forcefully, he said. "I doubt he's in there."

Or so he hoped.

"I just had an idea." Kat's eyes had gone all big. "How about this? Every home has a household god, right? Like we have Bastet."

Zet nodded, thinking of their ebony Cat Goddess statue back home. "And?"

Despite her pale face, Kat looked determined. "If we can get into Aziza's house, we can learn the name of his household god. We could make offerings, so the god takes pity on us and stops Aziza from haunting us!"

"Huh. You know . . . At this point, anything is worth a try."

Together, they ran across the hot paving stones. A cluster of pigeons rose flapping into the air. They crossed through a dusty intersection and skidded to a stop.

Men in uniform jammed the lane. More swarmed around Aziza's sprawling house. Most wore the colors of the Royal Guard.

Kat gasped. "Does this mean what I think it does?"

Zet's throat went dry. "The Royal Guards think Aziza really is the mummy."

"So Aziza *has* come back to curse our family. All because of that stupid jugnose business. I knew it!"

Zet fixed his attention on a big man dressed in a medjay police uniform. "Look." He grabbed his sister's arm and pointed at the officer. "It's Merimose! Maybe he'll tell us what's going on."

Zet and Kat had helped Merimose solve a few mysteries. Still, the medjay wasn't always happy about it. He liked to complain about them getting underfoot.

Zet and Kat hurried toward him.

Merimose swung around. "Keep away!" he shouted, making a chopping motion.

"Merimose!" they called.

Recognizing them, he crossed his muscular arms over his broad chest. "Zet. Kat," he growled. "I wondered when you'd show up."

"Hi, Merimose," they said.

"I'm on duty. I can't talk," Merimose said.

Despite this, Zet reached to shake hands and the man accepted. The medjay's palm was the size of a dinner platter and the texture of old leather.

Kat said, "What's happening? Is Aziza in there?"

Merimose regarded her. "It's not my investigation. Not this time. The Royal Guards are in charge, not us medjay police."

Zet said, "Why are they searching Aziza's house?"

"You two need to stay out of this," Merimose boomed in his low voice.

"We can't!" Kat said. "Everyone knows Aziza is haunting us!"

A man's sharp voice rang out behind Zet. "Merimose! Get rid of those kids. Do your job!"

Zet whipped around and came face-to-face with a massive Royal Guard. The man wore a gold-embossed breastplate. A long, curved knife gleamed at his waist and he carried a lightweight, fiber shield.

Zet bowed quickly. "Sir, we're the family that Aziza is haunting."

Kat said, "Please, tell us what's going on!"

The man's brows came together to form what looked like a giant black caterpillar. "Leave. Now."

"But sir, we can help—" Zet began.

"NOW!" the Royal Guard barked.

"Renni." Merimose hooked one thumb in the leather waistband of his kilt. "If you don't mind, I'll handle this. I'm familiar with these two. They mean no harm."

"Harrumph!" the Royal Guard said.

Zet swallowed. He had to try one last time. "We've solved mysteries before. And Aziza is haunting us. Surely we can help! It was our jug that—"

"HOW DARE YOU?" the man roared. "I am the head of the Royal Guard. Pharaoh himself appointed me protector of Egypt. I am an instrument of the Gods. If I wish to speak to you, it will be at the time of my choosing."

Zet wanted to explain that the Princess had asked for his help. But he knew better. What if he got Merit into trouble? He wanted to at least tell Renni about the mummy's visit to their street. But the man strode away. He slammed through Aziza's front door and was gone.

Kat said, "I can't believe he wouldn't listen to what we had to say!"

Merimose, however, looked unsurprised.

The scent of baking bread drifted from a neighbor's house. The medjay's stomach made a loud gurgle. He rubbed his belly. "Sorry, didn't have time for lunch."

Kat pulled a small packet from her pocket. "I have some dried figs here."

Merimose accepted a handful and wolfed them down. Swallowing, he said, "Thanks. Now you'd better move along and let me do my job."

Kat tugged at her braids, looking uncertain and worried. "We're in big trouble, Merimose."

"People are shunning our pottery stall," Zet added. "Pretty soon, we'll be out of business. Our family won't be able to put food on the table. Or keep a roof over our heads. We need this sorted out. Fast."

"Let the Royal Guard do that. Be patient."

"Patient?" Kat cried. "You wouldn't say that if you'd seen our mountain of returned pottery. And you especially wouldn't say it if a scary monster was after you."

Merimose grew stern. "Here now! Don't you go trying to track down that mummy."

"Why not?" Zet said.

A muscle flexed in Merimose's jaw. "I don't know what's behind this. But if a mummy is walking the streets . . . and if that mummy was once Aziza . . . well, it's no longer Aziza—not anymore. I don't want you kids anywhere near it. Hear me?"

Zet swallowed.

Merimose said, "This is no joke. It's not some mystery for you to solve. A mummy is more than dangerous. It's a creature of death."

Kat seemed to shrink into herself.

"But—" Zet began.

"No, Zet. What can you do to stop it? A mummy can curse you with a whisper. It can kill you with a touch. You want to chase it down? Then what? Put your hands on its body, and you'll turn to dust."

The way he spoke sent a cold trickle down Zet's neck.

Merimose went on. "The Royal Guards are protected by the priests. But you and me? Our weapons mean nothing. Renni and his men are the only ones who can solve this. That's why I've ordered my men to stand down." He grasped them both by the shoulders. "Stay away. That's not a suggestion. It's an order. Stay far away."

"Don't worry," Kat said in a pinched voice. "We will."

Zet's mind raced back to the mummy's awful whispers. Already, it seemed to have cursed their stall. Was Apu already cursed?

Zet was only a boy. He wasn't a holy man. He desperately wanted to fight, but what could he do? It could make things worse. Much worse.

He glanced at Aziza's dark, cavernous house.

Merimose had ordered his men to stand down. So who was Zet to think he could end this haunting?

He stared at the ground. "I see what you mean. I only hope the Royal Guard can fix this. Before something worse happens."

THE MUMMY STRIKES AGAIN

The Moon God, Khonsu, rose slowly in the evening sky.

Zet was pacing the rooftop when distant shouts drifted up from the streets below. He cocked his head, listening as the rising tide of babble swept closer.

Alarmed, he clambered downstairs, threw open their front door and ran outside. His mother and Kat followed close behind.

In the street, their neighbors stood in groups, talking in frightened voices.

Paneb, the brickmaker who lived next door, yelled, "Everyone get inside, lock your doors."

This only drew out more neighbors, all of them speaking at once.

Zet dashed up to the brickmaker. "What's going on?"

"Paneb?" his mother cried, "What's happened?"

Paneb was an honest man and a hard worker. Unlike other neighbors, he hadn't shunned Zet's family. In his raspy voice, he said, "The mummy is walking the streets again."

Zet looked around. "Here?"

"No—just off the Southern Road."

"The Southern Road?" A sick feeling struck the pit of Zet's stomach. "Uh oh."

Paneb said, "In Kanup Street."

"*Kanup Street?*" Kat screeched. "But that's where our friend Hui lives!"

Zet's hands went to his head. He didn't want to even think about what this meant. "I better go. It's attacking our friends. Mother, I'm going there."

"No," she said in a sharp voice. "You won't. I will alert the medjay."

"You can't leave. What about Apu? What if the mummy comes here?" Zet said.

Kat knotted the front of her nightdress. "The mummy must have gone to Hui's house because his mother helped us cart all that pottery back here."

"What do you mean?" their mother asked.

But Kat's words echoed Zet's own fears.

"Don't you see?" Kat's chin trembled. "The mummy is cursing Hui's family for helping us at the stall. Aziza is angry at them, now, too."

Paneb began backing toward his house. "You have no proof of that."

"By the gods!" Zet kicked his bare foot at the ground. "What if Kat's right? Mother, someone has to go. It has to be me."

"Fine." She nodded. A quick, jerky movement. "You will go for the medjay. Understood? Then come back to me safely. Now quick. Go."

Zet sprinted between the small crowd that had gathered. They parted to let him through. He rounded the corner and silence closed around him. Out of the darkness, he thought he heard footsteps. He drew to a halt. Yes, there they were. Coming up behind him.

He spun but there was no mummy, only the narrow silhouette of Kat in the moonlight. She was running hard.

"Kat!" he groaned. "You have to stay with Mother and Apu."

Her reply was heated. "Don't tell me what to do. Hui's my friend, too."

"Fine. But I'm not running for the medjay. Who knows how long they'd take. I'm going to Hui's. So let's just get there."

They reached the Southern Road. They were both panting by the time they turned into Kanup Street. Lamps blazed in every window and door. The crowds were thicker than at any festival in the Grand Plaza. Clearly, the mummy was long gone, but what had it done to Hui and his family? Had it hurt them?

"The back way, come on," Zet said.

They cut across a side street. Together, they clambered over the wall into Hui's tiny garden. Delilah was expecting them. She stood in the backyard with one hand on her hip.

"Not a step further," she said, her full cheeks flaming in the light of a lamp.

"Is everyone safe?" Zet gasped. "Did the mummy—"

"The mummy is gone," Delilah said.

"Is Hui—" Kat began.

"We're all safe. They're inside." She turned and roared over her shoulder, "I mean it boys, stay inside!"

A clatter could be heard. Footsteps and muffled voices. Something smashed. It sounded like a piece of pottery. The voices went dead still.

Delilah's mouth pursed. "Zet and Kat? I'm going to have to ask you to stay away."

Kat made a choking sound. "We're so sorry! We never should have asked you to help us."

Movement from the rooftop caught Zet's eye. Hui was up there but quickly pulled back. Zet frowned. He couldn't believe Hui would hide from his best friends, no matter what was happening. They'd always faced things together.

Zet's shoulders sagged. "We never meant to drag you into this. My mother's worried about you."

"We'll get through it," Delilah said. "But please, don't come back."

"Ever?" Kat squeaked.

Delilah relented. She was a big woman and used to handling rowdy boys. She swept Kat into a crushing hug and barked, "I'm only protecting my family. You can come back when this is over."

"What if it's never over?" Kat sniffed.

Delilah didn't reply.

Zet found himself reeling with shock. His life was being torn apart piece by piece. First the pottery stall, and now their friends. What next, their very lives?

Back home, Zet paused in front of Bastet, the cat-goddess carved of ebony. She watched him from behind silent eyes.

"I wish Aziza had never come to our stall," Zet whispered. "I'm sorry people called him Jugnose. Oh, everything is such a mess!"

Then, he thought of his father. He pictured that strong, smiling face. *Was he all right?* Merit's warning about the treasury filled his head. But there were other ways to curse a man on a battlefield. A mummy had dark powers.

Zet's heart squeezed in his chest. He touched Bastet's paws. "Is this curse affecting Father, too?"

Bastet continued to stare silently from her alabaster eyes. This ancient goddess of the home had guarded their family for generations. Even though her eyes were made of stone, Zet felt sure he read sympathy in them.

"Keep my father safe, Bastet. Please, keep all of us safe."

AN UNEXPECTED VISIT

It was late when Zet clambered up the ladder to the roof. As his feet hit the top rung, an alarmed gasp rang out. It came from the rooftop's far side. His instincts kicked into high gear when he spotted Kat struggling near the roof's edge.

Someone, or something, was trying to pull her off!

"Kat!" Zet cried, sprinting toward her.

"Hurry," she called. "Help me!"

He was nearly there. From below came a scrabbling sound. Whatever was pulling her off was thrashing around. Hard.

A boy's voice said, "By the gods, Kat, I'm going to fall."

Hui.

Zet raced forward to see his best friend dangling from the ledge. And Hui wasn't exactly the most nimble of the bunch.

"Hold on." Zet grabbed Hui's left hand. Kat pulled Hui's right one.

Together, they yanked him to safety.

Hui brushed himself off and grinned at Zet. "What took you so long?" he said. "I was about to be jackal dust."

Zet gave him a lighthearted punch. "How was I supposed to know you were coming over here?"

"When you were at my house, I made that bird noise."

"Bird noise?" Zet said. "I thought that was your brothers choking each other."

"Hmm, yes. Understandable."

Kat flapped her arms. "Will you quit joking around? What happened with the mummy?"

Hui flopped onto Zet's sleeping pallet. "Just let me catch my breath."

Kat turned sheepish and twisted her braid. "Thanks for coming. Even though now you're cursed because of us. You're the best friend we could ever have."

Hui gave Kat a dopey grin. "I wouldn't leave you guys in the lurch."

Zet laughed. "Lurch! That's funny."

Kat crossed her arms.

"Because mummies lurch," Zet said. "You know, when they walk?"

Kat said. "I got it. Thank you very much."

"Do you want to hear what happened or not?" Hui said.

"Yes," he and Kat said in unison.

"All right, well, I heard this creepy moaning outside our house. And so I opened the front door—"

"The mummy was there?" Zet said.

Hui looked almost sick as he dry swallowed. "Yeah. It pointed at me. It started whispering. This fast, muttering whisper."

"A curse," Kat breathed.

"I wasn't just going to stand there and let some monster curse me. So I slammed the door and ran around inside, looking for something to throw at it. But of course, Mother barred the door before I could do anything. And then—here's where it gets really weird—some lady screamed! From the opposite end of the street. No one could see who she was. She just screamed really loud."

Kat's eyes were wide. "That's what happened in our street! A lady screamed and everyone went to look for her."

"That is so strange," Zet agreed.

"And then, after the mummy left? My neighbors were running all over the place, looking for the screaming woman. But listen to this. I saw someone. Someone I *never* expected to see in my street."

"Who?" Kat said.

"That grouchy fisherman from the river."

This made Zet and Kat draw back in surprise.

"Are you sure?" Zet asked.

"The big, scary one? Who helped us get our raft unstuck?" Kat said.

Hui nodded. "Pretty weird, right?"

"Did you talk to him?" Zet asked.

"No. I was still inside and I doubt he spotted me through the window. But I know it was him. I'd recognize his big nose anywhere."

"This is all so odd." Kat stood and wrapped her arms around her middle. She paced a few steps, shivering.

A breeze pulled at Zet's hair. An idea was forming—one he couldn't quite catch. He frowned, thinking.

Kat spoke up. "Why would that scary fisherman be in your street?"

"Good question," Zet said. He was beginning to think they'd stumbled on a clue. *But to what?* "Maybe we should row downriver tomorrow and ask him."

"Maybe . . ." Kat said, although she didn't seem too fond of the idea.

Zet said. "Could they be connected? The fisherman, the screaming woman, and the mummy?"

Kat's brow furrowed. "It is a pattern." She stopped pacing. "Wait. What if that fisherman isn't a man, but a *ghost*?"

Zet groaned. "No, he's not a ghost."

Hui said, "Thank the gods for that. Who wants to fight a ghost? We already have a mummy on our hands. Yikes."

Kat said, "Then what *are* you saying, Zet?"

"What if this is all part of some big ruse?"

"A ruse? Impossible." Kat glanced at Hui. "Right, Hui? No way is this a trick."

Hui looked from Zet to Kat and back again. "Uh . . ." Hui hated picking sides.

Kat said, "Well? Who do you agree with? Me or Zet?"

"You?" he told Kat.

Zet smacked his forehead. "Only because she's glaring at you."

"Maybe."

Zet said, "The screaming lady that can't be found is a pretty strange coincidence. You have to admit, something weird is going on. Right now, our only lead is the fisherman from the river. Why was he in your street? We have to investigate."

Hui nodded. "Well hey, I'm free tomorrow." For some reason, he didn't sound happy about it.

"Why?"

"A palace messenger came before I left. I've been given the week off."

Kat said, "They must think you're cursed and don't want you bringing bad luck to the royal jewelers' workshop."

Hui nodded, looking glum. Did this mean he'd lost his apprenticeship? Did they honestly mean just the week off? What if it was forever?

"Wow. Bad news travels fast in royal circles." Zet slumped down beside his best friend. "I don't care what Merimose said. We can't just sit around. We have to do something. Fast."

SURPRISE ON THE NILE

The next morning, Zet and Kat asked their mother if they could go boating on the river. She agreed, saying it would take their minds off things. The siblings ate breakfast quickly and headed outside.

Early sun blazed down and Zet welcomed the coolness that rose from the paving stones. On their way to the river, Zet and Kat stopped to purchase a honey-cake, which they carefully wrapped in a clean cloth. Then, they detoured past their closed market stall.

A new pile of abandoned pottery lay before the tent. They sighed in unison.

"We better hide this away," Zet said.

Kat nodded. "Let's hurry. I bet Hui's waiting for us."

When they reached the Nile, the raft was still tied to the tree. Hui, however, was nowhere in sight. So they waited.

After what felt like ages, Kat groaned. "We told mother we'd be back before lunch. If we don't leave soon, we'll never make it downriver and back. Where is he?"

Zet rubbed his short hair. "I don't think he's coming."

Kat's hands went to her hips. Her brows furrowed with indignation. "Of course he's coming!"

"I bet his mother guessed what he was up to. You know he's not allowed to see us."

"Uh oh. I hope she didn't catch him sneaking home last night."

"That would be bad."

Nearby, a duck tipped underwater headfirst. Its tail feathers waggled as it foraged on the bottom. When it popped back up, however, its beak was empty. The duck quacked loudly and flew off.

"Maybe we should scrap this until tomorrow," Zet said.

Kat crossed her arms. "Why?"

"You want to go? *Just us two?*"

Kat said, "I'm not afraid of those river people."

Zet regarded her, thinking of how two days ago she didn't even want to investigate. "You should be."

"We have the honey-cake to give him," Kat said.

They'd come up with the excuse the night before. They'd give the fisherman the cake and say it was a thank you for his help the other day. After, they'd casually ask him what he was doing in Kanup Street.

Zet said, "What about the current? Remember how hard it was to paddle upstream?"

"Yes, I remember. But we already paid for the cake, and we got Mother to agree to let us come out. Who knows if we'll get another chance? The fisherman scares me, but the mummy scares me more. And right now, the fisherman's our only clue." She flexed one arm. "Besides, you know what? I think I'm stronger from carting those mountains of pottery home."

Zet grinned despite himself. "We don't have much time."

Kat said, "Let's go, before I change my mind."

Traveling downstream went quickly. The Nile carried their raft swiftly past Thebe's bustling watersteps. The city sights gave way to high walls. Here and there, buildings and shady homes peeked above them. The banks grew thicker with reeds and trees as the river wound its way along. Bees buzzed lazily in the gentle winds.

"We're almost there," Zet warned. "Look, there's that sandbank. Coming up on the left."

"I see it," Kat said.

This time, they were better prepared. Before casting off, they'd fashioned two anchors out of big rocks. "Get ready to weigh anchor. I don't want to get stuck again."

She lay down her pole. "It's really shallow. Now!"

Together, they tossed the rocks overboard. Great splashes sparkled in the sunlight. The raft came to a halt.

"Perfect positioning," Zet said.

Kat nodded.

They glanced toward the hut.

"Look," Zet said. "There's that ancient-looking block with the hieroglyphics I told you about."

She squinted. "I see two blocks."

She was right. *Had there always been two?* And where had they come from?

Something else was different. Footsteps had beaten a wide track through the overgrowth between the hut and the river. On the ground lay dozens of empty reed baskets. Some baskets floated, half-submerged, along the river's edge.

The mysterious sandbar had grown larger.

Zet and Kat slipped into the water and began wading toward shore.

"Hey!" came an angry shout.

The burly fisherman stood in the hut's doorway. Dirt and sweat covered his bare shoulders. He looked even bigger than Zet remembered.

Zet waved and called out a traditional greeting. "In peace, good sir."

"Get away, you!"

Water rushed past Zet's knees as he stood rooting his feet in the silty river. He plucked up his courage and called out, "We brought you a gift, to thank you for helping us."

"I don't want no gift," he snarled. "Didn't you hear me? Get lost!"

"It's a honey-cake."

"Take your stupid honey-cake and scram! Quit bothering us. Hear me?"

Kat's high voice startled Zet. "How rude! You can't order us away. This is public land."

"She's right," Zet said.

"Oh yeah?" the man snarled, advancing into the water. "Says who?"

Zet stepped back a foot. This had been a crazy idea. The raft was anchored; they'd never get free on time. He and Kat couldn't fight this fisherman!

"We'll call for the medjay," Kat said, raising her chin.

Zet knew by the way she knotted her fingers that she was terrified. But the man couldn't know that. Taking a cue from her, Zet puffed out his chest.

"Yeah!" Zet shouted.

The man's lip curled. "And how are you going to call for them, hey? Not like we're in town."

Kat pointed at the partially hidden wall that lay deeper in the overgrowth. "The Treasury Building is just on the other side of that wall. I scream really loud. Believe me, someone will come."

The man hesitated. His whole face flushed red. The flush spread to his neck. His fists balled at his sides. He looked ready to explode.

Zet pulled Kat back a step. He could sense her preparing to scream.

Then, the man's shoulders sank. His leathery face twisted into an apologetic smile. He spoke in a loud voice. "Look, now kiddies. Our poor daughter's in that hut. We don't got a home right now, and she's dead sick. We don't want any trouble."

Kat hesitated. Zet felt uncertain.

A faint voice called out, "Who are you talking to, father?"

"Don't you worry yourself, little dove," he called. "It's just some passers-by."

From the hut, there came the sound of violent coughing. "They won't try to make us leave, will they, papa?"

"No, kitten, don't you worry." Turning to Zet and Kat, he said, "Look here, I'm worried about my girl. We don't want anyone pushing us out of our home, even if it is only a poor hut. We're moving on soon. We're not lucky, not like you and your fancy royal friend."

Zet's face grew hot. "You knew who she was?" he stammered.

"I got eyes. I've been to a public ceremony or two."

"Why didn't you say anything?" Kat said.

"Didn't want any trouble. And I figured she wanted to be hidden, so I played along."

"Oh," Kat said. "I'm sorry about your daughter. Can we help?"

The coughing came again.

The man grimaced. "No. Some priest came and went. It's up to the gods now. We just want to be left in peace."

"At least accept the cake we brought you," Kat begged as the coughing fit grew louder.

"No. Leave us alone. Just like we left your royal friend alone."

"All right." Zet agreed. With all the commotion, he'd momentarily forgotten why they'd come. "One question," he called.

The fisherman scowled.

"Why were you in Kanup Street last night?" Zet said.

"Kanup Street?" the man spluttered. "I was nowhere near Kanup Street."

"But my friend saw you."

"He saw someone else, boy." The angry red color had returned to his cheeks. "Now let us alone. Get away and leave us poor folk in peace!"

NIGHT FRIGHT!

The sun god, Ra, beat down mercilessly as Zet and Kat rowed upstream. By the time they pulled the raft ashore, they were sweat-soaked.

Zet flopped down beside Kat to catch his breath. Starving, he unwrapped the cake and broke off a thick, sticky piece. "That man was hiding schomething," he said, his mouth full. It tasted delicious.

"What are you talking about?" Kat said. "His daughter is sick."

"Mmm. Maybe," Zet said.

"You heard her coughing."

Zet swallowed a large bite. "He looked weird when I asked about Kanup Street. He looked guilty."

"He wanted to get rid of us, that's all."

"Hui knows he saw him—he's an artist, he notices details, he wouldn't forget a face. I think that man was lying."

"Why would he lie? Even if he was in Kanup Street—what does it matter? A poor fisherman can't have anything to do with the mummy. He's taking care of his daughter."

Zet sat up. "Where was his wife? That woman?"

"Who knows? At market buying vegetables? Anyway it's almost lunchtime. Mother will be watching for us. Let's go."

That night Zet lay awake, unable to shake his suspicions. The fisherman had lied, he felt sure of it.

From the opposite side of the roof, Kat's snores drifted through the darkness. Zet's muscles ached from their hard row up the Nile. He rubbed his arms and yawned, exhausted even as his thoughts jabbered on.

If only he could see that mummy one more time, he'd have a better idea of what they were up against. But then what? Confront it? Beg it to stop? Ask what it wanted?

He only wished he knew where it planned to strike next.

An idea came to him.

Before he could pursue the thought, a familiar, bird-like whistle drifted from the street below. Zet bolted upright. He ran to the roof's edge and peered down.

"Hui?" he whisper-shouted at a shadowy form below.

"Who else?" Hui whispered back. "Come down."

"Hold on."

Zet grabbed his sandals and tossed them over. Then he clambered after them. His fingers and toes found foot holes in the mud-brick wall. He made quick work of it and soon landed beside his best friend.

"What happened to you today?" Zet asked.

"Mother."

"We figured," Zet said.

"Where's Kat?" Hui asked.

"Sleeping. Snoring actually. Anyway, good thing you showed up, I have an idea."

Hui rubbed his palms together. "Really?"

"I think the mummy's planning to strike again—tonight."

Hui's mouth gaped. "Tonight? Where?"

"Come on," Zet said. "I'll tell you while we run."

"What about Kat?" Hui scratched his neck and gazed up at the roof. "She'll be mad we took off without her."

"I'm not climbing back up there," Zet said. "But you can."

Hui hesitated. It was no secret he'd do just about anything for Kat. However, after his near-disaster climbing the other night, he gave a sheepish shrug. "Yeah, forget it. Why would she be mad? Let's go."

Zet and Hui ran through the darkness. Eerie shadows loomed in every doorway. A slip of torn, fluttering linen drifted past, swirling and tumbling. Cool air crawled over Zet's skin.

They reached the broad market square. Without the daytime bustle, the sprawling square looked creepy and forlorn.

Hui said, "You think the mummy is going to haunt your market stall?"

"Shh! Not so loud," Zet said.

Ahead, tents crouched against the earth. A breeze set the nearest one trembling. Its fastenings came loose and a linen panel billowed up into their path, striking them both.

Hui shouted, smacking at it. Zet grabbed the flap and tied it back down.

"This way," he hissed, pulling Hui by the elbow.

Hui leaned in and murmured, "Why are we whispering? You think that's going to stop a mummy from finding us?"

"Good point."

Still, they crept on tiptoe to Zet's pottery stall, glancing frantically this way and that.

"Where should we hide?" Hui said.

Zet pointed to their closed tent. "In there. We'll watch through a gap."

"What if the mummy's in there?" Hui asked and gulped, eying the large enclosure. "You first."

Zet squared his shoulders and slipped inside. He froze as his toe brushed something soft. Squinting, he spotted a pair of doves. They cooed in annoyance, but only shifted a few inches before going back to sleep.

Zet motioned to Hui. "It's safe. Don't step on the birds."

Together, they created a strategic hole to look out. That way they could watch the lanes between the other stalls.

"Now, we wait. Might as well get comfortable. I have a couple of cushions back there. Hold on. I'll get them."

Hui said, "No way. This place gives me the creeps. I'm coming with you."

A few moments later, Zet was still fumbling around in the blackness. Those cushions were back here somewhere. If only he could see.

"Hui, quit bumping into me," Zet said.

"There's no room."

"You could have waited," Zet said.

"Fat chance! Like I want to meet that mummy alone?"

Hui stepped on Zet's foot. Zet grabbed his toe and leaped around, knocking Hui sideways. They landed in a heap on something soft.

"Hey, look at that," Zet said. "Found the cushions. Let's go."

They stumbled back out, sending pots and plates rattling in their wake.

Hui hissed, "Shh!"

Maybe it was his terror or the absurd craziness of their situation, but Zet clapped a hand over his mouth as a snort of laughter escaped.

"This is insane," Hui gasped, cracking up. "I want my mummy. Get it? Mummy?"

"S—stop, that's not even funny," Zet said, holding his belly.

Hui banged into a tent pole. "Ow!"

"Seriously, quit it, I can't stop laughing!"

Finally, they wiped their eyes.

"One question," Hui said.

"What's that?" Zet asked, tossing down his cushion and sitting.

A shaft of moonlight lit Hui's face. "What are we going to do if the mummy shows up?"

"We're going to ask it what it wants."

Hui paled. "I was afraid you'd say that."

IT COMES TO LIFE

The moon god, Khonsu, drifted across the sea of stars above. In the tent, Zet and Hui had long since fallen silent. The breeze moaned. The air tasted of dust and a strange mishmash of spices. Neighboring stalls creaked and flapped, sending ghoulish shadows tilting across the square.

Hui grabbed Zet's elbow. "There! *Next to the date vendor's stall!*"

"Nope. That's not it." Zet stifled a yawn.

"What time do you think it is?" Hui asked.

"Past midnight."

"It's not coming," Hui said. "It would be here by now."

Zet hated to admit it, but Hui was probably right. This whole idea was a stupid dead end. And he was tired. Really tired. Rowing the raft had taken its toll. He wasn't looking forward to climbing the wall back onto his roof, let alone trek all the way home. He wanted to shut his eyes for a few minutes. Rest.

"Let's stay a few heartbeats longer," he said.

"You could have at least brought a snack."

"I didn't plan this, remember?" Zet shifted on his cushion. The giant vase supporting his shoulders felt solid. His eyes drifted closed. His head tipped back.

When Hui shook him awake, Zet was surprised to find himself lying down.

"Z-z-z-et?" Hui cried.

Zet's mouth felt fuzzy; his eyelids felt like a pair of stones. "Huh?" he asked, wiping drool from the corner of his mouth.

Hui squeezed his arm in a death grip. The boy's fingers were like rigid claws. They dug into Zet's forearm, practically to the bone.

"Yowza!" Zet yelped, instantly awake.

"L-look!" Hui gasped, still squeezing.

Zet tried to shake him off. "Calm down, will you?"

"Calm down? CALM DOWN?"

"What's the problem?" Zet said.

"The p-p-p-problem?"

"Yeah. Are you sick or something?" Zet said.

"O-over there!" Hui stammered.

"Over where—" Zet froze. His gulp was audible.

"Are you seeing what I'm seeing?"

Zet made a barely noticeable nod. His thudding heart sounded like drumbeats in his ears. His whole body went rigid. His eyes nearly popped out of their sockets.

"Zet?" Hui said in a high, pinched voice.

Zet made no reply. He was unable to find his tongue.

The mummy stood less than forty paces away.

And its burnt-black face stared straight at him.

"Run!" Hui tried to scramble to his feet. He tripped over his sandals and landed on his behind.

Hui tried again. He knocked over a stack of cooking pots. They flew left and right. Crashed down with small explosions. Pieces zinged everywhere. A large one landed in Zet's lap. Another struck him on the shoulder.

The shatter brought Zet to his senses. As the sounds died, he blinked and shook his head. Terrified or not, this was what they'd been waiting for, wasn't it?

"Don't move!" Zet hissed at Hui.

"Are you crazy? Let's go!" Hui backed away as the mummy lurched closer.

"No—this is our chance," Zet said.

The mummy paused. It tilted its head. Listening.

"Chance for what?" Hui cried. "To die?"

"To find out why it's haunting us!"

"Good luck with that. I'm out of here!" Hui backed up on all fours. He crouched behind a giant water jug, holding onto it like a shield.

Zet faced the creature of death. It looked awful. Worse than he remembered. The mummy's bandages were tattered and torn. Covered with brown stains and black blotches. And that disturbing burned face . . . It was a thing of nightmares. Nothing at all like the cute cat mummy he'd seen on the royal grounds.

A whisper issued from the mummy's scorched mouth. Fast and low. A hissing, otherworldly sound.

"What do you want?" Zet cried. "What do you want from us?"

The creature's right hand rose. It pointed straight at him.

Terror snaked around Zet's ribs; he could barely breathe.

The mummy's whispering rose to a shout. It went on and on. An awful, rhythmic chant.

Awoahaoh huhshhhhh ooohamamima awoahaoh huhshhhhh

The noise gripped the air. Soon, all around them, everything seemed to be vibrating. A wind rose, swirling dust into the air. And still, the mummy continued its awful chant.

Zet swallowed hard and forced his shaking legs to move. Everything inside him shouted *run!* Unsteadily, he got to his feet. Then he wrapped one arm around the nearest tent pole as though it was a friend. And perhaps, after sheltering his family for generations, this tent was.

"What do you want?" Zet shouted again. "Are you Aziza? Tell me what you want!"

The mummy's keening chant rose to a wail.

Zet could take it no longer. He would stop this now, or die trying.

"Who are you?" he cried, letting go of the pole and running out of the tent. "Tell me!"

He only made it a few steps outside. From the darkness beyond, a snarling animal launched through the air.

The jackal.

It dove at him.

Hui screamed.

Zet leaped clear and rolled beneath the tent's sidewall. Then he crouched behind a shoulder-high wall of dinner plates.

Outside the jackal, reeking of musk, could be heard sniffing and snuffling at the lowered tent flaps.

Voices rose from the market's fringes. People were coming. Lots of them. The shrill blast of a medjay's papyrus whistle shattered the air. Zet heard the slap of dozens of sandals weaving through the distant stalls along the market's outer edges. Weapons clanked. It sounded like both the medjay and the Royal Guards were arriving in full force.

"Who goes there?" shouted a man, his voice growing closer. "Show yourself!"

Zet recognized that voice: the Royal Guard—*Renni*—who'd tried to shoo him away from Aziza's house.

"Show yourself!" Renni shouted again, his voice drifting above the warren-like maze of shuttered stalls. Any moment and the crowd would find their way here.

Zet peeked beneath the flap to see the mummy turn and lurch off.

With a low growl, the jackal bared its teeth. Then it spun, claws scraping the ground, and loped off in its wake.

BEETLE-DUNG AND BREAD-WORMS!

"Quick," Zet said. "Out the back." He ran for it.

Hui followed and ducked under the rear flap.

"Which way?" Hui said.

Zet peeked around the side. The light of dozens of lanterns grew closer, sending shadows growing and shrinking, wavering like living creatures. Men shouted and fanned out across the square. They beat the canvas with sticks and yelled, *show yourself!*

Zet pointed in the opposite direction. "Head for that alley. That's where the mummy went."

He took off at a sprint. Hui charged alongside. Shadows closed around them. Only a wan moon lit their way.

"Forget the mummy," Hui gasped. "Are you crazy? Let's go home."

Zet veered left. "We have to go after it."

"Beetle-dung and bread-worms!" Hui cried, but followed anyway.

They reached the alley. Thebans were pouring out of their homes. Whispering. Clutching one another and heading toward the square.

As for the mummy and the jackal, they were nowhere to be seen.

Zet smacked his forehead. "How could we lose them? We were so close! How did they escape so fast?"

Hui grabbed Zet's arm. "Uh—Zet?"

"Hold on, I'm trying to think."

"Zet?" Hui yanked again.

"Not now—"

"Look! Over there!" Hui cried.

Zet looked. All he saw were more crowds. Swelling like the tide. "Look at what?" he demanded. "Did you see the mummy?"

"No—but I saw—"

"Forget it, later. Right now, we need to figure out how to get higher. We can't let the mummy escape again. Quick, this way." Zet dragged Hui down a narrow alley. A dozen enormous baskets filled the far end. Zet tried to pull one out. "Help me. Let's drag it over to that door. The one with the big lintel-overhang on top."

Hui latched onto the basket. "*Pee-ew!*" He clamped his nose shut with his thumb and forefinger. "What's in this thing?"

"Trash."

"Smells like a giant dead fish," Hui said.

"I'll turn you into a dead fish if you don't pull harder."

Hui laughed.

Zet fought a rising grin. "Just pull!"

But what a stench! His eyes were practically bugging out.

"Hey, what's a dead fish good for?" Hui said.

"What?"

"Scaling a wall! Get it? Because fish have scales?"

Zet laughed as he clambered up onto the sturdy basket, pulled himself onto the lintel, and then climbed the rest of the way to the roof. With a bit more effort, Hui scaled up after him.

They reached a small terrace. It was empty. They crossed to the far side and climbed over the partition onto the neighboring terrace. Everyone was down in the street. The boys kept going.

Finally, they reached the tallest house. It stood a story higher than those around it.

Below, the town of Thebes spread out around them.

The moon colored everything a sickly shade of gray. In the distance, mist rose from the Nile in eerie swirls. Fog pooled over its banks, sending thin wisps twisting up the adjacent streets.

And then Zet saw it.

The mummy.

It was moving at a fast pace. Mist curled around its legs. It looked as though it was floating. Flying even. Zooming along at a rapid speed. And it was headed for the edge of town.

"There!" Zet cried, pointing. "Let's go."

Hui groaned. "Look how far that is."

"We'll make it."

"It will be gone before we get there," Hui said.

"Not if we're fast." Zet crossed another three rooftops with Hui on his heels. "Besides, I have a feeling I know where it's going."

"How?" Hui demanded, stopping to catch his breath.

"Look at the path it's on. You know where that leads, don't you?"

Hui frowned. Then his brows flew up.

"No," Hui gasped. "*Noooo!* Not there!"

"Makes sense, doesn't it?" Zet tried to shove his friend forward. "Move."

Hui clutched his head and moaned. "We're dead."

"Hurry!"

"My life is over. And my mother's baking date buns tomorrow. Now I'll never get any."

Zet rolled his eyes. "They'd taste even better if you were a hero. Right? And just think of Kat's face, she's going to be so surprised. I can't wait to see that."

Hui pursed his lips. "Valid point." He motioned Zet forward. "Don't just stand around, lead on!"

Soon they were tearing ahead, legs moving at top speed across the rooftops. They caught a last glimpse of the mummy from their high vantage point. Then the rooftops ended. The boys dropped into the street. Mist swirled around their legs. The air grew briny with the Nile's scent. They kept running.

Buildings began to thin out. Palm trees stretched skyward, swaying like shaggy-headed giants.

They reached the Nile's shore. Out on its misty surface, they spotted an ancient-looking boat. And at the boat's helm, shining brightly in the moonlight, stood the mummy.

"Where's it going?" Hui said.

"It's crossing to the West Bank, the Nile's eternal side. That's where mummies are buried and become immortal."

Hui groaned. "Back to its tomb?"

"It must be. Let's get to our raft, it's close," Zet gasped.

Sure enough, their little raft lay safely where Zet and Kat had left it. The boys jumped on. They paddled into the moving current but the fog was growing thicker. Soon, they saw only misty whiteness in every direction. Sailing blind, they smashed into the far bank.

Together, they secured the raft.

Here the ground was dry and rocky. A rough road led up the sloping hillside. They darted up it. Stones scattered underfoot. Soon they reached a pair of iron gates.

"This is it," Zet whispered.

"Are we really going in there?"

Zet nodded, mouth dry. On the far side, shadowy tombs and statues rose from the ground. The boys eyed the famous graveyard: home of the mastabas, or burial chambers, of Egypt's powerful and wealthy citizens.

The Theban Necropolis.

Fear tickled Zet's scalp. Gooseflesh rose along his neck.

"I've never been inside a cemetery," Hui whispered.

"Me neither."

Gripping each other's arms, they pushed through the gate. The hinges creaked. In the distance, someone or something was murmuring. A low, hissing, rhythmic chant.

Awoahaoh huhshhhhh ooohamamima awoahaoh huhshhhhh

The boys stared at each other. Then the gate slammed shut with a bang.

AVENUES OF THE DEAD

The boys stood frozen, hands glued to each other's arms. Finally, the whispering died. A breeze swirled around Zet's ankles. The air in the necropolis felt cold. Avenues of graves climbed the hill before them. There was no mummy in sight.

Zet peeled his fingers from Hui's wrist and gulped.

They snuck forward, both hunched as if trying to become invisible. Something rustled to their left. The boys yelped.

"Just a mouse," Zet breathed.

"This graveyard looks like a creepy town," Hui whispered. "It's all laid out in streets."

"Look." Zet pointed. "Someone left food there, bread and fruit."

"It's all rotten. *Eeeeew.*"

The eerie moon lit the shadowy lanes between the graves. Some were small and simple. Others were marked by statues and steles inscribed with hieroglyphics. The largest were the mastabas, the tombs said to house whole rooms of treasures—objects the deceased might want in the Afterlife: furniture, jewelry, mirrors, vases, incense, jars of rich ointments, beer, and grains, and all manner of things.

Hui pointed at a mastaba. "That one has a door. But it's blocked up."

"Maybe to keep grave robbers out?"

"Yeah. I don't see the mummy, do you?" Hui whispered.

"There!" Zet cried as the mummy lurched past a stone slab in the distance.

The creature quickly melted into the mist.

But Zet had honed in on its position. The mummy wouldn't escape now. Their luck was improving—the jackal was nowhere in sight.

Swallowing his terror, Zet flung himself uphill after the monster. Hui, breathing hard, stayed with him. The air smelled of dirt and decaying flowers. Zet wiped his face. He couldn't rid his nose of the sweet, cloying odor.

"There," Hui cried. "The mummy's tomb!"

Zet followed Hui's outstretched finger.

The stone mastaba looked like all the others—except for one telling detail.

The mastaba's stone door was missing.

Powerful hands had smashed it wide open. Rocks lay crumbled at the gaping entrance. The sleeping chamber of the dead was no longer sealed for eternity like it should have been. Instead, the mummy had broken out of its tomb to walk the earth. It terrorized Zet, his family, and his friends.

The time had come to confront this mummy and put its haunting to an end.

"Zet," Hui whispered, "This is a bad idea!"

The ink-black hole beckoned, gaping like a screaming mouth.

Together, they crept forward until they reached it. Zet's hands shook as he grasped the tomb's broken walls. Jagged stone pressed into his palms. He raised a trembling foot. Held it over the threshold. Took a deep breath.

"Here goes nothing," he whispered.

Then he crossed over.

Into the blackness . . .

"*Zet?*" Hui whispered.

No answer.

"*Zet!?*" Hui shouted. "Are you still alive?"

"Shhh, I'm right here! But I can't see anything." His ankle bumped against something white-hot. "Ow!" he cried.

"*Zet!?*" Hui shouted.

"Stop shouting," Zet whispered. "Something burned me."

"Oh, by the gods, there's no flame, it's evil—it's black fire!" Hui cried.

"It's not. Just get in here, will you? I think I know what this hot thing is."

"Are you crazy?" Hui said.

"Hold on." Zet crouched and felt carefully around. His fingers sensed the warm glow of a small object on the ground. He touched the base, which was cooler, and moved his hands slowly up the sides. It grew hotter the higher he went. "I was right," he called to Hui. "It's a lamp. Someone was in here with a lamp. It's still hot."

"A lamp? Are you sure about that?"

"Positive."

A shuffling sound followed, then Hui banged into Zet.

"Ow. That's weird," Hui said.

"I know. Crouch down. Feel it?"

"Definitely a lamp," Hui said.

"I wonder if there's a flint?" Zet said.

Both boys swept their hands across the floor.

"Found something," Zet said. "I think it's—yes, definitely. A bow drill. Hold on, let me try to light it."

But using the bow drill wasn't easy. Fumbling in the dark, he worked the bow's cord rapidly back and forth. Hui took a turn. They kept working it, grinding the spindle against the wood block beneath it.

"I smell smoke," Hui hissed.

"We've got an ember. Blow on it—gently, gently!" Zet warned.

"I know how to do it." Hui used his breath to encourage the ember. "Touch the wick to the ember, quick."

Zet moved the wick into position. This was the moment of truth.

If the lamp blazed to life, nothing would be hidden. Not even a sleeping mummy. Or worse, a mummy standing over them.

The wick caught.

Zet leaped to his feet as the lamp devoured the darkness.

Everything stood out in hideous relief. Walls covered in hieroglyphics—curses neither Zet nor Hui could read. The gruesome canopic jars that held the mummy's internal organs.

What caught Zet's gaze, though, was the massive sarcophagus.

The ominous coffin lay dead center.

And they were standing right next to it.

THINGS THAT SLITHER IN THE NIGHT

S tanding stock-still in the wavering lamplight, the boys stared at the sarcophagus.

Hui's face was ashen. "Do you think the mummy's crawled back inside it?"

"I—I don't know," Zet said. "Should we look?"

"N-no way," Hui said.

Still, they shuffled forward, shoulder-to-shoulder, elbow-to-elbow, eyes fastened on the ornate coffin. Painted on its lid was the life-sized image of a man.

Was this Aziza? Zet couldn't be sure. Did he have a jugnose? Maybe. His gaze moved to the figure's arms, which were crossed over his chest. The figure's left hand held a golden ankh: the symbol of eternity. The right hand held something more menacing: a curved blade. A sickle.

This was madness.

No one was allowed inside a tomb!

No one, apart from a priest, was ever even permitted to see a sarcophagus. Or a mummy. Not like this. And these wall paintings—they had to be filled with spells and curses. Were all tombs like this inside? Painted from top to bottom with hieroglyphics and detailed pictures? And what was the price of Zet and Hui being there? Would they be cursed for all eternity?

Zet raised the lantern high over the sarcophagus. "Look," he whispered. "The lid! It's not closed all the way."

They leaned in close to study the gap.

A hissing noise began to issue from it.

"Oh n-n-no!" Hui cried. "I d-d-don't like th-this!"

Sweat trickled down Zet's sides and the lamp shook in his hand. The hissing intensified. He was rooted to the spot, unable to move a single step. Unable to run.

"Z-zz-et?" Hui gasped. "What's happening?"

"I can't move!" Zet cried.

"We need to leave," Hui said.

"We need to look inside," Zet managed through dry lips. "You know we do."

He pictured his family still at home, still safe. But for how long? What would the mummy do next?

"Aaargh!" Hui dug his fingers into his hair. "By the gods—the hissing's getting louder!"

His words broke the spell. Zet set down the lamp. He lunged forward and gave the coffin lid a shove. It weighed a ton. He shoved again and the wood groaned. On the third shove, the lid moved, widening the gap.

"Help me," he gasped. "Help me open it."

Hui's eyes were so wide they shone white. The boys placed their hands on the lid. Together, they pushed with all their might.

It began to shift.

Scraping.

Creaking.

Rasping.

Screeeeeeeeeeeeeech!

They got it halfway open when Zet hollered, "Stop! Aaaaaahhhh! Stop pushing, stop!"

Dozens, *no hundreds* of slithering snakes erupted through the gap. They swarmed, hissing, out of the coffin. Tongues flicking, cold eyes shining, serpentine bodies stinking. Everywhere. They were everywhere!

"They're on me," Hui shouted. "Get them off! Get them off!"

He stumbled back, arms and legs thrashing as he threw the snakes clear. His foot connected with a canopic jar. The jar toppled sideways and smashed into the one next to it, and then the next, until all four canopic jars crashed open.

But instead of organs spilling out, the contents came alive.

They were beetles.

Scarab beetles.

"AAAAaaaaahhhh!" Zet screamed.

"AAAAaaaaahhhh!" Hui screamed back.

Zet pulled Hui toward the door. "Run! Run for you liiiiife!"

The tomb walls vibrated with hissing and buzzing. Snakes writhed and beetles click-clacked. Horror whiplashed up and down Zet's limbs as bugs surged over his feet and swarmed up his ankles. He kicked out, trying to shake them off.

His foot hit the lamp. It clattered and broke. The tomb went dark.

"I can't see!" Hui screamed.

Zet lunged toward the moonlit gap. "This way!"

The friends leaped out of the broken door. They threw themselves to the ground and rolled, swatting and shouting.

"They're crawling out!" Hui screamed. "They're crawling out! Get up!"

"Gaaaaack!" Zet cried.

They stumbled backward, grabbing at each other for support.

Zet rear-ended into something. Something big and unmoving.

A giant pair of hands clamped down on their shoulders.

Zet glanced sideways and his eyes almost bugged out. The hand holding him firm was enormous. And it was no normal hand. It was the color of charred wood. The color of rot. Swallowing, Zet peered up.

He was staring right into the mummy's gruesome face!

He went cold all over. Then, he screamed with all his might.

WHO DISTURBS MY TOMB?

"*Who disturbs my tomb?*" the mummy intoned.

Zet and Hui thrashed, trying to free themselves from the monster's grip. Snakes and bugs continued to pour out from the mastaba's broken door. Glittering. Hissing. Clicking.

Louder now, the mummy cried, *"Who dares disturb my tomb?"*

Zet met Hui's frantic eyes. They'd been best friends since forever. Sometimes, they could practically read each other's minds. So when Zet shouted, "*kick*!" Hui knew exactly what he meant.

Zet drove his heel into the creature's shin. Hui did the same. The monster let out a barely audible *Ooof.* Its death-hold loosened, just enough. The boys ducked out of its grasp, ran a few feet and spun around.

Zet stared, mouth slack.

"Muh-muh-mummy!" Hui managed.

Bugs swarmed up its dirty, wrapped limbs. Up its ratty torso. Over its gaunt, grime-stained hands. The monster with its scorched head and charred eyeholes stood stock-still. Nestled deep in the burned folds of face linen lay a pair of terrifying beetle-black eyes. Watching. *Watching!*

Zet and Hui stood frozen in fear.

The mummy raised both arms. Wind shook its bandages. The monster spread its filthy fingers wide. Snakes slithered across the ground, wound up its legs, coiled over its shoulders, fell from its forearms.

The mummy lunged. Snarling, it grabbed both boys and dragged them into the dark, snake-infested mastaba.

They stumbled over the threshold, Zet and Hui yelling and punching. Zet found himself falling sideways and suddenly knew what he had to do. The lamp! He felt the doused lamp's heat before he touched it. Inside, the oil was still scalding hot.

"Hui, duck!" he shouted.

A shaft of moonlight caught the mummy's face. Zet threw the oil and the mummy screamed in agony.

"Run," Zet shouted, throwing himself out the door.

They ran helter-skelter down the avenues of tombs.

Hui's arms and legs pumped furiously as he ran alongside Zet. They leaped over a small statue. Kept going.

"Next time I think up something crazy," Zet gasped, "Tell me to jump off a dock."

"Gladly. Don't stop, it's after us!"

"Get out of this cemetery, hurry," Zet said, putting on more speed.

At the bottom of the hill, they hurled themselves out the gate and kept running until they reached the river. Their raft was still moored next to the Nile.

"Jump on. Paddle!"

Never had they paddled so fast in all their lives.

They reached the opposite shore, but this wasn't over. Who knew what the furious mummy would do next?

"We need to find Merimose," Zet said as they reached shore and tied up the raft with shaking hands.

"I bet he's in the marketplace," Hui said.

Hui was right. Chaos and blazing lanterns filled the market square. It seemed the whole town was awake. Merimose stood on guard with his officers while the Royal Guard questioned frightened bystanders.

"Merimose," Zet gasped, pushing through a knot of people to the big medjay's side. "We followed the mummy. We know where it went."

"Slow down," Merimose growled. "What happened?"

Zet and Hui started talking at once.

Merimose raised a hand. "Stop. Renni needs to hear this." He turned and shouted over his shoulder. "RENNI! Over here. We're in luck. We've got information."

Renni tore himself away from his men and approached, his blade rattling at his side. The head of the Royal Guard frowned at the boys as they stumbled breathlessly through their tale.

"You should have alerted us," he said. "Crossing to the West Bank on your own? What good would that do? Never mind—you'll answer for yourselves later." He made an angry face. "Take us to this tomb."

Zet and Hui led the search party to the river. Boats were gathered up and the small fleet of medjay and Royal Guardsmen crossed the misty Nile. On the far rocky shore, everyone embarked.

"This way," Zet said, leading the charge uphill and into the ancient mortuary.

But when they reached the mastaba, Zet got the shock of his life.

The tomb was empty.

No slithering snakes or clicking beetles. No broken canopic jars. No lamp. Just a heavy, silent sarcophagus with its lid firmly shut.

Even the signs of their struggle had disappeared. Their footprints had been smoothed over. It was all gone.

Renni said, "Where's the tomb? With the snakes?"

"This is it, right here. See, the door is broken open."

A few dried leaves blew across Renni's toes. "A broken door? That's all you have to show me?"

"Well, there were snakes and beetles. And the mummy was right here. We fought it ourselves."

Renni's lips pursed. "Did you, now?"

A couple of his men sniggered.

"You fought the mummy?" Renni sneered.

"I—I don't know where the footprints went. Someone must have gotten rid of them. Swept the ground or something."

"How dare you waste my time," Renni roared. He waved at his gathering. "You had me bring my Royal Guard all this way for nothing?"

"It's not nothing! I'm telling you, the mummy was here."

"I'll have you punished. My men should be in Thebes, not in some god-forsaken cemetery. I'll see you tried in court for your crimes, I'll—"

"Renni," Merimose boomed. "Can I speak to you a moment?"

"Whatever you have to say," Renni snarled, "Spit it out."

Merimose pressed his lips together. Then he blew out a breath. "I can vouch for these boys."

"Can you now?"

"If they say they saw something, they're telling the truth."

Renni said, "This is my investigation, Merimose, not yours. So keep out of it."

Merimose glared. Very slowly, he said, "With all respect—*sir*—if Zet says he saw that mummy, then I suggest you inspect this tomb."

"How dare you. I'll have your medjay-badge for this! I'll—"

Zet found his hands forming fists at his side.

"And another thing," Merimose said. "Since you're obviously unaware–Zet, Hui, and Princess Meritamen are friends. Good friends, in fact. Next time you speak to Pharaoh, I'm sure he'll also be happy to inform you that—" He leaned in close to Renni and spoke into his ear.

"They what?" Renni sputtered.

"It's true," Merimose said, "they helped Pharaoh solve more than one crime. So I think you best drop this talk of punishment. Immediately."

Renni had gone white with rage. He clutched at his head and let out a frustrated yowl. "Fine! Fine, just go. Just leave and we'll forget this ever happened."

"But the tomb," Zet said. "Aren't you going to search it?"

"Of course I'm going to search it!" Renni howled. "Now get off my crime scene. And keep your nose out of my business."

RUNNING FOR HOME

Zet could hardly believe it was still night as he and Hui paddled back across the Nile. It seemed like ages since he'd left home.

One thing was certain: dawn would arrive soon. The sun god, Ra, was nearing the horizon. When his gleaming rays burst across the land, everyone would wake. Including his mother. And Hui's mother.

If they hadn't already.

Despite the need to hurry, an idea broke into his worries and he froze.

"What are you doing?" Hui said. "Keep paddling! I have to get home. My mother's going to kill me!"

"I just thought of something," Zet said.

"Forget thinking. Think later! Paddle."

Zet said, "I should have told Renni to find out if that was Aziza's tomb."

"Not important right now," Hui said. "Focus!"

"Fine." Zet dug his paddle deep. He kept thinking though. He couldn't help it. Questions seemed to pile up, one after the other. Where had the snakes and beetles gone? And their footprints? It hadn't taken that long to alert the authorities and return to the tomb.

"We're here," Hui said. "Jump off."

The boys tied up the raft and sprinted up the bank. They ran through the mist-damp streets. At the Southern Road they split up, wishing each other luck.

Adrenaline surged through Zet as he neared home.

No sign of movement through the window. So far, so good. Silence gripped his street. He clambered up the rough wall to the roof. At the top, he quietly threw one leg over and then the other.

His sheets were exactly as he'd left them.

He squinted toward Kat's sleeping pallet. She was in bed, mouth open, snoring softly. She hadn't even noticed him missing.

Clearly, no one had.

Zet drew a hand across his brow and blew out a relieved sigh. At least something had gone his way. He only hoped Hui was equally lucky.

Instead of climbing under the covers, he crept over to Kat and shook her awake.

"You did *WHAT?*" she shrieked when he told her they'd chased the mummy to the West Bank.

"Shhhhh!" Zet hissed.

"*You did all that without me?*" she wailed.

"Keep your voice down, will you?"

Huffing, she whisper-shouted, "Why didn't you wake me up? This affects me, too, you know!"

"I know." He had to think fast. "Which is why I need your help."

She eyed him indignantly.

"I mean it. Please?"

"What kind of help?" she asked.

"You're smart," Zet said.

She rolled her eyes.

"So help me figure out what happened with that mummy tonight," Zet said. "Because I can't make sense of it, but maybe you can."

Looking slightly mollified, she pulled her knees up and wrapped her arms around them. "Fine. Tell me everything that happened. Slowly this time."

Zet did. He told her how the mummy showed up in front of the pottery stall, and how they chased it through the streets. He described how it escaped across the Nile in a boat lit by a ghostly glow. He told her about the tomb and the still warm lamp, about the snakes and the beetles. And how they'd rushed outside, only to be caught in the mummy's gruesome clutches.

"So it spoke?" Kat asked, winding her braid tightly in one fist. "When it grabbed you?"

"Yes, that's what I said."

She frowned. "Real words?"

"Yes."

"What exactly did it say?" she asked.

"Something like, *who dares disturb my tomb?*"

She toyed with her ear, thinking. "That is so strange. Since before it only whispered mumbo-jumbo."

"You're right. That is strange."

"I guess it wanted to get the message across—in plain words," she said.

"What's weird is, looking back, it's like the mummy wanted us to follow it. Why else did it light up its boat? It was glowing. It could have easily escaped in the dark."

"Maybe it couldn't help being lit up?" Kat said. "Maybe that's what happens when you're a mummy?"

"It wasn't glowing when it came to our house."

"True." She chewed her lip.

"Here's another question—where did the snakes and bugs go? And our footprints? It's all too unbelievable."

They sat in silence, pondering.

Kat shifted, wrapping her covers tighter around her shoulders. "What about before you got to the necropolis? Anything else you remember?"

"No."

"From the marketplace?"

"Nope." Then he bolted upright. "Wait—I totally forgot!"

"What?" Kat said.

"When we ran out of the square! Hui wanted to tell me something. *He saw someone.* But I didn't listen. I was too busy chasing the mummy. Hui seemed really freaked out."

"Who was it? Who did he see?"

"That's the thing," Zet said. "He never got a chance to tell me."

"Could it be a clue?"

"I'm not sure. We need to find out. But that won't be easy since his mother doesn't want us there. We'll have to sneak over."

Zet eyed the dawn breaking across the horizon. From the rooms below, Apu let out a long wail. These past few days, nothing seemed to comfort the once happy baby. Zet and Kat shared a glance, reading one another's thoughts. *Had the mummy cursed Apu?*

Quietly, Kat said, "I'm worried. Where's the mummy going to strike next? First it came here. Then to Hui's. Last night, our stall."

Zet stared out over the adjoining housetops. Crimson light pooled across tiles and balconies, streaked along walls and doors.

"Who's the mummy going to curse next?" Kat said.

"Good question."

Kat walked to the roof's edge. Fisting her hands at her sides, she gazed toward the center of Thebes. A breeze fluttered her dark bangs. "I'm pretty sure I know. And it won't be good."

WHO'S THERE?

Before Kat could tell him her suspicions, a loud hammering came from downstairs. Someone was banging on their front door.

"Who could that be?" Zet wondered aloud.

"I don't know," Kat said. "A visitor? At this hour?"

They bounded down the ladder and headed for the front room. They reached the door at the same time. Zet was about to yank it open but Kat stopped his hand.

"We don't know what's out there," she said.

In a loud voice, Zet said, "Who is it?"

"Geb," came the muffled reply.

Zet and Kat stared at one another. Geb? The spice-vendor from the market? What was he doing here at the crack of dawn?

Their mother appeared, wrapping a linen robe around herself. "Who's out there?"

"It's Geb, the spice vendor," Kat said.

"Well, open the door."

Zet liked Geb. The spice-vendor was a good man and an old family friend. The man stood on the front stoop, his weather-beaten face wearing a worried frown.

Zet said, "Is everything all right?"

"Er—" The small man hesitated and shuffled his fee

"Come in," their mother said.

"I shouldn't." Geb had his woolen wig in his hands. He wrung it like a dishrag. "Just a quick word."

"We'll be more comfortable inside," she said. "Please. Zet and Kat will bring refreshments."

Geb nodded, looking glum, and plopped his wig back on his head. "All right."

Zet and Kat took care of the refreshments as fast as they could, filling a platter with fresh figs and nuts in the kitchen and dashing back to the front room.

Geb was speaking. "I don't like it either, my lady, but you understand, don't you?"

Zet and Kat exchanged a fearful glance. *What had they missed?*

"Yes, I understand," their mother said, yet her face had lost all its color.

"Understand what?" Zet said, his fingers gripping the platter. "Mother? What's going on?"

"Set the fruit down," she said. "I'm sure Geb is hungry."

Geb looked anything but hungry. He looked sick to his stomach.

Kat said, "Why have you come, Geb? Please, tell us."

"It's not easy, children. I see how hard you work. It's . . ." Geb cleared his throat. "It's this mummy business. The vendors are scared."

"Of us?" Kat said.

"I'm afraid the mummy haunted the market last night," Geb said.

Zet flashed back to hiding in his stall, and the chaos with the medjay and the guards and all the villagers showing up in a panic.

Geb said, "The vendors held an emergency pre-dawn meeting. They're worried that your stall's presence offends Aziza and that his curse will spread to them unless something is done."

Kat said, "You make it sound like our stall is a disease."

Geb said, "I know your stall is one of the oldest. Your great-grand-father was one of the market's founders. Your grandpa was a friend to me, and a good man. Your father's a good man, too."

"But . . . ?" Kat said.

Zet said, "We've already shut our stall. We're only taking returns."

Geb licked his dry lips. "I must beg you to remove it."

"Remove our stall?" Kat screeched. "You can't ask that of us!"

"That's crazy," Zet said. "That stall is our life."

Damp spots appeared on Geb's forehead. "I don't like it any more than you do."

Zet's mother said, "We understand. We cannot risk the mummy hurting them because of us."

Geb wrung his woolen wig in his gnarled hands. "I'm sorry. If it were only me, I'd tell you to stay. But I'm an old man with little to lose. Many vendors have families to support. It's nothing against you, they simply can't fight the undead."

Zet could hardly believe this was happening. His world was crumbling. Lose the stall? Shut it down forever? It was their family's history and future. What would they eat? What about the roof over their head? What would their father come home to? Zet had sworn to keep life steady and safe while his father was away. He'd failed completely. And all because of that mummy!

His throat felt thick. He swallowed hard. He didn't want everyone to see the sadness written all over his face. Going to the door, he wiped his eyes on his tunic sleeve.

Geb said, "We vendors have always stood together. When times have been hard, we've stood behind you, as you've stood behind us. This decision was not made easily."

"No, I figured that," Zet murmured, believing him. Even grumpy Salatis, the date-seller, had come to Zet's aid in the past.

"I'll do whatever I can to help until you get back on your feet," Geb said. "I promise."

Kat's face was red. Her eyes brimmed with tears. "Oh Geb, that's kind, but I don't think we'll ever be able to get back on our feet. Without our stall, we'll have lost everything!"

Not on Zet's watch. He refused to let it come to that.

As Geb made to leave, their mother walked him out into the street. They stood murmuring together, but Zet no longer cared what they had to say. This had gone too far. He was furious and frightened all at once.

He had to stop that mummy, no matter what.

Kat sat on a cushion staring blankly at the floor.

"Kat," he said, causing her to start.

She blinked up at him with red-rimmed eyes. "Yes?" she said wearily.

"You said you knew where the mummy would show up next. Where?"

She unfolded herself from the floor and stood. Taking a shaky breath, she said, "I'll tell you. And we'll stop it together."

20

FUN AND GAMES

A short while later, Zet and Kat paced the roof, making plans. When the time came, they'd ambush the monster and take him down once and for all. Or be cursed for all eternity. Either way, this had to end.

"Zet, Kat?" their mother called up to them. "Get your sandals on. We're going out."

"Out?" Zet climbed down the ladder.

Their mother wore a simple linen day-dress and Apu was settled on her right hip. The baby chewed fiercely on his wet thumb. "I think we all need a break," she said. "There's been too much stress this past week. So we're going to take a picnic and spend the day in the public gardens."

"A picnic?" Kat clambered downstairs. "*Now?* But everything's falling apart!"

"Which is why we need to pull together as a family. The good news is that Geb has given us two days. If the Royal Guards fail to stop the mummy's haunting, in two days, we'll do as the market vendors ask. So yes, we're going on a picnic. I've packed a basket. Put your sandals on. It's lovely outside."

"But mother—"

"No buts. We're going to enjoy ourselves. We're going to eat and drink and play games. Everything else, we'll forget until tomorrow."

Zet and Kat stared at one another. What choice did they have?

The family trekked through the streets. Zet carried the heavy picnic basket. He longed to tell their mother everything. But it was too risky. What if she forbade him to act? By the gods, who was he supposed to be loyal to? His mother's wishes, or those of his father? And if he left things up to the Royal Guard, would they really solve the mystery? Could he afford to take that chance?

Kat sidled up to him and whispered, "Do you think Hui got caught sneaking home this morning?"

"I dunno. I wish we could tell him we figured out where it's going to strike next."

"*I* figured it out," Kat whispered.

"Yes, fine. Does it really matter? I just wish we could tell him."

"Well, we can't," Kat huffed.

It seemed they both were on edge. At least Apu seemed happier than he had been in weeks. The baby peered around with wide eyes as they left the dusty streets and entered the lush gardens. The air was heavy with the scent of flowers. Birds fluttered from branch to branch, twittering amongst the blooms.

Their mother laid out a big linen blanket.

At first, Zet felt too wound up to relax. Still, he flopped next to Apu.

It was a beautiful day. You wouldn't even know dark events were swirling around them. A leaf spiraled down and landed on Apu's upturned face. Apu squealed, waving his chubby arms. Kat smiled. Zet couldn't help it. He did, too.

"Want to try the fishing net?" Zet asked Kat.

"All right."

With hard work, swift lunges, and a few timely shouts, Zet and Kat managed to catch three big Nile perch. Their mother regaled them with praise. Then she grilled the fish until the fat crackled and popped, the meat turned deep golden, and Zet's stomach rumbled at the delicious scent. They ate perch and crusty bread until their bellies were full to bursting.

When the day cooled and they packed up, it felt like they'd gone on a long holiday.

Yes, there were troubles ahead. But as they walked together in the growing twilight, their eyes shone with happy smiles. They had each other, and that's what was important.

Back home, they once again faced the stacks of returned pottery.

Their mother ran a hand over a large soup-serving dish. "It's lovely, this tureen, isn't it?"

"I remember getting that," Kat said. "On last year's trip to the artisan village."

"Do you remember the boat ride home?" Zet grinned. "When we nearly got overturned by those hippos? Kat, you were screaming and screaming."

Their mother smiled. "We were all screaming."

"You're right," Zet said.

"Especially when that hippo started bellowing." Kat did a mock imitation of a hippo, which sounded more like a cow with a bad case of constipation.

The sound of her snorts and roars soon had Zet and his mother in stitches. They doubled over, laughing until tears ran down their cheeks and they had to beg her to stop.

Apu stuck out his tongue and sent a wet *PLLLFFHHLUT* at them all.

That sent everyone into fresh gales of laughter.

The following day dawned bright and hot. It offered a fresh distraction for the city of Thebes. The Wag Festival of the Dead was drawing near. As part of the celebration, Princess Meritamen's statue would be unveiled at the Temple of Isis. The unveiling would take place that afternoon.

Zet couldn't forget how much Merit dreaded having a statue of her likeness placed in plain sight. Zet didn't blame her, she'd never be able to walk around without being recognized, and she might never get to come out on the raft again or hang out like normal friends.

His own worries about the stall hung heavily on his shoulders: if this haunting didn't end tonight, tomorrow their beloved family stall would be forcibly removed from the market.

At home, no one voice their fears.

From outside came the lively chatter of people in the streets. Busy voices drifted through the open windows. Dressed in their finest, it seemed everyone was headed for the town center.

Kat said, "Mother, are you sure you don't mind us going to the unveiling without you?"

Their mother peered out at the crowds. "Of course not. Princess Meritamen is your friend. You must go. I'm sorry Apu isn't up to it. I think he got a little too much sun yesterday. Come, I'll walk you to the door."

Zet and Kat kissed their mother goodbye and joined the crowds.

They'd barely turned the corner when a figure darted out of an alley and grabbed Kat's elbow.

Kat screeched. Clutching at her chest she said, "Hui! You scared me half to death!"

"Sorry." Hui grinned. "Couldn't let your mother see me. Because she'd tell my mother and I'd be in huge trouble."

"She wouldn't," Zet pointed out, "Because our mothers aren't talking."

"Right. Good point," Hui said.

Kat said, "I heard about you and Zet chasing the mummy."

"Uh oh." Hui glanced at Zet. "Are you mad? I wanted you to come, I swear it!"

"Maybe," she admitted. "But it doesn't matter. Because guess what?"

Cautiously, Hui asked, "What?"

"I figured out where the mummy's going to show up next. And we're going to stop it this time. The three of us."

Hui gulped. "I don't know, Kat . . . you weren't in that cemetery. It was scary." He brushed at his neck as though recalling all those beetles.

"This time will be different," Zet said.

Hui had come to a full stop. "I don't see how."

"Because I have some serious suspicions about that mummy."

"Yeah, that it's going to curse us for good?" Hui asked.

"No, listen, let's cut down this side street. I'll tell you in a minute. After we climb onto that roof," Zet said.

They veered away from the crowds. The Temple of Isis where the unveiling would take place wasn't far now. But Zet, Kat, and Hui weren't going there. Zet and Kat felt certain that the mummy would put in an appearance. Soon.

This very morning, in fact.

In broad daylight.

They needed a good place to watch for its approach. Even more, they needed a spot from where they could track its escape.

"Perfect," Zet said when they'd climbed atop a row house. Like many row houses in Thebes, this house was attached on either side to at least a dozen more. "We can see the Temple of Isis and the whole square from here."

Kat pointed. "Look, there's Pharaoh. And Merit. Up on the Temple steps."

The Princess and her father, dressed in regal garb, shone golden in the light. Jewels glittered in an elaborate necklace at Merit's throat. Pharaoh wore the striped nemes headdress and carried a golden scepter. The royal father and daughter seemed larger than life.

Beside Merit stood a towering object draped in gilt-edged white linen: the statue.

As the square filled to bursting, musicians began to play.

The festivities had begun.

Zet had a bad feeling about this. He only hoped his plan worked.

21

SHE SCREAMED

From their perch, high on the rooftop, Zet, Kat, and Hui gazed across the crowd at the royal family. It was a glorious day.

Suddenly, Hui grabbed Zet's arm. "Get down!" he gasped, yanking all three away from the roof's edge. "Quick, get down!"

"What's happening?" Kat cried, throwing herself flat.

For a moment, the children lay there, panting.

"Is someone coming?" Zet hissed.

"By the gods, I saw them!" Hui said.

"Saw who?" Kat demanded.

"You know who, from before—oh what if they saw us!"

"Who?"

Hui scooted backward and angled himself behind some potted plants. "Get back here, will you?"

Zet raised his chin and chanced a look around.

Hui grabbed Zet's ankle. "By the beard of Ptah, what are you doing? Are you crazy?"

"Is it the mummy?" Kat said. "Did you see the mummy?"

"Of course not. I told you, it was that person I saw before. *Ohhh!* I hope they didn't see us."

In a fierce whisper, Zet said, "*Who* are you talking about?"

"The other night, like I told you."

"The fisherman?"

"No." Hui peered around the potted planter. "Oh gods, she's still there."

"*She?*" Zet and Kat crouched behind Hui and all three peeked around the big urn.

"Whoa!" Zet said.

A woman stood on a rooftop, not ten houses away. A line of flapping laundry partially hid her from view. Still, Zet would have recognized her anywhere.

"It's the lady from the river," Kat breathed.

Hands on her hips, the fisherwoman studied the crowd with frightening intensity. Maybe she just wanted a good view of the unveiling? Except that she kept scanning left and right as if to confirm she wasn't being watched. It wasn't normal. Something was up.

As if sensing his eyes on her, the fisherwoman swiveled toward Zet.

He hunched down, his thoughts spinning. "So that's who you were trying to warn me about the other night in the marketplace? When we were chasing the mummy?"

Hui nodded. "She was there, in the crowd."

Kat sat down hard. "Why? How?"

Zet said, "So let me get this straight. When the mummy haunted your house, the fisherman was in your street. Then, when the mummy haunted the marketplace, his wife—that fisherwoman—was there?"

"Uh huh."

Kat said, "But this means—"

"They have to be involved," Zet said, cutting in.

Kat frowned. "No. That doesn't make sense. How, by the beard of Ra, could a pair of fisherfolk be involved with a mummy? And what about their sick daughter?"

"I don't think there *is* a sick daughter," Zet said. "We never saw her. I think they made her up."

"*What?*" Kat gasped.

Zet rapidly reviewed the clues in his mind. The man and woman had appeared at every haunting. And there were strange facts about the mummy itself. Why had it been lit up in that boat? Why had it spoken real words in the necropolis? Merimose, their medjay friend, warned that the mummy's touch would turn them to dust. Yet Zet and Hui were both very much alive. He had to think fast, to put all the pieces together while the woman was still nearby. He had a terrible feeling, though, that everything was about to go wrong.

He burst out with a sudden revelation. "That mummy—it was using the lamp we found in the tomb. It must have been!"

Hui said, "I dunno. You think a mummy knows how to use a lamp?"

"And it left the lamp in the tomb for us to find. So that we'd light it and be scared out of our minds. So that we'd go and call the medjay and the Royal Guard."

"Why would the mummy do that? And if that's true, how did it get rid of everything in the tomb?"

Zet grew excited. "Easy. The mummy had help."

"Hah. Very funny. Who would help a mummy? More mummies?" Hui burst out laughing, and then slapped a hand over his mouth. "Wait—there are more mummies? That's what you're saying? Like, an army of mummies? And they're going to take over Thebes? That's why we're up here? I should have known. Oh, this is the worst. The absolute worst."

"There's no army of mummies," Zet said.

"No mummies?" Hui cried out, his face damp.

"Then w-w-what is t-t-THAT? *Over there!*" Kat cried.

She'd raised herself to peek at the Temple of Isis. Her finger shook as she pointed at the temple's rooftop. Zet stared at the mummified figure that was crawling across it on all fours.

Hui said, " By the wings of Isis, they're coming! The mummies are coming!"

"Shush!" Zet said as the mummy reached the temple's roof edge and leaned out over the royal pair below.

"Oh no," Kat gasped. "No!"

The awful sight made Zet's stomach somersault in fear. What was it going to do? He had to warn Merit and Pharaoh. But how? They were too far away!

The crowd hadn't spotted the monster. Their eyes were focused on the statue that was about to be unveiled.

Now, however, the mummy straightened. It angled upright in all its horrifying glory. As it raised both hands, several people pointed. A murmur spread through the crowd. Men, women, and children began to shout and scream. They shoved at each other, trying to flee. The square was so tightly packed that they were trapped.

Princess Meritamen and her father spun to look at the roof. Then Merit and Pharaoh disappeared from view as the Royal Guard closed around them. A protective net of spears and shields formed over their heads.

In the square, the medjay blew their whistles, trying to control the crowd.

On the temple roof, the mummy moved with stiff, jerky motions. It backed out of the crowd's view. Zet, from his vantage point on the roof, however, could see it perfectly. Who would chase the mummy, now that the authorities had their hands full?

The monster lurched into a jerky run. It moved with the speed of a strange acrobat, leaping across the ancient temple's roof.

And then a woman screamed. Her scream tore through air, loud and ringing, making the heaving crowd stop in shock. It was the same high scream Zet had heard that first night when the mummy had roamed his street.

AAAaaaaaaahhhhhhhh!

The bloodcurdling wail sounded like a woman's dying breath.

AAAAAaaaaaaaahhhhhh! AAAAAaaaaaaaahhhhhh!

Despite the chaos on the ground, people searched for the scream's source. The medjay abandoned their crowd control and ran to investigate. Merimose, his eyes fierce, led the chase. Clearly, the big medjay meant to get to the bottom of the mystery screamer.

But Zet now knew the screamer's identity. Everything was falling into place. He had a strong suspicion of what this was all about.

His eyes fastened onto the screaming woman, who stood partially hidden behind the hanging laundry.

"The screamer—" Kat gasped. "It's the lady from the river!"

22

THE CHASE IS ON!

The three children huddled behind tall vases, staring across at the fisherwoman.

"What does this mean?" Kat whispered.

"Stay down, let's watch where she goes," Zet said.

Hui said, "What about the mummy? It's getting away."

"Oh, shoot—come on, we need to move." On all fours, Zet crawled for the roof's far side. The sun-scorched surface felt hot under his hands and knees.

"Where are we going?" Kat said.

"To the river. Stay down!"

Hui scuttled along on all fours. "The river? You want to go back to that creepy tomb?"

Kat said, "*Zet?* What's going on? Hello!"

"There's no time, just hurry! To the raft!"

Zet wanted to explain, but he was pouring all his energy into running. They crossed several rooftops, and when they reached the shortest house they scrambled onto an awning and dropped to the ground. Except for the pigeons, here the streets were empty. The echoes of market chaos faded behind them as they made for the river.

Finally, they reached the Nile's shore. All three stood with their hands on their knees, bent double, breathing hard. Zet swallowed, his mouth parched.

"We've got to get to that fishing shack," he said.

Kat and Hui reeled in shock.

"The fishing shack?" Kat demanded.

"Something terrible is about to happen. We have to stop it."

"Stop what?" Kat said. "Zet, you're not making any sense. Is the mummy going to attack the fisherfolk?"

Zet smacked his forehead. "By the gods, I just realized something."

"*What?*" Kat and Hui demanded at once.

"One of us has to go for help. We need backup. Someone has to go for the medjay. Or the Royal Guard."

"ZET!" Kat said in a furious voice. "Unless you tell us what's going on right now, no one's going anywhere."

Zet nodded. As quick as he could, he explained. Kat and Hui's eyes grew wider and wider.

"I don't believe it," Kat cried. "This threatens all of Egypt!"

"Not if we stop it," Zet said. "So who wants to go for help?"

Kat said, "Don't look at me. I'm coming with you. This started at our house."

"What?" Hui said, brows flying up. "I'm not going for help! That Renni guy hates me. He'll clap me in chains if I bug him again."

Kat glared at him.

Hui, who hated disagreements, threw up his arms in defeat. "Fine. Fine, I'll go."

"Thank you," Kat said in a tight voice.

Hui puffed out his chest and adjusted his tunic. "But don't forget, this whole thing would fall apart if I hadn't volunteered."

At this, Zet had a horrible sense of foreboding. What if Renni and his Royal Guards wouldn't listen to Hui? But there wasn't time for a better plan.

Hui saluted. "I'm off!"

"Good luck," Zet said.

"You, too."

"See you on the other side," Zet said.

Hui dashed off and disappeared around a corner.

"Let's get the raft in the river," Zet said

The siblings splashed up to their knees in the cool water, pulling their raft. They clambered aboard, poles in hand. The current grabbed hold and they started moving. They traveled the familiar route, too tense to speak.

As they rounded a bend, Zet whispered, "We're almost there. Let's hide the raft."

They pulled it ashore, tucking it into a thicket of undergrowth. A sudden breeze sent tamarisk blooms raining into Zet's face, momentarily blinding him. He brushed them away and crept forward with Kat at his side.

Soon, the fishing shack came into view.

To Zet's surprise, the area was deserted. Baskets lay here and there. Dozens of them. Darting forward, the siblings peeked into the baskets and found them empty.

Kat grabbed Zet's shoulder and pointed. "Look how high the sandbank is!" she whispered. "They've been emptying dirt out there, using the baskets to do it. That's why it got so shallow. They must have been digging for days. And there's a boat!"

A big expensive-looking boat floated at anchor, just beyond the sandbank. The hull was made of wood and its sails were rolled up. The boat could carry dozens of people.

"Seems like no one's on it," Kat whispered.

"Not yet," Zet whispered back. "Let's check out the hut."

Kat swallowed. "All right."

Zet glanced inland to where the wall partially hid the Treasury Building from view. His muscles tensed in fear. Who was guarding the Treasury now?

With a mummy on the loose, all of Thebes was in chaos. Was it possible the Royal Guard had been forced to abandon the Treasury in order to protect the royal family?

Zet feared the worst.

He nodded at Kat. "Let's go."

23

THROUGH THE DOOR

Together, the siblings approached the wooden hut. A breeze moaned in the treetops and whispered through the grasses. Zet's wet sandals made squelching noises. He slipped them off.

"What if someone's in there?" Kat whispered.

"Shhh!" he cautioned and slowly pushed open the door. Just a crack.

Carefully, he squinted into the gloom.

"Empty," he whispered.

At his elbow, Kat gulped loudly.

They inched inside. Shafts of light stabbed through the rough-hewn walls. The place stank of sweat and old food. His foot squished down on something spongy. A moldy loaf of bread. *Eeew.* Gingerly, he kicked it away. Dirty sleeping pallets lay here and there. At least a dozen of them. The shack was bigger inside than it looked from outside, stretching backward away from the river.

Kat wrinkled her nose. "Someone needs a bath," she whispered. "Bad."

"Whoa, take a look at that!" Zet pointed at a massive gap dug into the earth. He covered his nose, hopped over reed mattresses and bee-lined for the dark hole.

"Stay quiet," Kat warned.

"I was right. *A tunnel!*"

That's where the sandbank came from. The fisherfolk had clearly been digging for days. They'd been carrying dirt out in baskets and dumping the dirt in the river. No wonder the raft had gotten stuck.

Zet thought of Hui. *Please let him bring the medjay and the Royal Guards. Fast!*

"I wish we'd brought a lamp," Kat whispered as they made their way into the tunnel.

"It's better we didn't."

"I can't see."

"Use your hands, feel your way," Zet said, dragging his fingers against the cool earthen wall as they shuffled deeper into the blackness.

At least the dirt was hard-packed, but was it enough to make the roof stable? What if the ceiling tumbled down and buried them deep underground? He tried not to shudder at his fear of being entombed alive.

His fingers touched what felt like a wooden beam pressed into the wall. He stopped to trace it in the dark. The beam seemed to connect with another slat overhead. A support arch. Clearly, the diggers had put a lot of work into this tunnel.

"How much further?" Kat whispered.

"I think I see a light ahead."

A glow flickered in the distance. It grew brighter as they drew near. Zet realized he no longer needed to use the wall to find his way. This was it. Any moment, he'd know if his suspicions were correct. Part of him wished desperately to be wrong. His heart thumped in his ears and he wondered if he'd ever again see the light of day.

Zet's knee slammed into something warm and solid. He tripped and fell flat on his face. Something thrashed and moaned under him.

"Zet?" Kat hissed. "There's someone here!"

Zet squinted in the half-light. He saw a man, bound and gagged. The man wore a gilded headdress and a robe of fine linen.

"He's tied up," Zet whispered. "Help me."

Kat got down beside Zet. But they had nothing to cut the ropes. Zet pulled the gag from the man's mouth. The man sighed in relief.

Kat whispered, "Who are you?"

"My name is Ptahmose. I'm the Overseer of the Treasury."

Zet nodded. He expected as much. "Are you all right, sir?"

"Yes. Thank you. But you mustn't worry about me. Go back the way you came, and bring help!"

"The authorities are already on their way," Zet said, hoping it was true.

Until then, though, they needed a way to prevent the evil intruders from escaping.

An idea came to him. "We'll have to cave in that tunnel-section up ahead."

"But the Treasury!" Ptahmose said.

"It's the only way to stop this," Zet said.

"Then go with my blessing."

"I just wish we had some tools to jab at the ceiling," Zet said.

"Then you must get into the Treasury. You'll find swords and spears and all manner of things if you can get inside without being seen," Ptahmose said. "And be careful the ceiling doesn't fall on you."

"We'll do our best."

Ptahmose nodded. "May the Gods be with you."

As Zet and Kat closed the final distance, Zet's heart hammered so hard he felt dizzy. Beside him, Kat was shaking. The increasing light was soon accompanied by chaotic sounds—clanking and shuffling, grunts and the rasp of heavy objects being dragged across a stone floor.

And then they arrived.

The tunnel mouth opened into a vast bright chamber.

Everything seemed to be glittering. Mounds of golden objects. Reams of spun fabric. Goblets and jewel-encrusted platters. Ceremonial daggers and breastplates. Trunks with their lids thrown open to reveal necklaces, rings, bracelets, and turquoise-studded amulets. There were objects from foreign lands—things that mystified Zet beyond all understanding.

He sucked in his breath. Kat did the same as they crouched in the tunnel's shadow and peeked out.

But it was clear that the Royal trove was only a fraction of what it had once been. The Treasury was nowhere near full. Princess Merit had been right. Worse, the remains were now disappearing into the hands of plundering thieves.

Lining each wall, stone-faced statues of long-dead pharaohs looked helplessly down at the awful scene unfolding. Eight men and two women shoveled plunder into sturdy sacks. Three more hulking men dragged the bags across the floor with filthy hands and heaved their booty into waiting carts.

Thirteen powerful, cunning thieves in all.

And they were just two children.

Zet swallowed hard, eyes searching for the weapons that the Overseer had mentioned. After a moment, he located a stand bristling with metal-tipped spears.

Could he possibly grab a spear and run back without being spotted? Would he be able to jab at the ceiling fast enough to bring down a section and trap the thieves inside? It seemed an impossible task. A stupid one, even. But what other plan did they have?

If only help would arrive!

He shot a hopeful glance toward the Treasury's colossal pair of front doors. Dust motes swirled in the vast space between them. How he wished those giant doors would fly open with Hui leading the charge.

But the Treasury doors stayed firmly shut. It was probably still chaos back at the statue unveiling. Merimose, Renni, and their men had their hands full protecting Merit and Pharaoh. The whole city had witnessed the mummy's gruesome visit. A vengeful creature from the dead. It was the only emergency for which the Treasury guards would abandon their post and rush to protect Pharaoh at all costs.

Days ago on the raft, Merit had said it would be impossible to bust down the Treasury entrance. But the thieves hadn't come through the front doors.

He turned to Kat and placed a finger to his lips. *"Wait here,"* he mouthed.

She looked white as a sheet, but ready to join him in a dash for the spears. He shook his head sharply, making silent gestures to argue that one person would be less conspicuous. Brows knitted with worry, she gave a frustrated, frantic nod.

Adrenaline ripped through him as he tiptoed out into the open. Every nerve stood at attention as he padded toward the stand of javelins.

A man grunted and the sound ricocheted through Zet with the force of a blow. He faltered and glanced right. A thug with lank greasy hair was tossing heavy bags into a narrow cart. He hadn't spotted Zet.

The stand of spears was so close. No more than a few feet. Almost there. He couldn't stop now. Except the thug was straightening. The thief lifted the cart handles and angled it toward the tunnel entrance. The wheels began to creak.

Zet closed the last few steps, pulled a spear free, and broke into a run.

"Hey!" the thug roared.

If Zet so much as stumbled, he was toast.

He reached the entrance and saw with relief that Kat was gone. But then he nearly stumbled over Ptahmose. Kat was on her knees beside the Overseer. She'd found a dagger and was trying to slice through his ropes. Suddenly the man's hands were free.

"They're coming!" Zet gasped, pulling his sister to her feet. "There's no time to bring the roof down. We have to scuttle their boat. Quick, it's the only way!"

"Go," the Overseer said, grabbing the dagger and sawing the bonds at his ankles. "It's up to you to save Egypt's treasures!"

24

THE MOUTHS OF CROCODILES

Zet and Kat ran. The tunnel soon swallowed them in darkness. With a jolt, Zet's speartip caught against the low roof. He staggered to a halt, nearly thrown by the impact.

Kat charged ahead, panting in the darkness.

From behind, the thugs roared with savage shouts that echoed along the passage. Zet yanked on the spear. It was stuck fast. He abandoned the weapon and pelted after Kat.

Ahead, the tunnel grew brighter. He could smell the dank shack before they reached it. They tumbled out of the passage, leaped across the mattresses, and burst through the door into the bright sunlight. They left the door flapping and ran for the boat.

Water splashed as they half-swam, half-dove to the bobbing vessel. The siblings scrambled up the side, using the anchor rope as leverage. When Zet's feet hit the deck, he heard a strangled shout.

Kat screamed and pointed. "The mummy! It's after us!"

She was right.

The mummy, its evil wrappings filthy and tattered, loped across the sand. It closed the distance, fast, the jackal on its heels.

"It's coming, pull up anchor!" Kat screamed.

Too late.

The mummy reached the vessel's side. Its dirt-blackened hands took hold of a rope, and beetle-black eyes glared from between the bandages. The siblings watched in horror as it hauled itself aboard. The deck creaked as the creature lurched toward them.

On the riverbank, the jackal pranced this way and that, snarling and gnashing its teeth.

Zet spun, searching for a weapon and finding none. The foul odor of rotting linen assaulted his nostrils as the mummy tackled him. The powerful monster threw Zet to the ground. Locked in a death-grip, they rolled across the deck.

Kat danced around them, screaming and kicking the mummy and trying to haul it off.

"The anchor!" Zet gasped, as powerful hands pinned him in place. "Pull up the anchor! We have to get away from shore before the thieves get here!"

Kat knew he was right, for she sped away.

An awful laugh bubbled up from the mummy's throat. Its glittering eyes glared, hard and cold. The deck lurched sideways. Together, the two of them slammed up against a railing. Zet drove his knee into the mummy's midsection.

It was a perfect shot. The mummy let out an angry shriek.

Zet rolled clear and leapt to his feet but the mummy was up, too. It pounced again. Zet tried to block and his fingers caught in the rotting bandages. As he jumped backward, the bandages came with him. They were unraveling.

The mummy roared.

Horrified and fascinated, Zet started to pull.

A dozen paces away, Kat struggled with the heavy anchor. She hauled it partway out of the water and the boat started floating downriver, fast. But she lost her grip and the anchor splashed into the Nile. A hard jolt sent Zet, Kat, and the mummy sprawling to the deck. They'd come to a full stop.

"Argh," the mummy groaned, rising and tottering away.

Zet ran after the mummy, grabbed a trailing bandage again, and pulled. As he did, the mummy began to unwind.

"Help me," Zet shouted.

Kat ran to his side and grabbed hold. They tugged, hauling at the long, grimy strip. Howling in shock, the mummy began to twirl and twirl. Faster and faster. The bare skin of one hand appeared. Then came a dirt-smudged arm. Followed by a bony shoulder.

Zet and Kat shared a startled look and kept pulling.

This was crazy!

Around and around the mummy spun until it was no longer a mummy but a tall bony man dressed in his loincloth undergarments. Finally, the last of the wrappings came free, except for the blackened bandages covering his face. The man kept spinning a few more times before he plonked onto his behind with a hard thump. Moaning, the man grabbed his head.

"Who are you?" Zet demanded, trying to pull the off the burned-black mask. "You're not a mummy! Who are you?"

But just then, on shore, the thieves burst out of the shack. The huge fisherman was in the lead.

"Stop those kids!" snarled the fisherman.

Zet and Kat shared a terrified glance. They'd never be able to pull the anchor up on time to sail out of reach. They needed to do something, but what?

"Those barrels," Kat gasped, pointing. "Are they food barrels?"

Zet knew exactly what she was thinking.

"Come on," Zet said. "Hurry!"

"Dried fish," Kat cried as she tore off a barrel lid.

"Perfect," Zet said.

Together, they tossed stinky fish hunks overboard. It took mere moments for the first crocodile to appear. Huge and brown, its leathery snout looked as long as Zet's whole body. Hungrily, it snapped up the first mouthful.

The thieves, who had plunged into the river, scrambled backward.

A second crocodile rose up, ancient-looking and knobby-headed. And then a third. The water churned with monsters.

The thugs screamed and retreated to shore.

From behind Zet and Kat came an enraged shout. The mummy-man was on his feet and they watched in horror as he peeled off his gruesome mask. It came away in sticky strips. Underneath, thick black smears of kohl lined the man's eyes. Now Zet understood: the kohl, grease, and singed mask is how he'd created his burned look!

Zet's stomach dropped. "You!" he cried.

"Yes, me," the man said.

It was the *Royal Mummifier!* The man who had once leered at Zet and Merit through a jackal's mask. No wonder he'd seemed suspicious that night when Zet had tried to question him about Aziza.

"But you're the Royal Mummifier!" Zet cried. "How could you do this?"

"How? I am gifted with the power of the gods. I will be rewarded with the gold and riches I deserve. And I will destroy you children for trying to ruin my plans!"

He dashed forward, reaching his bony hands for their throats. The boat, however, rocked unsteadily. The children leapt clear and the Mummifier sprawled to his knees.

At that moment, on shore, Hui came flying out of the shack.

Merimose was on his heels.

Behind Merimose came Renni.

And behind Renni came the whole of the Royal Guard and countless armed medjay police.

"Stop, you up there, whoever you are!" Renni shouted, pointing at the grimy-faced Royal Mummifier. "You're under arrest."

Zet and Kat cheered and whooped. On shore, Hui did the same.

"You've ruined everything!" the Mummifier screamed at Zet and Kat. "The gods will punish you for this!"

"Somehow, I doubt that," Zet said.

"Yeah," Kat said. "I don't think the gods are going to be too happy with you after this."

"You know nothing of the ancient religions. I alone know the secrets of the dead," the Mummifier said. Then he shook his fist at the gathered fishermen. "You fools! I should have never trusted you idiots to carry out my plan."

The big, burly fisherman shouted back. "You stupid cretin, you never should've talked to these dumb kids in your fancy temple. It's all your fault!"

The continued to shout insults back and forth, but Zet ignored them. Instead, he gave the bandages another tug and the Mummifier tripped, falling flat on his face. Zet and Kat dove onto his back and tied his wrists with the linen strips.

Then Zet glanced over the boat's side to see Merimose grinning broadly and rounding up thieves. The jackal, which turned out to be a huge dog, was tied to a tree. A medjay tossed the dog a bone and it flopped down to chomp away in silence.

The shack's door opened once again and the Overseer of the Treasury limped outside. His gold-trimmed robe was torn and his cheeks were grubby, but his face was lit up. He waved at Zet and Kat.

"Well done!" he shouted. "Well done, my young friends!"

It took ages for the hungry crocodiles to leave. When it was safe, Renni climbed on deck and tightened the Mummifier's bandages.

The priest said, "Let go of me. Or I'll make sure you're doomed for all eternity."

Renni shook his head. "I'm sure Pharaoh, the living god, will have something to say about that." He sent him over the side into the arms of a Royal Guard.

Zet and Kat jumped overboard and ran to Hui. The three friends whooped and cheered all over again.

Renni approached, curling his lip. "You reckless kids! You should have informed us about this place."

Hui looked offended. "Uh, excuse me, sir? I did inform you!"

With a howl, Renni said, "I meant *before* these two fools rushed down here!"

"Fools?" Kat demanded, her hands on her hips.

"They would have gotten away," Zet said. "They had a boat. They were robbing the Treasury and no one was here to stop them. Except us."

"Yes, well—"

Hui said, "I had to beg you to come. You didn't believe me. You were still mad that we dragged you to that old tomb on the West Bank."

Zet said, "We tried to tell you something was off up at the tomb. But you wouldn't listen. And then we only just figured out that this mummy business was all a ruse. They were doing it to throw Thebes into chaos and get you off the scent! That way the fisherman and his thugs could rob the place. And they almost did."

"Yeah," Kat said. "They got the Royal Guard to abandon the Treasury Building. They had it all to themselves, with a getaway ship waiting."

Zet said, "You were down in the square, thinking you had to protect Pharaoh and Princess Meritamen. While the thieves were inside, filling carts with loot."

Renni's face turned boiling red, whether with rage or embarrassment or both.

Merimose appeared and said, "All right, all right. Let's all calm down here. It's over."

Renni said, "Not until I say it's over. Merimose, haul away those thieves."

"Gladly." Merimose grinned. "After I congratulate Zet, Kat, and Hui for saving the day."

Ignoring the fact that Renni's head was practically smoking with outrage, Merimose bent to thank the children. One-by-one, he shook their hands in his huge leathery grip. Zet laughed with relief as Merimose clapped him on the back.

It was over. It was really over. They'd saved the Treasury funds. There was no evil threat hanging over their heads. No mummy's curse after all.

They were free.

A FESTIVE CELEBRATION

The long shadows of dusk cooled the air as the three children ran for home. Zet and Kat said goodbye to Hui and finally turned into their own street. When they reached their front steps and threw open the door, they heard something wonderful.

Apu was laughing.

Their baby brother, who'd been so unhappy of late, was giggling and chortling.

"Zet, Kat!" their mother cried and wrapped them in a hug. "The news is all over town. I'm so proud of you."

Zet and Kat hugged her back.

From a blanket on the floor, baby Apu called out to them in the best way he knew how. He stuck out his tongue, went PLLLFFHHLUT.

Zet swung Apu up. "Hello, baby brother."

"He has something to show you," their mother said. "Right, Apu?"

Recognizing his name, Apu flapped his chubby arms and smiled. And there, poking out of his little pink gums, was a tooth.

Kat's jaw dropped. "Is that why he's been so upset?"

"Yes, poor thing." Their mother stroked Apu's head. "Like I said, growing pains."

Kat flushed. "Oh! And here I thought—"

"You thought what?"

Kat shared a glance with Zet, who recalled how they both thought the mummy had cursed Apu. It seemed ridiculous now.

With a grin, Kat waved her hand. "Oh, never mind."

For the next two days, the house was alive with visitors. Neighbors had come to chat. Customers came bearing gifts of incense, food, cloth, and more. Zet, Kat, and their mother helped their guilt-ridden clients find their beloved dishes, pots, and plates in the stacks that filled the front room. Everyone agreed it had only been natural to fear the mummy's curse. No one bore a grudge.

Hui's mother, Delilah, baked cakes with their mother, which they served to everyone stopping by.

It was late afternoon when Zet, Kat, and Hui snuck away to the roof.

Hui flapped at a fly. "I still don't get why the Mummifier targeted you."

"Easy," Zet said. "He knew we'd make the perfect foil to distract the whole town. Everyone in Thebes knew about that Jugnose business, and that Aziza never forgave us."

"I bet the Mummifier was pretty surprised the night you showed up at his workshop!" Hui said with a laugh.

"Can you imagine?" Kat said.

"He hid it pretty well," Zet said. "But he did seem kind of fishy."

Kat placed another fold in the paper boat she was making for the Wag Festival of the Dead. Everyone in Thebes would be doing the same thing: preparing tiny paper boats to launch on the Nile to honor those who'd passed into the afterlife.

"I guess the Gods were looking out for us," she said.

Zet thought about the desperate prayer he'd made to Bastet days earlier, and how the ebony Cat Goddess statue had studied him with her silent eyes.

Hui frowned. "But what about in the cemetery? The mummy's horrible black face and hands?"

"Lamp soot, grease, and khol," Zet said.

"He sure fooled me," Hui said.

Kat held up her paper boat. "What do you think?"

"Impressive," Hui told her. "That'll be the best one there!"

Kat grinned.

His sister was holding her boat the next day as they stood on a set of freshly polished watersteps next to the Nile. Zet and Hui had boats, too, and so did Princess Meritamen, who stood at their sides.

The Mummifier's ears must have been buzzing, for they'd spent the last twenty minutes talking about him until there was nothing left to say.

"I'm just grateful to have such smart friends." Merit looked nothing like the girl who'd snuck over the palace wall and paddled downriver on a handmade raft. But although she shone with gold and turquoise, Merit had the same laugh and dancing eyes. "And Egypt is grateful, too. You three are heroes."

This left Zet, Kat, and Hui blushing.

Up and down the Nile, citizens of Thebes lined the waterway, crowding as far as they could see. Everyone held their paper boats, waiting for Pharaoh's signal to launch them. Zet, Kat, Hui, and their families stood under the shade of the Royal tent. They were excited to be right at the center of the whole festival.

Merit said, "I have a surprise for you. Well, actually, it was my father's idea."

"A surprise?" Zet said.

Just then, Pharaoh emerged from the royal tent. The crowds along the Nile fell silent, awed by his glittering presence. Pharaoh's face was deeply lined, but his shoulders were still broad and powerful, strong enough to bear the weight of the world.

Pharaoh nodded solemnly at Zet, Kat, Hui, and his daughter.

"If I'm not mistaken," Pharaoh said in his low rumbling voice, "It should be here at any moment."

At that second, the crowd parted to allow a breathless runner through. He was deeply tanned, glowing with sweat, and dressed in a light kilt and sandals. A royal messenger. And it was clear he'd come far.

Instead of approaching Pharaoh, the messenger knelt before Zet, Kat, and Hui. In his hands, he held two scrolls—one for each family.

"Where did you run from?" Kat asked.

"Open the letter."

Kat, who possessed the rare ability to read hieroglyphics, unrolled the scroll and gasped.

She looked at Merit and Pharaoh. "It's from our father!"

Merit said, "We sent a runner north and back because I know how awful it is to worry about your family."

Zet and his mother crowded close, with Apu in her arms.

"What does it say?" Zet said.

Kat's breath caught on a happy sob. "Father's safe. He knows we saved the Treasury. He says, *I always knew I could count on you. I'm so proud of you both. Give your mother and baby brother a kiss for me. I miss you very much. Your loving father.*"

Kat brushed away a tear and their mother did the same. Zet swallowed hard, doing his best not to choke up. Hui, who'd received a letter from his father, was all choked up.

It was a happy day for all.

Music began to play as Pharaoh, the Living God, stepped down to the water's edge. He knelt and spoke quietly as he placed a small paper boat on the Nile's surface. Zet wondered to whom Pharaoh had dedicated his Wag Festival boat. A relative that had gone on to the Afterlife, perhaps?

All along the Nile, a cheer went up. The water soon filled with gleaming white paper boats.

Kat, Merit, Hui, and Zet all knelt together to launch theirs.

"I know who I'm dedicating mine to," Kat announced. "Someone who I really want to be happy in the Afterlife."

"Who?" the others demanded.

"Aziza."

Hui laughed and said, "Good idea."

Merit said, "I'm going to do the same."

Zet said, "Me too." Then he grinned. "Just in case. *Live well in the Afterlife, Aziza.*"

The boat bobbed on the water. He gave it a little push and set it free.

A mummified cat

10 Fast Facts About Mummies

1. Egyptians started making mummies over 5,000 years ago.
2. In ancient Egypt, anyone could be mummified when they died, as long as they could afford it.
3. If you unrolled a mummy in one strip, the strip would be 10 football fields long.
4. Embalmers used tree resin or sap to make the linen strips stick together.
5. Without their wrappings, most mummies weigh only 5 pounds.
6. No mummy has ever been found inside a pyramid—they've only been found inside hidden tombs.
7. The mummy of Pharaoh Ramses II once received a passport to visit France.
8. Egyptians chose to get mummified because they believed they could use their preserved bodies in the afterlife.
9. Cleopatra's mummy has never been found.
10. Some mummy curses, including a handful associated with King Tut's tomb, have never been solved.

Get the study guide at: bit.ly/zet-mummy

Visit my ancient Egypt Website
For activities and facts
kidsancientegypt.com

Get free mazes, word searches and more, all made by me!
A new pack each month.
Tell me where to send it at:
https://www.subscribepage.com/scottpeters

Bestselling author Scott Peters has created over 300 museum, science center, and amusement park experiences for places such as Disney World, Universal Studios, and the Smithsonian.

Find Scott Peters online at:

facebook.com/ScottPetersBooks
pinterest.com/AuthScottPeters
bookbub.com/authors/scott-peters
amazon.com/author/egypt

Acknowledgements

My thanks goes out to Peter and Judy Wyshynski, to my sisters Jill and Sarah, to Scott Lisetor, Sharon Brown, Amanda Budde-Sung, Ellie Crowe, and Adria Estribou. And to everyone who had a hand in these stories, and who helped me along the way, I say thank you from the bottom of my heart.

Further thanks to the following sources:

Romer, J, 'Ancient Lives: The Story of the Pharaoh's Tombmakers', Weidenfeld & Nicolson, 1984

Booth, C, 'Ancient Egypt: Thebes and the Nile Valley In The Year 1200 BCE', Quid 2008

Casson, L, 'Everyday Life in Ancient Egypt, Revised and Expanded Edition', John Hopkins University Press, 2001

Brier, B, PHD, 'The Murder of Tutankhamen', G. P. Putnam's Sons, 1998

Morell, V, 'The Pyramid Builders', National Geographic Nov. 2001

Fletcher, J, 'The Egyptian Book of Living and Dying', Duncan Baird 2002

Oakes, L and Gahlin, L, 'Ancient Egypt, An illustrated reference to the myths, religions, pyramids and temples of the land of the pharaohs', Anness Publishing 2003

Muller and Thiem, 'Gold of the Pharaohs', Sterling, 2005

Klum, M, 'King Cobras, Revered and Feared', National Geographic Nov. 2001

MORE GREAT STORIES BY SCOTT PETER

THE I ESCAPED SERIES

I Escaped North Korea!

I Escaped The California Camp Fire

I Escaped The World's Deadliest Shark Attack

I Escaped Amazon River Pirates

I Escaped The Donner Party

I Escaped The Salem Witch Trials

I Escaped Pirates in the Caribbean

Coming Soon:

I Escaped The Tower of London